Nature Mage

Duncan Pile

Published in 2011 by New Generation Publishing

Copyright © Duncan Pile 2011

First Edition

Acknowledgments

This book has always been a pleasure to write. It's been the thing I want to do crammed into the small spaces between the things I have to do. As a result, this book has been written in pleasurable hours, and has been a joy to watch unfold.

Thanks must go to the guys at the Orange Tree in Nottingham, who have genially hosted many hours of creative time, letting me sit on one of their comfortable couches, tapping away on a laptop while a pot of tea cools besides me.

This has been a personal undertaking, done without much help throughout the writing stage, but since completing the book, several encouraging friends have offered invaluable support. They have read my book and generously taken the time to give helpful feedback. I want to offer thanks in particular to Caren Hattingh, Nature Mage's biggest fan, and a sufficient cheering section all by herself!

I fell in love with fantasy literature the first time I picked up David Edding's Belgariad. Margaret Weis and Tracy Hickman built on that foundation with their tremendous Dragonlance Chronicles, and before long, David Gemmell, Tad Williams, Raymond E. Feist, Terry Brooks and many other incredible writers added their portion of inspiration and magic to my burgeoning imagination. It is to these great writers that I owe the biggest debt of thanks, for giving me a love of magic and a passion for storytelling.

My thanks also go to you, the reader, for taking the time to get to know my beloved characters. As you enter their world, I hope you enjoy getting to know them as much as I have.

Chapter 1

Gaspi sat slumped at his desk, waves of warmth from the open fire blazing at the back of the small classroom sending him into a comfortable doze. A pleasant daydream featuring himself as the heroic goal scorer of the village Koshta team, was rudely broken into by the swinging clatter of hand-bell tones, followed instantly by the urgent scraping of chairs and the pounding feet of children, all convinced that every extra second of time outside the tiny schoolhouse's confining walls must be grabbed at all costs.

Ten seconds behind the pack now, Gaspi crammed his books, stylus and ink pot into his knapsack, and sprinted after his school mates, anxious not to miss out on the impromptu game of Koshta that would no doubt be starting up even as he ran. Over-garments would already be flung on the frozen village pond, heedless of mothers' scoldings to come later that night, and the hand-sized Koshta seed would already be skittering across the ice.

Gaspi's village was nestled in an upland valley, nearly two miles above the rolling plains far below that stretched into the distance. Surrounded by thick pine and fir forest, it was snowbound for the long stretch of winter, but that suited its inhabitants. The villagers of Aemon's Reach were not unfriendly, but winter was a time when the plains folk stopped their long treks into the mountains, and traffic across the peaks stopped completely. It was a time for family, and for community.

Once a week, roaring fires blazed in the Moot Hall, and everyone turned out in their Feast-Day best to gorge themselves on the plentiful game hunted and trapped in the thick forest surrounding their homes. Once the feasting was done the tables were dragged to the sides, and they would dance for hours to the rapped-out rhythms of the Tibor drum and the energetic scraping and wheezing of fiddles and the squeeze-box. Families would eat together every night, inviting those without companions to join them in their homes. And, all through the snowbound months, the villagers uniformly abandoned themselves to an obsession with Koshta. There were four other villages in the vicinity, all of a similar size, and all equally obsessed with their sport. As far as they knew it was played throughout the mountains, but they only ever had contact with these four villages, each of them reachable within two hours using the wide, flat snow shoes worn for such trips.

The villagers of Aemon's Reach practiced all week, but every third Feast-Day half the inhabitants of Vintarol, Steg's End, Steg's Nook or Petersvale turned up to try and take the lead in that winter's Koshta competition. The opposition villagers were welcomed warmly, but the competition was deadly serious. More than once a winter fights broke out around the pond, and once in recent history at the Red Stag Inn later at night, where the visitors stayed before trekking back the next day to their homes.

The village pond was the stadium for these epic battles, but for the next hour at least an equally savage game of Koshta would be played by the school boys of Aemon's Reach, each proud young breast filled with hopes of one day taking his place on the village team. Every boy was given a full size Koshta whacker on their first Nameday, but while very small they would use miniature versions of the stick, until big enough to try their own. Gaspi had been using his own whacker for a couple of years now, from the age of twelve, when he managed to wield it successfully for a whole game without tripping over his own feet.

Catching up with the other children, he flung himself on the floor at the edge of the ice and pulled his ice boots out of his bag. One of the village blacksmith's regular jobs was crafting blunted metal blades to be rigidly fitted into hard leather shoes, which the villagers used to skate over the pond. Gaspi tugged his boots on with a mighty heave and was quickly gliding over the ice, flowing into the general ruck of bodies and sticks. Gaspi's best friend Taurnil was already in goal. Plumper than the rest of the boys, Taurnil was always in goal, a position he seemed quite happy to fill. Gaspi flashed him a quick grin, and Taurnil beamed his guileless, open smile in response. Never one to hog the limelight, and utterly innocent of jealousy, Taurnil loved it when Gaspi showed off, easily twisting around other players, and punching home goal after goal.

Gaspi was about to skate over to Taurnil when something slammed into his side, and he fell, grunting, onto the ice. Pushing himself up onto his hands, cold against the ice even through thick mittens, he looked up to see Jakko, the blacksmith's son, standing over him, holding his whacker threateningly and leering with his unpleasant, piggish face. Flipping his whacker from hand to hand, and surrounded by laughing onlookers, his leer grew even broader and he was just about to speak when a sudden look of surprise stole over his face, and with glazed eyes he crumpled to the ice.

Gaspi looked up to see Taurnil standing over twenty yards away, lowering his stick. He rested the butt on the ice and stood casually, his unflinching gaze quietly challenging Jakko's group. Jakko himself was coming round, groaning as one of his friends helped him to his feet. He picked up the Koshta seed that had struck him and eyed up Taurnil uncertainly.

"Stay out of this, Taurnil. This is between me and Gaspi. I don't have a problem with you," Jacko grunted resentfully.

"Any problem with Gaspi is a problem with me. You know that, Jakko," Taurnil responded. The silent standoff lasted another few seconds, until Jakko spat in disgust and turned from the ice.

"You'll get yours, Gaspi," he threatened, as a parting shot.

"Anytime, Jakko. You know where to find me."

Taurnil skated over to Gaspi and helped him to his feet, grinning conspiratorially. Jakko had been out to get his best friend ever since Emea had gone to the midwinter festival with Gaspi instead of him. Emea and Jakko had been inseparable growing up, their parents being best friends, but Jakko had grown bigger than the other boys by his tenth Nameday, and Emea had started to draw away from him as he became pushy with his smaller schoolmates. Over the last few years she and Gaspi had formed a close friendship - though sometimes recently that friendship had become confusing - and Jakko had never forgiven Gaspi for stealing his friend.

He expressed himself through trying to hurt Gaspi at every opportunity, but so far Gaspi's phenomenal luck had kept him from any real harm. Only the previous week Jakko and three friends had caught Gaspi on his own behind the schoolhouse, and pushed him hard against the wall. Gaspi knew he was in for a beating, but on colliding with the wall a massive load of snow slid heavily off the roof onto the four bullies, giving him the few seconds he needed to make a getaway. There was no point trying to fight Jakko, who was much bigger than he was. Gaspi was a little small for his age, and wouldn't stand a chance, but he was fast, and once out of Jakko's hands there was no catching him.

Taurnil had silently elected himself Gaspi's protector, and, though a little plump, he was the strongest and largest boy in their year; even Jakko wouldn't take him on. Taurnil was well liked by everyone, and his support of Gaspi had saved his friend from the beating brewing in Jakko's limited imagination as many times as Gaspi had saved himself through speed or good luck.

It looked like the game was off, so Gaspi and Taurnil wondered over to Emea, who was watching from the side of the pond. A few blond locks escaped the confines of her thick, fur-lined hood, framing a face lively with intelligence and humour. A little line sat in the middle of her forehead, which deepened adorably when she was thinking. Gaspi found himself noticing the redness in her cheeks and on the tip of her nose, remembering when she had hugged him after the midwinter dance and pressed that little cold face against his own, as she kissed his cheek. He remembered with curious clarity the way their skin has stuck together, made tacky by the freezing air. All of these things came to Gaspi again in the moment he saw her, along with a tumbling ball of stomach-tightening emotions he could not name. And then she grinned at him and the moment was gone.

"Did you see that? Taurnil shot the seed at Jakko's head all the way from the goal!" Gaspi said, falling back into their usual banter.

Taurnil shrugged, but still seemed quite pleased with himself. "Well I wasn't aiming for his head. I was just trying to get his attention."

"Aww don't say that, Taurn," Gaspi said. "It was a heroic shot. One in a million. You should at least pretend it was deliberate. I know I would!"

Emea laughed at Gaspi, before turning to Taurnil with a more serious expression. "Yeah, it was a great shot Taurn, but I wish you'd not knocked him out. This'll only make him worse. You know what he's like." When Gaspi looked unconvinced she carried on, saying "Everyone thinks it was him who beat little Fredo up last summer."

"That's not what Fredo said," Taurnil responded.

"That's because he's afraid of Jakko," Emea said emphatically. "He just made up that story about strangers in the forest to keep Jakko off his back."

"You worry too much, Emmy," Gaspi said. "He's just a lot of talk and not much else. Anyway, I've got Taurn to look after me, and the worst that could happen is a beating. God knows, I've taken a few of those before."

And it was true. Gaspi had a bad habit of getting into fights, and always seemed to attract the enmity of one large boy or another, but his legendary luck had fished him out of most situations, and the few times he had come away with bruises and cuts had done nothing to calm him down.

Gaspi and Taurnil sat down to take off their ice boots, and then the three friends trudged home through the snow laughing and joking, the problem with Jakko out of their minds, kicking up snow at each other and eventually breaking into a snowball fight outside Gaspi's house.

As the light dimmed to a warm evening glow they each went their own way, to parents waiting at home and the smell of food cooking on the stove. As Emea turned away, the evening light caught her profile in soft hues, and Gaspi found his stomach tightening again with that ball of uncomfortable emotion, like his insides wouldn't stay still. Irritated with this unwelcome intrusion into his familiar feelings for his friend, he shook his head involuntarily, and turned into the house.

The door creaked as it swung open, the old metal hinges in need of repair, and Gaspi stepped into the dark hallway. Night came quickly in the mountains, and the lamps should be lit by now. A dim glow was seeping under the kitchen door, and, pushing it open tentatively, Gaspi didn't have to look far to find Jonn, his guardian. Unmoving in the corner chair, Jonn slumped unconscious before the fire, yesterday's growth still shadowing his face and a bottle of strong highland malt sitting on the floor below a dangling hand. Clasped tightly in his lap was a red scarf, and half-dried tear tracks glistened in the low light on his face. Sighing, Gaspi moved to his side and gently shook him, calling his name until Jonn began to stir. Helping him to his feet, Gaspi moved him to the bedroom. After putting him to bed he left the room, closing the door gently behind him and leaning back against the wall, breathing deeply and slowly, his head hanging loosely on shoulders too young to understand this sorrow.

Gaspi knew Jonn's story of course. Jonn and his wife Rhetta had been inseparable from Gaspi's parents, and when Gaspi was conceived they had proudly accepted the role of guardians, responsible for supporting Gaspi's parents in mentoring and guiding their child. Less than one year after Gaspi was born, Jonn and Rhetta had been deep in the forest on a hunting trip with Gaspi's parents, when a group of drunk trappers from the other side of the mountains had come across their camp. They had hit Jonn from behind before he realised they were there, and he had come around to see them running their knife across his best friend's throat. The two women were already dead, and if Jonn had been out for a minute longer he would never have woken. Jonn had never said much about what happened next, and all that Gaspi knew was that he had lost his mind, murdered the trappers, and nearly died out in the wilderness before he was found by a search party three days later.

He'd been unresponsive and speechless, staring incoherently into space, lost in a deep inner landscape where pain couldn't touch him. It had taken months to bring Jonn back to himself, and Gaspi had been taken in by Taurnil's family while he recovered. Jonn had taken Gaspi back when he was two years old, and the boy didn't remember any of these things, so for Gaspi life with Jonn was simply life as he knew it. Since that day in the mountains, Jonn had changed. He was no longer the warm, gregarious man he had been, when love and blessing had surrounded his days in a golden cloud. He was still kind, and helpful, and sincere, but in a distant way; he did not come often to village gatherings, and mostly kept himself to himself. He did odd jobs around the village to keep himself and Gaspi fed and clothed, and sometimes went out on his own hunting for a few days at a time, leaving Gaspi with Taurnil's folks while he was away.

The only person he ever showed real warmth to was Gaspi, his last remaining link to the friend he had loved like a brother. He loved Gaspi fiercely and protectively, and Gaspi loved him in return. Theirs was a rare loyalty and understanding, and when every now and again sorrow overtook Jonn and he fled into drunken oblivion, he was always filled with remorse the next day and apologised over and over to Gaspi, who just wished Jonn's pain could be taken away.

Jonn seemed most happy watching Gaspi on the ice, an unfettered smile of genuine pleasure bringing light to his usually solemn face every time Gaspi scored. Sometimes Gaspi watched with surreptitious envy through open shutters as families ate together, laughing and smiling in the warm glow of fire-lit kitchens, but mostly Gaspi felt he was lucky to have a guardian like Jonn. Although he was the only boy in the village to live in such a situation, the other children were too respectful to mock him for it. That is, with the exception of Jakko, who had recently started throwing barbed taunts about Jonn into his normal abuse. For the first time in his life Gaspi started to feel genuine hatred towards another human being, when Jakko stepped so cruelly on that sacred ground.

Gaspi found he hadn't the heart to do much that evening, so after getting some cured meat from the cellar, and munching on dried fruit, he sat in the kitchen until the fire died. He made his way to the bedroom he shared with Jonn and lay on his smaller cot staring at the ceiling - thinking of ways to make Jonn happier - until he, too, fell asleep.

Chapter 2

The red glow of morning radiated through Gaspi's eyelids, waking him comfortably into the new day. He was about to drift back to sleep when he heard the sound of pots clanking through the wall, and knew that Jonn was up and about. Pulling on some leggings and a shirt, Gaspi went into the kitchen, where Jonn was bending over the stove, frying some strips of meat for their breakfast. As the door closed behind Gaspi, he straightened and turned around, running a hand through his hair.

"Gaspi, about last night...I'm sorry," he said.

"It's okay, Jonn," Gaspi said.

"No, Gaspi, it's not okay. A boy shouldn't have to carry his Da to bed." The pain in Jonn's voice was palpable.

Gaspi was desperate to reassure him. "Jonn, really, I understand."

Tears brimmed in Jonn's eyes. "I know you do Gasp, I know it. But it doesn't stop me feeling ashamed. I just want you to know, I'll try not to..." Silence fell between them for a few moments.

"I know you will, Jonn." Gaspi moved to his guardian and hugged him gently, a hug Jonn returned self-consciously, but with gratitude. Jonn only fell into his drink once every few months, and Gaspi had never felt neglected by him. He just worried for Jonn, and silently shared his pain to a degree Jonn would never understand. More than anything else Gaspi just wanted Jonn to be happy, to maybe find another wife, have some children of his own. It wasn't the drinking that bothered Gaspi; it was the loneliness. Jonn seemed much more cheerful after that, and when Gaspi left that morning he even heard him humming a tune to himself as he cleaned.

The brilliant sunshine reflected off the snow in a blinding flare, and, looking around him, Gaspi drank in the sparkling beauty of the scene. The dark, bald undersides of tree limbs were iced starkly in white; the sheer black rock of the mountainside contrasted against its snowy covering. Birds flitted from branch to branch, chirping brilliantly in the still air. Breathing deeply, Gaspi shook off the last of the previous evening's darkness, and ran to the pond to meet his friends, as he always did on a Feast-Day morning.

Emea was helping her Ma that morning, so Taurnil and Gaspi practiced their goalkeeping and shooting skills on the pond, and after eating lunch with Taurnil's family they went back out that afternoon to carry on - only to find Jakko and his friends already using the ice. One of his friends pointed them out to Jakko as they approached, and turning to face them, he leaned confidently on his stick and stared them down, a customary sneer stealing over his face.

"Here comes the orphan. How's your useless Da, Gaspi?" he taunted. It was unspoken but common knowledge that Jonn sometimes fell to drinking heavily, but most people understood why and left him alone. Few things could make Gaspi's blood boil, but mocking Jonn was the worst of them. Seething, he froze momentarily, clenched fists turning as red as his face. Taurnil only just caught on to the level of his friend's fury in time, and grabbed him by the arm as Gaspi was about to lunge forward.

"Stop, Gasp!" Taurnil said firmly.

Gaspi tried to pull away, but after several attempts he stopped and stood glaring furiously into Taurnil's eyes. "Let go of me, Taurn, I'm telling you…"

"There'll be another time, Gasp. He has his ice boots on and you don't, and he has five of his friends with him."

"I don't care," Gaspi retorted. "He can't get away with that. I just..." But the moment was passing, and Gaspi's anger was easing to a simmer. "Okay, let's go then," he said angrily. Taurnil released his friend's arm and they walked away, Jakko and his gang's laughter following them down the street.

"I don't care so much what he says about me, Taurn," Gaspi said as his anger drained away. "It's that recently he's started bringing Jonn into it. You know what he's been saying? That Jonn was too much of a weakling to defend my parents that day. That he cowered in the bushes begging for his life while they killed them. I mean, I know it's not true, but if Jonn was to hear…"

"Jonn can look after himself, Gaspi," Taurnil responded. "You don't need to protect him."

Gaspi sighed. "Maybe not, but I just can't help myself. Jakko drives me insane. I'd love to pound his face in..." The two friends walked in silence for a few minutes, before Taurnil suggested they go and see Emea at her Ma's place and see if they could persuade her to come out with them.

Emea was sitting with her Ma, a plump woman of middle years who always had some sweet goodies for them hidden away somewhere. Emea's little sister Maria was playing with coloured wooden balls in the corner and the two ladies were at the kitchen table with cloth and thread strewn all around them. Looking up, Emea's Ma saw the boys as they approached the door. Smiling, broadly she called out to them "Come in boys, you're just in time," and bustled off into the pantry to find something for them to eat.

Gaspi and Taurn went in, and sat down at the table. Emea looked sharply at their faces. "What happened?" she asked.

It was Taurnil who answered, "Jakko was making trouble again." Gaspi huffed and looked at the floor.

"Well, that's not unusual. What's got you so riled, Gasp?" Emea probed.

"He was having a go at Jonn," Gaspi answered reluctantly, still looking at the floor. He glanced up, and seeing the sympathy in Emea's eyes he continued, "I just can't bear it when he goes for Jonn. He can say what he likes about me, but when he starts in on Jonn like that I just see red." Passing a hand across his eyes he blew out some air. "He was saying that Jonn was useless," he added, some seconds later.

Emea reached out a hand and placed it gently on Gaspi's. "Sorry Gaspi," she said.

Gaspi knew he should be feeling embarrassed, but looking into Emea's eyes he felt strangely comfortable. The moment extended warmly, until Emea's Ma came back in with a plate of pastries, and Emea withdrew her hand. The pastries were light, soft rolls of dough with fruit sprinkled throughout, one of the boys' favourites. Grabbing a couple each, all three of them gobbled them in silence apart from the occasional noise of pleasure, their host beaming at their enjoyment.

When the plates were clear, Emea's Ma shooed them out of the house. "Go on then, you three. Go and have fun. Just make sure you're back before we go to the Moot Hall tonight, Emmy!" Flinging rucksacks on their backs, the three friends bustled out of the door and into the cold, fresh air. It was a good day for exploring the forest, hunting imaginary boar, and shooting at game birds with homemade slingshots. They had some strips of cloth Gaspi had ripped from one of Jonn's old shirts, into which they placed rocks, spinning them round and round their heads and releasing them at whichever unlucky feathered target they chose.

Gaspi was particularly good at this, but Emea and Taurnil were fairly skilled too, and after an afternoon of high imagination and hunting they trudged home in the failing light with five plump birds to give to their parents and to Jonn. They wouldn't be needed tonight, as it was a Feast-Day, and they would eat in the Moot Hall with the village. Parting at the village well, they went to their homes in preparation for the night's festivities.

Just as they were separating, Emea caught Gaspi's arm. "Gaspi, save me a dance tonight?" she asked. Her sweet face looked oddly determined and intense, and, feeling suddenly nervous, Gaspi smiled weakly and nodded, before turning and walking away. He was suddenly aware of a storm of movement in his belly, and wondered why he felt that a pit had opened beneath him and that his next step would send him tumbling into it.

On entering the house, Gaspi was surprised to find Jonn sitting in the kitchen, polishing his best shoes.

He looked up as Gaspi entered the room. "Alright there Gasp? You'd better get a rush on if you want to be ready for the feast."

Gaspi grinned and ran to his room to get ready. Jonn hadn't been to a feast all winter, and even though Gaspi really enjoyed them, he always hated leaving Jonn on his own. On previous occasions his enjoyment had been overshadowed by images of Jonn sitting on his own in front of the fire, leaving him with a burden of guilt. This time would be different. Jonn would be there with him, enjoying the music and company. Maybe this would be the start of a new happiness for Jonn. Gaspi's imagination continued to create a happier future for him and Jonn as he got ready for the evening.

The villagers flowed into the hall in twos and threes. Some families would have to leave one parent at home with very young children, but almost the entire village would be out for the feast. In Gaspi's opinion, this was the best thing about winter: the massive tables groaning under the weight of platters of food, everyone laughing and happy, the wild swirling music and the stamping of feet going on long into the night. This was also a chance to dance with Emmy, something he was trying not to think about, but which kept intruding into his thoughts, bringing with it a fresh surge of discomfort in his belly.

He was sitting in the corner with Jonn, feeling proud of his guardian with his combed hair, brushed jacket and shining shoes. Jonn looked like the perfect highland gentleman, and Gaspi wanted everyone to notice how finely he had dressed.

Despite some minor signs of twitchiness, Jonn himself looked surprisingly comfortable, even among the large crowd of fifty or sixty people. He sat in the corner smiling and nodding to people as they called out greetings, Many of the women made a fuss over him, coming over and saying just how lovely it was to see him. One or two of them asked him to dance with them later, and to Gaspi's amazement Jonn agreed, smiling warmly at the requests. Suddenly tears were welling up in Gaspi's eyes, and he had to blink furiously and clench his jaw to avoid letting them spill onto his cheeks. A surge of pure, bright hope was filling Gaspi's heart, so strong he wondered if he could contain it, but he kept it to himself, and as the feasting began he found that incredible feeling fuelling his happiness to new levels. He laughed and joked with ferocity, drinking in every last drop of joy, earning amused, warm glances from Jonn and other adults around him.

After the feasting the dancing began, starting with a slow, rhythmic tune that relied heavily on the booming of the Tibor. Two lines of villagers faced each other, made up of men on one side and women on the other. Sleeves were already rolled up above elbows and the top few shirt buttons undone in anticipation of the exertion to come. Everyone was smiling already, and as the music started people began the careful pacing that later on would become a ruck, as steps and form were entirely forgotten and people abandoned themselves to rhythm.

Gaspi spun and twirled with person after person, swapping partners many times in the course of a dance. He was old enough to be allowed to drink some ale from the casks that sat in the corner, and two cool, creamy, flagons later he was feeling a great warmth spreading out from his belly that seemed to have reached his face, where a grin had fixed itself immovably. Out of the corner of his eye he caught sight of a lady taking Jonn's hand with a look of infinite kindness on her face, and leading him to the open floor. Jonn had a look of surprise on his face the whole evening, as if taken aback that he could relax enough to let some of the warmth in. He looked out of his element but happy to be so, and though a big man, he looked smaller to Gaspi in the company of all these other adults, dancing in the bright, flickering light of torches and fire.

Gaspi passed to another partner, and turned his head away from Jonn to find Emmy in his arms, smiling exquisitely at him. He became aware of the sweatiness of his fingers, and the complexity of the footwork he found himself suddenly unable to follow. He had never noticed before the flecks of hazel in her deep brown eyes, and found himself saying so. Emmy looked both pleased and nervous, and neither noticed they had stopped dancing. There was a long moment of stillness and unbroken eye contact, and then, following his instinct, Gaspi leaned forward and kissed her. It was only a brief kiss, but Gaspi would never forget the softness of that moment, and the sensation of her lips on his, her warm breath mingling with his own. It was a moment isolated from all others, with a meaning and sensation all of its own. What came before and after were just seas surrounding an island of bliss.

And then they pulled back, becoming aware of the smiles directed at them from nearby dancers, and the laughter of some of the men. One woman slapped her husband's hand as he playfully mocked Gaspi. Feeling embarrassed, Gaspi caught Jonn's eye, whose smile had no mockery in it, but was full of approval and understanding, and suddenly

Gaspi was not embarrassed anymore. Grinning, he grabbed Emmy and began to dance with her again. She too seemed unconcerned by the onlookers' attention, and though sometimes they passed shy looks back and forth, they were mostly comfortable with each other. The swirling in Gaspi's belly had diminished, and he was left with an excited feeling that this was the beginning of something new for himself and Emmy; something well worth exploring.

The dance drew to a close, and the two friends moved to the chairs left at the side of the moot hall where exhausted revellers were resting, to find Jakko sitting with two friends and scowling like a thundercloud. He stood up as they approached, anger radiating from him in waves. "Jakko, please don't!" Emmy pleaded.

"Why should I listen to you, you…whore?" The word fell out of Jakko's mouth uncomfortably, and he looked embarrassed to have cursed in such a way, but anger and injured pride would not allow him to back down, and his jaw firmed as he prepared to take it further. Lights flashed behind Gaspi's eyes, but before he was able to pounce on Jakko, Emea grabbed his wrist and pulled sharply, turning him towards her.

"Gaspi, don't be like him! Listen to me…please!" The words cut through the blaze in Gaspi's head and he held back, just. Standing there, fists still clenched, he stared at Emea in frustration. She span back on Jakko, fury sounding in every word. "Get out of here, Jakko. You can forget we were ever friends. You are a pig."

Jakko's face flared bright red, and for a moment regret and pain showed in his eyes. But unwilling to voice his feelings, he turned and stalked out of the room, his friends trailing behind him.

"Thank you, Gaspi," Emea said. "I know you wanted to hit him, and he would have deserved it. But I don't want to descend to his level."

Gaspi was smiling at her. "Why are you smiling?" she asked.

"I don't think anything I could have done would have been as harsh as what you said to him," he answered. Emea looked suddenly uncertain. "No, don't feel bad," Gaspi said firmly. "He deserves it. Let's forget about him and have another dance."

And they would have done that, but the musicians were packing up and it was time to go home. Jonn had volunteered to help clear up, so he and Gaspi and a few others were putting away tables and chairs and sweeping the floor. In the morning, some of the women would come in to clean properly, but this would make their job easier. Emea had gone home with her parents, and in the aftermath of the feast the men worked with easy companionship in the light of the dying fire.

When they were done, they threw dirt on the fire and made their way out. The other men departed, and Gaspi and Jonn turned alone from the large doors of the hall and began to walk home.

Before they had gone even ten paces, Jonn put an arm out to stop Gaspi, who was lost in a reverie and came to a halt in surprise. Following Jonn's gaze, he saw a flicker of movement from out of the dark near the pond. His hand on Gaspi's shoulder, Jonn stood still and waited for the shadows to resolve themselves. Two figures emerged from the gloom, and Gaspi was surprised to see it was Jakko and his Pa, Brock Hermon. Jonn seemed less surprised.

"Good evening to you, Brock. I didn't get the chance to say hello at the feast."

As Brock moved forward, his face caught the light from nearby windows. Gaspi had never really noticed before, but Jakko's piggish face was a close imitation of his father's, though bulk and years lent a worn quality to that unappealing look. Brock was the village blacksmith, the skin of his arms and hands scarred and reddened in places from his work, and in the lantern's glow his face looked red to Gaspi too. His face was set in a leer, aggression seething behind hard little eyes.

"Why did you turn up tonight, Jonn?" Brock asked. "You're a disgrace to yourself and to the village." The deep slur in Brock's voice showed him to be very drunk, and he was speaking so loudly that faces quickly began to appear in nearby windows.

"Brock, I think you should go home to bed and sleep this off," Jonn said.

"What was that? Don't you tell me what to do Jonn! You lost that right when you killed her," Brock slurred drunkenly. Gaspi felt Jonn go rigid next to him. "You heard me, Jonn. You lay in the bushes and cried like a coward. You may as well have killed her yourself." This was the first time Gaspi had heard anyone say that rumour to his face, and for a moment he was so shocked he couldn't even react.

"I didn't..." Jonn murmured.

"What's that...coward? I can't hear you!" Brock shouted. Jakko was sneering at Jonn, and then turned his face to Gaspi, a mingled look of hatred and satisfaction beaming unpleasantly from his face. The moment of shock was over, and Gaspi felt a burning fury building in him beyond anything he had ever known. Men were coming out of doors, feet crammed hastily into thick, fur-lined boots but otherwise dressed for bed, and freezing in the winter air.

"Brock, you need to calm down," called Seth Bertram, Taurnil's father.

"Don't you tell me what to do, Seth," roared Brock. "She should have been mine. But she got what she deserved."

Brock's attack had caused Jonn to withdrawn into a protective trance, trying to prevent the sharp edges of painful memories he tried so hard to submerge from scraping his mind once again. But at these words he came awake like a boar springing from concealment, an agonised roar sounding from his mouth. In a moment he was surging forward, arms outstretched, but he was stopped in his tracks by a mad rush of movement and wind sweeping past his head.

In the heart of unquenchable anger, Gaspi's fury broke free of the constraints of his body. He became aware of the environment around him: of trees and soil and ice, and of creatures sleeping or prowling in the night. They felt like they were a part of him, his to command, and he filled them with the fire burning in his heart. He sent his will swirling and spreading out through the air, leeching up through tree trunks and along branches, filling the breast of every bird nearby, crackling through the thick ice of the pond. Gaspi didn't know how he did it, but suddenly nature had become an extension of his anger, responding to his every thought.

Birds came awake and flung themselves from branches and nests, diving from the trees, gathering speed and momentum, before swooping down past Jonn and driving their sharp beaks into Brock and Jakko. They scraped them with scrabbling claws, flying in again and again to stab and scratch at the focus of Gaspi's hate.

Brock and Jakko were shouting fearfully, swinging their arms wildly at their assailants, before turning and running out over the pond. They slid and fell, scrabbling to their feet, falling again, crawling desperately away from the unrelenting swarm of cruel beaks. Blood was showing on their clothing, seeping through a hundred holes and tears. Gaspi's anger flowed through the ice, the inches-thick surface groaning as power coursed through it. He extended a hand, palm downwards, thrusting out splayed fingers. Massive cracks splintered the edges of the pond, sending a fine spray of snow and ice into the air and then, as Gaspi clenched his fingers fiercely into a fist, they lanced inwards from every direction. The thrusting fractures met in a violent explosion in the middle of the pond, shattering the surface beneath Jakko and Brock. The two terrified, bleeding men disappeared in a surge of spray.

"Gaspi, STOP!" yelled Jonn. Gaspi had been standing with a look of furious concentration on his face, with legs spread and planted on the ground, hand outstretched and pointing at the break in the ice, where

18

even now the birds were diving at the water, trying to get another stab at the drowning men. Jonn's shout did something to disturb his unrelenting focus, and as Jonn pleaded with him again he felt himself returning to his right mind. Seeing what he had done, and suddenly overcome by a massive wave of fatigue, Gaspi fell to his knees, head in his hands. A dark pit seemed to have opened beneath Gaspi, its draw irresistible, and he found himself plunging into unconsciousness.

Jonn ran to Gaspi and threw his arms around him, yelling to the onlookers, "Get them out, Seth!"

Like daydreamers snapping out of a reverie, the men of Aemon's Reach leaped into action, running to the shattered ice of the pond. Gaspi's attack had left giant breaks all through the ice, and Brock and Jakko had surfaced through two of these dark holes. The rescuers lay down on the edge of the frozen surface and reached out to the freezing, bleeding men, pulling them out of the water. One of the women ran into her house and brought back thick towels to wrap around Jakko and Brock, who were taken into Hahldorn's house to recover. Their faces blue and their bodies shaking uncontrollably all over, the father and son threw terrified glances around them constantly, checking for more bird attacks, but Gaspi's flock had dispersed the moment his trance was broken, flapping back to tree branches and away over the forest as if nothing had happened at all.

Hahldorn moved over to Jonn, who was still holding Gaspi protectively. As he approached Jonn looked up, his gaze defensive. Now was not the time to discuss what had happened.

Hahldorn spoke quietly so that only Jonn could hear him. "Take the boy home Jonn. I'll come by in a while after I've seen to Brock and Jakko."

Nodding gratefully, Jonn picked Gaspi up, who lay unmoving in his guardian's arms as he took him home.

Jonn closed the door behind him and lay Gaspi down on his cot, covering him with blankets and pulling up a nearby chair to sit in. Only then did he have a chance to examine Gaspi's condition. He was completely immobile, not twitching and rearranging himself like a normal sleeper, but statuesque, still as a stone, his breathing shallow and too fast. Panicking, Jonn ran back out and pounded on Hahldorn's door until he opened the door. Hahldorn was the village Healer and the only one Jonn could think of who could help Gaspi.

"Hahl you have to come and see Gaspi. He isn't moving."

"Hold on Jonn," Hahldorn answered. He poked his head back into the house and called out to his wife. "Martha, can you look after these two? I need to go and see to Gaspi."

Martha must have said yes, as Hahldorn grabbed his coat and followed after an anxious Jonn to his house. Hahldorn had a close look at Gaspi, opening his eyelids and peering at his eyes, lifting his arms and letting them fall, poking and prodding at him until eventually he grunted and sat down.

"I've seen people in a state like this Jonn," he said sombrely, "but normally they have to climb a mountain with a sack of rocks on their back to get there. Whatever happened out there tonight has drained him dry." Pausing to scratch his head, Hahldorn peered at Jonn from the corner of his eye. "Jonn, I think most people won't link Gaspi with the birds, and it may be best to keep it that way, if you get my meaning. But you and I know different. I don't have the ability myself, but I think this is the emergence of magic in Gaspi."

"Magic?" Jonn repeated, stunned by the concept. He had known in the moment that Gaspi was somehow linked to the birds' attack on Brock and Jakko, but hearing it said so starkly was still a real shock.

"Not just magic, but nature magic," Hahldorn added significantly. "He was angry enough to let it break loose, and the birds and the ice were responding to him. My gifts lie in healing, but it seems to me the amount of power released through the boy was immense, and without training that is really dangerous."

"But can't you help him…train him?" Jonn asked.

"I'm sorry, Jonn, this is outside of my knowledge. Nature magic is a rare gift, and Gaspi will need special training. I know one thing: he is going to have to leave here to get it." Seeing the look of protest on Jonn's face, he added "You don't have a choice, Jonn. You saw what happened tonight. Now that Gaspi's power has manifested, it will do so again, and unless it's managed properly, it will kill him. He's going to have to go to Helioport and study at the College of Collective Magicks."

Jonn stared at Hahldorn in unbelieving silence. "I can do something for him right now, though, Jonn. I will replace some of the energy he has lost. He'll still be weak as a baby deer when he wakes, but it'll put him back on the road to recovery."

Jonn nodded gruffly. Turning back to Gaspi, Hahldorn leant over him and, cupping his hands, placed them over Gaspi's chest. Hahldorn's breathing slowed down, becoming rhythmic and steady, and from beneath his hands light began to radiate, glowing pink through his skin. The pink glow intensified to a deep red, white light peeking out from the gaps between fingers, and then faded gently away again. Once the light was gone, Jonn noticed Gaspi's breathing was now deep and steady, just as Hahldorn's had been a minute previously, and his pale cheeks had a redness to them. Gaspi's arm twitched involuntarily, and he turn onto his side in his sleep.

"Thanks, Hahl," Jonn said, awestruck by what he had just seen, but mostly just relieved that Gaspi was going to be okay.

"Not a problem, Jonn," Hahldorn replied, sounding weary. "We can talk about this more tomorrow. Rest well." And with that he left the room, and Jonn sat down next to Gaspi, determined to be awake when Gaspi came around. Jonn began his silent vigil, watching over the boy who felt in every way like his own. A child of his own flesh couldn't mean more to Jonn than Gaspi did, and seeing him lying there, drained to exhaustion by such a hateful event, was painful.

In the deep of the night, a sob sounded from Jonn's lips. It was Gaspi who had brought him back from madness after Rhetta had been killed. His love for his friend's boy had given him a reason to live. In Gaspi he had found someone to love, and to protect, and earlier that evening he had thought for a short time that he might lose him. The thought of never seeing Gaspi grinning again, or fooling around with his friends, or shooting a goal on the ice, cut deeply into his heart, releasing an intensity of feeling he hadn't allowed to surface since losing Rhetta. With no-one around to see him, Jonn abandoned himself to the flood of feelings rising in him, and sobbed from the heart: deep, gut-wrenching sobs wracked his body as he sat huddled over, arms clasped tightly around his knees.

Later that night, when the flow of emotions had ebbed to a trickle, Jonn pondered what was going to happen to Gaspi. If this really was the first manifestation of magic in him, then his entire life was going to change. For starters, he was going to have to go to the great city of Helioport and join the College of Collective Magicks. He would have to say goodbye to his friends, to the safe and simple life he had known, and learn to embrace a dangerous discipline. Everyone knew magical ability was as much a curse as a blessing, hard to handle and potentially lethal to the user. Many students died as their magic blazed out of their control and turned on them. Last night Gaspi had drained himself to exhaustion with his first magical act, and it scared Jonn to think how close Gaspi might have come to killing himself. The only thing Jonn knew was that where Gaspi went, he would go.

His purpose was simple from now on - to be Gaspi's protector - and to do that, he would have to be strong. The night's release of feelings would be a new start for Jonn, and he would have to make it last. Getting up he went to the pantry, and fishing out the bottles of Highland malt he had stashed away in the back, he stepped outside and poured them onto the ground, a great golden patch growing in the snow at his feet, and vowed never again to touch strong drink. Returning to his vigil, he sat up all night as Gaspi rested.

Chapter 3

It wasn't until about midday the next day that Gaspi awoke. Rubbing his eyes, he peered around confusedly for a moment, then his eyes widened as memory resurfaced. Gaspi tried to sit up, but found himself unable to do so, and collapsed back on the bed.

"It's alright, Gasp," said Jonn. "Just lie still."

"But last night I..." Gaspi trailed off. He looked uncertainly into Jonn's eyes, and saw there the confirmation that his memory was correct, but also acceptance. "Brock and Jakko?" Gaspi asked tremulously.

"They're messed up, but both will be fine," Jonn answered. Breathing out a sigh of relief, Gaspi gave up trying to sit up. "How are you feeling, Gasp?" Jonn asked, concern evident in his tone.

"Very tired, but basically okay," Gaspi answered.

"If you're feeling up to it, can you tell me what happened?" Jonn asked tentatively. "I know what I saw but I'd like to hear it from you."

Starting uncertainly, Gaspi started to describe what had happened. When he reached the point about Brock's attack on Jonn he paused, looking again into Jonn's eyes, unsure if this was something they could talk about.

"It's okay, Gaspi. Carry on," said Jonn, with a wave of his hand. Gaspi described how angry he had felt when Brock had said what he did, how that anger had grown until it seemed to break out of his body. He talked about how he had become aware of every living and natural thing around him, touching the essence of wood, and ice and rock, and even the creatures creeping on the ground or sleeping in the trees. He had known in that moment all of those things were his to command, and he had sent his anger flowing into them, releasing it all at Brock and Jakko.

At this point Gaspi stopped, horrified by what he had done. He had knowingly made those birds attack other human beings, and had not stopped when blood began to show. He had been aware of the pounding of their feet on the ice, had waited until they were in the very centre of the pond, and had shattered it beneath them. It was a miracle they weren't dead, but Gaspi wasn't sure he would be able to live with himself, even though they had survived.

"Gaspi, I understand what you're feeling. I've never talked about it with you, but when those men killed Rhetta and your parents, I lost it completely. I'd been knocked out in the attack, and when I came around and saw...what they'd done, I became something else altogether - a kind of monster. There was a sword lying on the ground, and before they could even react I'd killed two of them. The remaining three men could probably have taken me, but my berserker rage must have terrified them, and they fled. I could have let them go, Gaspi, but I chased them down one by one. I murdered them, Gaspi, brutally and without mercy. The last one was begging for his life when I took it from him forever."

Jonn stalled for a moment, staring into space with an expression Gaspi could only think of as haunted. Gaspi knew the story of his parents' murder. Jonn had explained it to him when he felt Gaspi was old enough to hear the truth, but he'd never heard Jonn speak openly of his own experience of that evil day. It was hard to imagine his gentle guardian doing the things Jonn was describing.

Jonn started to speak again. "What I did that day drove me insane, Gaspi. It took me months to recover my mind, and it's been one of the hardest things for me to live with; almost as hard as losing Rhetta, or not being able to protect your Ma and pa. What I'm trying to say is...I know what it means to lose control."

"But Jonn," replied Gaspi, "what happened to you was much worse than what happened to me. I mean, someone killed your wife and friends. Of course you were going to lose it. Brock was just...saying things."

Jonn's brow furrowed in thought. "Well, for one thing, neither Brock nor Jakko is dead," he said. "I'm guessing you didn't actually want to kill them?"

Gaspi thought about it for a moment before speaking. "You're right, I didn't want to kill them. I don't even know what I wanted, but that's what worries me. After I'd started, well you know...once the..."

"Magic," Jonn interjected.

Astounded, Gaspi waited a moment before continuing. "Okay, once the...magic took over, I didn't think about the consequences. I was wrapped up in the moment, in the power....it was unbelievable. I'm scared, Jonn."

Placing his hand firmly on Gaspi's shoulder, he tried to comfort him. "Gaspi, we don't know anything about magic. Maybe that's part of how it works. The most important thing is that we find out about it as quickly as possible. We need to take you to people who can train you in it, as soon as you are better."

"You mean I have to leave Aemon's Reach?" Gaspi asked, cottoning on straight away to the implications of what Jonn was saying.

"We don't seem to have a choice, Gasp," Jonn answered gently, his voice overflowing with sympathy. "This....gift of yours will grow out of control without proper training, and you can only get that in

Helioport."

Gaspi was silent for a few minutes. He stared at the ceiling, his brow furrowed, and Jonn could sense him grappling with the idea of the immense change that was thrust upon him. Jonn sat silently, not interrupting Gaspi, giving him time to work through his thoughts.

Finally, Gaspi looked at him again, his eyes showing he already knew the answer to his question. "What about Emmy? Taurnil? I'm going to have to say goodbye, aren't I?"

Jonn sighed deeply. He looked steadily into Gaspi's eyes. "I'll be with you, Gaspi. You'll never have to say goodbye to me."

Gaspi sighed in return, and sagged back against the pillow. "When do we leave?"

Jonn hugged him then, speaking to him as he held him closely. "You're such a brave lad, Gaspi. I'm proud of you." Pulling back from him, he placed his big hands on Gaspi's shoulders. "I've never been to Helioport, but when I was younger I travelled with your father. We went to some big towns, even a city, and they can be great fun. And this gift of yours: Hahldorn says it's rare, so maybe it's really important that you develop it. Maybe you can help people, do great things."

Gaspi tried to smile to show appreciation for the effort Jonn was making to cheer him up, but all that Gaspi could feel was sadness at having to leave his friends behind. Jonn seemed to understand how deeply that would cut him. "Rest now, Gaspi," he said gently. "I'll make you some food when you wake up." Once Gaspi had closed his eyes, Jonn lay down on his own bed, and fell asleep too.

Later that day they were both up and sitting at the small table in the kitchen, eating fried strips of boar and venison, when Hahldorn knocked on the door. Pulling up a third chair he joined them at the table, and allowed Jonn to pour him a cup of water.

"How are you feeling, Gaspi?" he asked.

"Okay, I guess," Gaspi answered, unwilling to divulge his unexplored feelings about the previous night's events, or on the colossal change his life was about to undergo.

"Feeling weak?" Hahldorn asked.

"Yeah, just coming into the kitchen was tiring," Gaspi answered.

"You'll need to rest a couple of days, but you'll be fine after that," Hahldorn said. The Healer seemed to be rallying himself for something.

"Listen, Gaspi," he said seriously, "I don't know how much Jonn has said to you and there's no easy way to say this but what happened last night is going to change things forever for you. There's no going back. What emerged in you was magic - and more to the point - nature magic. It is a powerful and rare gift, and very dangerous without training. You are going to have to study with the magicians in Helioport, and you are going to have to go soon, or your power will grow out of hand and something bad could happen."

"Like last night?" Gaspi said quietly.

"Yes, like last night," Hahldorn responded. "The villagers don't really know what happened. Brock and Jakko don't know what happened either but I do, boy, and when that power erupted in you, I felt it. It was like nothing I've ever sensed, like a caged lion fighting to escape." Hahldorn's eyes widened as he spoke. "I'm not saying this to frighten you. Any magic can be a great power for good, but without training you are a danger to everyone around you."

Gaspi brooded silently, not responding to Hahldorn's comments.

"There's one more thing you need to know," Hahldorn continued, looking at both Gaspi and Jonn. "You two will not be going alone. Martha had a dream last night. She has a lesser talent than me for healing, but few people know she occasionally gets visions, and they always prove to be accurate: She knew when that blizzard was going to hit last winter; it was her sight that showed us where to find Jonn when he was wondering in the forest, after…" He glanced apologetically at Jonn, who just shrugged and waved for him to carry on. Sitting upright and placing a hand firmly on each leg, Hahldorn continued. "She has always, always known that you are important, Gaspi."

The people of Aemon's Reach were not anti-magic as such, but they preferred not to hear too much about it. They accepted Hahldorn and Martha's healing gift easily enough, as all villages in the mountains had a Healer, and it had become the norm, but prophecies and visions were another thing altogether, and were not spoken of.

"Martha dreamed last night of you and your friends. You were standing in a triangle, facing outwards, holding hands. She says it was a symbol of strength, that the three of you needed each other. There's more to it than that, but that's the essence of it. You will all have to go to Helioport."

Gaspi was looking at Hahldorn keenly. "When you say my friends, you mean Taurnil and Emmy…Emea?" He felt a twinge of guilt at the hope blossoming in his heart, but he couldn't help feel the burden that had sat on his shoulders all day lighten at this news.

"Yes, Gaspi," Hahldorn responded. "I probably shouldn't tell you this, but in Martha's picture you all had a symbol over your heads. Yours was lightning, and we already know what that is about. Emea had the sign of a Healer: a ball of light held in cupped hands. Taurnil had the great bear, which is a symbol of protection. It seems that Emea has an untapped healing gift, and Taurnil is in some way going to protect you, or both of you."

Hahldorn hadn't been able to keep the pride out of his voice when speaking of Emea's gift, and Gaspi was suddenly annoyed with him for finding any excitement in their situation. More than that he was annoyed with himself, for wanting his friends to have to leave their homes and everything they knew just so he could feel better.

"Have you spoken to them yet?" he asked.

"Not yet. I came here first, and will be going straight to their parents once we are done. I have one more thing to say to you, Gaspi," Hahldorn said, all excitement gone from his voice, and a look of gravity stealing over his features, his eyes curiously intense. "This vision of Martha's; she said it felt very significant, and not just for you. There is a sense of destiny in what she saw, and you three are going to be involved in something momentous. I'm asking you to take this seriously, Gaspi. More lives than your own may count on it."

"Okay, Hahldorn, stop scaring the boy," Jonn said firmly, placing a hand on Gaspi's shoulder. "What will be, will be. Gaspi and I will go to Helioport. We'll see what Emea and Taurnil's parents say before counting them in, shall we?"

"Of course, of course," Hahldorn responded, his face reddening in embarrassment. "Yes, let's head on over there now. Will you come?"

"I will, but Gaspi is too weak," Jonn responded. "He can stay here. I'll send Taurnil and Emea over to keep him company while we hammer this out." The two adults left the house, leaving Gaspi to his thoughts.

Not five minutes later, Taurnil and Emea burst through the door, and finding Gaspi at the kitchen table they pulled up some chairs and bombarded him with questions.

"What happened last night?" Taurnil asked.

"What's going on?" Emea joined in. "Da sent me away before I could hear."

"Why are Hahldorn and Jonn looking so serious?" Taurnil followed up, not giving Gaspi a chance to speak.

Gaspi answered their questions, filling them in on the confrontation with Brock and Jakko the previous night, on the eruption of his magic, on Martha's vision, and after many more questions his two friends eventually became quiet.

"Well, you know I will come, Gasp," said Taurnil, his gentle gaze steadfastly holding Gaspi's own. Gaspi was overwhelmed by the surge of gratitude he felt for his friend right then, his eyes filling with tears. He looked down at the floor, coughing and rubbing his face with his arm to cover his embarrassment. Taurnil was like a rock, and nothing more needed to be said. He had made his decision, and nothing could turn him from it. In his heart of hearts, Gaspi knew that to Taurnil their friendship meant more than life, and in that moment he began to wonder if there might be something to this talk of destiny. If he was to have a protector, he couldn't wish for anyone better.

Without meaning to, they both turned to look at Emea, whose face was a conflicting mixture of emotions more complex than either boy could interpret. She looked up, embarrassed at the attention, and feeling the pressure to respond as Taurnil had.

"It's okay, Emmy," Gaspi said, "If you don't want to…" He trailed off unconvincingly, vulnerability shining through his words like a beacon.

In that moment, Emea's confusion cleared up. "Oh Gaspi, of course I will come. That is not even a question." She reached out and held onto the hands of both her friends. "It's just that it's all too much. I mean…you having magic, and *me*, a *Healer*? And this is our home. And how will our parents feel? I just don't think they will let us go."

Gaspi barely heard any of it. The people who meant more to him than anything in the world - his two friends and Jonn - wanted to travel with him. Yes, he would miss Aemon's Reach, but to Gaspi home was where these three people were, and life could not be too bad if they were with him.

The three friends talked long into the afternoon - waiting for the verdict on their futures, imagining travel and adventure and the great city of Helioport - until Jonn came back and took them all to Taurnil's house, where all four parents were waiting, along with Hahldorn and Martha.

Taurnil's Ma looked like she had been crying, and his Da's face was ominously serious. "Sit down, you three," he said, which they instantly did. He was the kind of man you didn't disobey; not given to anger or ever harsh, but he carried the kind of soft-spoken authority people naturally submit to.

There was a long silence while he weighed them up, and then, rubbing the back of his neck he said "Hahldorn here has been telling us why we have to say goodbye to our children. I'm not going to drag this out, boys, Emmy. You can go to Helioport if you want to. We won't make you…but if you think it's the right thing, you are free to go." Emea's Ma let out a muffled sob, and turned her head away.

"The thing is," Seth continued, "you are fourteen now. Taurnil is already fifteen, so in just over a year all three of you will be free to do as you please anyway. We may not be happy with this, but Martha is adamant this is what must be done, and we need to trust her. Hahldorn has told us how her visions have helped the village again and again, and she has never yet been wrong. So we are going to trust you three to God, and let you go."

The two boys and Emmy sat in stunned silence. Not a single one of them had thought it would be this easy, and Emmy hadn't believed her Ma would let her go at all. She rushed to her feet and flung herself on her mother. "Oh Ma," she cried, "I'll miss you so much." Her Da, a gentle man, rested a hand on his wife's shoulder, a look of pained resignation on his broad face.

Taurnil hugged his Da, and then went and sat with his Ma, holding her hand. "He's my best friend. I have to go."

"I know, son," Seth responded. "We're proud of you." His Ma drew him into a long embrace. Jonn stood behind Gaspi with his hands on his shoulders. And right there and then, the matter was settled. They were going to Helioport. They didn't leave straight away, to give Gaspi time to get his strength back, but three days later the rising sun found Gaspi, Emea, Taurnil and Jonn standing at the border of the village, about to set foot on the winding path that many miles down the trail would join the Great South Road.

It was a tearful parting; Emea and her Ma were sobbing unrestrainedly. Her Da was more self-contained but was clearly upset at having to say goodbye to his daughter. Maria was too young to understand, looking around in confusion at her parents and big sister as they cried and embraced.

Emea picked her up and kissed her wetly on the cheek. "You be good now Maria," she said. Maria reached out a pudgy hand and pulled on a lock of her hair, cooing uncomprehendingly. Taurnil's Ma's tears were expressed more quietly than Emea's Ma's, but were no less heartfelt for it. Gaspi felt a little awkward, anxious not to intrude on his friends' sorrow, and he couldn't help feeling guilty that he was the cause of this separation.

Perhaps sensing his thoughts, Seth turned to him and said "Gaspi, I want you to know we don't hold you responsible for what destiny has decided. Taurn has chosen to go with you, but fate has chosen you all. Go with our blessing, son, and if you are going to be great, you will have great friends standing by you."

Jonn shook hands with Seth and Emea's Da, and when Emea's mother finally released her daughter, the four travellers turned and stepped out onto the road. Gaspi couldn't help the surge of heady excitement that thrummed through him, as morning lit up the landscape below. The tree line dropped away like a skirt, and thousands of feet below them many miles of plains stretched for as far as could be seen, shrouded thinly in golden mist. And through it all snaked a widening path, a great road to adventure, to magic, to destiny. Gaspi turned to look at his two friends, in whose faces he thought he could see some of that same excitement, despite the sorrow at parting from loved ones. As they walked he looked back several times, anxious for a last glimpse of life as he had always known it, but soon he could no longer see the village, quickly hidden by thick stands of trees. Turning back to face the road, his heart bursting with joy, Gaspi strode into his future.

Chapter 4

Jonn set them a good knee-jarring pace as they wound their way down the steep mountain trail. They had to attach snow grips to their shoes initially, but spring had been knocking at winter's door for weeks already, and as they made their way down the mountain the snow thinned and eventually stopped. Gaspi was amazed that, for his village, life was still snowbound and would be for weeks to come, and yet just a few hours down the mountain there wasn't a trace of white. If such a tiny change could bring about this remarkable transformation, how different might life be in Helioport?

At points the slope was so pronounced the trail wound back and forth in a long series of switchbacks, and very little forward progress was made, but as the day wore on they found themselves on the lower skirts of the mountain, the forest floor now carpeted in soft grasses. Jonn had them setting up camp as evening caught them, the sun-warmed air becoming chill; evidence of winter's lingering grip. But they were well provisioned for their trip, each of them carrying a backpack with a warm, fur-lined sack to sleep in at night. They were made from the skin and fur of white foxes, and though the fur was not thick it was incredibly warm, and rolled up so tightly they were easy to carry during the day.

Jonn sent them out foraging for dry wood, which they piled up next to him as he made a small pyramid of twigs and sticks. He struck a rock hard against a flint he kept in his pack, hitting it several times before a spark fell among dry moss stuffed between the twigs, and caught into a tiny flame. Blowing gently on it, Jonn teased the flame into life, smoke streaming from the moss as it was consumed. The twigs blackened and curled at the edges and then flared into flame, and ten minutes later the fire was burning merrily, needing only a little attention every now and again to keep it from going out. Jonn had brought some dried strips of meat and some dried fruit for them to feed on, so there was no cooking tonight, and the fire was for warmth alone; but Gaspi felt they were real adventurers, living in the wilderness.

Later that night, lying beneath the stars, he gazed in wonder at the familiar sky, enthralled by a sight he had looked at all his life. Everything felt new to him, full of possibility, and a million new thoughts seemed to enter his mind at once. After an hour or so the mesmerising sway of the treetops across his view of the sky gradually quieted those exciting new thoughts, and, lying snugly in his fur sack, the gentle sound of the wind ushered Gaspi into sleep.

The next morning Gaspi awoke to find Emea and Jonn already awake, but Taurnil snored on, undisturbed by the sounds of the camp being broken. Jonn pointed out a nearby stream for Gaspi to wash in, which he did, the ice cold flow from the mountains above them causing him to gasp as he splashed himself for as long as he could bear it. Emea smirked at him when he arrived back in camp, having gone through the same ritual earlier on. To his amazement Taurnil was still asleep, so he prodded his friend's face with his foot until he grunted and opened his eyes.

His eyes came slowly into focus on Gaspi's foot, now hovering a couple of inches over his face, toes wriggling. "That's not what I want to wake up to," he mumbled, and, continuing to grunt and groan, started to lever himself out of his sack.

"Come on, you big grumpy bear," Emmy teased. "Some of us have been up for ages!"

With muted grunting, Taurnil completed the operation of standing up, and shuffled over to the stream to wash. Emea couldn't help laughing at him as he ambled off.

"He's not at his best in the morning, is he?" she said.

"Not at all!" Gaspi responded with a chuckle. They had some more of the dried meat and fruit for breakfast and drank water from the stream, and after throwing dirt on the still-smouldering ash of last night's fire, the four adventurers started the day's hike. Jonn told them they would reach a hamlet by evening time and would stop for a proper meal and sleep in a bed, which they were all grateful for. Sleeping on the ground had seemed exciting the day before, but - carrying the bruises and stiff muscles a night on the forest floor had given them - the shine had been slightly rubbed off that once-gleaming notion. Gaspi didn't admit it to anyone, but he secretly looked forward to a warm bed, and something to eat that hadn't been dried weeks ago.

They travelled on easily that day, the pace steady but not too stretching, and talked about Helioport and about magic. They were getting ready to stop for lunch, when a rider emerged from the tree line in front of them. His horse was a big, hairy-footed beast, strongly marked with dark brown and cream mottling, which struck Gaspi as a little odd, as horses such as these were used for farming, not for travelling. The man on its back had the stiff movements of someone unaccustomed to riding, though he was doing his best to look comfortable.

As he neared them, he called out a greeting and pulled on the reins, stopping and climbing down from the horse. His face was too thin to be handsome, his nose long and pointed, and he had an unsavoury look about him, despite the smile that lingered on his face.

"Say, you wouldn't happen to have any spare food for a weary traveller?" he asked, head cocked on one side.

"Where are you from, stranger?" Jonn asked, and Gaspi was surprised to hear a hard undertone in Jonn's voice.

"Oh, from the north, a long way from here. You wouldn't have heard of it."

"Well, I'm sorry to say we don't have any spare food. Just enough rations to get us to the next way station," Jonn replied, which Gaspi knew to be a lie. All three young adults stayed silent, sensing something was wrong, but not being experienced enough to know what it was.

"Well, me and my friends are hungry, and I'm not sure I believe you," the stranger replied, his tone suddenly aggressive. The thin veneer of friendliness vanished like smoke, and as he spoke two scruffy-looking men moved out from the trees and walked towards them.

"We don't want any trouble," Jonn said, placing his walking staff squarely in front of him, his strong hands set apart and curling firmly around it in a familiar manner.

"Trouble is what you'll have if you don't give us your food; and while you're at it, you may as well give us your money too," the stranger replied loudly, his voice cracking at one point, his face twisted by a look of greed.

Jonn motioned for his three charges to move backwards, and as they did he swung his pack smoothly onto the floor, and hefted his staff into position in one easy motion. The first man came on suddenly, running at Jonn with a drawn sword in his hand, yelling incoherently as he attacked. Jonn waited for him to near, took a small step back, and cracked his staff hard on the attacker's head, who collapsed instantly and lay still. Jonn's attack had been lightning fast; just that slight step and his staff moving almost faster that the eye could see.

The other two men came on warily; one brandishing a battered sword with coarse wire woven round the handle, and the other a rusty, but wicked-looking, hunting knife. They looked less sure of themselves now, but not put off. They spread out to come at Jonn from both sides. The knifeman flipped his blade from hand to hand, looked at his partner, and then the two ran in at the same time. Jonn span his staff round his head, and just as they reached him stepped to the right, smashing the thick wooden stave into the outer side of the right hand man, his ribs snapping loudly under the blow as he was forced into his partner. The other man was thrown off balance, and before he could get his blade up Jonn stepped in and smashed the butt of his staff into his face. Blood flew from the man's shattered nose as he fell screaming into the dirt. The first man was still lying on the ground, moaning and holding his side as if he was about to fall apart.

Jonn placed his foot hard on the man's head and he was instantly still, his cheek grinding into the ground. "Don't follow us," Jonn said, his voice cold as steel, and, beckoning to his charges, he moved away from the three downed attackers. Before they had gone a hundred paces all three of them were yammering at him with questions, and even Taurnil was babbling excitedly.

"Keep moving, and shut up," Jonn said firmly. Glancing at their chagrined faces, he softened his tone. "We're not out of danger yet," he said in hushed tones. "I'll answer your questions later."

"What danger?" Gaspi asked. "You downed them in thirty seconds! They'll never come after us."

"Fighting skills are good to have, Gaspi; but all it takes is one mistimed blow, a lucky slip of a blade, and it's all over. Now shush!" After ten minutes there was still no sign of pursuit, and Jonn began to relax. "I'm sorry," he said seriously. "I didn't think we would meet this kind of trouble out here in the country. Maybe I should have asked Seth to come along."

"Where did you learn to fight like that?" Taurnil asked, a hint of serious intent in his voice.

"When Gaspi's Pa and I were young we travelled outside of the mountains for three years," Jonn answered. "For about a year of that time we joined the King's army in Dernoth, a city even bigger than Helioport." Gaspi was taken aback by this revelation. He had never really thought about Jonn's life before he came along, or heard this detail of his father's life. The image of Jonn's foot on the robber's head flashed into his mind again, the violence of the gesture shocking him. He remembered the harshness of Jonn's voice, and found it hard to reconcile it with what he knew of his gentle guardian.

Taurnil didn't seem phased at all, however. "Jonn, can you teach me how to fight?" he asked. Gaspi rarely saw him look so eager about something, so utterly focussed.

Jonn looked steadily at Taurnil, saying nothing for a few moments. "Why, Taurnil?" he asked evenly.

"Hahldorn said I was going to be Gaspi's protector. I can't protect him if I don't know how to fight, can I?" Taurnil sounded almost desperate, a tone Gaspi had never heard in him.

Jonn looked searchingly at Taurnil for a few moments, until he seemed to reach a decision. "Ok, we'll cut a branch next time we camp in the wild, and I'll teach you the staff."

Taurnil nodded, a look of satisfaction in his eyes. "Thanks," he said, and turned back to the road. As the day drew to a close they rounded a bend and saw the hamlet they would stay in that night. It was a small cluster of simple houses, one of which was clearly in use as the village inn, the door standing open, and warm, smoky light spilling out into the night. The sound of a squeeze-box drifted from the makeshift inn, and the four travellers began to think about cooked food and soft beds. Before they went in, Jonn advised them to stay quiet and follow his lead. The bar quietened as they entered, but the seven or eight locals quickly turned back to their pots, and they made their way to the bar unmolested. The inn-keep was a broad-faced, big-boned fellow, with heavy brows overhanging his face.

Leaning on the bar his eyes passed over Gaspi, Emea and Taurnil and came to rest on Jonn. "What'll be your pleasure, friend?" he asked, his face breaking into a welcoming smile.

"We'll be eating and staying the night, if you have room."

"No problems there," the inn-keep answered. "We have a couple of rooms free. One for your three, and one for the little lady I suppose?" He winked at Emea, the friendly gesture incongruous with his large, swarthy face.

Jonn nodded noncommittally, still a little wary of strangers after their experience on the road. "What have you got cooking?" he asked.

"We have a juicy roast lamb out back, with potatoes and some greens if that suits," replied the inn-keep.

"That'll be perfect," Jonn said, and led them to a table near the fire. They kept their packs with them during the meal, unwilling to trust strangers around them when they couldn't lock the doors to their rooms. The food came out on giant platters, served by the inn-keep himself, and accompanied by mugs of cool, creamy ale it went down a treat. All four of them were silent during the meal, apart from making a few involuntary noises of pleasure at a particularly juicy mouthful.

When his plate was clear, Gaspi pushed it away from him with a sigh of pleasure. His stomach was full and the ale was beginning to suffuse him with warmth. Grinning at his two friends, he listened to the tuneful wheezing of the local duo of musicians, tapping his feet to the rhythm. Emea looked particularly pretty; her cheeks glowing pink in the warmth, a big smile shining from her delicate features. They had not had much of a chance to talk about things since that first kiss in the Moot Hall. Everything had happened so fast since then they hadn't been alone even for a moment. As he looked at her, memories of that first, soft kiss played havoc with his mind. He wanted to go out for a walk with her, but he knew Jonn wouldn't let them in a strange village, and certainly not after the events of the day. So he had to settle for enjoying how lovely she looked, and looking forward to day they'd get to talk about what had happened. Taurnil badgered Jonn about his time in the army, and they spent the rest of the evening listening to some of Jonn's stories, before going to their rooms.

As the innkeep had suggested, Emmy had her own tiny closet of a room, and the three men shared a larger room with three simple cots in it. Gaspi grunted as he sat down hard on his bed. The mattress was thinner than it looked, and lay on hard wooden slats beneath. It wasn't luxury, but it was a vast improvement on the cold, bare earth. All three were quickly asleep; the two young men more exhausted than they realised, and even Jonn's rumbling snores couldn't wake them up.

Chapter 5

Gaspi awoke with a start in the darkness. It took him a moment to work out where he was. It was still dark and so he thought it must be the middle of the night. From the groans and scufflings in the room he knew he wasn't the only one awake. Through his sleep-befuddled haze he vaguely wondered what had woken them all up. Suddenly, a scream sounded that sent a shiver down his spine. Not a short scream, but a piercing wail of terror that dragged on for seconds and seconds.

"What the heck is that?" Taurnil asked in fright. Gaspi heard more fumbling and a loud curse, followed by a small blossoming of flame in the lantern Jonn was holding.

"Stay put!" Jonn told the boys, but as he was sprinting out of the door, staff in hand, he stopped. "On second thoughts, come with me, and don't leave my side for a moment!" They went past Emea's door, where Jonn ordered her to follow along, and ran down the steps two at a time, bursting out into the village green. Other villagers had come out of their homes, and they followed them to a small hut on the edge of the cluster of houses. Entering the open door, they made their way to a back room, where a woman leant over a bed, sobbing so deeply her breath came in painful gulps. Tangled blond hair obscured her face, and her body shook violently with each sob. Below her lay a man clearly dead, his face white as a ghost and drawn into a ghastly mask of fear: a mingling of agony and surprise that twisted his face into something barely human, a creature whose mind had been stretched beyond sanity before death took him.

Gaspi had never seen a dead body before, but he knew the scene in front of him was affecting him in ways beyond what he should be experiencing. His knees had turned to water, and he felt a numbing distance insinuating itself between his body and mind. Coldness filled him, and his nostrils were assaulted by a freezing, faintly metallic smell. He felt someone grab him by the arm and only came fully to himself once he, Emea and Taurnil had all been dragged outside by Jonn. He became aware of the ground beneath him, the warmth of his breath, and the familiar feelings of his own heart and mind began to flow again as the numbing cold receded. Looking at Emmy and Taurnil he could see they had experienced something similar. Taurn was pale, his normal quiet solidity turned to fragility, and Emmy was crying quietly, huddled on the ground. He moved to her, surrounding her with his arms, and she leant into him for support, crying onto his shoulder. Meeting Jonn's eyes, he could see even his guardian was shaken.

After a moment, Jonn got them to their feet and moved them back into the inn. No-one was in the bar, so they made their way silently back to their room. No-one seemed willing to speak, until Jonn urged them to start to pack their belongings. It was still hours from dawn, but there would be no sleep after this. They all froze when a tap on the door interrupted their hasty preparations. Opening the door a crack, Jonn checked who it was, tension showing in his stance, then swung it open to allow the inn-keep into their room.

"I thought I'd better come and see if you were okay," he said, genuine concern showing on his broad face.

"What the heck was that?" Jonn asked bluntly.

The inn-keep sank onto Jonn's bed, head in his hands, and sighed. "You deserve an explanation," he said wearily. "This hasn't happened for months, and we thought perhaps we would be left alone now." He looked up at them through his hands, eyes bleary with tiredness and sorrow.

Seeing the man's distress, Jonn softened his tone. "Tell us about it," he said more gently. "Please."

"It started last year," the inn-keep began. "One of the girls from Henting was taken - a hamlet several miles west of us," he said, indicating a general direction with a wave of his hand.

"She used to look after the sheep. Had something special about her, Alysia did. She was a simple girl...some would say a bit touched. But I just think her mind worked in different ways. She could see things sometimes, things that hadn't happened yet. And sometimes she could heal the animals just by touching them." The inn-keep paused, sadness stealing his voice for a moment. "They found her out in the fields, her sheep trying to wake her up. Looked like she'd had the soul ripped out of her, or been scared to death. I never saw a pretty face look so ugly."

He stopped again, unable to speak for several moments. "She wasn't the last," he continued, the dim orange lantern-light leaving the deep lines of his face in shadow. "There were others, spread out over the plains; one from this village, one from that, all people with something special about them. A village Healer, young Alysia, and there was old Jack from our village."

"What was special about Jack?" Emea asked, her face a picture of fearful fascination.

"Jack was the one folk used to ask to help when they needed to dig a new well. Somehow he always used to know where the water was; never got it wrong once. Easiest living any of us ever made. He just wondered around with his nose to the ground, and told them where to dig their wells. We found him dead in his bed six months ago, but there's been nothing since. We were just getting back to normal," he

38

added despairingly.

"And what about the man we saw tonight?" Jonn asked. "What was his...ability?"

"Harold? He can...he could read the weather. He wasn't always right mind, but he oft-times knew when a storm was coming, or an early chill. Of all the people who died his was the least...useful gift, 'specially as it didn't always work," he added with a pained smile. "We boarded up our homes against a storm that never came last year!"

Looking at their faces, he sighed again. "Well I don't want to frighten you. I just wanted to let you know what's been happening, and to say I reckon you should stop here the rest of the night. I know you might be wanting to leave, but this may be the safest spot around here right now. They have never attacked twice in a night."

"They?" asked Jonn.

"Well, whatever is killing these people, there has to be a 'They' involved in it somewhere - don't you think?" the inn-keep concluded.

"Alright," Jonn said. "You may be right. Now isn't the best time to be going out in the dark. We'll stay here till morning; but Emmy, you're staying in here with us."

The inn-keep bade them goodnight, and left them to move Emea's kit. Jonn put himself on the floor and gave the other three the cots, but as they lay down, sleep was harder to come by. After an hour or so, both Taurnil and Jonn's breathing had deepened, but Gaspi couldn't find any rest. Turning to look over at Emea's cot, he thought he saw a slight shuddering through her bedclothes.

"Emmy?" he whispered gently, at which the shuddering increased and a tiny sob sounded though the blankets she had drawn over her head. Moving over to her, he sat on the edge of her bed, stroking where he knew her head was through the blanket, until she pulled the covering down a little and he could see the silhouette of her face.

"Are you okay?" he asked awkwardly.

"I'm scared, Gaspi," she whispered tremulously. "I felt so...wrong in that room. So cold." She shuddered again, and this time not from crying.

"Me too," Gaspi admitted.

"And they're going after people with magic, Gasp. That could be us next time." She paused, and added even more softly: "It could be you." Even in the dark Gaspi could see her wide eyes glistening with tears, could hear the fear in her voice. Leaning in, he kissed her gently, a kiss she returned with trembling lips.

"I don't know what to say, Emmy," he whispered. "I'm frightened too. Once we reach Helioport we should be safe, I think."

"Lie down with me, Gaspi," she said. "I don't want to be alone." He climbed quietly into her bed, not wanting to wake Jonn or Taurnil, and they lay there quietly, holding each other, until they both drifted off to sleep.

Dawn stirred them all from sleep, and though Jonn gave Gaspi a level look he said nothing about his and Emea's sleeping arrangement. They packed quietly, and went downstairs to have breakfast before setting off. The innkeeper tried to keep the friendly banter up during their brief meal, and wished them well as they departed, but his façade was clearly strained and they were glad to see the back of the place.

After leaving the boundaries of the village, Jonn stopped them. "Are you three okay?" he asked, his eyes moving from face to face. Gaspi nodded as bravely as he could, Taurnil assenting more convincingly, but Emea had fear written all over her.

"Is this safe, Jonn? I mean, what about the…thing that hunted Harold? If it is looking for magical ability then it might come for us." Her voice trailed off, and Gaspi put his arm around her.

"I don't blame you for feeling that way Emmy," Jonn said gently, "but we can't let this change anything about our plan. I know you three must be worried about what we heard yesterday. Perhaps whatever killed these villagers is after people with mystical talents, but I don't think that puts us in danger." Jonn paused thoughtfully. "If they could sense magical ability, then why go for an old man who sometimes reads the weather when Gaspi is in the area?" he asked rhetorically. "I think we have to assume they find out who has talent the same way we do, by seeing it or hearing about it," Jonn concluded.

He looked at each of them as this sunk in. "Gaspi still needs training, and we don't really have a choice. We're halfway to Helioport now, anyway, and will hit the Great South Road tomorrow. There will be lots of travellers, and we should be safe. So let's just keep our heads down and carry on with the journey, eh?" He was trying to be upbeat and light-hearted and actually sounded halfway there, but Gaspi could hear the concern in his voice nonetheless.

Emea looked somewhat reassured, however, and after a moment she nodded. "Okay. You're right. We have to get to Helioport, and there's no reason to think going back is any safer." Gaspi fixed her with a searching look. "I'll be fine. I promise," she said, smiling bravely at him, and then at Jonn and Taurn.

"That's my girl!" Jonn said, kissing her on the cheek. As they started to walk, the four travellers spread out, each moving in their own space.

After a moment, Taurnil moved alongside Gaspi, speaking in an undertone. "If something was to attack us Gasp, would you be able to use your magic?"

Gaspi screwed up his face. "I don't know," he said truthfully. "Last time it just burst out of me. I don't think I can just make it happen. And..." he trailed off.

Looking at Taurnil, he said: "And I'm scared. What happened with Jakko and Brock was out of my control - I could have killed them. I never want to feel like that again." Looking into the distance, he shuddered involuntarily.

"No doubt!" Taurn said. "We'll just have to hope we don't meet anything too nasty, then." The two friends walked on in thoughtful silence.

Aside from a deer bursting out of the undergrowth in front of them, shocking the life out of the three young travellers and giving Jonn a good laugh, nothing eventful happened during the day. In the late afternoon, a movement in the treetops caused Gaspi to look up and see a couple of game birds in the higher branches. On instinct, he whipped out his slingshot and shot a stone right into the body of one of the unfortunate creatures, the other panicking noisily and making its getaway.

"Nice one, Gasp!" Taurnil said with a grin as the plump body flopped to the soil, and for the remaining hours of the day it dangled from Gaspi's backpack as they walked, promising more filling fare than dried old meat for their supper.

They stopped for the night while there was still enough light to gather wood, and made camp in a copse of trees, where they would be out of sight of anyone roaming the plains at night. After setting Gaspi and Emea the task of starting the fire Jonn told Taurnil it was time for his training to begin, and went into the trees looking for a branch that would become Taurnil's first staff. Returning with a leafy length of wood, freshly snapped from its trunk, Jonn sat down with his knife to whittle off the leaves and tiny branches, and square off the ends as much as possible.

"Hey, Taurn!" he called when the wood was ready, and hoisted the new staff at him over the clearing. Catching it firmly, Taurnil stood up and twirled it experimentally, flipping it from hand to hand to get used to the weight. With Gaspi and Emea looking on curiously, Jonn began to show Taurnil the basics of martial combat.

"Okay...the first thing is to get your balance," Jonn said. "You'll be leading from one foot like a swordsman, using the weight of your body to lend force to the staff. Are you right-handed?" Taurnil nodded.

"Then lead with your left foot, and place your right hand above your left on the staff, your hands about eighteen inches from each other."

"That's it! Perfect!" said Jonn as Taurnil shifted into position. "Now the staff is the most effective weapon for defence," he instructed. "Its advantage is speed and reach. You can move it very fast and with great force without much effort, and you can use its length to get beyond the reach of a swordsman. You can use it to disarm an enemy. A quick smack to the opponent's wrist will make them drop their weapon. Or you can use the end of the staff like a prod, driving into the face or belly while keeping your distance."

"The staff can also be used for attack, too," Jonn added, starting to spin his own staff round his head, then bringing it round in a vicious sweep that would have brained any would-be attacker. Jonn slid gracefully from move to move, effortlessly maintaining perfect balance, continuing to talk as he demonstrated.

"You can take out an opponent's legs," he said as he snapped out a brutal leg sweep. "Or the arms," he added, swinging the staff down hard where his imaginary enemy's torso would be. "Or you can go for the face," he said, as he thrust the end of his staff at such an angle and speed that any opponent would be lucky to walk away with a face at all. He paused, frozen in position, then turned his head towards Taurnil. "I don't want you trying to learn attacking moves just yet, Taurnil. The defensive discipline is good enough for now," he said, as he straightened up. In the light of Jonn's intense gaze and sudden seriousness, Taurnil didn't argue.

"Alright - get in position," Jonn instructed. The second Taurnil had his feet set, Jonn rapped his staff against Taurnil's wrist, making him drop the staff and jump back holding his arm, a look of injured pride on his face. Gaspi laughed out loud until Emea pinched him hard on the arm, and gave him a look that shut him up.

"Don't look hurt, Taurnil," Jonn said. "An enemy won't ask permission or tell you what they're going to do. This is your first lesson. Always guard your hands. An experienced opponent will go for them every time. Okay - let's try again." Taurnil took his position more warily this time, not taking his eyes off Jonn, a look of mild resentment still smouldering in his eyes. Jonn sprang into motion, going for the wrist again, and Taurnil managed to get one clumsy block in before another painful tap sent his staff to the floor, and left Taurnil nursing his (now bruised) wrist.

Jonn smiled tightly. "Okay, Taurn, I'll leave your wrist alone for a bit. Let's work on a few basic blocks." Gaspi and Emea watched as Jonn taught Taurnil the movement and contours of basic staff technique, showing him how to use his weapon to turn blades away from the body, to open the enemy's torso to a blow, and to keep an attacker off-balance. Taurnil seemed to be learning pretty well and, as Jonn was leaving his wrists alone, the two watchers became bored and wondered off a little way into the copse.

The sun had almost completely set now, but the light of the fire filtered through the branches enough to colour Emea's face in warm tones. Gaspi wanted to kiss her again as he had the night of the dance, but what if she didn't want him to? Neither of them said a word, and the silence threatened to stretch into awkwardness. She was certainly looking at him as if she wanted him to kiss her. She looked sweet and vulnerable and passionate all at the same time, and she kept looking at his mouth.

Just do it, Gaspi thought to himself, and made himself lean towards her. When she didn't pull back he kissed her gently and withdrew, searching her eyes for any sign of alarm. Her eyes were wide, and for a moment he wondered if he'd done the wrong thing, but then she put a soft hand against his face and returned a longer kiss. Gaspi stopped worrying and let himself thrill in the moment, his right hand tingling painfully with happiness.

Since they'd first kissed at the Feast-Day dance they'd not had time to talk about what had happened, and Gaspi realised he had been a bit uncertain about Emea's feelings; that is, until now. The moment felt like it would last forever, but far too soon the sounds of Taurnil's practice bout stopped and they could hear Jonn calling their names. Releasing Emmy's hand, Gaspi walked by her side back to the clearing, where Jonn was plucking the bird Gaspi had downed earlier. Looking up at them he caught Gaspi's eye and smiled ever so slightly, perhaps a little wistfully, before carrying on with what he was doing.

As Jonn cooked the bird, the smell of roasting meat set Gaspi's taste-buds tingling. The plump creature yielded a surprising amount of meat, and combined with hunks of soft bread it made a filling meal. They settled back as darkness fell, and talked comfortably in the flickering firelight. Gaspi found himself holding hands with Emea as Jonn told them stories of soldiering and travel. Unlike Taurnil, he was barely aware of the details of the stories, revelling in the simple pleasure of Emea's touch. After a while his palm became sweaty, and self-consciousness made him pull his hand back. Emea looked at him uncertainly until he flashed his warmest smile at her, and she relaxed again.

They slept early that night, and woke even earlier in the morning, getting a good start on the day's travel. Jonn set a strong pace for them, and the morning hours passed quickly as they journeyed onwards through the forest. Towards the end of the morning the trees began to thin out, beyond which Jonn said they would meet the Great South Road.

Chapter 6

Well before they saw the highway, Gaspi could hear the low rumbling of wagon wheels on hard stone, the cracking of whips and occasional shouts of the wagon drivers jostling against each other in a bid to make good time on the route to Helioport. For the merchants attempting the run, every hour counted if they were to steal a march on their competitors, which meant that courtesy took a back seat in the rush to make a profit.

As Jonn led them out of the last stand of trees, three sets of eyes widened in amazement at the sight spread before them. A road so wide and flat that four wagons could pass abreast curved broadly in front of them, filled with a steady stream of traffic in both directions. Gaspi had never seen so many people in one place. Brightly coloured wagons driven by equally brightly clothed men and women rolled alongside hard looking mercenaries. Farmers with wagonloads of produce travelled next to parents taking their children on an exciting trip to the big city, and the whole fluid crowd was sprinkled with stranger people still, who didn't fit into any obvious category.

Jonn addressed his amazed charges: "A major road like this has a certain amount of danger for us. Soldiers patrol it regularly, but there are too many people for them to be able to keep an eye on everybody, so I don't want you wandering off. Stick with me until I say otherwise." Looking searchingly into their, and seeing no sign of rebellion, he nodded and led them on towards the road. They travelled the last few hundred yards to the road and joined the ever-moving crowd, swallowed up in the greater flow of people.

Setting their pace according to the traffic around them, they turned their eyes to stare at the sights around them in continual amazement. Raggedly dressed children darted in and out of the throng, ducking beneath high-axled wagons, chasing each other and shouting in an endless game of 'Tag'. A bored-looking farmer sat atop his wagon, nudging a duo of shire horses forward as they dragged his load of beets to market. A small man in patched hose and tunic slumped in an afternoon doze in the back of the wagon closest to them, skinny elbows sticking out at funny angles like sticks. As if sensing their scrutiny, he lifted his head and turned to look at them from his perch. His nut brown-face was so wreathed with wrinkles and burnt by the sun, it looked as if his skin must feel like a leather shoe. Peering beadily into their eyes, a sudden grin turned the wrinkles into canyons, his eyes all but disappearing in the mass of deep lines surrounding them. Producing a large copper coin from his pockets, he began to roll it across his knuckles, making it disappear and reappear again with deft movements of his slender fingers.

The three youngsters stared goggle-eyed at this strange little man and his clever trick, and then gasped as one when a small, brown monkey leapt onto his shoulder from somewhere in the recesses of the wagon, and proceeded to stare at them with little black eyes. It had a pale, hand-sized patch over the top of its head, unhealthily luminous as if bleached by acid. Gaspi had never seen a monkey before, though he'd seen drawings of them in school, but it wasn't just the novelty that held his attention. As the monkey gripped the small man's shoulder, the gold coin slipped from the back of the small man's hand to the ground, and his face slackened, looking suddenly empty and unsure, even afraid.

The monkey seemed to be staring at Gaspi, leaning forward in intense scrutiny. One yellow-nailed hand clamped onto the man's face to get a better grip and he just sat there unmoving, even though a hard little hairy finger was curling right into his mouth. After a few moments of staring at Gaspi intently, the unnerving creature looked away, its interest passing to the crowd of travellers, seemingly scanning people face by face.

Gaspi continued to watch the monkey, discomforted both by its unusual behaviour and the incomprehensible reaction of the strange little man it clung to. Its little hairy face twitched slightly as its gaze moved from group to group, and then all of a sudden it tensed, its tail standing up rigidly above it as all the hair on its body stood on end. It was staring at a colourfully dressed gypsy girl who sat cross-legged in the back of one of her family's painted wagons, three cards turned down on the wagon bed before her. She was turning them over one by one, a far-off look in her eye, and talking in a hushed, sincere manner to the man walking alongside.

The little monkey stretched out a finger towards her and let out a hissing screech, lips pulled back tightly over bared, sharp teeth and bright red gums. And then it leaped to the ground, skittering through the crowd at frightening speed before springing up onto the back of the girl's wagon. The young girl started fearfully, and then, realising it was just a little monkey, began to smile; a smile which froze as the creature lashed out at her face. Emea shrieked as the monkey attacked the young gypsy girl, but instead of clawing or biting her it just slapped its palm across her cheek, and bounced off as quickly as it had arrived, shrieking excitedly until it disappeared among the wagons.

Emea recovered from her shock first and quickly made her way over to the girl, who was clearly unnerved, holding a hand to her cheek. Gaspi and Taurnil followed along behind her. "Are you alright?" Emea asked, full of concern.

"I'm fine...I think," the girl mumbled, still staring into space, in a lingering state of shock. Shaking herself out of it, she recovered a remarkable semblance of poise, and smiled warmly at Emea. Gaspi couldn't help noticing she was really very pretty when she smiled, her dark gypsy complexion so different from the paler girls he had grown up around. Taurnil was staring too, his jaw hanging open and eyes a little too wide. Gaspi snapped his own teeth shut self-consciously, hoping Emea hadn't noticed his reaction.

"Thanks for asking after me," she said. "I must admit I was a bit scared for a moment there. That nasty little creature and its horrible scream! But of course it's nothing to worry about, really. I was just being silly." Though she spoke calmly, Gaspi thought he could detect a lingering hint of unease. "I mean, after all, it's such a small thing," the gypsy girl continued. "What could it have done to me?"

Emea put her hand on the girl's arm. "I'm sure you're right, but I don't think you were being silly. Anyone would be a little jumpy after that."

There was a slight pause as they all stared at each other, reminded suddenly that they were strangers. "I'm Lydia," the gypsy girl announced confidently, holding her hand out to Emea, who took hold of it warmly.

"I'm Emea, but you can call me Emmy," she chirped, beaming at Lydia. "And this is Gaspi and Taurnil," she added, turning towards the boys.

"Hullo," they both mumbled awkwardly. Gaspi was a little red in the face and Taurnil was staring at his right foot as he toed the ground, earning a puzzled look from Emea.

"It's good to meet you all," Lydia said, thankfully dragging Emea's attention away from the two boys. "What are you three doing on the Great South Road?"

"We're going to Helioport," Emmy responded brightly. "Gaspi is going to train as a Mage," she announced proudly, beaming with excitement.

"Really?" Lydia responded just as enthusiastically. "That's fantastic! That's what I'm doing too. Helioport is the best place in the world to be if you have talent. As it turns out, I have a little myself," she said, with an air of mystery.

"Really? What kind of talent?" Gaspi jumped in, distracted from his embarrassment by genuine interest.

"My mother says I'm a Seer," Lydia said.

"What's a Seer?" Emmy asked.

"It's someone who has the natural ability to sense patterns in complicated events, to see the truth, if you know what I mean. Seers can even sometimes see glimpses of the future," Lydia answered. "Among my people, a few women in every generation are born with the ability," she continued. "That's what I was doing when that creature attacked me. One of the men in my family wanted a reading, and I was reading the cards to see what I could pick up. It doesn't seem to work like that though," she added after a pause, staring into the middle distance, a small frown marring the smooth, dark skin of her forehead. "The talent comes and goes when it wants to, and I can't just call on it when it suits me."

Looking back at her three new friends, her expression relaxed, and that lovely smile stretched her features and brought a sparkle to her eyes again. "Eat with me and my family tonight?" she asked.

"Oh, we'd love to!" Emea exclaimed. "But we'll have to ask Jonn. He's our guardian," she added.

"Well, he must come too!" Lydia insisted. "The traffic stops when it gets dark, and we'll make a circle just off the road on the west side in the lee of these hills," she said, indicating the raised ground sweeping up from that side of the road.

"What's a circle?" Emea asked.

"You've never met any gypsies before?" Lydia asked, receiving three headshakes in response. "It's what we do with our wagons when we settle down for the night, or for longer. We form a big circle and have a campfire in the middle. There'll be music, and dancing, and lots to eat. We love to have guests."

"Sounds brilliant," Gaspi said.

"I can't wait," Emea said brightly. "Thanks, Lydia. See you later, then."

The three friends parted from Lydia and found Jonn, who was walking not far from them, talking to a farmer taking his goods to market to get some news of the road

"Ah, there you are," he said as his charges appeared. "What's got you all excited, then?"

"We met Lydia, a gypsy girl," Emea said enthusiastically. "She's invited us all to dinner. You too, Jonn."

"Gypsies, eh?" Jonn asked eyeing Emea theatrically. "Well, we don't want to be rude now, do we?" he said, after a long pause. Emea gave a squeal of delight, and hugged Jonn. "Okay, okay," he said gruffly, patting her on the shoulder ineffectually.

They travelled on with the rest of the traffic for the short time the light remained. As dusk fell, travel slowed and then stopped, and the sound of tent posts being hammered into the ground sounded from all around them. Most travellers hauled their wagons off the road and set up camp for the night. Covers were pulled over produce and belongings, and soon the mesmerising sight of hundreds of cook fires spread up and down the road as far as they could see. Led by Emea, they wended their way through groups of travellers, all gathered round a fire, hungry for whatever was cooking over its coals, and the scent of a hundred meals brought a flow of moisture to Gaspi's mouth. In the darkness between fires they passed a few furtive individuals anxious not to be seen, and not a few couples breathing heavily and grunting in the darkness, but Jonn kept them to the wide pools of flickering light as much as possible, and soon came across the sight of a larger fire reflecting off the lacquered reds and greens of the gypsy caravans.

As Lydia had said, the colourful wagons, remarkable even by firelight, were set up in a wide circle. There were ten in all, and in the middle, lounging round the fire on the ground, were twenty or thirty gypsies, dressed as flamboyantly as their vehicles were painted. Recognising them as they passed into the circle of firelight, Lydia pushed herself gracefully from the ground and came over to greet them. Emea received a warm hug, and Gaspi and Taurnil a flash of that bewitching smile. Gaspi glanced at Taurnil, whose jaw was a little loose. Now that he thought of it, he couldn't remember Taurnil speaking since they'd met Lydia earlier that afternoon.

One of the men lounging round the fire looked up at the new arrivals, and levered his tall, rangy frame from the ground to come over. Resting his hands on Lydia's shoulders, he smiled at the strangers. His hair was as dark as Lydia's, his intent eyes a rich brown. A long moustache hung over a prominent jaw, his well-tanned face framed with strong, clean lines.

"I'm Roland, Lydia's father," he greeted, smiling affectionately down at his daughter. "Welcome to our fire, friends. It would be our pleasure if you could join our circle tonight." His invitation was accompanied by an outstretched hand.

"Thank you, Roland," Jonn answered, who seemed to be genuinely touched by the warmth of the invite. "I'm Jonn, and these are my charges: Gaspi, Emea and Taurnil. We'd love to join your circle this evening." Roland's smile turned into a grin, and throwing an arm round Jonn's shoulder, he steered him into the camp, gesturing expansively with his free hand and falling into easy banter.

This left Lydia with the three friends. Gaspi noticed that her cheek still bore the mark where the monkey had struck her earlier that day. Her skin was pale where it had struck her – pale, like the light patch of fur on its head. Gaspi felt vaguely uneasy, but pushed his worries aside for the moment as Lydia led them into the circle. If Lydia wasn't bothered by what had happened earlier, then he really didn't have a reason to be.

There was a scattering of logs around the fire in a rough circle, within the greater circle of wagons. Jonn was already seated among a group of colourfully dressed adults, and Lydia led Emea, Gaspi and Taurnil to another spot on the other side of the fire. They were passed dishes of an unidentified but delicious-smelling stew, a creamy concoction of white meat, onions, and a delicate sauce infused with the invigorating taste of herbs that Gaspi couldn't identify. Gaspi was thrilled at the subtle but delicious taste, his tongue tingling with satisfaction at each mouthful. A strong wine was poured into goblets and placed in their hands, which Jonn insisted be watered down before they were allowed to touch it. Lydia drank hers un-watered. After they ate, Roland picked up a guitar and began to strum a lilting tune, which rose and fell hypnotically, accompanying the earthy sound of his voice as he sang.

As Roland sang Emea felt herself transported, her mind slowing and warming, thickening like hot treacle as she fell softly into a trance. The music swelled and fell away like breath, natural as the moonlight and gentle as the wind that brushed against her hair and caressed her cheek. She glanced at Gaspi, who was sitting hunched over his knees, staring hypnotically into the fire. His often intense face looked as relaxed as she had seen it since leaving Aemon's Reach.

Letting her gaze rest on Gaspi, Emea allowed her heart to feel. Somehow he seemed more real in that moment - or maybe it was the moment that felt more real - but whatever the cause, she felt that the ground beneath them was more solid, the fire more comforting, the shadows they cast richer and darker, and her feelings stronger than she had known before. Watching the firelight flicker against Gaspi's hair, she noticed a furtive movement in the shadows between the wagons behind him.

She searched the darkness lazily with her eyes, waiting for the telltale movement, but nothing more happened. About to settle back into her trance again, Emea suddenly sat bolt upright, and grabbed Gaspi's arm.

"The monkey!" she hissed.

50

"What? Where?" Gaspi said, scrambling to his feet. Emea pointed at it, until Gaspi spotted the bobbing patch of white, which resolved into the unhealthy light patch on the little creature's head as his eyes adjusted to the dark. It was under an axle, neck extended to full stretch, hard little eyes glinting in the firelight as it scanned the circle of revellers. Its whole body hardened with whip-taught tension when its eyes fell on Lydia, and raising an outstretched finger it released a grating screech, a natural sound underpinned by an inexplicable darkness.

The whole enclave froze in mid-motion, the unearthly sound awakening a primal fear in every breast. Gaspi found his heart beating wildly, and Emea had covered her ears with her hands. They expected the monkey to attack Lydia as it had earlier that day, but it remained stiff as a statue, bony arm and finger pointing at Lydia, its mouth pulled back in a rictus, revealing sharp teeth grinding against each other as it continued to hiss and drool.

Out of the night behind the demented creature, the shadows began to stir and to coalesce into a denser patch of darkness; a glob of night separated out from the shadows, and taking a rudimentary human form. Sitting on top of what mimicked heavy shoulders was a dark head, without form except for two denser points of darkness; blacker than black and swirling with power, swallowing all light into their gaze.

The campfire shrank to a bare flicker, repressed by a pervading cold seeping across the clearing. Freezing mist rolled out across the grass, each blade instantly coated in ice, which crept with frigid fingers over the wagon wheels and tarpaulins, crackling its way over axles and up wooden supports.

A cold, metallic scent filled Gaspi's nostrils as he felt the world closing in on him, the bright light of his mind shrinking and dimming to a wavering glimmer. Abject terror gripped his insides, making him want to squirm and shriek but so frozen by fear was he that he couldn't move, staring impotently at the approaching menace.

The creature followed the monkey's outstretched finger with its eyes. Its gaze settled leadenly on Lydia, and it began to glide heavily towards her across the clearing. Lydia had curled up in a ball, her head tucked under her arm, shoulders shaking from involuntary sobs. Gaspi faintly heard a whimper nearby, and in the deep recesses of his mind recognised Emea in that sound. Somehow, her terror penetrated the frozen fog of Gaspi's brain. The almost-extinguished fire of his heart was suddenly re-stoked, burning up fiercely against the cold, shaken from incapacity by anger. He couldn't lie there uselessly while this monster terrorised his friends, and as he fought against the freezing fear something snapped inside him: a doorway flew open that was normally held tightly shut.

In an instant, Gaspi's awareness stretched beyond the boundaries of his own body, and flowed out into his environment. He could feel the brittle grass cracking under the onslaught of the ice, the wood of the wagons constricting and creaking, the waning heat of the fire as it battled to stay ablaze, and the thumping hearts of terrified individuals writhing on the ground. And in the midst of all this was a swirling black hole, sucking all energy into its gaping maw. Gaspi could sense the flow of life-force draining from every living entity in the clearing into that endless sucking vacuum.

Without knowing how he did it, Gaspi whispered in his mind to the flame of the campfire, willing it to burn more brightly, to battle the leeching cold that almost put it out. And burn it did; not merely burn, but blaze! It soared and leaped towards the sky, roaring in defiance against the invader.

The dark creature moved hurriedly back from the fire, its head swivelling angrily, looking for the source of resistance. But Gaspi was already advancing, hands upturned, a look of furious intensity etched across his face. He lifted his hands, and the fire shot upwards in great spears of flame. The creature took its black gaze off Gaspi, and for the first time showed some hesitancy, as trails of fire curved upwards and out over its head in five thick streams. It lifted its own hands towards the advancing flame and for a moment it slowed in its flight, but Gaspi thrust out his arms aggressively, the firelight shining in his eyes, and the five trails of fire shot down to the ground, enclosing the creature in a great burning cage of light. Gaspi pushed the blazing bars inwards, pressing them against the creature's dark bulk.

The creature lifted its head, glaring at Gaspi with utter hatred and black intention, and released an unearthly howl, like a gale roaring through a canyon; a sound that turned Gaspi's bones to water and ripped at his sanity. Gaspi could sense the wood fuelling his cage of flame was nearly spent, and dizziness began to assail him. That dreadful sound shook him in ways he didn't know a person could be shaken, and just when he thought he couldn't sustain the effort any longer the creature howled one last time, its eyes boring hatefully into Gaspi, and then folded into itself and disappeared.

As warmth returned to the clearing Gaspi pitched forward into darkness, his mind swallowed up by shock and exhaustion. The fuel for Gaspi's cage of flame was utterly spent; the charred logs collapsed, sending a cloud of the finest grey ash billowing into the air.

Emea, Jonn, Lydia and Taurnil ran to Gaspi the second he fell to the ground, faces white with their own shock, and full of fear for him. Jonn was especially worried, as Gaspi had not just fallen into a comatose state as he'd done after his magic burst free from his control the first time, but he was moaning and writhing on the ground - his face screwed up so tight the skin around his eyes had turned white, and his hands clenching and unclenching over and over.

Knowing how close Gaspi came to dying when he had attacked Brock and Jakko with his magic, Jonn was not willing to wait around and see what happened. "We need to get him to Helioport as soon as possible!"

"Wait until morning, Jonn, and we'll carry him with us in one of our wagons. My wife can look after him while we travel," Roland said, white faced and trembling, his voice unsteady. He reached a hand out to touch Jonn's shoulder.

Jonn shook Roland's hand off. Recognising his rudeness, he explained, "Sorry Roland, but we can't wait. Gaspi could die if we don't get him some help right now. I know we don't know each other, but can you give me a horse? I will carry him with me, and ride to Helioport without stopping."

Roland accepted his apology with a nod of his head. "Of course, Jonn, what's mine is yours. And before you ask, I'll bring Emea and Taurnil along with us and will find you at the college when we arrive."

"Thank you, Roland," Jonn said. "I can't tell you what this means." His eyes communicated sincerity and relief. "Now, I must be off".

Roland muttered something to one of the young gypsy men, who left the ring immediately and came back leading a large, coal-black horse. "Ramoa will carry you best. He's strong and pretty fast, and won't tire out quickly." Jonn vaulted into the saddle and reached out to take Gaspi from Roland, placing him in front of him on the saddle and holding him in place with his arms.

Roland's wife, Miriam, came running with a small bundle she'd fetched from one of the wagons, and pressed it into Jonn's hands. "Here's some hard cheese and a small loaf to keep you going," she said, her round face flushed and grave.

"Thanks, Miriam," Jonn said, pushing the bundle into a pocket, and turned to Roland. "Find me at the College of Collective Magicks!"

He turned his gaze to Emea and Taurnil, who stood together looking lost and afraid.

"Look after her, Taurnil," he said; and with that, he kicked his heels into Ramoa's flanks, and sped off into the night.

Chapter 7

It was a long night for Jonn, racing Ramoa as fast as he dared along the Great South Road. Where the wagons gathered thickly by the roadside, enough light spilt onto the road to make his path clear, the surface of which was kept in good repair by regular patrols sent out from Helioport, but when the wagons grew sparse and the only light was from the half-moon and stars above he had to slow to a canter, to avoid any potholes or straying from the road.

He didn't allow himself to contemplate what might happen to Gaspi, but became a man focussed on one task only – to get to Helioport. No other thought entered his mind, his eyes riveted to the road to spy out safe passage, his thoughts all of speed and urgency. His breathing flowed in and out with the galloping rhythm of the horse's pounding feet, the two becoming one in their onward plight through the dark.

The diffuse glow of dawn meant nothing more than light on his path to Jonn, and the chance to draw nearer to Helioport, but he knew he could not continue to race Ramoa this way without killing him. He would have done that if Ramoa would die at the gates of Helioport, but there was still most of a day's ride before them, and necessity spoke strongly enough to force Jonn to stop and rest the horse for a while and eat something himself. He ate with one arm wrapped around Gaspi, pulling his unresponsive body into his own, unwilling to let go of him for a moment. Soon he was back on the horse, and driving for Helioport again.

They passed waggoners rising early with the dawn, who peered at them curiously after they'd blazed past. People shouted after them, telling him to slow down, or just making fun, but Jonn ignored them all. As the road began to fill up he was forced to ride on the very right hand side of the thoroughfare, where lone horsemen were expected to pass the slow-moving wagons. But even there Jonn had to weave his way through the mass of travellers, until his pace became frustratingly slow, and he began to become desperate. What if he couldn't get Gaspi to Helioport in time? What if he...? Ruthlessly shutting down his thoughts, Jonn pressed on as best he could.

Sometime about midday he came across a mounted patrol. As he raced past them the patrol leader called out to him to stop, but Jonn didn't even turn his head. The patrol immediately went in pursuit of the fleeing stranger, driving their horses at a gallop, and quickly gaining on the overburdened and exhausted horse Jonn was riding. As they overtook and surrounded him, Jonn knew he had no further choice, and pulled on Ramoa's reigns till he stopped.

Hand on the hilt of his sword, the patrol leader warily approached Jonn. "What's the hurry, stranger?" he asked, keeping several feet between him and Jonn.

"Captain, it's my son. He's dying. Please let me go on," Jonn pleaded, hands already gripping Ramoa's reigns again.

"Hold on!" the patrol leader commanded. "Dying of what?"

"He has magical talent, but is untrained," Jonn answered. "We were attacked on the road, and he has drained himself so dry defending us he is barely clinging onto life. I must get him to the College of Collective Magicks straight away. Every second counts here, sergeant."

The patrol leader's face lost its sternness. "I have no reason not to believe your story, friend, but if you go another mile on that horse you'll kill it." He was eyeing Ramoa with a keen eye, noting the sweaty froth smeared thickly along his flanks. He made a quick decision. "I will go with you, help clear the road, and get you through the gates fast. Helioport is still four hours ride away."

He turned to a swarthy guard among his crew. "Jim, you're in charge. Continue as planned, and report to me when you return tomorrow night." Jim nodded. "And bring this horse with you. We'll take Alberich's instead." He waved at a speechless Jonn, asking him to get off Ramoa, which he did after a second's hesitation, carefully sliding Gaspi down after him and holding him protectively. One of the patrol climbed off his own horse, handing the reigns to Jonn with some reluctance, and eyeing Ramoa doubtfully. Ramoa hadn't moved during the whole exchange and soon his heaving flanks began to slow their huffing and puffing, and he began to chew on the grass.

When Jonn had mounted his new horse, and had Gaspi secure before him, the patrol leader wasted no time in bidding his patrol farewell, and led the way along the road to Helioport at a strong pace. Every time the road was blocked by meandering travellers he would shout in warning and clear the way forward as quickly as possible, and the two horses continued their journey with barely a pause for the next few hours.

Jonn did not communicate a single word to the patrol leader, but kept his attention on the road and on Gaspi, who had ceased moving several hours ago, and was in the same comatose state Jonn had seen him in earlier that year. He was deathly still, the jostle of the horse's movements doing nothing more than cause his limbs to flop around, lifeless as a puppet.

Late in the afternoon, Jonn caught his first sight of Helioport. His thoughts were all of Gaspi and the unusual appearance of the city went unnoticed. On any other day he would have stopped to stare at the flowing contours of low domes and spires; all shaped from the same rich terracotta-coloured stone, organic and sinuous, feminine as a city could be, with barely a straight line in sight.

As they approached the gates, the patrol leader, who had taken just a moment on the ride to tell Jonn his name was Erik, hailed the cluster of guards surrounding the main gate, pulling up just long enough to let them know what was happening.

In moments they were ushered into the city, and in the cool of the wall's shadow they slowed their horses to a canter, the clack of eight hooves on hard stone echoing in the enclosed space. Erik led him on a broad street that swung anti-clockwise around the inner edge of the wall, and then gradually curved in towards the centre of the city, rising steadily towards the densest cluster of minarets, set on a rise above the rest of the city – the College of Collective Magicks.

Erik and Jonn, who continued to carry the unmoving Gaspi in his protective arms, cantered along the road's inward curve towards the heart of the city, passing curious onlookers and city dwellers of every type, until they reined in their mounts at the gate of the college itself. The college was surrounded by an enclosing wall of creamy, polished stone, much paler than the reddish stone of the city itself. The gateway was a graceful arc of this stone, spanning the entryway and meeting over the travellers' heads. These walls were not made for physical protection, but marked the boundary in exquisite contours, emanating a diffuse glow that announced the presence of magic.

Two booths sat like bookends at either end of the encircling wall, shaped from the same pale stone without any apparent seam or join, and in each booth a red-robed man sat at his ease. Even in his hurried state Jonn noticed there weren't any actual gates between the two booths, but only the broad span of pale stone arching over their heads, leaving an open entryway wide enough for two carts to pass through side by side. And no armed guards stood at attention at the gateway, either.

A small group of what must have been students in brown robes flowed through the gate, nodding respectfully to the two red-robed men in the booths. Pressing through the traffic, Jonn rode up to the right booth, where the gentleman had stood up and was peering intently at Gaspi's comatose form.

"Please help my son!" Jonn pleaded, all restraint abandoned in the presence of hope.

The gatekeeper's eyes widened with urgency. "What happened to him?" he asked hurriedly, bustling out from behind the booth and coming to look more closely at Gaspi.

"He exhausted himself with magic," Jonn said, his voice cracking under the strain.

"Magic? Say no more." And with that, the gatekeeper rang a tiny silver bell hanging from his waist. Jonn didn't think anyone inside the college could possibly hear such a gentle tinkling sound, and was about to object when two brown-robed students came rushing out of the gate. "Take him to the infirmary immediately," commanded the gatekeeper, "and tell them it's burnout. Quickly, now!"

One of the students waved his hand in a precise motion, and Jonn was stunned when Gaspi's body lifted out of his arms and floated to the student's side, hovering off the ground as if he was lying on an invisible bed. Jonn tried to follow the two students as they took Gaspi through the gates, but the gatekeeper would not let him through. He held his hand out in front of Jonn.

"There's nothing you can do now, good sir," he said kindly, "but you can go to the guest suites and rest while we tend to your son." He must have seen the reluctance on Jonn's face. "He really is in the best of hands," he added gently. "Please…" His compassion got through to Jonn, who nodded once in agreement. The gatekeeper rang another bell that hung in the booth, summoning another student to lead Jonn to the guest suites.

Before departing Jonn turned to Erik. "I can't thank you enough, Erik," he said. "If you've saved him, I owe you my life."

Erik smiled, and gripped Jonn by the shoulder. "Let's just hope he'll be okay." Jonn nodded. "I'll be at the barracks by the city gates," Erik said. "When you find out how he is and have some time, let me know, okay?" he added, before turning to lead the horses away.

Looking back over his shoulder he called back. "And when my patrol get back, I'll make sure your horse is looked after. You can pick him up when you want to." Jonn thanked him again, and followed the student into the college.

Chapter 8

Gaspi was lost in a sea of pain. A red haze filled his vision, surging and swirling in an agonising tide. His grasp on his identity was faint at best, slipping away through his fingers, and all he knew to do was to hold on, to fight. But hold on to what? Fight for what? There were no obvious answers to these questions but some gritty part of him insisted he continued to do these things, and so hold on he did.

He had no awareness of the journey by horse, or of Jonn holding him, or the passing of night into day, but he could feel the thread of his life slipping inexorably out of his grasp, moment by moment.

The pain seemed endless, its objective cruelty racking him beyond his ability to endure, and at some point even his stubborn insistence to hold the darkness at bay began to diminish. Dark, empty spaces floated through his red inner vision. The darkness was empty of pain, but felt cold and lifeless, worse almost than the hot pain he fought. Oblivion called to him from that darkness, calling him to let go, to submit; and perhaps if it had taken longer to reach those that could help him, he would have done so.

At the point where darkness began to fill his vision, where blackness swept through the red in powerful waves, where the fingers of his soul began to loosen their grip, there was a sudden inrush of light, as if a door had been flung open, and blessed whiteness flowed over Gaspi's eyes, filling his vision and ending his pain. And then, there was nothing.

When Gaspi regained consciousness again, he was disturbed to find his vision again blank and tinged red, but as he moved out of the deep sleep of recovery he identified the colour as the warm pink glow of sunlight through his closed eyelids. Slowly, tentatively, he opened his eyes, the motion heavy and unnatural. It took several moments for his eyes to adjust to the bright glare of the sun, but when he stopped blinking against the brightness he was able to look around.

He was tucked into a narrow but comfortable single bed, enclosed by starchy white sheets, in a high-ceilinged room big enough to contain the five other beds set opposite each other in rows of three. The other beds were all empty, as in fact was the room. Warm swathes of sunshine beamed down through the high windows and spot-lit the wooden floor in broad rectangles of light. Dust motes drifted lazily in the sunbeams, and through the windows Gaspi could see the swaying tops of elegant trees, and hear snatches of laughter and muffled conversation carried to his ears by swirling breezes.

Memories of his encounter at the gypsy campfire filtered through Gaspi's sleep-fuddled haze, and if he had the strength he would have sat up in alarm. Where was he? Why was no-one here with him? But he had no time for further thought, as at that moment the door was pushed open by a matronly woman carrying a tray, and following her was Jonn.

"Ah - I thought you'd be awake!" said the nurse.

"Gaspi!" Jonn cried with relief and rushed to his bedside, falling to his knees on the floorboards to give Gaspi a bear-like hug. "How do you feel?"

"I'm think I'm fine, Jonn," Gaspi said, tiredness making it hard to focus. "I'm just exhausted…can barely keep my eyes open."

"Well that's to be expected, young man," interjected the nurse, placing her tray down on a small table next to Gaspi's bed. "Go back to sleep, and you can eat this when you're awake again."

"But I want to know where I am…what's happened…" Gaspi fought with his shutting eyelids, which slid down and closed with irresistible finality, and with Jonn's hand on his head he was reclaimed by sleep. Several hours later Gaspi awoke again, feeling much more alert and keenly aware of his growling stomach. Jonn was asleep in the comfortable chair next to him, breathing noisily through his open mouth.

Unable to restrain himself, Gaspi prodded Jonn until he awoke and immediately began to question him. "Where are we?" was the first thing on Gaspi's mind.

Jonn rubbed his eyes. "If I answer that question, will you eat before asking me anything else?" Gaspi nodded impatiently. "We're in the infirmary of the College of Collective Magicks."

Gaspi couldn't help feeling excited. "But…" he began, but was cut off by Jonn placing the tray of food firmly in his lap.

"Eat!" Jonn said firmly. Gaspi did as he was told, wolfing the food down as fast as possible, barely noticing the freshness and delicacy of the fruit, or the wonderful flavour of the nutty bread in his hurry to return to interrogating Jonn. Finally, he pushed his tray aside and looked at Jonn expectantly.

Gaspi wanted to know what happened after the confrontation at the gypsy camp, where Emmy and Taurnil were, if Lydia was okay, how they got to the college, how long he'd been asleep, and if he was alright. Jonn patiently answered his questions, even explaining the help he'd had from Erik.

"I wonder how close Taurnil and Emmy are," Gaspi sighed, once Jonn had answered all his questions to his satisfaction.

"I'm sure they'll be here in a day or two," Jonn replied. A frown marred Jonn's forehead as he stared hard into space. "What I want to know," he added, "is what on God's green earth was that thing that attacked you at the gypsy camp?"

"It didn't attack me, Jonn," Gaspi responded. "It attacked Lydia."

"Lydia? But why?" Jonn asked in surprise.

Gaspi realised Jonn hadn't seen the monkey strike Lydia earlier on the same day they had been attacked at the gypsy wagons. "Jonn, we only met Lydia that day because she was attacked by that demented monkey. You know, the one that made such a horrible screech at the campfire?" Jonn looked thoughtful for a moment and nodded. "Well we were watching the same monkey earlier in the day," Gaspi continued, "when it suddenly went mad and sprinted at Lydia. She was sitting in one of the gypsy wagons doing a reading for one of her family."

"A reading?" Jonn asked quizzically.

"Yeah, Lydia can read the future sometimes," Gaspi explained. "She called herself a Seer. She must have been using magic when the monkey saw her."

A grim understanding dawned on Jonn's face. "Mmm...the thing you fought must be the same type of creature that attacked Harold in that village we stopped at."

"And the monkey is some kind of scout!" Gaspi finished. They both sat in silence for a moment, thinking through the implications of what they had deduced.

"We may not be right about this, Gaspi," Jonn said. "It's more than a little bit strange."

"I'm sure of it, Jonn!" Gaspi insisted, pressing himself up onto his elbows, his face full of zealous conviction.

"Easy now, Gasp," Jonn said gently. "You may be right, but this is way beyond us. We need to take this to the Mages."

"But maybe they should send someone out, someone who can do magic," Gaspi urged. "Lydia might still be in danger." His eyes widened suddenly. "And Emmy!"

"Good point, Gaspi," Jonn conceded. "I'll go straight away, if you don't mind me leaving you."

"I don't mind," said Gaspi, leaning back on his pillow, temporarily mollified by Jonn's urgency.

Jonn paused before he passed through the door. "Stay in bed, Gaspi!"

Jonn exited the infirmary into a large open courtyard, surrounded on all sides by ivy-covered buildings, and crisscrossed by rambling paths that wound around fruit trees and old willows. Not knowing where he was going, Jonn looked for the first Mage he could see, and guessing the man sweeping past him in deep red robes was a candidate, he stopped him with a hand on the arm.

"Excuse me, but can you take me to…the leader here?" Jonn asked, unsure of the correct title assigned to the head Mage.

"To the Chancellor?" the red robed man responded. "But why? He's a busy man, you know."

"I assure you, it is a matter of urgency," Jonn said. "My son is in the infirmary after a magical attack, and we have news he will want to hear."

The conviction in Jonn's tone must have convinced him. "Follow me, then," he said briskly, and strode across the courtyard, red robes flapping around his ankles as he went. Jonn allowed himself to be led out of the courtyard, and on a winding uphill journey through low arches, narrow corridors, up and down stairways, past various buildings both grand and meagre, though all having a certain grace of their own. Jonn was taken aback by the sheer variety of styles of the buildings they passed. There was no sense of uniformity, and in fact even the more sedate, traditional section of the college that housed the infirmary was not consistent with the reddish stone used to construct the city itself.

After several minutes of walking past the endless variety of bizarre constructions, some of which Jonn could have sworn should not be able to support their own weight, they came to a stately tower situated on then highest point of the complex. Its scale made it look narrower than it in fact was. Its tapering height was dotted with windows all the way up and around, until it swelled at the top into a large bulb, which itself tapered to a fine point, like the stopper in an alchemist's apothecary jar. The bulb-shaped peak of the tower had a series of large glass-filled windows looking out in every direction, several of which reflected the morning sun into Jonn's eyes in dazzling rays.

Squinting, Jonn entered the large, open doorway at the foot of the tower, following his red-robed guide, who urged him to wait there until he returned, indicating a row of deeply-cushioned gold-coloured armchairs spaced along the wall of the atrium. The Mage spoke to a silver robed magician sitting behind an enormous desk near the entranceway, then walked towards a series of platforms set against a wall opposite the armchairs. Each platform was made of the same creamy stone as the outer wall of the college, glowing faintly from within. There were twelve of these circular platforms in all, each one standing just under a foot tall, the wall behind them marked with arcane symbols. Reaching the twelfth platform, the Mage stepped up and moved to its centre. Placing his hands by his sides he spoke a single word, and to Jonn's amazement he simply disappeared. There was no warning; one second he was there, the next he was gone.

Mentally exhausted, Jonn blew out a lungful of air and sank down into one the comfortable chairs with a shake of his head. He decided that too many new things at once made them lose their appeal. Even so, he couldn't help staring curiously at his surroundings. The inside of the tower was much larger than it appeared, and it took him a moment to work out it wasn't a magical trick, but merely the deceptive proportions of the tower that gave a false impression from the outside. Reasoning the tower must be extremely tall, Jonn let his eyes roam over the contours of the spacious entrance hall. Rich tapestries of every hue hung around the cool, creamy interior of the building. Spaced in some kind of design he couldn't discern, they formed a pattern that was unpredictable and yet comfortable to the eye, as if part of an order beyond his ability to detect.

Letting his eye roam further, Jonn was curious to discover the ceiling swept upwards on all sides to a hole in the very centre of the room, about twelve feet wide, below which there was another of the cylindrical plinths of the same width, glowing gently against the floor. Jonn almost jumped off his seat when a pair of feet came out of that hole, followed by the hem of a multicoloured robe, and then the whole robe, and finally above outstretched arms came an enigmatic face framed by long hair and a dark beard. The cause of Jonn's fright descended quickly to the floor, where he gently pulled his arms in to his side as he neared the plinth. As he pulled in his arms, the figure slowed and then stopped just as his sandaled feet touched stone. Stepping off the plinth with cheerful aplomb he strode towards Jonn, a look of wild enjoyment on his broadly grinning face.

"Welcome, friend!" he said, pumping Jonn's hand with enthusiasm, his hands exerting an unexpected strength. "My name is Hephistole, and you would be...?"

Jonn gave his name, trying his best to sound normal, but the strain of seeing vanishing and flying magicians must have showed in his voice.

"My good man, you must be tired," the colourful stranger said, "being dragged up and down the grounds like that! Come up to my office, and we can sit down and have a nice cup of tea." Jonn couldn't stop his eyes flicking nervously towards the hole in the ceiling. Hephistole laughed. "No, not that way," he said, and taking Jonn by the arm led him towards the glowing plinths on the floor.

"Ahem…" Jonn cleared his throat nervously.

Hephistole glanced sideways at Jonn with a mischievous glint in his eye. "No need to worry. No need at all. It's perfectly safe," he said confidently, his lips upturned at the edges in a repressed smile. Leading Jonn onto the twelfth platform, Hephistole turned to Jonn and said "Now just stand still, arms by your side....that's right! You might feel a little disorientation." Once Jonn was standing as directed, Hephistole brought his own arms in, and looking Jonn in the eye spoke a single word with annunciation: "Observatory."

The strangest vibration ran through Jonn's body, as if he were buzzing like a giant bee. His vision blinked off entirely, seeing nothing but a blank greyness emptier than darkness. It couldn't have been longer than a heartbeat later when Jonn's sight came rushing back, along with the welcome presence of something solid beneath his feet, but his relief was quickly overridden by astonishment at the sight of a completely different room.

Hephistole hopped off the platform, and turned to Jonn with a grin. "See, it's not too bad!" he said cheerfully. Jonn wasn't sure he agreed, but didn't want to offend his unusual host. Hephistole gestured at Jonn, encouraging him to seat himself in a chair near the platform. Jonn stepped off the platform, with some relief, and sat down in the well-cushioned chair. Hephistole was already pouring hot red-yellow liquid into delicate cups with tiny handles.

"Erm, yes, not too bad," Jonn mumbled bravely. "How on earth does that work?" he asked, more to distract himself from shock than from any real desire to know.

"Well, my dear man, that is not quickly answered," Hephistole said with a smile, passing one of the cups to Jonn on a matching plate only a little bigger than the cup itself. "In fact, we're having something of a debate about this very subject at the moment." Jonn's sense of urgency, temporarily suspended since entering the tower, began to swell again now that Hephistole looked ready to launch into a lengthy monologue.

"It's been understood for some time now that we are as much energy as we are matter," Hephistole started enthusiastically, "and the transporter acts as a focus for just that activity – turning matter into energy, and energy into matter." Hephistole beamed as if that explained everything, but Jonn's look of utter confusion prompted him to divulge a little more information. "Did you feel a kind of resonance when you stood on the platform?"

"I felt like my whole body was buzzing," Jonn said, politeness forcing him to answer with a semblance of interest.

"Ah yes. I forget how strange that feels the first time," Hephistole said with a sympathetic smile. "Well, that 'buzzing', as you call it," he continued, "was what it feels like to be transformed into an energy signature of your whole being."

"You mean I was no longer there?" Jonn asked, curiosity momentarily overriding his need to bring up what he had come to talk about.

"No, not at all!" Hephistole answered, with a laugh like a thunderclap. "You were there, but expressed as energy instead of matter. The reason you couldn't see was because you had no eyes!" Hephistole's grin broadened ever further.

"But isn't that dangerous?" Jonn asked.

"Dangerous?" Hephistole said slowly, as if examining a new concept for the first time, turning it over in his mind for a good view of it from all sides. "Well, I suppose so if it went wrong, but it rarely does - and if it does, it is rarely something we can't fix." There were too many "rarelys" in that for Jonn, who said nothing, but inwardly vowed to take the stairs on the way down.

"So, anyway," Hephistole continued, "once you have been converted to energy you can be moved around at great speed. The transporters connect to each other through a magical field that contains the energy, and you literally travel through the walls and ceilings, furniture and people until you reach your destination and are reformed into matter. Isn't it wonderful?" Hephistole exclaimed.

"Yes…wonderful," Jonn repeated, unconvincingly. Jonn opened his mouth to bring the conversation round to the subject he'd come here to discuss, but Hephistole had started talking again.

"Some of our learned colleagues believe the transforming of matter into energy is the way forward for magical development in the area of transport, but others believe that manipulating matter to serve us is the better approach."

Mistaking Jonn's look of frustration for confusion, Hephistole continued. "You've already seen a perfect example of the two methods. Argent used the transporter to come up here, but I flew back down to the Atrium to meet you. Argent went through an energy conversion, but I manipulated matter to float down to you." Hephistole's eyes grew intent, as if sharing a deep personal secret. "I made myself lighter within a confined field, and manipulated my density so I could fall through the air at a speed of my choice. You can speed up or slow down by changing the relative densities."

Jonn finally lost all patience. "Please!" he said, a bit louder than intended. Hephistole's eyebrows climbed up his forehead. "Please," Jonn repeated, more quietly this time. "We need your help."

"My good man, I'm sorry," Hephistole said, sitting down abruptly and giving Jonn his whole attention. "I've been told I ramble on sometimes. Tell me all about it!"

After waving for Jonn to continue, Hephistole settled in to consider Jonn's tale, resting his bony elbows on his knees and placing his head on his open hands, piercing green eyes probing deeply into Jonn's as he began to talk.

Jonn tried to rush through the details of his story but Hephistole continually stopped him with probing questions, and in the end he started from scratch and told him everything, from the day Gaspi's magic emerged until their arrival at the College. Hephistole listened intently, asking further questions, examining what Jonn told him with intense scrutiny. He didn't seem remotely concerned about Gaspi's previous comatose state, but at the description of Harold's death, and the attack of the creature at the gypsy camp, his long face became grave; losing its vibrant energy for the first time since Jonn met him, wreathed in deep lines of concern.

"So what we're worried about," Jonn summarised, "is that these creatures seem to be searching for magic users, and they already know of Lydia and Gaspi. Gaspi is safe here at the College, I assume, but Lydia is still on the road, with my other charges Emea and Taurnil. What if they come under attack again?"

Hephistole remained motionless for a few moments, staring deeply into space. Jonn was about to cough politely, when the Chancellor shook his head like a dog shedding water and returned his attention to Jonn. "Well, that's quite a story," he said with a snap of decisiveness in his tone, "and you're absolutely right; we can't leave your young friends out there unprotected." Hephistole's eyes unfocussed for a moment; he appeared to be concentrating on something.

His eyes refocused on Jonn. "I've called someone who can help," he said, before springing to his feet and beginning to pace back and forth. Jonn didn't know whether to sit or stand. Bringing his movement to a sudden halt, Hephistole turned back to Jonn. "We have noticed some strange signs in the last year. Stories of magicians going missing have reached our ears; and some stranger, darker tales too. We have one Mage out there in the north investigating the truth of the rumours, and your story makes it harder to deny. There may be a force out there intent on our destruction, and one with some power." Hephistole's expression lightened. "But I mustn't burden you with my worries! Rest assured, we will bring all our knowledge to bear on this. And there is some good news, of course."

"Good news?" Jonn asked.

"We have a Nature Mage! That is no small thing, Jonn."

Hephistole's broad grin returned to his face. "And by your own account, we have a Seer and Healer on their way to us as we speak."

The sound of a small gong being struck pervaded the room. "Ah, here is Voltan," Hephistole said. The room pulsed with the quiet buzz of the transporter (a much less intrusive sensation than Jonn had felt when he was the one being transported), and suddenly a slender, dark-skinned man appeared on the glowing platform. Hephistole gestured towards the arrival, by means of introduction. "Jonn, this is Voltan. Voltan, this is the father of the young boy we have in our infirmary."

Voltan smiled at Jonn, a slight uplifting of narrow lips set against a fine bone structure and tight, dusky skin. Voltan's narrow nose was finely sculpted, delicate nostrils flaring under an aquiline bridge, his eyes dark and deep beneath an angular forehead. His hair formed a widow's peak and was drawn back tightly across his head into a pony tail at the back, held by a leather thong. Jonn stood up and shook Voltan's hand; the magician's grip was firm, but not overly so.

Turning to Voltan, Hephistole briefed him on the situation. "We have three young friends of our guest here travelling with a family of gypsies, heading to us. They are in some danger, and need an escort of magicians capable of defending them against attacks." Voltan's gaze was intense, and he did not speak once while Hephistole described the attack Gaspi had turned aside, and the theory Jonn and Gaspi had concocted.

"Is there anything you want to add?" Voltan asked, once Hephistole had finished.

"No, that about sums it up," Jonn answered.

"Well, it seems like fire works against them," Voltan said thoughtfully. "We have no Nature Mages, of course, but there are other ways of using fire. I'll go myself, and I'll take another of the warriors. I'll go straight away." Turning to leave, he paused at the edge of the transporter. "It's amazing your son survived the attack, and the use of his own magic, Jonn. He must have an unusual talent. I look forward to meeting him." And with that he nodded once at Hephistole, stepped on the transporter, and was gone.

Hephistole smiled brightly at Jonn. "So let's go and meet this young magician of yours!" he said enthusiastically, gesturing for Jonn to step onto the transporter.

"With all due respect, could I use the stairs?" Jonn asked, glancing with distrust at the plinth.

Hephistole's eyes widened. "Stairs?" he asked incredulously. "But my dear man we don't have any stairs here. Why would we need them when we can travel so much more efficiently using the transporters?"

"Of course....no stairs," mumbled Jonn. "Can we at least fly down?" he asked, though without any obvious enthusiasm for this option either.

Hephistole scratched his beard. "Well, yes, if you'd prefer that. I can stretch the field of varying density around both of us and control the descent. But what's wrong with the transporter?" he asked, in an injured tone.

"I would rather stay in one piece and float down through the air than be split into a thousand little pieces." Jonn asserted bluntly.

Hephistole's mouth twisted in a confused smile. "That's not exactly how it works, but if you prefer to fly then we will fly. This way, if you please." Hephistole led Jonn round the extensive curve of the large office, which circled the outer edge of the tower's giant bulb-shaped peak. Jonn was surprised as they passed several areas where the sinuous inner wall recessed deeply back into the centre of the tower, creating unexpected spaces. The first such space they passed was unlit, its dark interior filled with small cages, each with a red velvet cloth draped over its door. The next recess had exactly the same contents, but the cages were twice the size. The third area seemed to have nothing in it, but was lit from a source Jonn could not detect with a dim purple glow.

In all there were seven recesses, the last filled with the kind of calibrated instruments Jonn associated with taking measurements, or comparing weights, along with many others he couldn't compare to anything he'd ever seen. They were made of all kinds of materials, and each was placed on plinth of its own. Some items were non-descript and clunky and some were intricate and sparkling with gold, silver, or even jewels. An earthenware mug sat next to a delicate set of gleaming silver scales, which was adjacent to a hand-sized sculpture of a golden wyvern, its eyes set with flashing rubies, its head curled around and resting on a wing. Jonn was amazed at the size of Hephistole's office, and said nothing for the entire walk around the edge of the tower's cavernous peak, until they came at last to the end, where a large hole in the floor ended the walk from the podium to this end of the room.

Hephistole held his arm out to Jonn. "Hold on to my arm, and step off when I do." Jonn was having second thoughts about flying, but he was too embarrassed to ask to go back all the way to the plinth. Taking Hephistole's arm, he walked to the edge of the hole, and then as Hephistole stepped forwards he gulped and stepped out into space. Everything in him tensed as he expected to plummet through the hole, his hand gripping Hephistole's arm like a vice. But the air he stepped into caught and held him suspended over the drop. Looking down, Jonn couldn't help grabbing even more tightly onto Hephistole's arm.

Hephistole smiled at him, and with a wave of his hand initiated the descent. They dropped unhurriedly down through the levels of the tower, passing through several floors that appeared to house comfortable offices, and several more that contained expansive laboratories. On the lowest floor above the atrium, Jonn was afforded a fleeting view of a group of young men and women, all in brown robes, sitting cross-legged in a circle with a white-robed Mage in their midst. They were hovering three feet off the floor. Finally, they passed through one more ceiling and emerged into the wide open space of the atrium, just as Hephistole had done a couple of hours previously.

Jonn was immensely relieved when his feet came to rest several inches above the glowing plinth, and he was able to hop off onto the floor. Hard ground beneath his feet slowly banished his anxiety, and he couldn't help ask one more question of Hephistole.

"If you use your own magic to fly, why do we need a plinth at the bottom here?" he asked. "It's not like we're being transported."

Hephistole looked pleased. "Excellent question, excellent question," he said, rubbing his long-fingered hands together. "The plinth is not a transporter. It is there in case a magician loses concentration and falls!"

Jonn could hardly believe his ears. "You mean we could have fallen?"

"Well, technically, yes," said Hephistole patiently, "but that hasn't happened to me in years. Besides, that's what the plinth is there for. If anything approaches it at any kind of speed, it slows and halts it before impact. So there's nothing to worry about, see?" Jonn didn't have the chance to say anything, as his eccentric guide was already striding towards the wide doors of the tower, long hair and robe flapping behind him. Jonn caught up with him and matched his pace, and the two men walked through the grounds to the infirmary.

Chapter 9

Gaspi was way past impatient. A view of the ceiling had lost its appeal several hours previously, and the walls were not much more interesting. Despite a lingering exhaustion, he had tried to lever himself out of bed several times without any notable success, and the last attempt had seen him sliding down onto the floor next to the bed. It was in this position that Hephistole first laid eyes on Gaspi.

With a twinkle in his eye and a bark of a laugh he bounded over to Gaspi, and helped him back into bed. "A bit restless, are we?" he asked.

"Er, yeah," a red-faced Gaspi answered, taken aback by this dynamic stranger.

With Gaspi settled back on his bed, the newcomer pulled up a chair for himself and sat down, his sparkling eyes peering enthusiastically at Gaspi. "So, my young fellow," he said. "My name is Hephistole and I have the honour of being the Chancellor of this fine institution."

"Nice to meet you, sir," Gaspi said politely.

"No need for that, young man. The students call me Heppy behind my back. Feel free to abuse the familiarity," he said, with a broad smile.

A slow grin spread over Gaspi's face, and after a short pause he thrust out his hand. "Then you can call me Gaspi," he said.

Hephistole shook his hand solemnly, then let out a spontaneous laugh. "Good lad," he affirmed. "Well, now we have that out of the way, let's talk about why you're here. Jonn here has told me all about your journey. You've been through quite an ordeal! I think it's best that we start looking into your training."

"Heppy," Gaspi ventured courageously, "sorry to interrupt, but are you sending out someone to get my friends?" Deep concern for Emmy and Taurn overrode any remaining shyness.

"Of course, of course," the Chancellor answered briskly. "I should have told you that straight away. I sent two Mages out over an hour ago. All being well, they should be with you by tomorrow." Gaspi breathed a sigh of relief and let his head fall fully back onto the soft pillow.

"Thank you," he said sincerely. He looked up, meeting Hephistole's gaze. "You said something about my training?" asked Gaspi. "Does that mean you will be taking me on as a student?"

"Absolutely! And if it's alright with you, we'll begin as soon as we possibly can."

"That would be great," answered Gaspi.

Hephistole's face grew more serious. "There's something we need to sort out before you can get down to the business of learning magic,

Gaspi. You have a powerful form of magic rarely seen these days. It is so powerful it almost killed you - twice, from what Jonn tells me." Gaspi shuddered, the memory of those terrible events making him fearful. "I don't want you to worry about that, Gaspi," the Chancellor said reassuringly. "We won't let that happen to you again; but the first thing you must do is gain control of the forces within you."

"Can you help me do that?" Gaspi asked.

"Of course," Hephistole answered, with a smile. "But your magic is so powerful we've had to put a block on it to stop you using it until you are ready. When we brought you in here you were still connected to the magic, and if we hadn't blocked you there's no way you could have recovered."

"I don't understand," Gaspi said.

"It doesn't benefit us much going into the technicalities of it right now. Experienced practitioners of magic would disagree on the exact cause of the phenomena, but suffice it to say that without control you were unable to let go of the power once you'd released it this last time, and every time you gained a little strength back the magic sucked it out of you, trying to harness your life force. So I apologise for the intrusion, but I had to enter your mind and put a block between you and the source of your power, to save your life."

Gaspi stared into space, trying to make sense of what he was hearing. Finally, he asked "But how am I to learn to control magic if I can't use it?"

"Good question!" Hephistole barked so loudly Gaspi jumped. Gaspi got the impression that there was little Hephistole liked more than a good question. "We will be teaching you the mechanisms of control - an interface to your mind, if you like." Gaspi looked confused. "Sorry Gaspi. Look at me going on like an old fool, using technical jargon where a simple explanation will suffice! We are going to teach you to meditate, which is a relaxed state which enables you to examine and control your thoughts and feelings. Trust me, you'll enjoy it!"

"Okay, Heppy," Gaspi said, still unsure as to what it all meant.

"I'll ask the matron to give you a restorative, and we'll move you into your dormitory tomorrow," Hephistole said. "You should be strong enough by then, and we don't want your friends arriving to find you in a hospital bed, now, do we?"

Gaspi grinned. "Sounds good!"

"Okay, Gaspi, I'll take my leave now. We don't want to exhaust you! I'll see you soon," the enigmatic Chancellor concluded. Bounding out of his chair, Hephistole left with a wink and a grin, banging out through the infirmary door; which, as if energised by his touch, swung vigorously on its hinge for several seconds after he was gone.

Before Gaspi fell asleep that night the matron brought him a small glass filled with a bright green drink. "Drink up, young man," she said in a tone that brooked no argument. "By tomorrow you'll be back to your normal self." Gaspi sipped the strange looking brew, and found it to be not unpleasant. Its taste was earthy, bursting with the unfettered freshness of growing things, and Gaspi thought that it was somehow both hot and cold at the same time. As soon as the liquid had slid down his throat a slow warmth begin to tingle in his stomach and spread languidly through his body, seeping down his limbs and along his fingers until every part of him thrummed with a soothing inner vibration. Sleep approached irresistibly like a giant wave, sweeping up over him, sucking him down into its depths and crashing down, plunging him into the depths of dark, oblivious rest.

The next morning, Gaspi awoke feeling quite back to normal. He immediately got out of bed, relieved to find no remnant of the malaise that had kept him in his bed for the past day. Jonn had left some clothes for him on a chair, and Gaspi had just finished dressing when Jonn arrived along with a boy who looked to be around Gaspi's age. The boy was taller than Gaspi, with the kind of handsome features the girls at home liked. He was broad-shouldered and blonde-haired, and wore the brown robes of a student.

He introduced himself without making eye contact, and without shaking hands. "I'm Everand," he announced, as if that statement should mean something in itself. "I'm here to show you to your dormitory," he said, waiting impatiently for Jonn to gather Gaspi's things together. As soon as they were ready, he led them briskly from the room. As they walked through the complex, Gaspi sped up to walk alongside Everand.

"Are you in my year?" Gaspi asked, trying to think of something to spark up a conversation.

"Yes," replied Everand without embellishment, chin thrust high into the air as he walked. Gaspi lapsed into silence, slipping back to walk alongside Jonn, who just shrugged when Gaspi gave him a questioning look. Everand led them to a long, single-storey building, set along one side of a large courtyard, which unlike the other enclosed areas of the college was just an open square of hard, dusty ground, not planted with trees or covered in grass. It was marked all over with white lines, forming a pattern Gaspi didn't recognise. The square was enclosed on all four sides by low buildings. The one Everand entered was twinned by an exact replica on the opposite side of the courtyard, and the other two sides were filled with a mismatched selection of buildings, whose use was not immediately obvious.

As Gaspi followed Everand into what he assumed was to be his dormitory, the smell of wood-polish filled his nostrils; the kind of strong, resinous scent that instantly takes you back to the place it was first smelled. Everand stalked at his unyielding pace along the long, narrow room, between two rows of six beds on either side, before stopping at an empty bed at the end of the row.

"This is yours," he said, looking briefly at Gaspi before turning to leave.

"Thank you," Gaspi murmured, feeling put out by Everand's cold manner.

As Everand reached the door he turned around. "They say you're a Nature Mage," he said, his tone edged with disbelief.

"So they say," Gaspi answered shortly, disinclined to say anything more.

Everand said nothing for several seconds. "The Dean asked me to tell you to come with the first-year boys to class tomorrow morning," the tall bay said reluctantly, as if it were beneath him to be passing on messages. "You will be joining us straight away." And with that, Everand turned on his heel and was gone.

"Well, he was nice!" Gaspi said to Jonn.

Jonn smiled ruefully. "Don't let him worry you, Gaspi. There are all kinds of people in the world. A little bit of rudeness is nothing to worry about."

Gaspi said nothing, but didn't agree with Jonn at all. Why should Everand have treated him like that? He had done nothing wrong at all. Years of being singled out by Jakko had imbued him with an instinct for idiots, and Everand looked like a clear candidate. He inwardly resolved to make an impression on the arrogant Everand as soon as possible.

The floors and walls of the dormitory were made of dark grainy wood, polished up to a fine sheen. The wide, heavy beds were of the same dark wood, and at the back of each were two shelves sitting directly over a half-moon shaped bedhead. At the side of each bed was a small cabinet, with a single upper drawer and a larger open space below it, and a small wooden chair. The other beds, shelves, cabinets and chairs all showed signs of habitation; books were stacked on the shelves, sheets, though tidied, had clearly been slept in, and clothes were hanging on the backs of chairs. The other students' cloaks and robes hung from brass hooks which protruded from the wall at the side of each bed.

Jonn put a sack containing Gaspi's few clothes and belongings on the bed, and sat down on the chair. "Get yourself sorted, Gasp, and we'll go and see if there's any news of Emmy and Taurn, maybe see some of the city," he said. Glad of the distraction, Gaspi emptied his sack on the bed, quickly finding a home for all its contents; the only thing of any real personal value to him a hard Koshta seed, which went in the drawer in his bedside cabinet.

Gaspi and Jonn made their way to the main entrance of the college to ask about the arrival of the gypsy caravan, but there wasn't any news, so Jonn took Gaspi into the city. While Gaspi had slept, Jonn had learned his way around the main streets of the town, and visited the barracks several times. Today, he took Gaspi to a café with a view of the main gate. Jonn ordered a plate of cured, spicy meat, and they sat at the side of the street watching people go by. Each table had the same centrepiece; a kind of covered clay bowl, with several long, flexible pipes snaking from it. Other customers were sucking on those pipes, drawing smoke out of the clay bowl as it gurgled noisily.

Gaspi was intrigued when Jonn asked for theirs to be lit. He watched as Jonn drew in a deep lungful of smoke and let it stream out of his nostrils with a contented sigh. When Jonn invited him to take a pipe for himself, Gaspi quickly snatched the nearest one and sucked. Jonn couldn't contain his laughter as Gaspi gave an explosive cough and spluttered uncontrollably, the inhaled smoke violently expelled from his mouth as soon as it touched the back of his throat.

Gaspi was put out by Jonn laughing at him, and pulled a face. "Come on Gasp, lighten up!" Jonn said with a smile. Gaspi couldn't help smiling in return. This trip seemed to be doing his guardian the world of good. Gaspi couldn't remember Jonn looking this relaxed in Aemon's Reach, and was happy with the change.

"I've got something to tell you," Jonn said. Gaspi looked at him expectantly."I'm signing up as a guard. I'll need something to keep me occupied as you study."

The source of Jonn's good mood became clearer to Gaspi. He had been wasting away in Aemon's Reach, with nothing to do but odd jobs, and everything he saw reminding him of what he had lost. But here he was free from all that, and the prospect of soldiering was clearly doing something for him.

"That's great, Jonn," Gaspi said, genuinely pleased for his guardian. "Now I won't have to worry about you being bored," he said with a grin.

"Cheeky young pup," Jonn muttered good-naturedly, taking a

playful swipe at Gaspi's head. "Now, come on, and try this Tabac again." A couple of hours later they were still sitting in the same spot, replete with the local, spicy sausage they had indulged in, and after several embarrassing attempts Gaspi had given up on the Tabac. It had a subtle cherry flavour as well as the harsh tang of Tabac, but Gaspi couldn't work out how Jonn could call it smooth, whatever he had said about passing the smoke through water to filter it. Jonn had explained to Gaspi that smoking Tabac was only an occasional pleasure, and that some people became so addicted to it they'd smoke it all day every day until their lungs filled with giant growths that led to a painful death. Gaspi, whose throat felt like he'd been swallowing sandpaper, didn't feel he needed the warning.

They were still waiting for their friends to come into the city, and as they had watched everyone coming through the gates they knew they had not missed them; there was no reason to go elsewhere. Jonn was sitting back in his chair, feet extended and resting on a small stool. They talked on and off, comfortable in each other's company, and as they talked, Gaspi let his eyes explore his surroundings. The thick red outer walls of the city were smooth and rounded at the top, just like the houses and shops of the outer city. Gaspi thought the whole place looked like nothing more than a giant anthill.

His eyes fell on the guards at the city gates, who were each dressed in shining light chain-mail over a burnished leather cuirass - a piece of hard leather armour covering the chest and back. The chain mail hung to just above the knees, and beneath them the guards wore leather-trimmed trews to protect their legs. The only weapons they carried were short swords, sitting tightly in scabbards attached to thick leather belts. It didn't seem to Gaspi that they were very well armed, but then he noticed the rows of spears, heavier swords and bows fitted to brackets set into the walls of the gatehouses on either side of the gate, within easy reach of the soldiers if the need to use them arose.

The gatehouses rose up to the top of the wall, a series of steps cut into the side of them to provide easy access to the top of the wall, where a path wide enough for two to pass abreast had been cut deep into the top of the wall. Gaspi could see the head and shoulders of sentries pacing along the path around the city wall, until they completed an entire circuit of the city and started again.

A troop of soldiers passed them by, booted feet tramping noisily in unison. "They must be changing the guard," Jonn said. Gaspi's eyes were drawn past the soldiers to the gate itself, where a group of wagons was entering the city. As the first wagon passed through the gates, its green lacquered sides caught the sun.

"It's them!" Gaspi exclaimed, his seat clattering to the ground behind him as he surged to his feet.

"Hold on, Gaspi!" Jonn called, to no avail. Gaspi darted through the traffic, weaving between groups of people, until he came to the enormous gates of the city, through which three colourful gypsy wagons had now trundled. Gaspi scanned the faces of the wagon drivers, a broad grin bursting onto his face as he saw Roland.

"Roland!" he called, waving his arm energetically, until the wagon driver looked down and saw Gaspi, and his own face was drawn into an expansive smile. Roland pointed behind him to the fourth wagon emerging through the gates, and to Gaspi's sheer delight there were two dusty but familiar faces poking out over the driver's seat, staring goggle-eyed at the city before them, and with them was Lydia. A mischievous urge came over Gaspi and he raised a finger to his lips, receiving a wink from Roland in response. Sneaking up close to the wagons, he stealthily made his way back to the side of the fourth wagon, where his friends were still ogling Helioport like uncultured peasants. He climbed up the wooden ladder at the side of the wagon, sidled in behind the driver's bench, and with a quick heave swung himself over the back and landed heavily between his two friends.

"Impressive, isn't it?" he said, the astonished faces of his much-missed companions transforming from shock to joy in a heartbeat.

There was a fraction of a second's silence. "Gaspi!" Emea screamed, and suddenly her arms were around him, her head buried deep into his neck.

Taurnil clapped a large hand on Gaspi's shoulder and returned Gaspi's grin, but the tightness of his grip and something around his eyes showed Gaspi the immense relief he was experiencing. "Good to see you, mate," he said, and Gaspi was sure there had been a catch in his voice. Emea must have heard that same catch, as at that moment her embrace turned into a death-grip, and she began to sob into his shoulder.

"Emmy, don't cry. Emmy, what's wrong?" Gaspi asked.

"Oh, Gaspi!" she gulped after a few seconds. "I was...so worried...we thought you might be...you know...but you're okay!" She looked up, her eyes bright with tears, and met Gaspi's gaze, smiling a watery smile.

"Yes, mate," Taurnil said, "it's a bit of a relief to see you...er...here. You looked totally out of it last time we saw you, if you know what I mean." Gaspi was taken aback by his friend's seriousness.

Lydia reached over shyly, and placed a hand on Gaspi's. "I'm glad you've recovered, Gaspi," she said gravely. "You saved my life."

Gaspi hadn't thought of it that way, and didn't know what to say. "Oh. Don't mention it," he said, not knowing what else to say. A sudden realisation sent an icy shock to his core.

He'd known something wasn't right about his friends' reaction, and now he knew what it was. "But Heppy, I mean Hephistole, the Chancellor of the college - he sent out a couple of Mages to find you. They should have told you I was okay," he said, deeply concerned.

"We've seen no-one, mate," Taurnil answered.

Emmy shook her head. "Maybe they missed us?"

"I don't know," Gaspi answered, filled with concern. "We'll have to let Hephistole know. Did you have any more trouble on the road?"

"Nothing at all," Taurnil said. By this time the wagons had pulled to a halt inside the city wall, out of the way of the main gate, and Roland and Jonn were walking over to them.

"Good to see you, Gaspi," Roland called.

"And you, Roland," Gaspi called back. Gaspi's relationship with Jonn had always been more like two friends looking after each other than guardian and child, and Gaspi felt comfortable being on first name terms with adults.

Gaspi quickly told Jonn what he had discovered, unable to shake a feeling of dread.

"I'll go tell Hephistole straight away," Jonn said worriedly. Jonn turned to Roland.

"Thank you, Roland, for bringing them here safely," he said, his tone grave and sincere. "The local guard will take you to where Ramoa is stabled. How long are you staying?"

"We're here to bring Lydia to the college," Roland answered, "so at least a week while she gets settled. We might even set up camp and stay for a while. We've been on the move for months now, and a rest might do us some good."

"Where will you be staying?" Jonn asked.

"In the wagons, of course," Roland answered, sweeping his arm in the direction of the bright gypsy caravans. "We'll get permission to set up a circle outside the city wall."

"Let me buy you a meal tonight!" Jonn insisted. "Then we can catch up properly about the rest of your journey."

"That would be a great pleasure," Roland answered.

"Meet me here by the gatehouse at third watch," Jonn said. "If you're not here, I'll come find your circle."

"Third watch it is," Roland agreed.

Jonn turned to Gaspi. "Gaspi, will you lead everyone up to the college? I'm sure the gatekeepers will know what to do from there."

"Sure," Gaspi answered, and taking his leave Jonn set off up the road to find Hephistole.

Chapter 10

Gaspi led his awe-struck companions up the long curve of the road that led to the College, followed several paces behind by Lydia's parents, pointing out the couple of landmarks he could remember from Jonn's more thorough tour earlier that day. He adopted an air of bored familiarity when drawing their attention to some of the grander buildings, until Taurnil stopped him.

"Gaspi, how long have you been out and about here?"

"Just today," Gaspi answered reluctantly.

Taurnil and Emea laughed freely, and even Lydia couldn't hide a smirk. "So you're going to stop the experienced traveller act now?" he said, not letting any hint of a smile show on his face.

A red-faced Gaspi didn't know where to look. "I don't know what...well..." he blustered. "Oh fine!" he said at last, an embarrassed smile spreading on his face. All four of them burst out laughing, and Emea leaned over and gave him a peck on the cheek. Gaspi led them up to the college, where they approached the creamy, glowing stone of the outer wall, and the two gatekeepers sitting in the booths on either side of the gateway itself.

Gaspi waited for Roland to catch up with them before approaching one of the magicians. "Could you help us please, sir?" he asked. The gatekeeper was an aging man with shoulder length, messy grey hair, and enormous bushy eyebrows.

He leaned forward, raising one of those extraordinary brows. "And what kind of help would you be looking for?" he said, with a warm smile that cracked his wizened features.

Roland stepped up behind Gaspi. "Gaspi here has already been enrolled in the college by his guardian, but these two are also here to enrol," he said, indicating Emmy and Lydia. "This is Lydia, a talented Seer and my youngest daughter," he said, making no attempt to hide the pride he took in his child and her talent. "And this is Emea, one of Gaspi's friends from Aemon's Reach, who is believed to have a healing gift," he finished with a flourish of his hand. Roland's flamboyant introductions seemed to embarrass Emea, whose cheeks had turned pink.

"Very good," the gatekeeper said with enthusiasm, and reached over for the small silver bell sitting on the desk, ringing it three times in short sharp bursts. A green-robed Mage arrived shortly. She was the youngest magician Gaspi had seen so far, though there was nothing youthful about her. Gaspi didn't know if it was her hair, scraped back into a severe bun, or the firm set of her thin, straight lips, but she carried an air of unyielding sternness.

"So we have some new students?" she said, peering down at a board she carried with her through small square glasses. "I'm not expecting any today."

"Did we have to tell you we were coming?" Emea asked.

"Don't fuss, child!" the woman answered with a touch of irritation, as if flapping at an annoying insect. "We'll not turn you away." She looked them up and down more closely, examining them intently over the long narrow point of her nose. "At least, not yet," she added. Before they could ask what she meant by "not yet," she had turned and was walking briskly back the way she came. "Follow me," she called unctuously over her shoulder. Emea directed a wary look at Taurnil, who just shrugged, and the small party walked into the college.

Emea and Lydia spent the next hour filling out forms for the formidable magician, whose coldness stood out in stark contrast in Gaspi's mind to Hephistole's almost overwhelming warmth. Jonn had already filled out Gaspi's forms while he had been recovering, so he and Taurnil sat and chatted while the girls finished up. They discovered that Lydia and Emea would be sharing a dormitory, and that they too would be expected at class first thing the next day, but along with this good news there was something more disturbing to contemplate. The unfriendly magician, whose attitude was starting to rankle, referred to something called 'The Test', which she'd explained was a way of determining if they had sufficient magical talent to be trained at the college. It would take place a few weeks into their training, once they had learned to safely release a magical force; and they were dismayed to learn that, if they failed, after all they'd been through, they could still be turned away.

Roland had helped carry their baggage to the dormitory, and had gone to seek permission to set up a circle outside the city walls. The girls settled in, then found Gaspi and Taurnil sitting on a bench at the side of the dusty quadrangle. They sat down and began to talk animatedly of the Test.

"Well, now we know what she meant by *not yet*," Gaspi said.

Emea looked worried. "But what if we fail it?" she asked. "I mean, we know you have ability Gasp, and the same goes for you, Lydia, but we don't really know anything about my healing gift, do we? We only have Martha's vision to go by. I mean...what if you pass, and I don't?"

Gaspi put his arm round Emea. "Don't worry, Emmy," he said comfortingly. "I'm sure Martha was right," he said, with more confidence than he felt.

"Gaspi's right," Taurnil added. "Remember what Hahldorn said; Martha's never been wrong. She predicted all of the disasters and troubles the village has been through, and always got it right." Gaspi didn't think Emea looked comforted by Taurnil's words.

An idea that could help encourage Emea flashed into Gaspi's head. "Emmy, why don't you try and do some magic now?" he said excitedly.

Emmy looked doubtful. "But I don't know how," she said uncertainly.

"Well, when I released my magic I just thought about what I wanted to happen, and sort of commanded it to happen. Maybe you should try something like that."

Lydia's expression brightened. "You're meant to be a Healer, right?" she said thoughtfully. "So maybe that's where you should start. Gaspi has nature magic, so he can use natural forces. You're a Healer, so you should try and heal someone."

Emea laughed. "Right now I don't feel like a Healer at all," she said, "but I'll give it a go. Anyone sick?" she asked, with a wry smile.

"Actually, I scraped my leg getting down from the wagon," Taurnil said, pulling up a trouser leg to expose a small graze above his ankle.

Emea looked at it dubiously for a moment. "Well...here goes nothing," she said, and, hopping off the bench, she knelt in front of Taurnil and put her hands over his cut. She tried to think about Taurnil's flesh, but her mind kept wanting to focus on how her knees were beginning to hurt, and how hungry she felt. She stayed there for a few moments, trying to imagine the damaged skin healing under her hand, but nothing was happening. A group of girls came around the corner and burst into fits of giggles as they walked past, at which point Emea jumped up, her pretty face flustered and red with embarrassment.

"That's it!" she stated angrily. "I'm not trying again until they teach me what to do." She shot Gaspi an accusing glance.

"What?" he said in an injured tone. "It was her idea too," he accused, pointing at Lydia.

"Charming!" Lydia said, and put her hand on Emea's shoulder. "Don't worry Emea," she said. "It was a stupid idea anyway. I'm sure we'll learn how to release our magic once we start lessons."

They spent the rest of the afternoon exploring the college, and were amazed by its size and complexity. Just when they thought they'd explored every part of it, they would discover another secretive nook, or an archway leading to a whole new section of eclectic buildings; some grand and imposing, some cosy and cottage-like, and some piled up with unpredictable wings, corridors, towers and extensions. What amazed Gaspi most of all was that apart from the more formal section of the campus around the dormitories, there weren't two buildings in a row that were built in the same style, and non of them matched the uniform red-stone dwellings of the outer city. Perhaps a city of magicians couldn't resist using magic to stamp their own personalities on the campus. Or maybe they got homesick, and some of these buildings were a nostalgic reminder of how things looked back home.

Whatever the reasons behind the amazing constructions, the campus contained a riotous mixture of uniquely designed buildings, some so bizarre they must be held up by magic. There was one building that looked like nothing more than a giant tent, the entranceway flapping perpetually in a breeze that didn't exist. Emea was excited by a house that was covered in thousands of colourful butterflies, their wings moving gently in the sun, causing an unpredictable ebb and flow of rippling colour.

As the afternoon wore on, they found themselves in a quiet section of the college, hidden away behind the giant tower that stood at the centre of the grounds. None of the buildings seemed to be in use, and the streets themselves seemed unnaturally quiet. The colourfully-robed magicians parading through the rest of the campus were conspicuously absent here, and Gaspi became very aware of the echoing clack of their shoes against the paving stones. In the middle of this strange district they came upon the oddest building they had yet seen. Standing on its own, and un-shadowed by other structures, was a solid pyramid made of a smooth black material. It could have been marble or granite for its smoothness, except that it reflected absolutely no light at all. There was no entryway cut into its unmarred sides, and it was surrounded by a high wall of the creamy, gently glowing stone that they knew held an enchantment of sorts. There was no break in the enchanted wall, and Gaspi wondered how anyone was meant to approach the building without climbing over it.

After circling the outer wall a couple of times they stopped for a moment, staring at the anomalous structure. Both girls were feeling tired, and Emmy sat down on a nearby bench while Lydia leaned against the wall. After a few moments, Gaspi was stunned to see Lydia slide down the wall until she was sitting on the ground. Perspiration had broken out on her forehead and she looked unnaturally pale.

She drew the back of her hand across her forehead. "I don't feel good," she said, her voice strangely quiet.

"Lydia, are you ok?" Emea asked worriedly. "Taurnil - help Lydia up," she said with a snap of command in her voice. Taurnil easily lifted

Lydia to her feet, supporting her with an encircling arm.

Lydia looked like she was going to faint. "Can we get away from this building please?" she said.

"Uh, sure," Gaspi answered, a befuddled expression on his face. "I think it's this way back to the dormitories," he said, and led them off in that direction.

After a few minutes, the colour had returned to her face. "I think I'm alright now," she said. "Sorry about that." She stepped away from Taurnil, leaving him looking disappointed.

"Don't be sorry," Emea said.

"I just felt sick and dizzy all of a sudden, and not myself at all," Lydia said. "I felt really miserable, and cold."

Gaspi was reminded uncomfortably of the way they'd felt in the village after the attack, and, sharing a glance with Taurnil and Emea, he was pretty sure they were too. "Maybe it's nothing," Gaspi said with deliberate lightness. "It was probably just a funny turn."

Lydia didn't say anything in response, and Gaspi didn't think she was any more convinced than he was. The disturbing event had exhausted their sense of adventure, so they returned to the dormitories.

Jonn and Roland arrived shortly after they did, and took them out to an inn near the college, where the adults spent the evening talking about their experiences since their precipitous parting several days earlier. Lydia had fully recovered from her earlier discomfort, and was joining in with the banter. Emea and Taurnil had gotten to know her on the ride to Helioport, and Gaspi could see how comfortable both his friends were with this new companion. As the night wore, on he began to see why. Although not chatty like Emea, Lydia had a warmth that shone through her mysterious demeanour. She laughed freely and was quick to affirm, and Gaspi found himself becoming quickly comfortable with the idea that their three had become a four.

He couldn't help noticing that Taurnil listened very closely whenever she spoke, and the thought that his friend may be interested in her was enough of a reason on its own for Gaspi to accept her unconditionally. Gaspi had never known Taurnil to like a girl before, and if it wasn't for an unusual vulnerability Gaspi detected in his friend, Gaspi would have found Taurnil's bumbling attempts at flirting funny. He clammed-up around Lydia, and when he summed up the courage to speak to her, he was tripping up over his own words. Seeing his friend so smitten, Gaspi could only hope Lydia wouldn't break his heart.

The night wore on pleasantly, until Jonn and Roland decided it was time for the new students to go to bed, and took them back to the college. Gaspi said goodnight to the girls, and to Taurnil who was staying with Jonn at the barracks, and made his way into the dormitory. It was well past dark now, and Gaspi quietly made his way past the sleeping humps of his fellow students to his bed. Getting changed quickly into his nightclothes, Gaspi slid into bed, and pulled the covers tight up around his chin.

Though he was very tired, sleep did not come easily, and thoughts of the coming day drifted through his mind. Tomorrow morning, he would begin to study magic. He could barely believe it. The word magic evoked enticing childhood images of mysterious incantations and beguiling powers, of bubbling cauldrons and swirling alchemical substances brewing in a haze of red smoke and cloying incense; but the magic he had experienced was more like a whirlwind tearing through his being and leaving him thoroughly scoured. Thoughts of an unknown tomorrow circled in his brain until the onset of sleep softened the boundaries of his consciousness, and fantastical images stepped lightly through his imagination, their languid progress lulling him gently into unconsciousness.

It was over half way through fourth watch, deep into the heart of the night, when thoughts grow long and the day's memories echo silently in the darkness, when the few souls who are awake stare at winking stars and glowing moon, their minds turning ponderous thoughts over in slow hands. The guards on duty at the gate had long since dropped any pretence at alertness, leaning heavily against their upright spears, mastering a fine balance between wakefulness and sleep. But the night's lazy progress was about to be interrupted.

At first, the guard thought he was mistaken, seeing just a phantasm of the night, a dark movement within the greater darkness. But then a strange sight resolved itself before his eyes. A creature with four legs was lolloping slowly towards the gates, cloak flapping behind it in the breeze. Its gait was cumbersome and tortured, as if it was injured, and indeed it did look to be hurt: two of its legs were not moving, dragging along the ground behind it. The guard nudged his fellow awake, who had slipped into an upright doze, pointing at the creature as it neared the pool of light.

Both guards drew their swords in readiness. "Who goes there?" the first guard shouted. The creature continued to shuffle forward, dragging its useless legs behind it, a low groan emitting from the darkness. Another guard, finishing his round up on the city wall, saw the commotion and drew a bead on the shambolic creature, holding his crossbow in readiness to shoot.

"Hold where you are!" he shouted, "or I'll shoot!"

The creature took one last step forward, stumbling into the pool of light surrounding the gate, and collapsed. The first guard gasped and the patrollers raised his bow as two men rolled onto the floor. The illusion of a single creature had been created by one man carrying his unconscious fellow. The first guard ran over to the injured men, crouching down to asses their injuries. The conscious man had a widow's peak and penetrating dark eyes; eyes which right now brimmed with horror and pain, and he wore a wizard's cloak. Reaching out a grasping hand he grabbed the guard's arm, pulling him close.

"Get...Hephistole," he said, each word forced out with great effort, and fell to the ground, unconscious.

Chapter 11

A warm buzzing sensation ran gently up and down Gaspi's body, lightly stimulating his recumbent muscles. A gentle humming began, separating into harmonic strands of sound, like a choir of angels whispering in his ear. Gaspi emerged from the depths of sleep, called to awareness by the beautiful sound in his ears, and as he opened his eyes the sound swelled to a warm concluding cadence, the perfect resolution of suspended harmonics. Gaspi took a deep breath and sat up, blinking at the warm light that flooded in through the windows, which Gaspi noticed now were stained glass shaded in varying golden hues, from light cornflower to a deep orange. What was it that had woken him? The echo of something beautiful lingered in his mind.

Around him, other boys were also waking. At the far end of the room, against the wall, Gaspi recognised Everand, sitting on the edge of his bed and rubbing the sleep out of his eyes. Gaspi couldn't help noticing that Everand's body was well built and athletic. He had the kind of broad, slender, but well-muscled physique that spoke of both strength and flexibility. Leaning back he let out a mighty yawn, thrusting long arms into the air, and finished off with a shake of wavy golden hair that framed what could only be called a handsome face. Lying in the next bed along from him was a smaller, dark-featured boy, trying to ignore the room waking around him. He hid his head under the covers and buried it in the pillow. Everand let out a resounding guffaw and pulled the blankets off the other boy's bed. "Get up, Ferast, you lazy slob!" he said.

Ferast groaned, and slowly dragged himself up to a sitting position. "Leave me alone, Rand," he said, head in his hands. Ferast couldn't have looked more different to Everand. His chest and shoulders were narrow, and his ribs showed slightly through pallid skin pulled tightly over a sparrow-like frame. His chin-length dark hair was lank and greasy, hanging over pointed features and black, inscrutable eyes that shone with the light of razor-sharp intelligence.

Gaspi felt suddenly self-conscious, surrounded by the group of boys who all knew each other, and yet was not comfortable making the first move after Everand's frosty reception the previous day. As they went about their morning ablutions, trailing in and out of an adjacent bathroom, nobody spoke to Gaspi, and his agitation increased. His uniform had been delivered to his bedside the previous day, brown cloak included, and Gaspi pulled on his grey shirt and woollen trousers, which fitted well, and slipped into a pair of leather shoes that had also been left by his bed. He had also been left a small leather satchel on his bedside table, identical to one carried by the other boys. Gaspi was still being universally ignored by the time he had finished dressing, and it was tempting to say nothing about it and skulk in the background; but it just wasn't in his nature to put up with unfair treatment, and he decided to break the deadlock.

Gaspi turned to the boy in the bed next to him, and caught his eye. "Hi, I'm Gaspi," he said, as confidently as he could. The boy looked away quickly, making a gruff kind of non-verbal response that could not be interpreted as friendly.

Gaspi turned to face the boy in the bed opposite him. "Hi, I'm..." he started, but the boy had already turned his back. Gaspi was embarrassed. Everyone had seen him get snubbed, and no-one seemed to want to break the tension. Looking around, he saw a couple of the boys looking uncomfortable, shooting anxious glances at Everand and looking anywhere except at him.

Anger flared in Gaspi. "What's this all about, then?" he challenged, glaring straight at Everand, who was the only boy meeting his eyes. "Picking on the new boy?"

"Just so you know your place, Nature Mage!" Everand said, his eyes hard and cold. "We don't believe any of this rubbish. There's not been a Nature Mage at the college in the last two hundred years, and somehow I don't think you're anything special," he said, with a sneer. He walked over to Gaspi until they stood face to face, Everand the taller boy by a clear six inches. He poked Gaspi in the chest. "*If* you have any kind of talent, we'll find out what it is. As for me, I don't think you'll even pass the Test, village boy."

An astonished Gaspi stood speechless, as Everand turned away, grabbed his cloak and school bag, and stalked out of the room, the other students trailing after him. Astonishment turned to anger again in Gaspi at the injustice of the situation. Why did he always get picked on by one idiot or another? It was Jakko in Aemon's Reach, and now this strutting peacock. What had he done to deserve it? Always quick to ignite, Gaspi's anger boiled into a cold fury, but then an image flitted into his mind that muted his anger; an image of Jakko being carried from the village pond, frozen and half pecked to death by birds. Gaspi took a deep breath and tried to calm himself. Whatever happens, he mustn't lose control this time. Picking up his school bag and cloak, he made his way out of the dorm, and tried to catch up with the other students.

He caught sight of them passing into a large building set just off the quad, and jogged up behind them. The building turned out to be the refectory, and as Gaspi walked into the expansive room filled with long tables and low benches, he looked around to try and catch sight of Emea and Lydia. Everand and many of the boys from Gaspi's dorm sat down together at a large table by the window, where they were quickly joined by several girls. Older boys and girls sat at other tables in smaller groups. Gaspi assumed they were students because they were also dressed in brown robes. At last, he spotted Emmy and Lydia sitting nearby, with bowls full of cereal and fruit in front of them. Gaspi used the few minutes it took him to queue up and get his breakfast to calm down. He didn't want Emea to be dragged into the conflict with the other boys, and by the time he joined them at the table his face showed nothing of the anger and frustration he was feeling.

"Hi Gaspi, sleep well?" Emea asked. Lydia smiled at him.

"Yeah, not bad. And you?" he asked.

"Not really," Emea answered, screwing up her face. "I kept waking up and wondering where I was." Emea chuckled at herself. "I suppose I'll get used to it in time," she said.

"I wonder what will happen today," Lydia said, her voice filled with calm expectation. Emea looked so nervous she could barely keep her food down. If Gaspi was honest, his own feelings were closer to Emea's than Lydia's, whose long practice at magic lent her a familiarity and comfort he couldn't attain. They didn't have time to discuss it further, as a chime sounded brightly in the air. The three friends scrabbled to grab their belongings and followed along behind the other students, who were heading quickly out of the refectory and across the courtyard to a small, cosy-looking building Gaspi assumed was their classroom. It was built in the same style as the other buildings around the quad: formal in construction, the buildings showed their beauty in the intricate carvings and reliefs decorating the pale, creamy stone of the bricks. Ivy sprawled expansively up the walls, spreading its embracing arms around the long, multi-paned windows.

The other students were filing in through the door and into what was indeed a classroom. There was nothing overtly magical about the classroom; rows of desks faced a chalkboard, and a raised platform for the teacher's desk. The walls were lined with rows of shelves, crammed to overflowing with well-thumbed books. A green-robed magician stood with his back to the students, scribbling energetically across the board. The students only filled two thirds of the desks, leaving Gaspi a choice of seating. Picking a spot by the window next to Emea, he slid sideways into the chair.

Hushed conversation and restrained giggling rose in the room as the teacher continued to write on the board, his chalk banging percussively against the hard slate. Putting his chalk down, the teacher finally turned around to face the class. He had a friendly, nondescript face, with even but unremarkable features, topped with tidily parted hair.

"Good morning, class," he said with a warm smile, surveying them with proprietary approval. His gaze stopped on Gaspi, then moved to Emea and Lydia. "And today we have the tremendous privilege of welcoming new students of magic to our class," he said, beaming at the three new arrivals. "Three at once, how wonderful!" he exclaimed. Uncomfortable under the class's scrutiny, Gaspi wished the teacher would stop gushing over them and get on with the lesson, but he obviously had no intention of doing so.

"Young lady," he said, waving a hand in Emea's direction. "Would you be so kind as to tell us your name?"

"Emea, sir," she answered self-consciously.

"Emea," repeated the teacher. "That's a lovely name. And what kind of magical talent do you bring to us?" Emea went pink with embarrassment and muttered something so quietly no-one could hear her.

"Come again? No need to be shy, now!" the teacher said cheerfully.

"I'm a Healer," Emea repeated, just loud enough to be heard.

"A Healer. Wonderful! Emelda will be pleased," effused the teacher. Gaspi looked around anxiously, expecting the same kind of derision from the class that he had received in the dormitory, but everyone was looking at Emea with interest. It seemed to him that Everand and several other boys were looking at her with *too* much interest. A tall, willowy girl in front of Emea directed an encouraging smile at her.

"And how did your powers first manifest?" the teacher asked.

Emea looked stricken. "Erm...they haven't," she answered, devastated by the admission.

The teacher looked confused. "But...ahem...well...that is most unusual. How do you know you're a Healer if your powers haven't showed themselves?" Haltingly, Emea explained that a Seer in her village had told her so.

The professor looked curious. "Well, we will have to do what we can to release your talent then, won't we?" he said encouragingly. Emea looked panic-stricken. "Please don't worry, my dear," he implored, unable to ignore her obvious distress. "We are very skilled at releasing talent, and I'll make sure someone starts on that with you today." Emea nodded once, looking at the floor, and the professor kindly moved along.

"And the other young lady," said the teacher, moving on to Lydia. "You are...?"

"Lydia," replied the gypsy girl calmly, with the quiet confidence that added mystery to her demeanour. She also was receiving admiring stares from the boys, and Gaspi couldn't help feeling indignant on Taurnil's behalf, whose interest in Lydia was obvious - at least, to him.

"And where does your talent lie?" asked the teacher.

"I'm not entirely sure," Lydia answered, "but I have the Sight." Noticing some confused looks, she added: "I can see the future sometimes. My people call me a Seer."

The teacher looked fascinated at this, an eyebrow rising sharply into his forehead. "A rare gift indeed," he said, "and not one that normally comes unaccompanied by others. And who are your people, my dear?"

"I'm a gypsy," Lydia answered proudly.

"Ah yes, of course," the teacher said. "I should have known. A people with a long history of talent. I shall look forward to seeing your gift unfold."

He turned his attention to Gaspi, who had been dreading this moment.

"And what about you, young sir?" he asked.

Gaspi didn't see any way to avoid the inevitable. Faced with the flat stares of Everand and Ferast, he forced a confidence he didn't feel. "I'm Gaspi," he said. "I'm a Nature Mage." Emea looked around in puzzlement as some of the boys snickered. Ferast leaned across and whispered something in Everand's ear, who snorted with laughter, but the teacher didn't seem to notice any of it.

"A Nature Mage!" he said quietly. "A rare gift! We are lucky indeed to have you with us. And how did your power first manifest itself?" he asked eagerly.

Gaspi knew he had to give some kind of answer, but he desperately didn't want to expose painful memories in front of the class. "Someone I know was being attacked, and I defended them. It just kind of happened," he finished vaguely, hoping that would be enough.

"*What* kind of happened?" the teacher asked, insensitive to Gaspi's discomfort. Gaspi didn't know how to answer. He paused for a few moments, trying to think of something to say that would satisfy the teacher's curiosity, but he couldn't come up with anything.

Gaspi's shoulders drooped. "I took control of the birds around me and attacked them," he said in a defeated tone. The hush in the classroom was palpable, until it was broken by Everand snorting with laughter. Several students followed his lead.

The teacher looked around in confusion, before turning his attention back to Gaspi.

"I'm sure you had a good reason," he said, looking at Gaspi intently for a long second. "A Nature Mage, eh?" he said, evidently fascinated by the prospect of having such a student under his tutelage. Gaspi squirmed uncomfortably under the teacher's scrutiny.

"Well, fair is fair," he said, briskly. "I should introduce myself too. I am Professor Worrick, teacher of all things arcane, and specifically matter manipulation - though none of you are ready for that, yet. I am also the Dean of students, and responsible for your care."

He continued to direct his attention to the three newcomers. "You must have many questions. Most of them will have to wait, but is there anything you're burning to know before we begin our class today?"

Lydia's hand shot in the air. "Yes, Lydia?"

"I was wondering where we fit into this class?" she asked. "I mean, how can we catch up with the other students? Shouldn't we be in a beginner's class, or something?"

"Ah, I see you are labouring under a misconception," said the professor, with a smile. "None of your classmates here are experienced magicians." Some of the students puffed themselves up defensively, feeling their prowess was being underrated. "They only embarked on their studies within the last few months. The truth is that magical ability always manifests itself around your age, a year after at the latest. All your fellow students in this class have only just started touching their talent. If anyone else arrives in the next few months, we will allow them to join the class. After that, they will have to wait until we have enough new students to start a new class. We call this the first year for simplicity's sake, but in reality we'll teach you as a group until you're ready to move on to the next stage of your studies, and the class will be disbanded. That normally takes between a year and eighteen months. You'll all be assigned special tutors according to your abilities, so you'll find it easy to catch up with anything you've missed."

Gaspi was relieved that they were not so far behind; he felt like Everand and his friends had less of an advantage over him. He inwardly determined to develop his powers as quickly as possible, so he'd be able to hold his own against the other boys if necessary.

"Any more questions?" Lydia's hand went up again. "Yes, my dear?"

"If we all have different talents, then why do we study together? Shouldn't we learn on our own, from someone with our talent?"

"Ah, I see," responded the professor. "No-one has explained how this all works to you yet. Well, permit me to enlighten you. Your talent is how magic has found its first manifestation in you, but it is not the only magic you can do. Studying magic is like exploring a broad and complex landscape. There are endless varieties of power, and each is expressed uniquely through an individual, as each individual is unique!

The fact that you started with healing or prophecy, or even nature magic, means that is the most natural form for arcane power to find its outlet in you, and your talent, will be most strongly expressed in that way. But you can learn something of other forms of magic. Some you'll have success with and some will be like wrestling a bear, but no-one practices a single branch of magic on its own."

A thoughtful look stole across Professor Worrick's face. "There are some who seem to be able to practice almost any branch of magic, but they are few and far between, and here at the college we teach you to focus on your strengths and to learn the basics of other disciplines. Does that answer your question?"

Lydia looked a little confused, but nodded anyway. Obviously feeling he had explained the essence of magical talent, the professor began the class, which was on imbuing physical objects with magical properties.

"The most notable example of this is surrounding us at this very moment," said Professor Worrick, at the end of a lengthy explanation of which kind of materials take an enchantment most effectively, and something of the theory of how it is done. He pirouetted slowly in a full circle with his arms turned outwards. When he was facing the class again he asked, "Does anyone know what I'm talking about?"

"The wall," answered the girl who'd smiled at Emea earlier.

"Exactly, Temalia," said the professor. "The wall! It is not made of naturally magical stone - there is no such thing, of course. It's actually constructed from a mineral found not fifty miles away that takes enchantment extremely well. In the distant past we mined, shaped and enchanted it, imbuing it with the properties that make it the effective barrier it is. The enchantment shows itself in the glow, which no doubt you have noticed."

Gaspi's hand went up. "What exactly does it do?" he asked.

"It forms a barrier against certain forces. When a creature is driven by a destructive intent they exude a kind of energy, which we can identify if we know what to look for. Anything trying to cross that threshold exuding that energy would be resisted, and if they continued to force their way through they would be consumed."

"Consumed?" asked Ferast, with a kind of curious intensity.

"Burned to a crisp," said Professor Worrick lightly.

A small, curly-haired boy raised his hand. "But professor, what if one of us was really angry at someone, wouldn't it…get us too?"

"Angry at someone in particular, are we, Matthius?" he asked, with a smile. "I'm only pulling your leg," he said, when Matthius protested. "It's a good question. There's a vast difference between anger and murderous intent. All emotions cause us to emit an energy signature. Have you ever walked into a room and found it taut with tension you could cut with a knife, but nobody has spoken?" Several students grunted in assent.

"The wall is enchanted to detect and resist only the kind of murderous hate a truly evil person could feel," Professor Worrick continued. "Even if one of you were to hate someone enough to want to harm them, you would still be conflicted in your conscience, feeling guilt and uncertainty, maybe fear, and these counter-feelings would muddle the energy signature. The only creatures that would be detected by the barrier are those who have a single, destructive thought in mind with no balancing emotional signatures. In fact, the barrier was not designed to resist human evil, which is complex in nature, but the kind of evil you find in summoned creatures such as demons, who carry nothing but darkness and know nothing of warmth or love. If the barrier ever resists you, Matthius, you would have travelled so far down the road to evil as to be irredeemable."

The professor's explanation left a palpable silence in the room; the air seemed heavier, and the light gloomy and oppressive. Gaspi shook his head to clear it, as the professor spoke again. "I think it's time for a demonstration."

Indicating that the students should follow, the professor picked up something that was not much larger than Gaspi's schoolbag from the shelf behind him. It was cylindrical and covered with a red velvet cloth. He led the students out of the room and all the way to the main gate at the entrance to the campus.

"Line up just inside the gate, if you will," he said, indicating a spot some yards inside the arching span of glowing stone. Gaspi wondered what he could be doing, as he had a quick discussion with the gatekeeper. What was under that cloth? Professor Worrick placed the covered item on the ground just outside the wall, and walked back to stand with the class.

"This," he announced, gesticulating in the direction of the covered object, "is a dJin," - and with a purposeful flourish of his hand the cloth flew off what revealed itself to be a cage, landing on the ground beside it. The second the cloth was off the cage, a bundle of fury ripped into the silver bars, hissing and growling with unrelenting venom. It was hard to see what the creature was beyond an impression of blazing eyes and flashing teeth and claws. Its hard little arms banged noisily against the cage, its feet scrabbling at the floor. What was not hard to identify was a single-minded will to destroy. It was filled with hate - not a tempered, steel-edged anger, but a slavering, mindless intent to rend limb from limb - and the focus of its hate was them.

Professor Worrick kept his eyes on the cage while addressing the class. "Whatever happens, don't move through the gate!"

Before anyone had a chance to ask any questions, a flick of his wrist released the catch on the cage door, which sprung open, and the dJin spilled out onto the ground. Not even stopping to right itself, it lurched forward into a headlong sprint, using its hands as much as its feet to gain purchase, sharp claws digging jagged furrows in the dirt. Most of the class uniformly leapt back in horror, recoiling from the ferocity of the aggressive dJin, which clearly wanted nothing more than to tear them apart. Emea grabbed Gaspi's arm and half-hid behind him.

The dJin veered towards Professor Worrick, letting out a grating snarl that sounded like it was tearing its own throat apart. When it reached the gate and tried to pass under the arch, its frantic movements were suddenly arrested as if it was caught in thick treacle, affording the class a clear view of its form. It had a small, potato-like head, lumpy and ill-formed, with flashing little black eyes that were flitting back and forth angrily, trying to find the source of its sudden restriction. Its mouth was a narrow gash crowded with sharp, pointed brown teeth, below the slightest hint of a nose, barely a bump in its face. It was hard and hairless, rippling with chorded muscle so rigid the rough grey skin was pulled tight almost to splitting.

This creature seemed built for killing alone, each muscular limb ending in thick, wicked black claws. Heavy veins bulged on its neck as it strained against the invisible barrier, its feet digging into the ground again and again as it surged fruitlessly forward.

"Now, watch!" said Professor Worrick. "It has nothing but hate. It won't stop, even though it will destroy it to keep going. The enchantment held in the stone is designed to resist evil, not to kill indiscriminately, but if something continues to push against it, unrelenting in its hate, then the barrier will begin to cause them pain, burning the invader with increasing heat, and if that doesn't stop them, they will burn up." He said nothing more, but stared at the dJin, waiting for the inevitable to happen.

The dJin's snarl turned to a hiss of pain when smoke began to curl from its skin. As the pain increased, the creature spat and roared alarmingly, its fevered gaze flicking from person to person as its anger swelled, stimulated to new heights by escalating pain levels. The hiss of pain turned to frightful cries as tiny flames flickered along its arms and torso, and then its legs and shoulders. Emea hid her face in Gaspi's shoulder at the horrible sight, but Gaspi couldn't feel sorry for the dJin. Even in the face of its own death its only feeling was hate, its only thoughts of killing them. Its cries turned into screeches of torturous agony as its head went up in a ball of flame, and all they could see was a writhing ball of fire flailing with dying strength against the barrier. The sound stopped as its lungs finally gave out, and it collapsed in a ball of smoking dust, utterly consumed by the magic of the barrier.

The class stood in shocked silence. Gaspi glanced around, and saw Ferast staring at him, or more precisely at the way Emea leaned into him. No-one had known until this moment that there was something between them, but the lank-haired boy had clearly taken notice. Gaspi could have sworn that Ferast's gaze had a calculating edge, but then Professor Worrick was speaking again and he looked away.

"Could you manage that level of hate, Matthius?" Professor Worrick asked. Matthius shook his head mutely. "Then you don't need to worry about the barrier." As he led them back to the classroom, whispering broke out in small groups, excitement replacing the shock of witnessing the horrid creature's painful death:

"Did you see it burn? Whoosh!"

"Never seen anything like it..."

"I thought it was going to get through for a moment!"

Professor Worrick had to calm them down when they were all back in their seats.

"I've been teaching long enough to know that you won't listen now if I bore you about enchantments. What would you like to know about the dJin?"

"Where does it come from?" a slim, dark-haired girl at the back asked. Professor Worrick looked thoughtful, and was silent for so long that they began to think he wasn't going to answer. He stood staring out of the small window by his desk, hands clasped behind his back.

"The dJin is from Hades," he answered at last. "It is a demon." Lydia gasped, hand clapped over her mouth. Everand looked incredulous, Ferast almost eager. Gaspi didn't understand the reactions of their classmates. He'd heard of demons, but not in any way that made him believe they were real. They were the subject of fireside tales told by old folks to scare youngsters.

"Demons are very real," Professor Worrick said, as if reading Gaspi's mind. "They inhabit a plane far harsher than this one, where it is kill or be killed, where the mighty crush the weak without a thought. They are summoned to our realm to do our bidding by those with the skill, bound with powerful spells so they cannot attack their summoner. The dJin is the lowest of all demonic forms. It has no magical power and is not physically strong, though in our realm it is a ferocious killer despite its small stature. In the demonic realm, they are no more than ants. They live in giant underground complexes, finding safety in numbers, but are no more than a nuisance to the real forces of that plane."

Faced with the fact that demons were real, Gaspi started to wonder about the creature that had attacked them at the gypsy camp. Was it a demon too? Something else niggled at Gaspi, something that didn't add up about what Professor Worrick had said, but it remained just out of reach.

"Any more questions?" Professor Worrick asked.

"Did you summon it, sir?" asked Emea. And then Gaspi understood what was bothering him. If the dJin couldn't get past the wall of the college, then how did it get in?

"Me?" exclaimed the Professor with dark amusement. "No, my dear. Summoning is forbidden. It is a dark art punishable by Severing." Professor Worrick must have spotted Gaspi's confused expression. "Severing is the ultimate punishment for a magician," he explained. "It's the full and final severing of your magical power."

A heavy silence reigned in the classroom for several seconds, before Professor Worrick continued with his lesson. "To summon and control an evil creature, a demon of any type, takes the kind of magic you would not want to be involved in. And besides," he added, "I wouldn't have the power. It takes extraordinary talent to be able to summon even the smallest demon, and my skills lie elsewhere." He lapsed into silence.

Gaspi put his hand up. "So, how did it get here?" he asked.

"And that is where I cannot go any further," the professor answered. "It's an important question, but it takes us into areas Hephistole would not have you study yet. Please accept my apologies, young Mage, but for now you must suspend your curiosity." Professor Worrick clapped his hands together. "And now it is time to return to the topic of enchantment," he said, accompanied by the disappointed groans of the students.

Chapter 12

Gaspi listened intently as the lesson continued, eager to learn as much as he possibly could as quickly as possible.

"The practice of enchantment is not complicated," the professor explained. "As with most magic, it is a question of focus, willpower and release. For instance, if you wanted to enchant this piece of chalk to divine water, you would have to first of all focus intently on the chalk; the stronger your focus, the more effective the enchantment. Then you would have to imagine the chalk being able to achieve divination. Picture it in your mind until you can feel it, until you know in your bones that the chalk is able to sense water. Developing a fertile imagination is one of the keys to exceptional magic. Once the picture is strong, the last stage is to release your power. This is the interesting bit. Everyone releases power in different ways. Some use a motion of the hand, some use words. Healer Emelda sings her magic into being. I've known a man who could only release his magic through dance.

As some of you already understand, the release of your magic is like a signature. It is something unique to you, and something that will come quite naturally. Watch!" The professor picked up the piece of chalk, took out a small knife from his pocket and made a nick in one end of it, and placed it on his open palm. There was nothing dramatic to see as the professor imbued the piece of chalk with the desired property. After a couple of moments of quiet, he simply shut his eyes, closed his fist around the chalk, whispered something under his breath and opened his eyes again. Gaspi was certain that as Professor Worrick whispered he had felt something, a kind of tingling in his belly, a tickling against his skin, and then it was gone.

In the professor's still-closed hand was the same stick of chalk, but in the dim light of the classroom they could all see that the top of it, peeking out of his closed fist, was now glowing gently. It was subtle, but there could be no doubt that the previously normal piece of chalk had been magically altered, imbued with magical properties. Professor Worrick opened his hand. The small stick of glowing chalk burst into movement the second it was free to do so, spinning rapidly for a moment on his palm. It stopped, twitching like a navigator's compass, before settling into position, the end with the nick in it pointing right at a half full glass of water sitting on the professor's desk. Gaspi was impressed. This was the first magic he had seen consciously performed, and the excitement of the possibilities it opened up to him sent a thrill along his spine.

"Everand, you're able to release your magic consistently now,"

Professor Worrick said. "Come and have a go." Everand slid out of his desk, and walked straight-backed up to the front. Professor Worrick gave him a different piece of chalk, again marking one end of it. "Now remember to focus, Everand, and imagine the chalk is able to detect water. You want the marked end to be your pointer."

Everand screwed up his eyes in concentration, staring forcefully at the chalk. He stood like that, shoulders hunched, for several moments, before closing his fist tightly around the chalk. "Seek!" Everand pronounced in a loud, ringing tone. He looked down at the now glowing chalk sticking out from his fist, and smiled. Looking confident, he held out his arm, and opened his hand. The chalk twitched into life, but instead of spinning in a circle it flew right out of his hand, across the front of the room (narrowly missing a surprised Professor Worrick), and smashed into the glass of water. The chalk exploded into shards, white dust billowing into the air, and the glass, perched on the edge of the table, toppled off and smashed on the floor, its contents flowing away from the glass and pooling at Professor Worrick's feet. Several students burst out laughing, but a furious look from a red-faced Everand silenced them.

"What did you imagine, Everand?" Professor Worrick asked, without a hint of mockery, though Gaspi thought he could detect a twitch at the corner of his mouth.

"I imagined it finding the water," Everand said indignantly, glaring at the smashed chalk as if somehow it was to blame.

"Ah yes, perhaps I should have made it clearer," Professor Worrick said. "A divining device points to water; it does not itself go to the water, or find it. Well, well. Let's not be discouraged. This is a good lesson in the importance of focus and accuracy, wouldn't you say? And anyhow, Everand, your enchantment may not have been right, but it was certainly powerful."

Everand straightened his shoulders, mollified by the inference of potency, and went back to his desk. Professor Worrick set the class some homework; to imbue a small fragment of rock with the power to resist heat. He handed out the fragments of rock to each student except for the three newcomers, who he asked to stay behind once the other students had left.

He explained to them what the rest of their day held. Students only attended communal classes in the morning, and in the afternoon divided their time between personal studies, projects and one-on-one tutoring. Professor Worrick explained that each of them was to be paired up to an appropriate tutor; one who best understood their talent and could train them in its use. Emea was to study with Miss Emelda, one of the

Healers at the infirmary and a teacher at the college. Professor Worrick's secondary gift was prophetic, and so he would be Lydia's mentor. The professor explained that as there were no Nature Mages, Gaspi would study under Voltan, a warrior Mage skilled in martial magic.

Before they began their mentoring, however, they had to learn to release their power, a process which would begin after lunch in the adjacent classroom. Gaspi was full of conflicting emotions when the professor sent them on their break. Seeing magic performed up close had awoken a kind of hunger in him. Up till that morning, magic had been something that had threatened his life, something very serious and frighteningly powerful. Having seen the controlled way in which magic could be used had started to make Gaspi feel for the first time that he might actually want to be a Mage, but it wasn't easy to cast off the terrible memories of his first experiences with magic. He just hoped that whoever taught him how to safely use his power was able to cope with the strength of his gift. After all, they didn't have any other Nature Mages around, so how could they be sure they knew how to teach him to control his magic? Full of uncertainty, Gaspi followed his friends out of the classroom.

The three friends went to the refectory, where lunch was still being served. They each grabbed a steaming chicken pie, and piled their plates with roast potatoes and onions. They chose an empty table and sat down, pulling up the long bench with a loud wooden screech. On the tables around them, the other first-year students were talking excitedly about the dJin; Everand, recovered from his embarrassment in the classroom, was holding forth on demonic creatures, the attention of several pretty girls raptly fixed on him. Gaspi felt a sudden surge of resentment at this pompous boy, who seemed to have taken it upon himself to make his time at college harder than it needed it to be. It was hard enough learning to tame his magic, without having to deal with this kind of thing.

Emea caught him glowering at Everand. "Gaspi, why are you staring at that boy?" she asked. Unable to hide his feelings, Gaspi told the girls about the conflict in the dorm that morning. "Oh Gaspi, I'm sorry," she said sympathetically. "You really don't need this."

"Tell me about it!" he said. In a transparent effort to distract him, Emea started talking about what their next class would be like, and was inadvertently successful. She couldn't hide her nerves about what would be revealed about her, or more to the point what wouldn't be revealed, and Gaspi's sympathy for her did what her conversation failed to do, and drew his attention away from Everand. He put his arm around her shoulders. "You'll be fine Emmy. I know you will," he said. It sounded vacuous, but it was all he could think of to say.

"I know you will too," Lydia added confidently. "And I'm a Seer, remember?" Emea smiled unconvincingly.

The lunch hour passed quickly, and soon they were heading back to the classroom next to the one they'd studied in that morning. No-one was in the room and the door was slightly ajar, so they went inside.

"Oh, how lovely!" Emea exclaimed in surprise. The desks they expected to find were nowhere to be seen, and across the floor were scattered deep, comfortable cushions, surrounding three padded armchairs in the middle of the room. The light coming through the windows was warm and golden, almost orange, filtering through stained-glass windows, caressing the leaves of enormous plants that sprung out of giant pots placed liberally around the room. Gaspi felt immediately restful; the worries that had plagued him over lunch seemed somehow less of a problem, less urgent. Emea began to explore, pinching the large, heavy leaves of the plants, testing out the cushions. She was humming happily to herself, obviously delighted by the peaceful atmosphere, until her musings were rudely interrupted by a large cushion slamming into the side of her head. An impudent Gaspi grinned at her from across the room, daring her to retaliate. She had caught the cushion reflexively, and held it defensively before her.

"Gaspi, we're not here to play!" she admonished. He laughed and bent to pick up another cushion, not spotting Emea's cushion sailing across the room until it caught him across his face.

"Oh, it's like *that*, is it?" he said, raising his arm to toss another missile. Emea was grabbing frantically at the nearest cushion on the floor, when the door swung open and an enormous, white-robed woman entered the room. They froze - Gaspi holding a cushion behind his head, ready to throw, and Emea stooped over, hands reaching towards one on the floor, head raised and turned towards the door, a grimace fixed on her face. Only Lydia looked innocent, standing over by the window, no cushion in her hand or anywhere near her. The large magician stopped in her tracks, staring at the now frozen tableau before her, then let out a throaty chuckle and entered the room, the door swinging shut behind her as she shuffled over to a chair at the front of the room.

"Make yourself at home," she said with a wave of her hand, then sank into her chair with a sigh of relief. "I'm Healer Emelda," she said. Emea, red faced, looked mortified that her mentor had met her in this way. The three students looked at each other, at the cushions on the floor and at the three chairs, and sat down in the chairs as one. Emelda chuckled again; a warm sound filled with mirth.

"Do you like the room?" she asked.

"Yes, very much," piped Emea, still looking thoroughly embarrassed. Lydia and Gaspi said they liked it too.

"Well, that's good," said Emelda. "How you feel in this room will influence how quickly you learn to connect with your talent."

"What do you mean...Healer Emelda?" Gaspi asked, a little formally.

"Gaspi, is it?" Emelda asked. Gaspi nodded. "In the classroom I like to be called Miss Emelda, or just Miss if you like. Healer Emelda is a bit of a mouthful," she said warmly. Gaspi immediately liked her. She was friendly and informal and he suspected she'd be a good mentor for Emmy. "And what I mean, young Mage, is that a calm atmosphere, where you feel comfortable and rested, will help you achieve the optimum state for connecting with your talent," Emelda explained. "Your magic lives in the deepest part of you, in the very seat of your being, and I am going to help you get in touch with it. I am going to teach you to meditate."

Gaspi felt a surge of anxiety. He raised his hand. "Yes, Gaspi?"

"Miss, I've already connected with my talent, and don't know if I want to do it again," Gaspi said.

"Don't worry, Gaspi," Emelda replied in a comforting tone. "Hephistole has told me about your experiences, and you are not in any danger here. I think he has already mentioned to you that we have put a block on your power, and however powerful you are, you won't be able to get past it. Your talent is what makes you powerful, and if you can't touch it then you have nothing to fear, do you?" Gaspi nodded, but must have still looked uncertain. "What I'm going to teach you today," Emelda continued, "is a technique that will enable you to control your talent. Once we release the block you can start to use it straight away, and if we have any problems we'll put it right back, okay?"

"Okay," Gaspi responded, with a little more confidence this time.

"Just relax, and enjoy the lesson," Emelda said. "Let us worry about releasing your block when it's the right time. Can you do that?" Gaspi said he could.

Emelda waved her hand in a deliberate-looking motion, and a gentle hum filled the room. Gaspi recognised it as similar to the sound he'd woken up to that morning, but this one had deeper, bass sonorities underpinning the harmonies, and was more steady and repetitive. He found it extremely relaxing, and one look at his friends' faces showed them that they did too.

100

"We use sound and light to help you achieve the optimum state for performing magic," Emelda explained. "The greatest magical innovators of our day work in enclosed, restful environments like this to enhance their work. All of our enchantments are done in just such an atmosphere to ensure the highest infusion of power into the object. You will find, with magic, that peace is power." Gaspi noticed that Emea was listening to Emelda with rapt attention, eyes wide as she drank in every word. Again he felt that this wise, assured woman would be a good mentor for her.

"Magic resides in the deepest part of you," Emelda continued, "where everything is pure and your potential is unlimited. As we grow we all learn to consciously restrict ourselves, to live in the outward part of the soul that interacts with its environment, struggling with the strains and stresses of daily life. But the deepest part of you, your spirit, is unaffected by these struggles, and is all-knowing. The techniques I'm going to teach you will enable you to touch that part of you, and that means to touch your talent. If you're all ready, I'll take you through a simple exercise."

She paused, looking intently into each of their faces. "So, are you ready?" she asked significantly. She received a mixture of nods and murmurs in response. "Then get yourselves comfortable. Until you're used to attaining an optimum state, you may fall asleep lying on the cushions if you try to meditate lying down, so the chairs are the best place to start. Just settle yourselves in, legs and arms uncrossed, your feet flat on the floor and your hands resting separately on your lap. Feet uncrossed, Gaspi. That's it. Now, roll your shoulders a few times to iron the kinks out...that's good. Now close your eyes, and allow your breathing to deepen..."

As Emelda took them through some breathing exercises and simple visualisations, Gaspi found himself teased by feelings of elation. His toes and fingers tingled, as he became increasingly relaxed. Emelda's voice drifted in and out as his own imagination took over at points, creating fantastical visions, the warm-hearted imaginings of his soul. Once Emelda had taken them through the initial relaxation exercises, she took them deeper into a trance.

"Imagine you are in a safe place...somewhere you feel completely at rest...it can be anywhere at all, somewhere you've been or somewhere you create...allow the image to form in your mind..."

In Gaspi's mind's eye he saw a secret mountain valley, hidden from everyone but him. It was tucked away between two peaks, sheltered from the wind and bathed in sunshine. Thick green stands of firs skirted the slopes, surrounding a shining blue lake in the centre of the valley.

"What can you see?"

Gaspi found himself in the centre of his vision, standing by the lake. A gentle wind caused the crystalline water to ruffle, sunlight flashing off each tiny wave, and piercing into the depths of the sparkling water with long, golden shafts.

"What can you hear?"

Behind him, the sweet sound of birdsong bubbled from the throat of a thrush. Other birdcalls sounded crisply from the trees. Water lapped gently at the lake shore, making a shushing sound as each tiny swell swept over pebbles.

"What can you feel?"

A gentle breeze tickled against Gaspi's cheek. Cool grass and soft, springy soil pressed comfortably against his bare feet. But, above all, he felt a deep, peaceful rush of contentment, and surging joy, as if a deep well of his spirit had been opened. In a semi-rapturous state, Gaspi found himself wondering where this joy was coming from. What produced these feelings of bliss and filled his two-dimensional pictures with colour and depth and sound? What caused him to feel the wind on his cheeks, to taste the moisture in the air on his tongue? What made him feel more comfortable in his own skin than he had ever felt? Was this some form of magic?

"Affirm to yourself that you are in a safe place. Nothing can enter your secret place unless you allow it..." Gaspi didn't think he had ever felt more safe, more comforted.

"As your feeling of safety grows, let your attention turn inwards. Let your consciousness search in, towards the centre of your being..."

Emelda's words drifted through his consciousness as he moved more deeply into stillness, scraps of sentences catching his attention, directing his thought.

"Become aware of your flesh, strong and solid...now move deeper...past the body and into the soul...become aware of your emotions...examine them from a distance...unaffected...let them go one by one...leaving them behind...until all you have is stillness..."

Gaspi was a small, softly glowing light in the heart of his being, still as a pond, utterly restful, gently curious.

"In the centre of your being, residing in perfect stillness, is your spirit...feel it drawing you in as you approach this sacred, inner space, where you know all and all is known..."

Emelda raised herself out of her chair, and moved quietly to behind where they sat.

"Expand your senses, exploring the depths of your spirit, and become aware of your power."

Gaspi peered intently with the eyes of his soul, searching for something in that inner light of his spirit. At first, he could sense nothing at all, and intensified his gaze, feeling a glimmer of frustration mar his otherwise peaceful experience.

"Not being forceful..." Emelda said. "Your inner senses gently exploring...remaining open to your power."

Gaspi breathed deeply, letting go of his frustration and softening his inward gaze, sending his probing thoughts gently roaming through his inner landscape, until he sensed it. Within his spirit there was a force; not obvious at first, but there nevertheless. It swirled within his being, a light within the light, part of him and yet separate, moving in perfect harmony with his own spirit. Gaspi thought he smelled a faint scent of freshly turned earth, of greenery and new growth. The faint scent grew stronger in his nostrils, so that he almost opened his eyes to see where it was coming from, but he instinctively sensed that this was all part of connecting to his magic, and kept his eyes closed.

The swirling globe-light of Gaspi's spirit was no longer the gentle white he had first perceived, but was coloured with tinges of green, which, as he watched, grew stronger and more pervasive. He peered deeply into the mesmeric light, wooed by its vibrant depths, and then abandoning caution he plunged into it, letting it surround him, watching it surge around him in a hypnotic orbit. It was many-hued, ranging from the fresh green of new life to the emerald hues of ancient forests. Allured by the beauty swirling around him, moved by its purity, Gaspi reached out with his hands, then with his heart, trying to harness the flow of this power, trying to get into its flow, but it remained out of reach. It was as if he was looking through thick, clear glass that separated him from the object of his desire. It came to him that this was the block placed between him and the source of his power, the block intended to keep him safe, but right now all he wanted to do was shove it aside and draw deeply on the magic within him. Try as he might, he could not touch the power he could see, and after a few minutes he stopped trying and contented himself with resting in the centre of his being, observing the flow of magic around him. Emelda's voice cut through his trance and into his consciousness once again.

"Allow yourself to become aware of your physical environment once again..."

Reluctantly, Gaspi turned his attention outward.

"I'm going to count from one to ten. Affirm to yourself that with each number you will become more alert...one...two...becoming aware of your body..."

Gaspi wriggled his toes and stretched out his arms.

"Three...four...taking what you've experienced with you as you re-enter full consciousness...five...six...become aware of the chair you're sitting on..."

Gaspi rolled his feet to work out the stiffness in his ankles.

"Seven...eight...re-orientate yourself to the room... nine.... ten.... and open your eyes."

Gaspi found himself blinking in the light of the warmly lit room, and, looking around him, saw the others doing the same. Lydia looked radiant and relaxed, but he couldn't read Emea, whose forehead was marred by the tiny vertical frown line he found so endearing.

"So...let's talk about our experiences," said Emelda, a look of childlike fascination and delight written across her face. "Remember, what you experience is private, and you don't need to talk about anything if you don't want to, but in the interests of learning, it would help if you can be as open as you feel comfortable with. So - who wants to start?"

Lydia went first, talking confidently about her inner journey. Her secret place was a plushly decorated Gypsy caravan, expansive and luxurious inside, scattered throughout with the softest cushions, the air perfumed with expensive incense. She had connected with her talent, visualising a crystal ball filled with deep crimson light, which filled her with magical energy when she placed her hands on it. Gaspi went next, briefly explaining his experience of the swirling green light, and also how the block had restrained him from connecting with it.

"And what about you, Emea?" Emelda asked.

Emea was quiet for a moment. "I don't know. I mean...I think I felt something, when we were relaxing. I felt...happy, and something else. But every time I started to go there I'd be distracted. My hair felt like it was pulled too tight, or I couldn't stop itching. Maybe I've got fleas!" she said in disgust.

"Ah yes, I know the feeling," said Emelda with good humour. "Some people find meditating very easy, and others have to work at it. It's like a muscle you have to train. Don't be discouraged, Emea, you'll get there." Emea looked doubtful.

"Well, now you've tried to connect with your talent, let's try and use it, shall we?" Emelda said cheerfully. "Not you of course, Gaspi, but your turn will come soon. Now, girls, I want you to close your eyes...and you, Emea. That's right. Now, try to recapture some of that calmness you have been feeling. Allow the magic to draw you in..." Gaspi watched his friends' faces. Lydia looked beatific, Emea like she was trying to thread a rope through the eye of a needle.

"Cup your hands in front of you, as if you are holding some water,"

Emelda continued. She moved over, and adjusted their hands. "Now, draw near to your power, visualising it in whatever way feels most natural." Emea's frown deepened, as Gaspi watched.

"Imagine your power channelling into your cupped hands, forming into a ball of light. Gently now, don't force it..."

At first nothing happened; but to Gaspi's amazement, a hand-sized globe of red light slowly filled the gap in Lydia's hands after a moment. His gaze flicked involuntarily to Emea's hands, desperately hoping something would happen for her. The moments ticked by excruciatingly, but the pause was becoming too painful, and Gaspi saw Emelda shift in her chair, about to speak, when all of a sudden he caught sight of the slightest pale white glow within Emea's hands. Emelda had seen it too, pushing herself quietly out of her chair and shuffling forward to get a better view, but the movement distracted Emea and she opened her eyes. For a fraction of a second the glow in Emea's hands lingered, and then it winked out of existence as if it had never been there. Her hopeful gaze lingered on the spot where she thought just *maybe* she had seen something, before looking up at Healer Emelda with an uncertain expression.

Emelda smiled at her, and rested a hand on her shoulder, but said nothing, not wanting to disturb Lydia, whose hands still cupped a merrily glowing ball of red light. Emea gasped gently in surprise when she saw it, but Lydia was undisturbed.

Emelda spoke softly to her. "Lydia, when you feel ready to do so without losing your focus, open your eyes, and keep your power flowing into the ball of light."

Lydia continued to sit as she was for a few moments, breathing steadily in and out, and then slowly opened her eyes, which widened slightly on seeing what was in her hands, but the surprise didn't break her concentration. The red light continued glowing in her hands for several heartbeats, her face breaking into a smile, but then the light began to falter, flickering dimly, then brightly, and then disappeared in an instant.

"Bravo! Wonderful. Good job, both of you," Emelda exclaimed enthusiastically. She must have seen Emea's sceptical expression. "Lydia, you managed that marvellously - but that doesn't mean you weren't successful too, Emea. I saw light begin to form in your hands, and I think Gaspi did too?" she enquired of Gaspi.

"Absolutely. I definitely saw something," Gaspi said, silently willing Emea to believe him.

Emea's pretty face glowed pink. "I think I saw it too," she said, "just for a moment after I opened my eyes." Beneath the embarrassment and mixed with a lingering uncertainty, Gaspi thought he could detect a hint of determination in Emea, a determination born of hope, and as he breathed more easily he realised just how worried he had been about the release of Emea's power.

Emelda set them some homework, asking them to try and achieve a meditative state on their own, once this evening and once the next morning before breakfast. They weren't to use their powers outside of the classroom for now, until she felt they had them under control. Gaspi asked when the block would be taken away.

"We'll wait at least a week, until you can confidently approach and let go of your power," Emelda said. "The problem you had on your journey was due to not being able to let go, and not knowing how much you can safely draw on. For now, just work hard on familiarising yourself with the magic within you."

Chapter 13

They talked animatedly as they gathered their bags up. "Who'd have thought it?" Lydia breathed elatedly. "That I could connect with my power so easily?"

"Or that meditating would feel so amazing?" Gaspi added, remembering the euphoria he'd experienced.

Even Emea, whose experience had been less intense, was excited. "I found it hard to relax, but whenever I did, it was like touching the edge of something beautiful. And that was just the edge." Gaspi smiled, happy that Emea had gained a little confidence.

They emerged from the classroom door into the dusty courtyard to find an object flying towards them. Gaspi instinctively reached out, and caught what appeared to be a large bundle of leather rags bound tightly in a ball. All the boys in their class had stopped in mid-action, positioned all over the strangely marked quad.

"Throw it back, then!" one of the boys shouted, and Gaspi passed it back to him with an easy overhand lob.

Emea looked at Gaspi with a knowing smile. "Want to watch, Gasp?" she asked.

"Sure," he said, not taking his eyes from the ball. The three friends sat down on the nearest bench to watch what was happening. In a way, it was similar to Koshta. The aim of the game seemed to be to pass the ball between two coats placed at each end of the quadrangle. The coats lay on the white lines at each end of the courtyard, marking out two goals. The difference was that the ball was much larger than a Koshta seed, and there were no sticks involved. It could only be kicked and not picked up, except by the boy guarding the goal, or when it went over the boundary of the quad.

It seemed strange to Gaspi at first - all that kicking, and not being able to use your hands - but soon the speed and skill needed to control the ball with just your feet had him mesmerised. He leaned and shifted in his seat as the boys played, jumping to his feet when it looked like a goal was going to be scored. Some of the boys were clearly better than others, and Gaspi grudgingly noticed that Everand was pretty skilled, scoring over half of his team's goals. Ferast was not playing, but watched from the sidelines.

Some time into the game Everand clashed with one of the other boys, leaving him writhing on the ground, clutching his ankle. His team mates gathered round, urging him to get up. When it became clear he was not going to get up, the captain, a tall blond boy called Owein, turned to Gaspi, who was the only boy apart from Ferast who was not already playing.

"Want to take Alek's place?" he called out. Gaspi didn't need asking twice, but got up and walked out into the courtyard. The other boys didn't show any outward friendliness, but neither were they hostile. It seemed as if hostilities were to be suspended while the game lasted.

"Have you ever played before?" the tall blond boy asked him.

"Nope. Doesn't look too hard, though."

"Well, just try and put the ball through the goal, yeah?"

Gaspi nodded.

"Want to hang back for a bit, play in defence while you get a feel for it?"

"No," Gaspi responded. "I'll do what Alek was doing." Alek had been playing near the goal, picking up long balls and trying to score. This is what Gaspi had been really good at in Koshta, and he was itching to put the ball through the goal.

"Everyone alright with that?" the blond boy asked.

"Yes, Owein," a thick-set boy with tightly curled, wiry hair answered. The others nodded.

"Fair enough," Owein said. "You're up the front of the pitch. Keep your eye out for the ball when we pass it to you, and if you get clear of everyone, yell for the ball." Gaspi nodded.

"Everyone ready?" Owein asked. He placed the ball on the ground, and Gaspi sprang into motion, sprinting down the pitch past the other boys, getting into the kind of position Alek had been holding. Owein passed to the thick-set lad, who muscled through the pack by sheer force more than skill, keeping the ball close to his feet. Half way down the pitch he saw that Gaspi was in a few feet of clear space, and passed the ball forward to him. Gaspi had been running backwards, keeping his eyes on the ball, and saw it coming. It bounced high several feet in front of him and Gaspi knew what he had to do.

He lifted his leg to trap the ball, and amazingly it worked, the ball slapping against his thigh and dropping to the floor at his feet. Turning round, he brought the ball with him, and as the defenders closed in he aimed for the narrowing gap between them, through which he could see the open goal. He thrust out his foot and struck the ball - but he only hit it with the outside of his foot, and the ball went spinning off to the right, bouncing off the pitch.

Gaspi's face flushed red with embarrassment, and as he turned round to face the team he expected derision, but to his surprise there was no laughter, and Owein clapped him on the back as he turned to run back down the pitch. After that Gaspi grew in confidence. His speed came in handy, and his team mates soon grasped that he could get himself into open space very quickly, and out-pace anyone on the pitch if they gave him the ball. Though the ball sometimes bobbled over his feet and he occasionally lost control, his touch on the ball was becoming defter by the minute. Everand's team scored another goal, putting them ahead by three, and it was Owein's team's turn to kick off from a marked spot in the centre of the courtyard. When a goal was scored, all the players had to return to their half of the pitch, and couldn't move until the ball was struck from its spot by the team who had lost the last goal.

Owein put the ball on the spot, and murmured intently to Gaspi and the thick-set lad, "Gav, go right, Gaspi go long. I'll act as if I'm passing to Gaspi but will put it through to you instead, Gav. Gaspi - get in the middle and make some space, and Gav will pass it across to you. Your job is to put it in the goal before the defence can block you. Got it?" Gaspi and Gav nodded.

Owein kicked off, passing the ball back to a small, dark-haired boy. The second the ball had been touched Gaspi was off, sprinting up the left hand side, trying to draw players to him to create space in the middle. The ball was passed back to Owein, who kept it under control with some clever footwork as Everand tried to take it off him. Gav was most of the way down the pitch on the right by now, and, picking his moment perfectly, Eric made a long pass. The ball curved high over everyone's heads and came down right in Gav's path, who brought it under control after a couple of bounces, and looked up to find Gaspi.

Gaspi waited until the moment Gav looked up, then ducked around two boys and sprinted into the middle, several yards out from goal, finding clear space just as Gav's foot struck the ball. It was as if everything was happening slowly. The ball sailed towards Gaspi, turning in the air as it came, passing over the head of a leaping defender and curving down towards Gaspi. It was coming down at waist height, and Gaspi knew from the sounds of feet pounding the floor behind him that he didn't have time to bring it down before aiming. Leaping into the air he swung his foot around, powering the stroke from his hip, trying to catch the ball in mid-flight. His foot struck the ball solidly, re-directing it towards the goal. The goalkeeper leaped at the ball, but Gaspi's strike was fast and accurate - and though he leaped with outstretched arms, the boy landed with a loud "Umph!" several feet from the ball, which had sailed past him, through the goal.

There was a loud cheer from some of the boys on Gaspi's team, who seemed to have momentarily forgotten they were meant to be ignoring him. Gaspi was elated, both by the cheering of the team and the satisfaction of scoring. This was almost as good as Koshta! Turning around, he grinned wildly at Emea and Lydia, who were also cheering. Owein looked pleased and Gav flashed him a grin, but as he surveyed the other boys' faces he saw uncertainty, or a kind of blankness as they controlled their reactions, flicking nervous looks at Everand. Everand's face was dark with dislike, and no-one on his team was smiling.

His excitement muted but not quenched, Gaspi jogged back down the pitch, anxious to get back into the fray. The game lasted another twenty minutes, and although Gaspi didn't score again he came close twice and made a good pass to Gav, who put another one through the goal.

The game ended with Everand's team winning seven to six, and the boys traipsed off the courtyard looking dusty and tired. Gaspi was under no illusions that his exclusion from the group was over, but felt that at least with Owein and Gav that the ice had thawed a little. Telling Emea he'd see her at supper, he followed the other boys into the dormitory to clean up.

That evening Taurnil came to meet them at the college, and they went out into the city to find a tavern. It turned out they didn't need to wander far, as only two streets away there was an inviting place called the Travellers Rest. It wasn't built in the curvaceous style or the reddish stone of the rest of the city, but was made of large blocks of squared-off, pale stone. It was a sprawling maze of a building, two stories high, made without any apparent design. Its contours didn't show a single straight line and unexpected wings of the structure sprang out of nowhere, golden light spilling out of many windows. Gaspi led the way up to the bar and ordered in ales for him and Taurnil, and wine for the girls.

"Students, are you?" the barmaid asked, with an amused look.

Gaspi and the girls nodded. "Not me," Taurnil said. "I'm training with the guards."

The barmaid was pretty and young, and gave Taurnil an appraising look. "City guard, eh?" she asked, twirling a lock of blond hair around a finger. "I can't deny a city guard his ale, but I can't serve these three...unless you buy it for them, of course. Got to be fifteen to buy beer, you know!" Gaspi was crestfallen, but to Taurnil's credit, he didn't gloat as he bought the drinks, even if his chest was a little more puffed out than normal. Gaspi thought he saw his friend's eyes flicking towards Lydia. Every last corner of the bar was filled with people, and a loud buzz of conversation filled the air, rising and falling in waves, peals of laughter regularly rising above the general thrum.

They had to search for several minutes to find seats, wondering through the unexpected twists and turns of the enormous establishment. At the front of the tavern was the main bar, large and open and decorated in old brass and dark, heavy wood. The walls were ornamented from floor to ceiling with curious items; currency from different regions, aging parchment announcing events long past, polished brass tools, and even the stuffed heads of dead animals covered every last foot. In the back was an equally large room with a raised stage in its back corner, which Gaspi assumed was for musicians to perform on, although it was empty at that moment. Round tables filled the rest of the room, and the walls in here too were festooned with musical curios. Numerous small nooks led off both rooms into cosy snugs stuffed with deeply-cushioned benches and chairs and small, round-topped tables, and it was in one of these that the four friends found somewhere to sit.

"Nice one getting the drinks in, Taurn," Gaspi said.

"Yes, but wasn't that a bit risky, pretending to be a guard?" Emea asked with concern.

"I wasn't pretending, and anyway I'm fifteen, so I could have got the beer anyway," Taurnil said, flushing slightly at the attention, his eyes again flicking involuntarily towards Lydia.

When Taurnil didn't say anything else, Gaspi punched him on the arm. "Well...tell us!" he said.

"Oh yeah, sorry. Jonn took me there this morning, and once they found out I was fifteen they said I could join up. I'm officially enrolled now, and start training tomorrow."

Gaspi could see how pleased Taurnil was, even though he was trying not to show it. "That's great, Taurn," Gaspi said with a big grin, his excitement teasing more of a reaction from his friend, who returned the grin foolishly.

"We start with weapons training," he said, and it was clear there was nothing that could have pleased him more. Emea leant over and gave him a big hug, which he accepted stoically, accustomed to Emea's shows of emotion.

"Is this something you want, then, Taurnil?" Lydia asked, her penetrating gaze resting on him while he searched for an answer.

Looking directly into her eyes, he answered simply, "Yeah. I've got a feeling in my gut that this is what I'm meant to be doing." Lydia nodded, accepting his answer unquestioningly, and placed a hand gently on his forearm. Flustered by Lydia's touch, Taurnil quickly changed the subject. "Enough about me," he said. "How was your first day at college?"

All three began talking at once; about the dJin and their first experience of trying to release their magic, which fascinated Taurnil, and they had to relive the experience several times before he was satisfied. They started talking about the football game, when Emea mentioned the behaviour of the other boys towards Gaspi. Gaspi had been hoping to avoid talking about this, but now it had been brought up Taurnil didn't look like he was going to let it go at that.

"So who's this Everand, then?" he asked.

"Rich boy? I dunno," answered Gaspi sullenly. "He just seems to have taken a dislike to me, and the other boys pretty much do what he says."

Taurnil barked out a laugh, shaking his head. "I don't know how you do it, Gasp. Everywhere you go you make an enemy with the biggest, pushiest lad."

Gaspi laughed reluctantly, his face breaking into a roguish grin. "Must be my natural charm."

Emea slapped his shoulder playfully, giving Gaspi an exasperated look. "Just don't wind him up, Gaspi," she said.

"As if I wound him up!" Gaspi retorted indignantly. "Honestly Emmy, I've practically bitten my lip off trying to be polite to him, but he has it in for me. So does his nasty little friend…Ferast."

"Mmm…I must admit, there seems to be something odd about that one," Emea conceded.

Lydia had been listening intently up to this point. "I think Everand's jealous," she said conclusively.

"Jealous? Of what?" Gaspi asked incredulously.

"Because you're a Nature Mage, of course," Lydia answered. "You've joined a group where he's the top dog, and threatened him by having the most rare and powerful form of magic in all the lands."

Taurnil nodded slowly. "It makes sense, Gaspi," he said, his eyes lingering a bit longer than was necessary on Lydia's serious face.

"Well, I didn't ask for it, did I?" Gaspi said bitterly. "I mean, this supposed *gift* has nearly killed me…twice!"

"We know, Gaspi," Emea said, placing her hand on his knee. "But try to give them time to adjust. Maybe it'll all blow over in a week or two." Gaspi grunted noncommittally.

"So how does football compare to Koshta then, Gasp?" Taurnil asked, changing the topic. Gaspi immediately perked up.

"Brilliant!" he enthused. "You wouldn't think so, with that big ball bouncing all over the place and not being able to use your hands, but you get into it."

"Gaspi scored, you know," Emea announced proudly.

"In your first game?" Taurnil said. "Good going, Gasp!" He

sounded genuinely impressed. "Let me know when you're playing again, and I'll try to come and watch."

"Sure thing, Taurn," Gaspi responded. "Maybe you can join in. You could play in goal."

"Well, I don't know about that," Taurnil responded. "I mean, you three are all magicians now, and I'm...well...I'm not." He seemed suddenly shy, glancing questioningly at Lydia.

"Yeah, but you don't need magic for football!" Gaspi asserted.

"Well, yeah...maybe," Taurnil responded, avoiding eye contact by staring at the pint glass he was playing with. "Let's just see how it goes." Lydia's gaze was fixed on Taurnil, her head cocked on one side as she scrutinised him, but she said nothing. The silence extended for several moments. Gaspi wanted to break it, but felt that somehow this was between Taurnil and Lydia.

It was Taurnil who spoke next. "There's a guard's tournament in a couple of months. Will you all come and watch me if I compete?"

In all his life, during which time Taurnil had always been Gaspi's best friend, he had never asked him to watch him compete at anything. Gaspi was the competitive one, and Taurnil was always there faithfully to back him up. Gaspi felt excited at the prospect of returning the favour. "Of course mate," he said, clapping Taurnil on the back.

"But Taurn, you've not even started training yet," Emea said. "How will you compete with the other guards?"

Taurnil shrugged. "I'll just have to get good quickly," he said seriously, then grinned. "Besides, it won't be dangerous. All the weapons will be padded or blunted. Will you come, Emmy?"

"I'll come," she said, her concern mollified. "And Lydia will too, won't you Lydia?"

"I'd love to," the dark-haired gypsy girl answered with her usual serious intent. Gaspi nearly laughed at Taurnil's utter failure to hide how pleased he was.

"Well, we'd better be getting back," Emmy said. "It's getting late, and it's bound to be another big day tomorrow."

"Yeah - anything could happen, really," Gaspi said. "Alright, let's get going."

Taurnil walked them back to the college and said goodnight, promising to come by the next evening if he could, and strolled off down the hill towards the barracks. When they reached the dormitories, Gaspi took his opportunity to spend a little bit of time alone with Emea.

"Want to go for a walk, Emmy?" he asked. Emea looked at Lydia, who smiled and said goodnight, giving them both a kiss on the check, and disappeared into the dormitory. Emea and Gaspi walked slowly round the courtyard. Gaspi was surprised by how suddenly awkward he felt. He was unnaturally aware of the cracks in the paving-stones, and had to resist the urge to scuff uncomfortably at the ground. Why did he all of a sudden feel unable to talk to Emmy after feeling comfortable with her all day? Being around her made him feel amazing, but sometimes it dried his mouth up too.

Emea broke the silence. "Taurnil looked happy, didn't he?"

"Yeah," Gaspi answered with relief. "He really wants to be a guard, doesn't he?"

"I've never seen him so determined." A few more seconds passed in silence, until Emea spoke again. "I'm not sure about him entering this competition though. I mean, he could get hurt. What do you think?"

Gaspi grinned. "I think you worry too much, Emmy."

"I don't!" she replied indignantly. "Well...okay, maybe I do, but it's only because I care about my friends!" she added, with a little fire.

"Okay...easy now!" Gaspi said with a laugh, putting his arm around Emmy's shoulders, turning her towards him as they stopped walking. "Sorry, Emmy I was only pulling your leg. I like that you care so much." Emea relaxed and smiled back, her eyes deep and sparkling in the orange lamplight.

"Well, I do... I mean, I do care," she said softly. Gaspi's heart was thumping all of a sudden, right up in his throat, so much so he was sure Emmy could see it. His eyes took in the soft shimmer of her hair, the openness of her face, which was tantalisingly near to his own. Gaspi leaned in to kiss her, and they stood together in the lamplight for a long moment, until by some mysterious communication they both gently pulled away and broke the connection. "I'm glad we're doing this together Gaspi," she said, and he understood she was referring to the whole thing; the magic, the journey, their relationship, everything.

"Yeah, me too," he said. "This would be a lot scarier on my own." Gaspi felt a heady flow of happiness, and they walked around the quad a while longer, talking more comfortably now, and kissed once more before saying goodnight at the door to Emmy's dorm.

As he walked across the quad back to his own quarters, Gaspi wondered whether the wondrous but disconcerting emotions he felt for Emea would ever settle down. At the moment he seemed to flip from friendship to romance several times a day, without any warning. It was exhausting. She'd been his friend much longer than she'd been his girlfriend, and in some ways he was still getting used to it. He supposed that in time it would all hang together, and life would be much simpler when that happened. He entered the dormitory and made his way through the sleeping forms of his classmates in the dark, finding his bed without tripping over, and he sat down on it as he began to undress. Lifting his arms to pull his shirt over his head, he caught the glitter of Ferast's eyes in the near darkness, and somehow Gaspi knew he had been watching him and Emea The thought gave him the creeps. When the shirt was off his head he looked again at Ferast, whose eyes were now closed, but Gaspi couldn't forget the dark glitter of Ferast's invasive gaze, and as he lay down to sleep he shuddered involuntarily, and pulled the covers up over his head. It took him some time to drift off.

Chapter 14

On the other side of the campus, at the top of his tower, Hephistole was awake, and he was not alone. Standing at a window, looking out over the dim lights of the city at night, Voltan furrowed his brow in thought, drawing his dark widow's peak even further down his forehead than normal. Hephistole was wrapped up in a mauve velvet dressing gown, and sat comfortably in a deep chair behind his guest, a glass of sherry in his hand. A fire roared in the grate next to them, and a second glass of sherry sat on the tabletop, untouched.

"What are your thoughts, Voltan?" he asked. The warrior Mage remained still for a moment.

"I think we need to mobilise our Mages," he said. "We can't be unprepared for whatever is coming."

"What makes you think something is coming?" Hephistole asked, his own brow furrowed in thought, his gaze far off.

"As I said to you this morning, Hephistole, I've never come across anything like the creatures I fought in the plain. They were…powerful. And the boy's story…"

"Powerful, yes," Hephistole added, his gaze still unfocussed. "And yet, Gaspi fought off one of them on his own." Hephistole turned his glass slowly back and forth between his thumb and index finger as he spoke, mesmerised by the lamplight glinting off the sharp facets of finely-cut crystal.

"He's a Nature Mage!" Voltan retorted with feeling. "And he nearly died!"

Hephistole looked up at his friend in surprise. "Forgive me, Voltan," he said gently. "I did not mean to belittle your encounter, nor question your powers. You are one of our finest warriors. I merely meant to say that we are not without hope." Silence lingered between the two men; the unselfconscious silence of people who have known each other a long time, and whose minds are busy with thought.

Hephistole was the one to break it. "I know he is a Nature Mage, Voltan, but he is untrained, and still he held the demon at bay. We haven't known anyone with his particular gift in our lifetime. We don't have any real knowledge of the boundaries of his skill, and what I'm hoping…" Hephistole looked off into the distance again, "…is that he can show us a thing or two."

It was Voltan's turn to look surprised. "That's a heavy burden to place on young shoulders."

"Which is why I won't be placing it on him," Hephistole answered. "Not yet, at least. I want to give Gaspi as much of a run at being an apprentice Mage as possible, and it may be years before we have to face whatever force is driving this incursion into our lands. That's if there is anything behind it at all..." Hephistole lost his faraway expression and pushed himself up straight. "So be it," he said decisively. "Start preparing the Mages for battle. I agree that we can't sit here twiddling our thumbs, even if we don't know what we're facing. But let's keep this quiet. Meet with the heads of each discipline and tell them everything - but only them. As far as the students need to know, we're just focussing on martial magic for a while. It's not the first time we've done that in recent years."

Voltan looked grimly satisfied at the prospect of doing something useful, the hard lines of his mouth drawing tight with purpose. "I'll try and get some creative ideas out of the heads of each discipline," he said, "and see what we can come up with that might be effective against this type of demon."

"That would be good," Hephistole agreed. "Threat or no threat, we have to be able to combat this kind of attack."

Voltan moved as if to leave, but hesitated, looking back at Hephistole with an uncharacteristic display of uncertainty. "Do you still think it's got something to do with...your old acquaintance?"

Hephistole met Voltan's gaze grimly. "Maybe, maybe not," he said softly. "But there's something familiar about this I can't shake off. Either way, we need to be alert to every possibility."

Voltan nodded. "Rest well," he said, as he turned to leave again.

"And you, old friend," Hephistole answered softly, seconds after Voltan stepped onto the transporter and disappeared.

Hephistole stayed up long into the night, not moving from his comfortable chair except to top up his sherry glass. His mind drifted back to a time when he had been a young pupil at the college, in the first flurry of excitement at the discovery of his own considerable powers. He had found every lesson scintillating, every piece of knowledge another key to opportunity and possibility. He had excelled in his year, advancing quickly beyond the abilities of his fellow students, and had been itching with frustration at the snail's pace he was forced to progress at, until a particular teacher had taken an interest in him.

Shirukai Sestin was Chancellor of the college when Hephistole was a student. He taught both neuromancy and healing, a powerful combination of talents enabling him to influence both the mind and the body. Hephistole's own talents lay in the direction of neuromancy and, drawn by his unusual strength in the discipline, Shirukai took him on as his student. Hephistole remembered the heady excitement he'd felt when he heard the news of his selection, as Shirukai rarely took on a pupil, and was known to be both secretive and powerful. The long tutoring sessions in Shirukai's pyramid soon eclipsed his regular classes both in terms of the complexity of magic he was learning, and the energy he applied to them. He looked forward to those times with his mentor with an almost feverish hunger, and every day it seemed his mind and abilities were stretched to the limit by the endless cascade of esoteric knowledge and practice.

Shirukai showed Hephistole how to sooth and agitate the mind, how to remove memories and place blocks of various types. He taught him how to speak from mind to mind, how to read unspoken thoughts, how to put the mind to sleep and influence the emotions. By nudging certain parts of the brain, he could stimulate emotions without a natural cause. He could cause a sudden rush of happiness, or fear. So caught up in his thirst for knowledge, Hephistole never stopped to question the use of the magic he was being shown. Hephistole carried the youthful presumption that all magicians worked for the good of others, and managed to ignore any internal discomfort he might have felt when the topic of their discussions sometimes turned a little dark.

However talented Hephistole was at neuromancy, he struggled constantly with the frustration that he had no appreciable ability in the area of physical healing, and so could never combine the powerful control of the mind he had gained with influence over the body the way his mentor could. It was during a session where Shirukai was trying to develop Hephistole's unimpressive healing skills that Hephistole was first forced to face a dark side to him that was impossible to ignore. The memory came back to him with peculiar clarity.

Hephistole entered the pyramid and made his way down the single, long corridor to Shirukai's study as usual. He pushed open the door and was surprised to find a dog strapped to a metal table in the centre of the room. The dog was breathing calmly, relaxed under the influence of Shirukai's neuromancy.

"Come in, Hephistole," Shirukai said, his long, slender fingers caressing each other in a gentle, weaving motion. "Today you are going to try your hand at controlling both the body and the mind."

Hephistole looked unsure. "Is the dog sick, professor?" he asked, peering uncertainly at the healthy-looking animal.

"No, not sick," Shirukai said, closely observing Hephistole's reaction as he spoke, "but how can you practice without a live subject?" His eyes explored Hephistole's face for several seconds.

"Don't worry Hephistole," he said. "The dog will not be harmed."

"Of course," Hephistole said, not entirely satisfied, but still eager to see what would happen. He placed his bag on a chair, and came to stand beside Shirukai.

"I have the dog in a trance," Shirukai said softly. "It is currently convinced it is safe and it can feel no discomfort. I'm going to hand the reins over to you now. Ready?" Hephistole nodded. He slid his own controls in place, holding the dog's mind in the same illusion, restricting the release of feelings that could disturb the creature's equilibrium. As Hephistole's controls slipped into place, Shirukai simultaneously withdrew his; a seamless transition they had practiced many times.

"Now, I want you to hold the illusion, no matter what happens. I will cause the dog a little physical discomfort; nothing major, but enough to agitate it, and as the body responds the illusion will become harder to hold. I want you to hold the dog's mind in place. You must keep it convinced it that it is safe and in no physical pain."

Shirukai must have detected Hephistole's unease. "How do you think we heal people who are in agony?" he asked angrily. "We do exactly this, stilling the mind so we can work on the body. It's important you understand the principle, and I've told you the dog will not be harmed. Now you either trust me, or it is time for us to end this arrangement." Shirukai didn't blink as he stared flatly at his pupil.

Hephistole considered his mentor, the man who had trusted him with so much knowledge, who shaped his learning with such skill, and found there was only one answer. "I trust you," he said.

Shirukai's mouth tightened at the corners. "Then let's begin. Are your illusions still in place?" Hephistole nodded. "In a moment I will start to cause the dog some discomfort." Despite Shirukai's words, Hephistole couldn't escape the feeling like they were doing something wrong. It was true that injured people needed exactly the kind of intervention they were practicing, but this time they would be causing the harm and not just bringing the healing. Whatever his reservations, it was too late now, and when it came down to it he did trust Shirukai, even if he couldn't understand him sometimes; a dark man shrouded in mystery. His thoughts were cut off by the intrusion of a magical sensation he had never felt before. It was like a slow grinding motion or discordant sound, grating on his inner self with each second of its endurance. His stomach flipped uncomfortably as strange magic was worked in his presence. The dog began to shift on the metal table. A leg twitched, and in his anxious state Hephistole almost let go of his magic.

"Hold your illusion!" Shirukai commanded, his eyes boring angrily *into Hephistole's own. He strengthened the outflow of his power, soothing the creature with a wave of assurance, subduing its ability to feel pain. Sure enough it settled back on the table again and was still, though the morbid flow of Shirukai's power flowed unabated. Hephistole's breath started to come too swiftly, in deep gulps, and sweat broke out on his skin, which prickled as if stung by a thousand tiny needles, but just as he began to feel dizzy the source of his discomfort was gone. He blinked twice, released his own magic, and looked up at Shirukai, who was busying himself around his desk. Hephistole's sweat was drying on his skin, and he was already wondering if he imagined those strange sensations that had made him feel so out of sorts just moments earlier. But no, surely something had happened, something unpleasant. He realised Shirukai was speaking to him.*

"...can see that combining disciplines can be very powerful," his mentor was saying. "The possibilities are endless if you are willing to be creative." There was a long pause, during which Shirukai looked steadily at his pupil. "Well that's enough for today, he said finally. "I'll let you know when it's time for your next lesson."

Hearing the dismissal for what it was, Hephistole mumbled a goodbye and left, not even remembering to shut the door behind him. He walked with unsteady steps down the long corridor, and out into the sunlight. The slight breeze chilled him as it dried the remaining sheen of cold sweat as he walked. He was turning the experience he had just been through over in his mind. What had caused him to feel so dreadful? Was that Shirukai's magic? Another form of magic Hephistole didn't know yet? It had certainly felt different from anything he had yet channelled, and left him shaken. Suddenly, he realised with a touch of panic, that he had not got his bag with him. He must have left it in Shirukai's pyramid, and much as he didn't want to go back there he couldn't go to class without it the next morning.

Reluctantly, he made his way back to the pyramid, feeling uneasy the whole way; an unease that doubled and then tripled as he entered the pyramid and walked quietly down the corridor to Shirukai's study, hoping his mentor had left the room and he could retrieve his bag unnoticed. He could see down the gloomy corridor that the door stood ajar, dim red light filtering round its edge, and as he drew near he heard a whimper. Hephistole froze on the spot, sure that what was happening behind the door was not something he was meant to see.

Everything in him was urging him to leave, but some stubborn, curious part of him refused to do so, and he edged closer and closer to the open door. He was just two steps away from the door when the whimpering began again, louder this time, followed by a startling yelp, a sound of fear and pain so shocking Hephistole jumped and almost fell over. Reaching the door he leaned into the wall on its open side, leaning forward to get a glimpse of what was happening inside. Red light washed the room in its sullen glow. Craning his neck he could see several feet of floor and the edge of the metal table. He stretched just a little further, and more of the table came into view, on which he could see the hind legs of the dog, and the edge of Shirukai's robe, who was standing over the creature, facing away from the door.

Hephistole could see his bag on the other side of the room, but there was no way he was interrupting Shirukai and getting it back that day, not when he was so terrified of what was going on in that room his knees had turned to water. The dog let out another loud yelp, its legs twitching violently. Horrified, Hephistole turned and fled back the way he came, scurrying as quickly as possible to put distance between himself and his mentor.

Hephistole's thoughts returned to the present. There was a reason to connect the recent attacks with Shirukai. The sorcerer had been exiled from the college and country several years later when he was caught performing the most heinous of experiments on a guard that had gone missing. Those experiments had included the forbidden practice of summoning a minor demon and using it to torture his victim. The Council of Magicians had banned Shirukai from the borders of the known lands in punishment. Nobody had heard from him since. Logic told Hephistole that his old mentor should have been long dead by now. He had been well into his years when he'd been exiled, and another forty years had passed since then; but in his heart of hearts, where the memory of his complex boyhood relationship with Shirukai still lingered, he could feel a familiar signature, a resonance that he couldn't dismiss. Sitting in his armchair, staring deeply into space, Hephistole brooded long into the night.

Chapter 15

Gaspi woke early. None of his classmates were up yet, and the light showing through the windows was only just transitioning from the grey of pre-dawn to the first golden glow of sunrise. Rising quietly he washed and dressed, and made his way out into the courtyard. The lingering chill of night goose-pimpled the flesh of his arms, and he drew his coat around himself to keep warm, rubbing his arms vigorously and breathing in the sharp, clear air.

Gaspi wanted to practice his meditation every day as Emelda had instructed, and the early morning seemed the best time to do it without distraction. Looking for a secluded spot, Gaspi walked around the edge of the courtyard, looking down the passages leading off into other areas of the campus. Before getting even halfway round, he came to a passageway that led to a low-walled garden in a courtyard of its own. Carpeted in lush grasses, the garden was laced with wandering hedgerows and flowerbeds. Willows hung their languid branches over the lawn, and gentle streams meandered through its length. The trees and plants were not consistent with what grew throughout the city, and Gaspi could only presume that some botanically minded magician had cultivated this lovely garden, and sustained it with magic.

Though not large, the higgledy-piggledy nature of the garden provided a variety of shady places where you wouldn't be overlooked, and Gaspi quickly found a spot by a stream, where a well-placed bench enabled him to take his ease without watering his behind with morning dew. A large willow hung its long, lazy branches over his head, dappling him with shade. Sitting as Emelda had shown them, feet uncrossed and flat on the floor with his hands resting on his lap, Gaspi tried to repeat the breathing exercises he'd performed the previous day. At first he found it hard, the kind of focus required for relaxation slipping through his grasp as he thought about every last distracting thing he was trying to let go of. But somehow the gentle tinkling of the stream and his repeated efforts to slow his thoughts and focus on the moment enabled him to slip, almost without noticing it, into that altered state Emelda had led them into the previous day.

It was the steady flow of peace that alerted Gaspi to his achievement, a kind of tickling, refreshing caress that breezed gently through his mind, and for a few minutes he was content to remain like that, enjoying the natural harmony of his inner world. Once he was fully immersed, Gaspi allowed his senses to rove inwards, searching without force for the core of his being. With very little effort, he drew near to the warm globe-light that represented his spirit, and sank deep into its core. The gentle peace he'd been experiencing deepened to a profound inner silence, and he moved correspondingly from contentment to reverence. He was aware of the nearness of love. It caressed his soul like the softest silk, spoke wordlessly with the fulsome, echoless quiet of snow-covered forests. To Gaspi it almost seemed sentient - love with a capital L - and he allowed himself to be wooed.

The previous day, Gaspi had found it hard to maintain control. Intoxicated by his inner experience, he had tried to touch his magic, despite the dangers it posed. Today he felt more in control, and though captured by love, enraptured by its tangible warmth, he maintained a kind of detachment, a part of him observing the experience instead of losing himself in it entirely. That conscious part of him directed his attention to his power, seeking its flow within the depths of his spirit, and soon enough a wash of refreshing green light mingled with the white, the colour deepening as he observed it. It pulsed with his heartbeat, surrounding him in a rhythmic dance of delight. He could sense it waited eagerly for his command, coiling lovingly round his hands, but this time he didn't attempt to touch it, and was content to simply draw near.

Just before withdrawing from his trance, Gaspi reached out with splayed fingers to feel the barrier between him and his power. Ever so gently, he rested his fingertips against it. It had no texture or temperature, but simply was. It stood invisible and unbreachable between him and his magic, and after a few seconds he withdrew, and slowly brought himself out of his trance. When he opened his eyes he was almost surprised to find himself still sitting on the bench, hands resting in his lap. He stood up and stretched, enjoying the lingering after-echo of peaceful contentment, and made his way to the refectory. The other students were awake now, some of them stumbling bleary-eyed out of their dormitories, squinting at the bright morning sun, which had fully risen now, and shone brightly down on them.

Emmy and Lydia were sitting on their own in the refectory. Gaspi grabbed some steaming, freshly baked bread and some fruit that had been sliced and stirred into thick yoghurt, and went to join them.

"You look cheerful," Emea said, smiling at him warmly.

"Have you been meditating?" Lydia asked.

Gaspi grinned. "Yeah. You too?" Lydia smiled and nodded. "It's great, isn't it?" Gaspi said. "How about you, Emmy?"

Emea's mouth twisted in frustration. "Well, I tried. It wasn't a total waste of time, I suppose. I mean, I did start to feel relaxed towards the end, but I couldn't…do anything." Emea's eyes flicked towards Lydia. "Unlike Little Miss Magic here!" she added in disgust. "Show him, Lydia!" Lydia gave Emea an understanding look, then extended her hand towards Gaspi. Her palm was empty for a moment, and then the deep red globe of light she had conjured the previous day blinked into existence. It was tiny this time, swirling beguilingly over her palm like a living pebble. Gaspi caught Lydia looking at it fondly for a moment, like it was a pet, and then she snapped her hand shut and it was gone.

"I can make it bigger, of course," she said, "but I don't want everyone to see what I'm doing."

"That's great Lydia, that's really great!" Gaspi said sincerely. He was amazed at how comfortable she seemed with magic, as if she'd been practicing it for years, but then he supposed that in a way she had, acting as a Seer for her family. Emea, on the other hand, was clearly wrestling with the idea of herself as a magician, and he had not even had a chance to touch his magic in a controlled way yet, with the block still in place. He determined to speak to Emelda about it today to see when it could be removed. Breakfast ended when the bell rang, calling them into class, and they all filed out of the refectory and into their classroom.

Emelda was taking the class today. Her large body was stuffed into the armchair behind the teacher's desk, and she smiled indulgently at the students as they walked in, saving a wink for Emea, who trailed in at the tail end of the group. Gaspi, Emea and Lydia had to sit in separate seats as the others were already taken, which wouldn't have bothered Gaspi had he not seen Everand smile at Emea and invite her to take the seat next to him with a wave of his hand. Gaspi knew Emmy was too nice to say no, and that she wouldn't be interested in such a pompous idiot, but had to subdue a wave of anger at Everand's presumption. The self important idiot knew he and Emea had something going, and was flirting with her anyway. What riled him most of all was Ferast's smirk. Everand's dark-haired, skinny friend was sitting on his other side, his lips curling in a knowing smile as Emea took her seat. Gaspi took a deep breath and chose to focus on the lesson. Those two could wait.

Emelda taught from the chair, mostly, her manner matronly and comforting. Gaspi found her voice soothing and full of warmth, and her frequent chuckles infectious. The topic of the lesson was healing. The other students had started the series two weeks previously, so Emelda went over the basics briefly to help the newcomers catch up a bit.

"Healing is more about deftness of touch than it is about power," she said. "It's about tuning into the delicate processes of the body -

where bone is knitting, or flesh is rebuilding itself - and stimulating that process. The more you try to speed it up, the harder it is to get right. It doesn't take a lot of power, but just a sliver of magical pressure exerted in the right place at the right time. There are times not to heal, and times to wait for the body to align itself before encouraging its natural process. If you want to study healing you have to use patience, and become intimate with nuance."

"Not very exciting is it?" she said with a smile, looking round the room from face to face. "Well - it is to me!" she said in answer to her own question, her broad face beatific with sincere pleasure. She let her eyes roam from face to face. "Remind me," she said, "how many of you here have a primary healing gift?"

Emea's hand didn't go up straight away. Emelda gave her a level look, until Emea's hand shyly rose into the air. "So we have Emea," she said, her eyes scanning the rest of the room. "Ah yes, that's right - Ferast." Gaspi looked round in astonishment, sure he must have misheard, but Ferast's hand was still in the air, an inscrutable look upon his shrewd, intelligent face. Lydia was looking at Ferast with an arched eyebrow. Ferast didn't seem to notice the attention he was receiving, and Gaspi and Lydia exchanged questioning looks before turning their attention back to Emelda, who had started talking again.

"A practical demonstration always helps arouse the interest, don't you think?" she said, before ringing a small bell on her table. A minute later the door opened, and a brown-robed magician came in, carrying a black cat, slack and drooping in the way only a sleeping cat can manage. Gaspi assumed from the robe that the girl, who looked only a year or two older than them, was one of the older students. She placed the slumbering creature carefully on the desk.

"Thank you, Salomé," Emelda said. Salomé smiled at Emelda, and then briefly at the first year students, before leaving the room.

Emelda shifted the cat around, until the students could see a long gash in its side. "So you can all see that this cat has been injured," she said. "It's been given something to keep it asleep for a few hours, and it doesn't feel any pain. In a minute you will come up in groups of three. As you know, healing takes place through contact, so I want you to place a hand on the cat, and then probe with your senses. I want you to explore the wound, identifying where the healthy flesh ends and the torn flesh begins. Feel that break, until you can pinpoint the exact place of transition. Okay you three - you go first," she said, pointing at the students sat nearest her.

In groups, the students all had a turn exploring the cat's damaged tissue with their minds. When it was Gaspi's turn he tried to do what

Emelda said, and found he was unable to do so. He couldn't "send his thought" anywhere. Emelda caught his look of frustration. "Ah, sorry Gaspi...I wasn't sure if you would be able to do this with your block in place. You'll get a chance at this soon enough."

Gaspi sat down, disappointed he'd been unable to join in the class, but more interested in what Emea would experience when it was her turn. This class was more important to her than to him. Soon enough her turn came, and she went to the front of the class with Everand and Ferast.

Emea made her way to the front of the class, nervous and excited at the same time about trying her hand at her first bit of healing.

"Any questions before you begin?" Emelda asked.

"Yes," Emea said. "How do I send my thought out? I don't know what you mean by that."

"Well everyone does this differently," Emelda said, "but I just imagine my thought is a tiny probe, a ball of light if you will, or a breath of wind, something non-physical, and then send it into the cat. It is a function of magic to do this, which is why Gaspi was unable to do it, but it requires almost no power at all. You're not doing anything other than observing. Want to try?"

Emea nodded, and focussed her attention inwards. She allowed a tiny point of awareness to form, barely a flicker of power, and was surprised to find she could do it. With the minimum of effort she directed that point of awareness into the cat, and immediately became aware of the living and breathing casing of flesh surrounding her probe. She moved it back and forth, sensing the difference between healthy flesh and the torn and ragged tissue of the wound. She could feel the exact point where the damage began, could feel the change of texture beneath her fingers, see the ruined ends of torn blood vessels. At some point her perception moved from a simple awareness to an almost visible perspective, as if she were inside her probe, viewing the injury from inside the cat. She could "see" the healthy and torn flesh all around her, sensing its transition in minute detail.

"Very good Emea," said Emelda. "That's enough for now. Gently withdraw your awareness." Emea released her concentration and realised she had been so immersed in the exercise she had closed her eyes. She opened them, delighted to have found the exercise so easy, and thrilled by the vivid sights and sensations she had experienced.

"Very interesting, Emea," said Emelda with a thoughtful look. "What were you looking at there?"

"The wound, like you said," Emea answered confusedly.

"With your eyes closed?" Emelda asked.

"Well, yes. I was looking at the tissue; where it was torn, and where it was healthy."

"And what was your perspective when you were looking?"

"What do you mean?" Emmy asked.

"I mean, where were you looking from?"

"From inside the cat, of course," Emmy said.

Emelda clapped her hands. "Well, well," she said. "That's very clever of you. Most people can send in their thoughts to probe the flesh they are still seeing from the outside, sensing the flesh through the probe as if through touch, but not seeing it visually. It's another thing altogether to enter the body like that. It's not unheard of, but very sophisticated, young lady. Well done."

Emea went bright red with embarrassment and pleasure at Emelda's praise. As she took her seat, she determined to ask Emelda more about what she had done at the end of the lesson. The rest of the class all had their turns at laying hands on the cat and searching out its wound, with mixed success, and no-one was able to duplicate Emea's feat of perception.

"I'm really pleased with how you've all done this morning," she said with a genuine smile. "So pleased, in fact, that I want to take this a step further and give some of you a chance to actually heal the cat. Emea, why don't you come first, seeing as you are the most familiar with the wound?" Emea looked suddenly unsure of herself, but made her way out to the front anyway.

"Okay, now you're going to do the same thing as before - but instead of looking at the quality of the tissue, I want you to sense the body's natural healing process. It will be very subtle, and very slow, but there should be a kind of growth you can pick up on if you can be still enough to sense it. Can you try and do that?" Emea nodded, determined, and placed her hand on the cat before closing her eyes. Emelda looked on with approval.

"Now, send in your senses," she instructed. Emea closed her eyes, letting her awareness form once again into a tiny probe of consciousness, and sent it into the warm casing of the cat's body. "Okay, good," Emelda said, softly. "Now, listen very carefully with all your senses, until you can sense the body's healing process."

This was harder to do, and for several moments all Emea could hear was the rushing of the cat's blood and the deep bellows of the lungs; but slowly she became aware of a gentle movement beneath that. It wasn't a physical movement, nor did it make a sound, but it was more of a direction, a gentle pressure towards mending, towards the knitting together of bones and flesh, towards health. It was like an intricate weaving, and had the kind of patient, timeless quality she would expect a tree to have in its slow growth towards the light, and it infused every cell of the cat's body. Emmy felt she was sensing health itself, the very opposite of decay, and allowed herself to get in sync with its living force.

"Can you sense it yet, Emea?" Emelda asked.

"Yes, I can," said Emea.

"Good," said Emelda gently, not wishing to disturb Emmy's concentration. "Now comes the interesting part. I want you to draw on your power and release it in a tiny, steady outflow, directed not into the flesh but into the healing force of the body itself, encouraging it to speed up. Don't force it or use too much power or the body will probably not respond. You are just to massage it, tease it, show it what you want it to do as you release your power. This takes a steady hand. You can begin whenever you're ready."

Emea tried to tune in to her spirit, into the core of her being, but found herself unable to summon anything that could be described as power. She used the meditative technique Emelda had showed them the day before, and for a moment was sure she could sense what she was looking for; an alluring, spinning core of healing light. Sensing she was close to her power, Emea tried to grab it and release it into the cat's body, but it was like grabbing at air, and the nearness evaporated into nothing.

Emea opened her eyes in frustration. "I can't!" she said angrily.

"Don't worry, don't worry!" Emelda said comfortingly. "I would have been amazed if you had been able to do this on your second day of using magic. It was a good try. How about you, Ferast?" she asked, turning to the dark-featured boy, who came forward eagerly, his fingers clenching and unclenching involuntarily in anticipation of using his powers.

"Now put your hand on the cat...oh!" Emelda stopped in her tracks, as Ferast was already touching the cat, his face twisted into a mask of feverish concentration, not waiting for Emelda to instruct him. His eyes narrowed so tightly they were almost shut as he bent his thought on the cat. For a few moments nothing happened, and then a girl sitting at the front of the room gasped as the cat's wound began to close. Flesh filled out the gash, the raw tissue replaced with healthy muscle, until the skin stretched itself out over the wound and was knitted together, leaving no mark at all, as if the animal had never been injured.

"Very good, Ferast," Emelda said, as he stepped back, looking excitedly at the place where the wound had been. "But next time, wait for me to instruct you." He looked up at Emelda and gave the briefest of nods, and walked back to his desk, his eyes gleaming. Emelda watched him all the way back to his seat.

"Right, class," she said. "Well done today. We've made real progress. Next time we'll have a purely practical class, and see how many more of you can turn theory into real healing." And with that, she dismissed them.

Gaspi stayed in his seat, deliberately taking a long time to pack away his things so that he could catch Emelda, and ask about removing his block. He waited until the last of the students had left the room before approaching her.

She looked up as he drew near. "Yes Gaspi, how can I help you?" she asked, placing her things to one side and giving him her full attention.

"It's about my block, Miss," Gaspi said a bit nervously. He really wanted to start using his magic, and if Emelda said no he'd have no choice but to wait. "I meditated this morning before class and want to be able to touch my power."

Emelda looked at him thoughtfully. "What makes you think you're ready, Gaspi?" she asked.

Gaspi thought for a moment. "I don't know," he said honestly, "but I'd rather face this now, and I can't see how waiting will help. The meditation is really easy for me, and it makes me feel amazing."

"And that is exactly what you have to be careful of, Gaspi," Emelda responded. "Magic is very addictive - and yes, it can make you feel wonderful, or powerful, or both. How easy did you find leaving your meditation this morning?"

"I had to make myself do it, but it wasn't too hard," he answered.

Emelda wrinkled her brow in thought. "Letting go of magic is much harder than letting go of the peace you feel while meditating." She paused for another long, thoughtful moment. "Ok, I'll talk to Hephistole. He's the one who put your block in place, and no-one can undo his work but him. If he is happy to do so then we'll arrange something. How does that sound?"

"Great!" Gaspi responded eagerly, unable to hide his excitement.

"Don't get your hopes up, Gaspi," Emelda said. "He may not think you're ready." Gaspi nodded, not discouraged. He felt sure that Hephistole would let him try. Full of excitement, he made his way to the refectory, where he found Emmy and Lydia tucking into a spicy lentil stew. Helping himself to a portion, he joined them.

"How come you're sitting on your own?" he asked.

The girls looked at each other. "Everand asked us to join him and his friends," Emea said carefully, "but we didn't think you'd want to sit with him, so we came over here."

Gaspi looked pained. "But I don't want you two to miss out on making friends just because I'm having some problems."

"Gaspi, we don't want to be friends with him if he's such a pompous idiot," Emea said heatedly, two little pinpricks of pink blossoming in her cheeks "If he wants to be friends with us, he can make an effort with you."

Gaspi felt gratified, but was still unhappy. "Thanks, Emmy. But still, why can't you hang out with the girls?"

"Have you seen the way they follow him around?" Emea asked. "It's like whatever he says goes...so until he accepts you, we're not going to be friends with any of them."

"It's a bit different in the dormitory though," Lydia said. "They're friendly enough in there. It's just when we're all together that there's a problem. I think it will blow over, Gaspi."

"I just don't want you to miss out, that's all," Gaspi said.

Emmy put her hand over his. "Don't worry about us, Gaspi. We're fine, and you matter far more to us than all of this lot together."

Gaspi smiled gratefully at both of them. "Thanks," he said. Over lunch he told them about Emelda's promise to ask Hephistole if he would consider removing Gaspi's block.

"That's great, Gaspi," Emea said. "Do you think he will do it?"

"I hope so," Gaspi said. "I can't see any point in waiting."

"I don't think you should get too excited, though," Lydia said, "just in case he wants you to wait."

"That's what Miss Emelda said," Gaspi said with a touch of irritation, "but I'm not very good at being patient."

Emea laughed. "I guess we'll find out soon enough," she said.

Chapter 16

After lunch, they went back to the cushion-filled classroom to practice releasing their power. Gaspi entered first, and his heart leaped into his throat when he saw that Emelda was not alone. Hephistole sat next to her, his charismatic face breaking into a dazzling smile as Gaspi entered the room.

"Ah, there you are," Emelda said. "There's been a slight change of plan today." She waved the two girls towards the seats. "Lydia, Emea, we'll stay here and carry on practicing meditation. Gaspi, you'll be working with Hephistole," she said, with a knowing smile.

Hephistole popped up out of his chair. "Come along then, Gaspi," he said enthusiastically. "No time like the present!" He strode out of the room. Gaspi swung his backpack over his shoulder, swapping hopeful looks with Emea as he left.

Hephistole's long-legged stride set a fast pace for Gaspi, who had to do a little hop every few steps to keep up. Gaspi thought about all the reasons he would give to persuade Hephistole to let him touch his power, running through them in his head over and over so he wouldn't forget any of them when the time came. Gaspi's mind was so busy he didn't notice any of the fascinating scenery he was passing, until they reached the enormous tower at the centre of the campus. Hephistole led them through the cavernous space of the atrium, pausing briefly to say hello to the magician behind the enormous reception desk, before weaving through the bustle of colourfully robed magicians and brown-robed students; traffic that streamed from or to the line of glowing transporter plinths, where magicians were appearing and disappearing with a word.

Hephistole led Gaspi to the last of the plinths. "Step on!" he said. "Yes, that's right. Now stand still, arms at your side. This may feel a bit strange, but it'll be over quickly." Gripping Gaspi's shoulder with his hand he enunciated "Observatory!" Gaspi's awareness was instantly swamped by an overwhelming vibration, a kind of high-pitched buzzing that ran through his whole being. His vision disappeared entirely, replaced by blank, grey, nothingness, and for a heartbeat he felt pulled in all directions, thoroughly disoriented. Gaspi was relieved when everything snapped back together and he found himself standing on a plinth in Hephistole's large study at the very top of the tower. He knew he was at the top of the tower as massive, curving windows showed him an impressive view over the college and city, and beyond the walls into wide open wilderness. In the distance craggy mountain peaks rose from the plain, their edges softened by a light haze, and cushioned by feathery wisps of white-spun cloud stretching across the pale sky.

Hephistole caught Gaspi staring in wonder at the scene. "Best seat in the house, eh, Gaspi?" Gaspi wasn't sure which house he meant, and just nodded in response. Hephistole waved him towards a well-cushioned seat facing the glorious view. "How about a drink?"

"Yes please," Gaspi responded politely, minding his manners. Hephistole went to a recess in the wall and peered thoughtfully at a row of small, glazed pots, ranging in colour from deep red to a vivid blue.

"This one, I think," he said decisively, picking a burnt-orange container and bringing it to an enormous desk set in front of the window, where he took a large pinch of tiny, dried leaves from the jar and placed them in a small mesh bag. The bag had a drawstring that Hephistole tightened and tied off in a knot. He held his hand over an ornate pot with a curving spout, and Gaspi felt that tingling sensation behind his navel that told him magic was being worked. Seconds later, steam was piping from the spout. Hephistole took the lid off the teapot and placed the small bag of dried leaves in it, before placing the lid back on.

"Have you ever had tea before, Gaspi?" he asked conversationally. Gaspi said he hadn't. In the mountains you could only buy tea from travelling peddlers who came through in the summer, and so for large portions of the year they didn't have any. Even when they had it the adults kept it for themselves, as it was a rare and expensive commodity.

A warm, spicy smell was emanating from the teapot, making Gaspi's mouth water. It smelt a bit like the wine they drank at the Midwinter Festival in Aemon's Reach, and Gaspi felt suddenly homesick. The terracotta city of Helioport couldn't be more different from his mountain home, and his eyes inadvertently slipped to the horizon, where massive peaks loomed in the distance. Even those peaks looked different though – hard and rocky. The mountains he had grown up in were cloaked in deep fir forests, and for at least half the year were softened by thick blankets of snow. Gaspi's mountains were places of adventure, of secret dens and rampant wildlife.

Hephistole's voice brought him back to the present. "So, how are you settling in at the college, Gaspi?"

"Fine, thanks," Gaspi replied, unwilling to voice his troubles with Everand to Hephistole. "It's all still a bit new."

"Ah yes, the heady excitement of your first taste of magic," Hephistole responded, interpreting Gaspi's comment as positive. "Anything you like in particular?"

"The meditation is great," Gaspi enthused, warming to the topic.

"Miss Emelda showed us how to connect with our spirits," he said, his face glowing with excitement.

"Do you find it easy to do?" Hephistole asked.

"Yes, very easy," Gaspi answered. "I was up early this morning before dawn, practicing. It was incredible! I can't believe I never knew about this before."

Hephistole smiled warmly. "I'm glad you're enjoying it," he said, with the genuine pleasure of an enthusiast whose hobby has been taken up by another. "And now you want to try some magic," he added.

The list of reasons for letting him try and use his power was still running through Gaspi's head and poured readily from his lips. "Yes, I would. Miss Emelda says I am good at meditation, and this morning I was able to stop easily, even when it felt amazing. I knew I could come back to it anytime, and Emelda, I mean Miss Emelda, she said that was what I needed to learn – to let go. I can't see any point in waiting. And besides, I don't want to get behind Emea and Lydia, and the other students are already ahead of me anyway and I need to catch up." Gaspi looked at Hephistole intently, out of breath and out of reasons.

Hephistole rubbed his chin and looked at Gaspi thoughtfully. "Well, I can see you're passionate; but I need to caution you, Gaspi. You must be careful, where magic is concerned. If you don't learn how to use it with the utmost caution, you will endanger yourself and those around you – especially with a gift like yours." Gaspi nodded, trying not to look impatient, but Hephistole was not fooled. "I know you're champing at the bit, but please take me seriously." Hephistole's face was unusually grave. "Just last year a young Mage tried to channel too much power too fast. One student was seriously injured and the boy himself will probably never be able to use magic again. He burnt himself out Gaspi, and destroyed his ability to channel power."

Gaspi was immediately sobered by such a horrible thought. "Will he ever recover?" he asked.

"I don't know," Hephistole answered. "It's very rare for that to happen, and far more likely that misusing your magic will result in death. Only time will tell what happens to that young student. For now he is back on his parents' farm, learning to live without his power." Gaspi shuddered at the thought. "I want you to promise me, Gaspi, that while you attend this school, you will always exercise caution when using magic."

"I promise," he answered, without hesitation.

"And if you are unsure if you can do something safely, will you promise to ask a teacher about it before doing it?"

"Yes," Gaspi answered solemnly, without a hint of impatience.

"Then I will help you to touch your power, if that is still what you want."

To his credit, Gaspi actually thought about it for a second or two. "Yes please," he said, after a moment.

Hephistole's serious face suddenly brightened, a broad grin spreading from ear to ear. It was like the sun breaking through clouds after a storm. "Oh, good!" he said. "I do like doing this!" Gaspi was taken aback by the sudden transformation of the enigmatic magician. Hephistole's demonstrated a broad range of range of moods, and sometimes flitted from gravity to playfulness with little or no warning.

Hephistole took the lid off the teapot, releasing a small cloud of fragrant steam. He sniffed at it a couple of times, and breathed out a sigh of satisfaction. "Just right!" he said, replacing the lid. He poured the tea from the pot in a long, amber stream, filling two finely made porcelain cups with the brew. Hephistole gave one of the cups to Gaspi, passed on a delicate matching saucer. Up close the warm small of spices was even more enticing, and Gaspi eagerly raised the cup to his mouth.

"Oh! Hold on!" Hephistole admonished. "It's very hot. You'll burn yourself. Just give it a couple of minutes to cool down, and it'll be about right." Gaspi gently placed the cup and saucer on the table.

"We make these teas here in the college, you know," Hephistole stated conversationally.

"Oh really?" Gaspi said, unsure why they were talking about tea when there was magic to be done.

Hephistole responded as if reading his mind. "There are ordinary tea leaves in each blend, of course, but the rest is mixed up by our resident herbalist to have a different effect on the drinker. The orange," he said, indicating the cup in Gaspi's hand, "has a calming herb in it, to help you enter a trance-like state. Though from the sound of it you won't need much help with that." Gaspi immediately thought of Emea. Perhaps she could use the herbal drink before practicing mediation. He made a mental note to ask Hephistole about it later.

"The tea should be about right now, Gaspi," Hephistole said, settling himself in a chair opposite the young pupil. Gaspi raised the cup to his lips and took a sip. The tea tasted as good as it smelled, the warm spices of the brew making his tongue tingle. It tasted of warm winter nights, of home and hearth, and had an instantly relaxing effect on him. Gaspi sank more comfortably into his chair.

"What I propose we do is remove your block before you meditate, rather than in the middle of the process." Gaspi nodded, keen to get on with it. "This way, you can approach your power from a distance, get as close as you want to it, and then withdraw. If we released your block when you're already deep into meditation, it might be a bit overwhelming," Hephistole explained. "How does that sound?"

"Sounds fine to me," Gaspi said.

"As you approach your power," Hephistole continued, "try to engage it very lightly. Don't grab it, and don't go too fast." He waited for Gaspi to show he understood. "Once you're in touch with it, try to relax and keep letting it go and retreating. Once I know you can control it I will be happy to remove the block for good. Okay...are you ready?"

Gaspi had a fleeting moment of uncertainty, awoken by an image of Jakko and Brock covered in specks of blood, fleeing for their lives. Hephistole must have sensed his hesitancy. "Don't worry, Gaspi," he said. "If it gets out of control I'll put the block right back in, okay?"

Reassured, Gaspi's enthusiasm came rushing back. "Okay...I'm ready," he said.

"Good lad," said Hephistole. He pushed himself out of chair and came over to Gaspi's chair. Placing his hand gently on Gaspi's head, Hephistole closed his eyes. Gaspi closed his eyes too, trying to sense what Hephistole was doing. He was still ranging inwards, when Hephistole began to hum. It was a curious little tune, strangely jumpy and counter-intuitive, and then it stopped. Hephistole took his hand away and stepped back. "It's done," he said.

"I don't feel any different," Gaspi said.

"No, you wouldn't," Hephistole responded. "The difference will be obvious when you touch your power."

"Why were you humming, Hephistole?" Gaspi asked curiously.

"That's how I chose to create your block," he answered. "I infused a musical signature with magic, and simply hummed it backwards to release the block."

"Oh!" Gaspi said, remembering what Professor Worrick had said about ways of releasing magic, intrigued by the possibilities this opened.

"Some people use the same methods for releasing magic every time, whereas I like a bit of variety," Hephistole enthused. "But enough of that – it's time for you to experience your power." Without waiting for a response, Hephistole waved his hand in a clockwise motion, and sound filled the air. The music was similar to that conjured by Emelda, but deeper somehow, more complex and compelling. The effect of the tea seemed to intensify, gentle waves of warmth drawing Gaspi down into an increasingly relaxed state. "I'm not going to lead your meditation," Hephistole said. "It's best if you do this for yourself. Just practice what Miss Emelda has taught you, until you become aware of your spirit."

"Okay," Gaspi said.

"You don't have to let me do this," Hephistole continued, "but it would be easier for me to help you if I can observe what's happening. Do you mind if I send a probe into your consciousness?"

"That's fine," Gaspi said, comfortable that Hephistole was someone he could trust.

"Thank you Gaspi," Hephistole said, sincerely gratified. "Then let's begin."

Gaspi closed his eyes and began the exercises Emelda had taught him, breathing evenly and deeply and allowing his worries to evaporate as he tried to enter an altered state of consciousness. It didn't surprise him that it came very easily to him, and, aided by the tea and the hypnotic sonorities of Hephistole's music, he attained a deep state of peace more quickly than he'd yet managed. He allowed his imagination to form his secret place around him, and soon he was appreciating the glistening water and lush foliage of his inner sanctum. Gaspi became aware of a presence with him, and was momentarily confused until he recognised it for what it was; Hephistole was with him, an invisible, silent presence at his side. Putting his concern aside, Gaspi turned his attention back to the scene, drinking in the details, allowing his meditative state to deepen further as the sights and sounds around him became crystalline in clarity. He felt the desire to lie down on the grassy banks of the lake and let the movement of the clouds mesmerise him, to take off his shoes and rest his feet in the cool water of the lake; but today he had a greater mission, and didn't allow himself to linger.

As soon as he felt able, he ranged further in, searching for the swirling white core of his spirit. It took a while, but finally sound and sight began to dissolve into greater stillness, where all quieted itself in reverence of the soul's true essence. Gaspi drew near to the simple glowing light of his own spirit, spinning gently in its own space. Endless creativity and love beamed from his spirit, and it felt so immense to Gaspi that he had to remind himself that this was actually part of him. He wondered for a moment how something so endless and pure could exist within him. It felt so much greater than him, timeless as the mountains. Not wishing to be distracted when he was so close to his goal, he put the thought aside, determining to ask Hephistole about it later.

Gaspi drifted into the light of his own spirit, letting it surround him as he had done in Emelda's class, and turned his thoughts to magic. He would have perhaps felt anxious if not in so relaxed a state, but as deeply focussed as he was, no fearful thoughts entered Gaspi's mind as he began to tune his awareness in to power.

At first nothing happened, but then the slightest strands of green appeared in the white. The rich colour expanded slowly, of varying hues, permeating the globe-light of his spirit until all around him was a deep flow of green. It was as if his magic cried out to him: "Own me! Embrace me! I am your birthright." For one last moment he hesitated, deliberately reminding himself of Hephistole's caution. He was to engage it lightly and release it again; something that sounded easy but felt very difficult in the moment when all he wanted was to grab it with both arms and contain as much of it as possible.

Gaspi carefully extended a hand, calling the green light to his control. Tendrils of colour flowed towards his hand, circling it, twining through his fingers, settling in his palm. The last time Gaspi had tried to reach out to his power the block had been in place; an impenetrable, invisible barrier between himself and his magic. This time he felt magic's touch: the vibrant sensation of something very much alive, coiled within him. It felt completely natural, an extension of his will, though it contained an energy of its own - something strong and eager. It wanted an outlet, somewhere to go, something to do. It was raw potential, a primordial soup of energy waiting to be drawn on. The desire to embrace it became stronger. He wanted to breath in as deeply as possible, filling himself up with life until he couldn't contain another drop. But he remembered Hephistole's caution once more, and released his hold. He let his hand drop to his side, consciously letting go of the magic that moments earlier had curled lovingly round his fingers.

He wasn't sure what would happen, then. Would the magic leave him as he intended? Or would he be unable to let go? The response was instantaneous, tendrils of green retreating from his touch as if recoiled by a gentle elasticity, flowing back into the general mass of colour. Gaspi felt a sense of approval from Hephistole, whose presence he had forgotten about. Gaspi smiled, satisfied at his first successful control of magic. For the next few minutes he repeated the exercise, drawing power to him and releasing it, holding it a little longer each time. It was never easy to let go, getting harder each time he did it. He managed it several times, and on the last attempt was only just able to let go of the magic before he felt Hephistole nudging him, asking him to release his trance completely. Obediently, Gaspi went through the exercises Healer Emelda had shown him to come gently out of an altered state. When he opened his eyes a few minutes later, he was swamped by a wave of fatigue. Grunting, he slumped down in the chair, surprised at his body's reaction to the magical exercise he'd been performing. Hephistole was at the desk, brewing another pot of tea, this time with leaves taken from a bright green jar.

He fixed Gaspi with a beady eye. "Tired, are we?" he asked.

"Yeah...very!" Gaspi said. "Why do I feel like this? Did I do something wrong?"

"Wrong?" Hephistole responded, sounding surprised. "Oh no - everything went very well." He brought a steaming cup of tea to Gaspi. The liquid was a light green colour and smelled of spring rain and fresh, growing things.

Gaspi started to speak: "But why...?"

He didn't get the chance to finish his sentence. "Drink up, Gaspi," Hephistole interrupted. "Question time can wait a few minutes," he said, with a smile. "You'll feel better once you've finished this." Gaspi took a sip of the steaming brew, then another. He wasn't surprised when he quickly began to feel revived. He was still tired, but manageably so, his body resting comfortably and his mind sharp. Hephistole waited while he drank the whole cup down.

"Okay," the Chancellor began. "Let me explain a few things, and if I miss anything else out you can ask me afterwards, okay?" Gaspi nodded.

"Using magic is just like using any other part of your mind or body," he continued. "Imagine that the part of you that uses arcane power is like a muscle. At the moment yours is unused, and therefore very weak. Follow me so far?"

"Yep," Gaspi said.

"When you first touched you power today you were able to let it go relatively easily, am I right?"

"Yeah, sort of," Gaspi answered. "It was still hard to let go, but it was easier than the other times."

"Exactly," Hephistole said. "If you lift a big rock over your head it will be easiest the first time, then it will get harder and harder, until you can't lift it at all. It's just fatigue, and the more you practice the stronger those muscles will get. Even the most powerful Mages get tired, Gaspi. Many a duel between equally-matched spell-casters has been decided by who has the most endurance. They can both throw powerful spells at each other and defend against the other's attacks, but if you run out of energy, the simplest spell can kill you if you can't defend against it. This is particularly dangerous with magic, Gaspi, as it takes a certain kind of effort to release it, too. If you're in a weakened state it can not only be difficult to use magic, but also to release it at the end. If you're really weak, you may not be able to sever the connection, and then you end up being drained by the magic until all your life force is gone. Does that explain why it became harder and harder for you to release the magic?"

"Yeah, that makes sense," Gaspi said. "But I wasn't even doing any actual magic! I was just holding and releasing it."

"Quite true, young Mage," Hephistole said. "Imagine how much harder it will be to let go when you're actually using it to do something? I'm glad you can see that, Gaspi. The important thing for you to remember is not to rush. Your endurance will build surprisingly fast, but you must stay within your limits."

"Okay," Gaspi said, feeling a little discouraged at how much he had to learn, and at how little strength he had.

Hephistole must have picked up on Gaspi's despondency. "Gaspi, you did incredibly well today. I didn't know if you'd be able to touch and release your magic even once. I was ready to put the block back in at any moment. But you managed a lot more than that. I'm proud of you," he said, looking steadily into Gaspi's eyes. Gaspi flushed with pleasure and self-consciousness. Hephistole's praise meant a lot to him.

"So the question remains," Hephistole said more lightly, "as to whether we leave your block off or not." He fixed Gaspi with a searching look. "What do you think, Gaspi?"

"Well, I managed the exercise okay," Gaspi answered thoughtfully. "I mean, shouldn't it be safe to leave it off now?"

"Maybe so," Hephistole answered. "To be honest with you, Gaspi, what I'm concerned about is what would happen if you try to do something too stretching, and can't let go again.. If I leave the block off, will you promise me to be extremely cautious, and if you're even slightly uncertain about trying something, to come and ask me or Miss Emelda?"

"Definitely!" Gaspi answered emphatically. "I don't ever want to experience that again. I'll be careful."

Hephistole smiled. "Okay then, Gaspi, we'll leave it off for now. But I'll give you a tool to use in case things go wrong and I'm not there to help you. As I said earlier, your block was put in place using a musical spell. I'm going to teach you the tune so that if things get out of hand you can replace the block yourself. How does that sound?"

"That sounds fine," Gaspi said, curious about how to make a spell work with music. Hephistole spent the next half an hour teaching him the tune for replacing his block, until he was sure Gaspi knew it.

"The spell obviously doesn't work just by humming the tune, or you'd be blocked again by now, wouldn't you?" Hephistole asked rhetorically. Gaspi had worked that much out, and said so. "That is why you won't be able to remove the block once you've sung it back in place," Hephistole continued. "If you can't touch your power, the spell-song won't work even if the tune is right. It's quite simple though, Gaspi; you just channel your power into the tune as you sing it. Do you think you can do that?"

"Can't see why not," Gaspi answered.

"Good," Hephistole responded. "You can head off now, then."

Gaspi was about to leave, but then he remembered the profound contact with his own spirit that had caused him so much wonder during the meditation. "Actually can I ask you something before I go?" he asked. Something about Hephistole made it easy to ask questions.

"Absolutely," the Chancellor answered, beaming. "I shall endeavour to answer it for you to the best of my ability."

"Well, it's about what happens when I meditate," Gaspi began. It's like my spirit is incredibly deep...bottomless, maybe. And it's so…loving. I know it's meant to be a part of me, but somehow it feels…bigger." Gaspi couldn't find any words to express what he was feeling more clearly, and fell silent, hoping Hephistole understood what he was trying to say.

"Ah, yes," Hephistole said quietly. "You've stumbled across one of the great questions. I have to let you know that my answer will disappoint you, as I don't know any better than you do! But I can share a few thoughts with you." He looked out of the window at the distant mountains.

"There are many theories about magic, and about our spirits, Gaspi. Some would say that when you use magic you are tapping into a universal source; a power that exists in all beings, in every rock and tree and in the deep, fiery core of the world. Some believe that force to be mindless, just an underlying powerful source of life, but that would not explain the sense of love you so accurately describe. Others feel that meditation is a way to contact a Supreme Being. Do you worship a God, Gaspi?"

"Not really," Gaspi answered. "There's a chapel in my village, and they hold services every Rest-Day, but I never enjoyed them very much. Well, the singing was okay, I suppose."

Hephistole laughed. "Found it a bit boring, did you? Well that's quite understandable. I'm not one for services myself. But what you'll find is that all over the world different cultures worship God, or something that you or I may understand as God, in diverse and wonderful ways. Some people paint themselves up and stamp round a fire, chanting themselves into a trance. Others sit quietly, and listen to the silence. For some reason, some people prefer to sit on hard wooden seats and listen to someone talk until their buttocks are numb."

140

Gaspi laughed freely. Hearing about these other ways of doing things felt liberating.

"What I'm trying to say, Gaspi," Hephistole continued, "is that many people consider that that endless source of love and purity you experience when meditating to be something of God residing in you. If they are right, it is both part of you and part of God, and it's probably impossible to separate the two!"

Gaspi nodded thoughtfully. "I like that idea. But what about the magic? That feels different, more…" He couldn't think of the word.

"Active?" Hephistole asked.

"Yes, sort of," Gaspi answered. "The love seems endless, intelligent maybe, but it's observing rather than actually doing something. The magic feels alive, and wants to get out."

Hephistole laughed once more. "Well, that might be more about you than the magic - but yes, it's been said that if your spirit is a connection with God, then magic is something solely about you. It is a harnessing of your own power, focussing it on specific tasks. I'm sorry, Gaspi, I can't say anything more specific than that. I have my own suspicions, but this is the kind of thing everyone has to work out for themselves."

"No, that's fine," Gaspi answered. "It's exciting. There's so much I don't know about. And I like the idea of something powerful out there that's full of love."

"Good," Hephistole said. "You'll have to let me know what you discover." Hephistole seemed to be entirely serious.

The headmaster clapped his hands and stood up. "Well that ends our lesson. I'm happy for you to practice what we've done today before tomorrow's class, but promise me you won't actually do anything with your magic between now and then? I'd rather your first experiences of performing magic were under the supervision of a teacher!"

"I promise," Gaspi said, more than happy just to be able to touch his power.

Hephistole stood up. "It's been my pleasure, young Mage. Now, if you step on the transporter and say "Atrium," you'll be back on the ground floor again."

Gaspi stepped onto the transporter. "Just say the word?" he asked.

"Yes. The transporter has been enchanted to do the work for you, and the word alone will suffice. Bye for now, Gaspi," Hephistole said with a smile.

"ATRIUM," Gaspi said, a little louder than was necessary. The unnerving buzzing sensation ran through him instantly, and sound and sight were obliterated, until he arrived in one piece on the corresponding plinth near the wide entrance to the tower. Gaspi didn't think he'd ever grow to like the transporters. Stepping off the plinth, he walked out of the tower into bright afternoon sunlight, and set off back to the dormitory, anxious to tell Emmy all about what he'd learned.

Chapter 17

The sound of clashing swords echoed through the practice yard. Taurnil watched eagerly from the sidelines, as two guards practiced before the drill began. He was equally bewildered and fascinated by swordplay. Where the staff came naturally to him, he still wrestled uncomfortably with a blade. The heavy length of steel felt unwieldy in his hand, and the movements of basic sword-fighting were all very forceful - hacking and slashing, powered by the strength of his arms and upper body. The staff, on the other hand, had a subtlety to it. You could move your hands only slightly, and the attacking end of the staff would whizz through the air with crushing force. Taurnil liked the economy of movement required to use the staff, as well as the range it provided, but he still wanted to learn other weapons skills. He had been drilling with sword, staff and mace for the few days he had been in the guards, and was covered in flourishing and partly-healed bruises. He was yet to win a one-on-one bout with any of the guards, though he'd come close to beating one of the other guards with the staff. Not many guardsmen favoured the staff and it was not compulsory to learn it, so Taurnil only had twelve other guardsmen he could spar with.

The Drillmaster entered the yard from the barracks, a stocky man whose body was not toned or sculpted like some of the young guards. His torso and arms were solid columns of undefined muscle, strong as tree trunks. He was covered in wiry, dark hair, and his body was marked all over with the hard-won scar tissue of an old campaigner. Tobias Trask was a good Drillmaster. He worked his guards hard, but was always fair, and he looked after his own. His drill sessions started with exercise - running laps of the practice yard, harassed by his constant calls for this or that guard to speed up when he thought they were not pushing themselves. He didn't do this from the sidelines, but would run with the guards, moving from group to group, encouraging and admonishing as he saw fit. This was followed by push-ups, which Taurnil found hard, pushing his heavy frame off the ground with the strength of his arms and chest over and over until his muscles burned with agony. Drillmaster Trask ranted on and on about stamina and strength. *It's all very well and good to be able to swing your weapon hard*, he would say, *but a battle is won more by an ability to endure rather than by strength.* His guards were in peak condition, as well as skilled with their weapons.

The exercises began as normal, and by the time Taurnil had run twenty laps of the large yard and strained through fifty push-ups all he wanted to do was sit on the floor and be allowed to breathe. Today, he wasn't going to get his wish.

"Taurnil, Kristos, the staff!" Tobias ordered. Taurnil stumbled to his feet, dismayed that he had to fight without even a moment to catch his breath. His opponent was a rangy guard several inches taller than him. He was broad-shouldered and slender, and looked as taut as a whip. The combatants each chose a staff from the weapons rack, and were quickly ringed by the other guards, eager to watch the fighting.

"Fight!" commanded Trask.

Taurnil and Kristos broke into a slow clockwise circle, sliding their feet across the ground in a careful pacing movement, almost dance-like. Taurnil had learned how to move in a fight on his first day as a guard, and although it was still new to him, he was able to keep pace with an opponent without tripping over his own feet. Kristos was in his late twenties and was an experienced fighter, better by some distance than the other guards he had fought so far. Taurnil couldn't help wondering why the Drillmaster had paired him up against someone who'd probably have him flat on his back in under a minute.

Kristos leapt forward, thrusting his staff at Taurnil, testing his defences. Taurnil blocked the thrust easily enough, but the tall, wiry guard kept him constantly on the defensive, pushing Taurnil to see if he could keep up a strong defence. Taurnil held his ground by the skin of his teeth, struggling to keep his exhausted body moving under Kristos' onslaught. Just when he felt he couldn't go on any longer, Taurnil realised that he had known where the last few attacks were coming from.

Concentrating fiercely, Taurnil realised there was a pattern to Kristos' attacks. Every time he went for a high thrust it was followed by a blow from Taurnil's right side. He watched the next few attacks until he was certain, and sure enough Kristos always seemed to follow up a high thrust in the same way. Taurnil's weakness fled in a moment, replaced by a surge of adrenaline. When the next blow came from the side, he would make his move. Kristos' staff swept in as anticipated, but this time Taurnil didn't just block the weapon, but pushed it down and aside, trapping it against the floor. Kristos met his eyes as Taurnil brought his staff across in a vicious sweep. Kristos' feet went flying from under him, and he tumbled to the floor in a heap.

As Kristos fell, Taurnil kicked him over onto his back, and moved in for a killing blow to the throat. Killing moves were never completed, of course, but as soon as you were in position to deliver one the Drillmaster would bang the gong, and the winner was declared. Taurnil leapt forward with excitement, his heart beating wildly as he anticipated his first win. But Kristos was faster than him, rolling out from under the blow before it could be delivered. Before Taurnil could react he felt the end of Kristos staff crash against his back, swung up at him from Kristos' low position on the ground. Pain lanced through his back as Taurnil stumbled onto his hands and knees. He tried to recover, but knew he was taking too long to get up, and that Kristos would already be coming in with a killing blow. Sure enough, the gong sounded as he finally surged upright. Taurnil's shoulders sagged as he turned to face the victor, whose staff was levelled at his head. Kristos lowered his staff, his hard, lean features breaking into a tight smile.

"You did well, boy," he said. Taurnil was still frustrated at missing out on his first win, and didn't acknowledge the praise.

"It's true," Trask interjected. "That was a good sweep you pulled off there. You nearly had him."

Taurnil's cheeks glowed red. "Thanks," he said, conscious of his age, and desperate not to appear as inexperienced as he in fact was.

"Your reflexes are good, Taurnil," Trask continued, running a hand over his thick dark stubble as he sized up the young fighter. "We'll turn the rest of that puppy fat into muscle and build your strength in just a few months. I'd wager you'll be a fine fighter with that stave soon enough, laddie."

"Shame he can't hold a sword without sticking himself," one of the other guards called out. Everybody laughed, including Trask, and Taurnil couldn't help cracking a smile of his own.

"It's early days yet," the Drillmaster said. "We'll see about the sword in time." He turned to the rest of the guards. "Okay, pair off! We'll see how good you all are with short-swords." Taurnil breathed deeply with relief now the attention was taken off him. One of the other young guards paired up with him and for the rest of the session Trask took them through their paces with the short-sword, walking up and down the line, sometimes grabbing a guard's sword, demonstrating, correcting. By the end of the session Taurnil's hand was numb from the constant jarring of blade against blade, and, after placing the weapon back in the rack, he trudged wearily to the showers to wash off the sweat of another hard day.

The morning after his block was removed, Gaspi rose early to meditate. No-one else seemed to use the garden he had found, at least not so early in the morning, and his practice was blissfully undisturbed. As usual the meditation was invigorating, but Gaspi had no intention of lingering in a peaceful state that day, and quickly tried to reach his power. He practiced connecting with and releasing magic several times, as Hephistole had taught him, and managed to resist the temptation to do anything with it. He was itching to put his power to some use, even if it was just summoning a ball of light; but his promise to Hephistole meant something to him, and he refrained. After all, he would get his chance in class.

Breakfast came and went quickly as he anticipated the lesson, and when they made their way into the classroom it was Voltan who greeted them. The class was quiet and respectful as they waited for the start of that day's lesson, and Gaspi guessed he wasn't the only one who found Voltan intimidating. When they were all settled, Voltan rose from the teacher's desk.

"Good morning, class," he said in his quiet, serious voice. "Today you will be studying martial magic." His announcement sent a thrill through the students, who broke into urgent whispers.

"...not been studied in years," someone said a little too loudly.

The whispering stopped instantly, as Voltan spoke again. "I will be setting up a kind of shield, and teaching you a basic attack. One by one you will attack the shield and see what kind of force you can muster." Again, the class broke into murmuring, fuelled this time by excitement.

"I'm going to teach you the most basic magical attack – the force strike. It's very simple to conjure. You simply form energy into a bolt of pure force, and thrust it at a target."

Voltan reached down to a cavity in the rear of the desk and brought out a curious-looking instrument, placing it dead-centre on a table at the front of the room. It was all of one piece, made of a darkened silver metal and covered in intricate carvings. It had a circular base and a slender stem. The stem rose about a foot, where it split and curved outwards into two matching half-moons. The two halves formed a circle that didn't quite meet at the top, and looked like it should contain a lady's mirror.

Voltan addressed the class again. "Anyone know what this is?"

Everand's hand went up. "A force shield," he said confidently.

"That's right. The frame contains a shield that absorbs and measures force. Observe!" He tapped the device on the top of the open circle, and immediately a pearlescent disc of gently-swirling energy filled the gap, glimmering with a light sheen. "The shield will absorb all but a very strong force," Voltan continued, "and reflect the strength of that force by changing colour. Allow me to demonstrate." He strode to the back of the classroom, and turned to face the force shield. The pupils swivelled in their chairs to get a good view, eager for a demonstration.

"Now, I'm not going to use all my strength, as there's a chance it could break the shield." His arm swept up, palm facing outwards, and a ball of pure force began to coalesce against his open hand. The deep tingling sensation in Gaspi's belly told him powerful magic was being conjured. The furrow in Voltan's brow deepened suddenly as he thrust out his palm, sending the ball of power hurtling across the room. It hit the force shield dead centre, and it glowed a vivid red as it absorbed the force. At the moment of impact Gaspi felt rather than heard a kind of detonation, a deep but muffled resonance like a large bell being struck underground.

"The harder the strike, the deeper the colour," Voltan said. His eyes moved round the class, observing the eager faces of pupils itching to have a go for themselves. "Gavin," Voltan said, "do you want to try it?"

"Yes sir," Gavin said, rising from his desk and walking over to the professor.

"Okay, let's see if you can summon the force strike first," Voltan said. "Just summon your power as you would normally, but instead of forming it into a ball of light, summon it as raw energy in your palm."

Gav held his hand palm upwards, staring at it in fierce concentration, his brows knotted above squinting eyes. Slowly, a ball of magic took shape in his hand, opaque and alive with energy. The tingling behind Gaspi's navel was less this time, but still noticeable.

"That's good, Gavin. Now keep the strike there, and think about firing it at the shield." Gav looked up to set his sights on the target, but his ball disintegrated into thin air. "That'll happen if you lose concentration," Voltan said. Gav looked embarrassed. "Summon it again," Voltan said, "but this time concentrate on both things at once; maintaining the ball's integrity, while focussing on the target." Gav squared his shoulders, and lined himself up with the force shield. A force strike gathered in his hand again as Gav lifted his hand, palm towards the target. His brows knotted even more tightly than before, and the ball flickered as he looked at the shield, but he managed to keep it together, almost glaring at the force shield while the ball of power swirled against his hand.

"Good," Voltan said. "When you're ready, send it at your target. Just imagine it flying from your hand and hitting the target, and release your power." Gav stood rigidly for a few moments, then suddenly flung out his arm, and the force strike left his palm, sailing across the room much more slowly than Voltan's strike. It hit the target, which turned a straw yellow colour as it absorbed the force. The detonation was so subtle Gaspi almost couldn't feel it. Gav looked at Voltan uncertainly.

"Excellent," the teacher said. "It's not easy, is it?"

"No, it's not," Gav answered, looking drained.

"Take a seat Gavin," Voltan said as he walked back to the front of the room. "There are a lot of things you have to think about when doing this," he continued. "First of all, there is summoning the ball. Then you have to maintain it while you focus on your target, and then you have to impart both direction and speed to the force strike. Gavin's strike would have had more of an impact if it had been faster, but he got the direction right. If you can summon a powerful strike and send it with speed and accuracy, you can get a devastating result. But if you get any of it wrong, it will be ineffective."

He looked around the class slowly. "Who else wants to try?" Several hands shot up but fell again when Everand stood up and walked to the back of the class.

"Okay, Everand, in your own time," Voltan said. Everand stood with his legs apart, planted firmly on the ground, and raised his arm as Voltan had done. A ball of energy formed in his hand much more quickly than it had for Gav, and without waiting he pushed out his palm, sending the ball of power he'd created spinning quickly across the room into the forceshield. The shield absorbed the strike as before, but this time it glowed an orange colour. Everand's strike was clearly more powerful than Gav's, and as he strode back to his seat, arrogance etched all over his face, Gaspi felt annoyance at Everand balling in his stomach.

Several other students had a go at the force strike with varying degrees of success. Some delivered a successful strike, though no-one achieved as deep a colour as Everand until it was Ferast's turn. Pushing his lank hair out of his eyes, he squinted at the target. There was something about the way he carried himself that made Gaspi uncomfortable. The small boy was fidgety and awkward, his movements jerky and somehow spider-like. Ferast brought his hand up, a ball of power filling it almost immediately, and with an almost casual flick of his bony fingers it sped across the room. It moved faster than anyone's strike except Voltan's, and the shield glowed burnt-orange as it absorbed the strike, a deeper colour than the one Everand had produced. Gaspi glanced at Everand, catching a look of surprise on his face, which was quickly suppressed. Ferast wore a smirk as he slunk back to his desk.

"Very good," Voltan said. "That was a good, swift strike. Now, let's give our new pupils a chance. Emea - how about you?"

Emea had uncertainty written all over her, as she pushed back her chair and walked to the back of the classroom. She held her slender palm upwards, that neat little line Gaspi liked so much appearing in her forehead as she concentrated. Gaspi crossed his fingers, desperately hoping that for her own sake Emea would be able to conjure the force strike. At first nothing happened, but then Gaspi saw something swirling in her palm, a walnut-sized ball of force that flickered on the edge of existence. The small ball of power didn't disappear when Emea raised her eyes to the shield, nor when she held her hand out in front of her, palm facing the target. She stretched out her arm, trying to push the ball forwards, but after disconnecting from her palm it span slowly forward for a couple of seconds before dissipating into the air. One of the girls started to snigger, and Emea went bright red.

"Who's laughing?" Voltan asked calmly, but with an edge to his voice that instantly shut the culprit up. He turned back to Emea. "Well done, Emea," he said. "You're much newer at this than most of this lot. Miss Emelda tells me you have a deft touch, and power will come with time. You can sit down now." Emea bustled back to her seat, relieved to be out from under the class's scrutiny.

It was Lydia's turn next, and with quiet confidence she summoned a force strike and hit the shield with it, which glowed a light orange colour in response.

"Gaspi, your turn!" Voltan said, once Lydia had taken her seat. With a mixture of excitement and trepidation, Gaspi walked to the back of the classroom. This would be the first time he would use magic to actually do something since his block had been removed. Unlike the meditation classes, there was no time to enter an altered state, and he had to engage directly with his power without any preparation. Digging deep he sought out the inner flow of magic, finding its currents after just a few moments of inward searching. The magic felt eager, strong, hungry.

Gaspi raised his palm upwards, drawing magic into his hand as a sphere of raw force. The magic came at his call, forming into a swirling ball of power. The sense of gathering force was intoxicating, and Gaspi was filled with a determination to do better than Ferast and Everand. He continued to summon his power, the force strike swelling in his hand beyond the size of anyone else's. A slight wave of giddiness washed over Gaspi, and, realising he had become caught up in the moment, he stopped the flow of magic to the strike. Or at least he tried to, but it didn't want to stop. It was like throwing a rock in a river – the water just flowed around and over the block and carried on its way. Suddenly nervous, Gaspi doubled his efforts to stop the flow, the ball of force now double the size that even Voltan had produced.

Gaspi started to panic, terrified of letting the magic get out of his control. He tried to strangle it like a snake, cutting it off from the source, but it just squeezed through his fingers. The ball of force grew larger and larger until it was a swollen sphere of power held against his open palm. Dizziness came rushing through him in greater waves, and

Gaspi felt his knees weaken, his legs in danger of buckling.

"Gaspi, stop drawing on your power!" Voltan said sharply, stepping nearer the young Mage, but not too near. Gaspi looked at Voltan helplessly, desperate to regain control, and then he remembered the spell song Hephistole taught him. Urgently, he recalled the tune, humming it as quickly as he could. Some of his classmates gave him a puzzled look, and a few began to push their chairs backwards away from him as his still-growing ball of force churned potently against his hand.

"Gaspi, stop!" Voltan said again, louder and more urgently. Fighting through dizziness and pushing away panic, Gaspi sang the spell song again, directing his rampant magic to flow into the notes of the song, unlocking the power Hephistole had lent it. When the last note of the short tune passed from his lips the uncontrollable flow of power was suddenly ended. Gaspi stumbled backwards into the wall, and if it wasn't for Voltan leaping forward and catching him he would have slid down to the floor. Voltan half-carried him to his seat.

"Are you okay?" he asked. Gaspi had not lost consciousness. He may have been on the brink of it, but he had cut off the magic in time, and was just left with a pervasive weakness. His limbs felt like they were made of lead.

"I...I think so," he said, in a quavering voice.

Voltan peered intently into his eyes for a moment and nodded. "You replaced your block," he said. It was not a question. Gaspi nodded. "Quite impressive really," Voltan muttered, "managing to spell-sing under that pressure." He stood up snappily.

"Well, young Mage, I think we need to think about other ways of restricting your magic. A partial block may be an option. After class we will talk to Hephistole about it." He turned back to the class. "Okay, that's enough excitement for today," he said. "I don't want you practicing the force strike unsupervised. No martial magic is to be used outside of class. Is that understood?"

The pupils groaned grudgingly. "Does that mean we have no homework, sir?" Matthius asked.

"Thank you for reminding me, Matthius," Voltan said, as several pupils groaned, glowering resentfully at the small lad. "For next class I want you to have all read the first three chapters of Soltere's *Theories of Magical Combat*. There will be a test." The class grumbled unhappily as Voltan waved them out the door. Gav smacked Matthius round the back of the head.

"Why d'ya have to go and ask?" he asked as they left the room.

Soon Gaspi was the only student remaining. Voltan glanced at him.

"Go and have some lunch, Gaspi. You need to get some energy back. Come back here afterwards, and we'll work on your block with Hephistole." Gaspi said he would and left the room, where Emmy and Lydia were waiting for him. As they walked into the refectory, laughter burst out from Everand's group, and from the looks he was getting Gaspi was pretty sure what they were laughing about.

"Never mind him!" Emea said firmly, placing a hand on Gaspi's arm. "Go and sit down, Gaspi. We'll bring some food over." Gaspi hated being seen to be weak, but he had no strength left at all, and sat down wearily at an empty table. He could hear the mockery from across the room.

"The Nature Mage can't even summon a force strike!" Ferast's nasal voice evoked a flush of anger in Gaspi. Why couldn't they just leave him alone? What galled him most was that there was nothing he could do about it with his block in place. Until he learned control of his magic, they would never shut up. He was still fuming when Emmy and Lydia brought his food over. It was a vegetable soup accompanied by two thick slices of cheese and a small loaf. Grateful for the distraction he tucked in, and slowly the girls' company calmed him down. They wanted to know what had happened in class, which he explained as well as he could.

"I'm going to get control of this," he said determinedly. "Voltan said something about a partial block. Maybe that will help," he added hopefully.

"I'm sure it will," Lydia said, with her usual calm certainty. Conversation moved to the coming evening. Roland and the gypsies would be moving on soon now that Lydia had settled into the college, and they'd invited the three students to feast with them at the circle.

"So...is Taurnil coming tonight?" Lydia asked. Gaspi blinked and looked up at her. Usually she was measured and sure in everything she did, but all of a sudden she had sounded...vulnerable. Emea was taking a great interest in her soup, moving it round and round in the bowl.

"Yeah, he said he'd come over after practice with Jonn," Gaspi responded. "We'll all go down together."

"Oh...good," Lydia said, and Gaspi could have sworn he saw a faint red tinge beneath her tanned skin. He resisted smiling to himself. He was sure that Taurnil liked Lydia, but until now hadn't known what the mysterious girl thought about his friend. He might be wrong, but it looked like the feeling might be mutual. He certainly hoped so, for Taurn's sake.

After lunch they returned to Miss Emelda's classroom, where Emea's mentor was waiting for them, along with Hephistole and Voltan.

Hephistole stood up as they entered. "Ah good - here you are. With your permission, Voltan and I will be borrowing Gaspi for just a short time, but will return him to you shortly for the rest of this afternoon's class."

"Of course, Chancellor, as you wish," Emelda said, playing along with his exaggerated courtesy.

He inclined his head in Emelda's direction, and sketched a bow in the direction of the girls. "Ladies," he said as he left the room, followed by Voltan and Gaspi. As it happened they didn't have far to go, as the main classroom was free.

"So," Hephistole said once they were seated. "You had to replace your block during class this morning, I hear?" They sat in a kind of triangle, and Gaspi felt strangely equal, like he was being treated as a peer.

"Yeah...I could summon my magic and make the force strike, but when I tried to stop drawing on the power I couldn't cut it off. It just kept flowing, and the strike was getting bigger all the time. I had to use the spell song to stop it."

Hephistole peered at Gaspi with his head cocked slightly on one side. "Interesting...most interesting!" The Chancellor paused. "Don't be dispirited, Gaspi," he said, after a moment's thought. "You did well to use the spell song."

Gaspi didn't look at all encouraged. "But I still can't control my magic!" he blurted, full of frustration. He hadn't meant to get angry at Hephistole, but he couldn't help it.

"Yes, but there's a good reason for that, Gaspi," Hephistole responded calmly. "If you had the same magical strength as your classmates you could do it as easily, but your power is much greater, and therefore takes greater practice to control."

Gaspi sat up straight, his anger leeching away as Hephistole's words sunk in. "Am I more powerful than the other students?"

Hephistole looked at him intently, his mouth turning up at the corner in a slight smile. "Let's put it this way. They are trying to tame a cat, and you're trying to tame a tiger."

"What's a tiger?" Gaspi asked.

"A very big cat!" Hephistole answered.

Voltan folded his arms. "It's probably best not to boast about this to your classmates, though."

"Yes sir...I mean, I won't," Gaspi answered, and tried very hard not to think of Everand.

"So!" Hephistole said ringingly, clapping his long-fingered hands together. "We need to find a way to help you tame your tiger. Voltan has suggested a partial block. This is similar to the block you've had in place, but it works more as a limitation, allowing only a certain amount of power to flow through at one time. This will give you time to gain strength and control the flow of magic. As you continue to use your power the block will erode, allowing more power through in increments, which you can adjust to as you get used to it. How does this sound?"

"It sounds great," Gaspi answered. "I was worried I'd have to stay blocked again for a while, or not be able to do any magic at all." He paused. "Can you do it now?" he blurted, his eagerness overriding any attempt at politeness.

Hephistole laughed. "Yes Gaspi, right now! You can still re-establish the full block using the spell song I taught you, but hopefully that won't be necessary." He stood up and lifted his hand, holding it over Gaspi's head. "Are you ready?" he asked.

"Yes," Gaspi answered. Hephistole's hand rested on his head. Gaspi sat still while Hephistole stood there, unable to sense any magical activity. After a minute, Hephistole stepped back, and sat down again.

"Is it done?" Gaspi asked.

"Why don't you try and see?" Hephistole said. Gaspi nodded, and closing his eyes, sent his senses inward. He was quickly able to draw near to his power, and, reaching out, he summoned it to his control. He held it for a moment, released it, and opened his eyes.

"Yes...that works," he said, relieved.

"Then let's return you to your studies with Miss Emelda," Hephistole said. The headmaster and teacher walked with him back to the main classroom, taking their leave of Gaspi as he re-entered the room.

"That was a good idea, Voltan," Hephistole said with a smile, after the door had closed behind Gaspi.

Voltan nodded. "We don't know the limits of the boy's power, and this will keep a control over how much he uses until he's ready to use more." The fierce-looking teacher fixed Hephistole with a direct gaze. "I'll tell you this much - if he'd fired that force strike, it would have blown half the classroom away!"

Hephistole didn't seem phased about this at all. "Interesting," he said as they turned to walk back through the campus. "Definitely interesting!"

Chapter 18

Taurnil came to meet them that night as planned, and met Gaspi outside the dormitory.

"How's the training going, mate?" Gaspi asked as they sat on a nearby bench, waiting for the girls.

"All right. I won a bout today," Taurnil said, breaking out into a big smile.

"That's great!" Gaspi said enthusiastically. "With the staff?"

Taurnil let out a gruff laugh. "Yeah, with the staff. I couldn't beat a girl with swords at the moment."

Gaspi laughed in return. "So how did the fight go?" he asked, hungry for the details.

Taurnil shrugged. "Well, to be honest it was pretty straightforward. It was Bret, one of the younger guards. He's better with the sword, but likes to fight with the staff too. He just came on a bit too strong and I floored him with a leg flip, and went straight for the kill shot. It lasted about twenty seconds."

"Sounds like you well and truly had his number," Gaspi said.

"Looks that way," Taurnil said, smiling broadly, and then the smile slipped off his face as quickly as it had arrived, his jaw falling open foolishly as he stared goggle-eyed across the courtyard. Gaspi turned to follow Taurnil's gaze, and saw Emmy and Lydia stepping out of their dorm. Both girls were dressed in full gypsy garb. Emea was dressed in a luscious skirt and scarf of saffron yellow, but it was Lydia who had caught his friend's attention. She wore a billowing white shirt tucked into a flowing skirt of deep and vibrant shades of red. She wore a rich scarf over her shoulders that matched her dress, and had large, painted wooden jewellery around both wrists. The girls glowed like gold and flame in the evening light. Gaspi was entranced, and shared a look with his gobsmacked friend.

"Close your mouth, you big lumphead!" Gaspi said to Taurnil, who looked blankly at his friend for a moment, then snapped his jaw closed as realisation hit. The two boys walked over to the girls.

"You look lovely, Emmy," Gaspi said, his eyes taking in her rich clothing, and the way it flowed over her like water. She flushed a little, her eyes sparkling. Gaspi kissed her on the cheek and offered her his arm.

Without meaning for it to happen, Gaspi and Emea walked away from Taurnil and Lydia, leaving them standing alone together.

Once Gaspi and Emea had walked away, Taurnil was suddenly very aware of himself. What could he say to make things comfortable? Gaspi was always so good at these things, but he just felt as if his tongue had turned to wood. After a pregnant pause, he broke the silence. "Nice dress," he said clumsily.

"Thank you, Taurnil," Lydia said, and they started walking, falling in behind Gaspi and Emea, who were too wrapped up in each other to notice the awkward moment. Taurnil thrust his hands into his pockets, scuffing the ground with his feet.

"So, what's happening tonight?" he asked, more to keep the conversation going than out of genuine interest. Taurnil was surprised as Lydia enthusiastically started talking about the evening's entertainment. His clumsy attempt at conversation seemed to be working. He'd never been comfortable with long conversations, at least not if he was expected to do much of the talking, but maybe all he had to do was ask questions and Lydia would do the rest.

"...my Da will play his guitar, and we'll all dance round the fire," she said enthusiastically.

"Dance?" Taurnil asked, a little too quickly.

Lydia threw an amused glance at him. "You know, moving your feet around to music, maybe even your body too," she said mischievously. "Don't worry Taurnil," she said, patting his arm. "I'll show you how to do it." If anything, this made Taurnil worry even more!

They wound their way down through the town, and met Jonn at the gate to the city. He smiled warmly at them. "Ah, there you all are," he said. "Well, come along then. Food awaits!"

He led them through the city gates and a short distance around the outer wall, until they came across the gypsy circle; the vibrant reds, yellows and greens of lacquered wagons shone in the evening light. The sun was perhaps half an hour from setting, and in preparation for the evening's festivities Roland had already started the fire going, its leaping flames pale in the lingering daylight. When Lydia caught sight of her da tending to the growing blaze, she let out a little noise of delight and trotted ahead of Taurnil, who didn't know whether he ought to keep up, or just carry on walking on his own. As if sensing her approach, Roland stood up, the line of his broad shoulders framed against the light as he turned around. Grinning, he took a few long strides towards his daughter, and swept her up in his arms. He planted a kiss in her hair, lifting her clean off the ground.

Taurnil was touched by the unselfconscious display. There was obviously a lot of love there between father and daughter. Lydia normally had a sort of knowing calm about her, but moments like this revealed her passionate side to Taurnil, who watched the greeting hungrily, imagining what it would be like to be the one Lydia ran to.

Roland had put Lydia down, and strode towards the rest of the small party. He spread his arms expansively. "Gaspi, Emea, Taurnil - my daughter's good friends - welcome to our fire." His sincerity was easy to respond to. Emea smiled sweetly in response, and Gaspi wore a broad grin. Roland put an arm around Taurnil's shoulder as they turned into the camp. "So Taurnil, Lydia tells me you're a city guard now."

The feast was exactly that. A whole deer roasted slowly over a cooking fire, hot juices dripping into the flames, releasing a smell that made Taurnil's mouth water. There were wooden bowls of steaming vegetables, and a communal pot of roasting juices to pour over the meal. Some of the colourfully dressed gypsies had already filled goblets with spiced wine from the kegs set up around the edges of the circle, and a group of musicians were strumming and plucking tunefully. The musicians gave Taurnil an uncomfortable reminder that he would have to dance later that night, and the nervousness that had been balling in his gut all night escalated to new, even higher levels.

The gypsies were leaving the next day, and in anticipation of being separated from her family, Lydia was lit up like a lantern. She was flushed with high emotion, dancing most of the night away with friends and more often with her Da, beaming out a complex mixture of vibrancy and vulnerability. Taurnil's evening thrummed with a different kind of emotional intensity. He was desperate to comfort Lydia, aching to sooth her hurt, but felt wooden and restricted. Surely his presence would be unwelcome in such a private moment.

As promised, she pulled him into the circle of dancers a couple of times, but on each occasion he couldn't manage to conjure the kind of easy banter Gaspi was so capable of. His legs felt stiff as stilts as he tried to follow Lydia's amused instructions, which might have been fun if he could have laughed at himself, but he felt like the whole world was watching him stumble and trip through the dance. He felt humourless and without personality, and all he knew at the end of each dance was relief. He spent most of the night well back in the shadows at the edge of the circle, watching with pangs of jealousy as Lydia twirled with handsome, smiling gypsy boys, their confident chatter enticing peals of laughter from the beautiful young woman he admired so much.

Taurnil felt like he'd reached a crisis point. It was as if his previously healthy heart was shrivelling and darkening like a prune. What had he been thinking of? Why would this magical, beautiful girl be interested in a plodder like him? All his obsession was doing was making him miserable. He took a long last look at Lydia, dancing once more with her father, laughter beautifying her already lovely face, and deliberately turned his back, walking away into the shadows.

Chapter 19

Over the next several weeks, Gaspi didn't see much of Taurnil. He went to visit him a few times at the barracks after training, but he hadn't come up to the college or met them in the Travellers Rest. Gaspi could tell that Taurnil didn't want to talk about what was bothering him, and their conversations had been limited to magic, football and combat; so when Emea asked him what the matter with Taurnil was (which she frequently did) he couldn't answer her, though he suspected he knew something of the problem. Lydia didn't mention Taurnil's name even once, and if someone else did her face would stiffen until the subject was changed. Emea had said enough for Gaspi to know that her behaviour had something to do with the way Taurnil disappeared during the feast at the gypsy circle, but that was all he could figure out.

He didn't have much time to think about it, however, as those weeks were very busy for the three trainee magicians - they had been exposed to all manor of magical learning. They continued to study enchanting and healing, but also began to look at prophecy, neuromancy and matter manipulation. Now that his block was released Gaspi was able to use magic along with the rest of the class. This silenced most of the murmurs about his lack of ability, but not entirely. The partial block meant that his magic was only as powerful as most of the other students', and certainly not as strong as Everand's. The Nature Mage was suddenly very ordinary, and Gaspi didn't feel like explaining about the partial block, even when Ferast made snide comments behind his back.

The martial magic lessons continued to cause a stir among the students. As far as anyone knew, lessons in offensive magic hadn't been given in a long time, and all the students were murmuring about what this could mean. They were talking about this one evening in the Rest. Gaspi had persuaded Taurnil to join them, but wasn't so sure any more that it was such a good idea. Lydia was nervous and quiet in the presence of an equally uncomfortable Taurnil, who couldn't join in with the conversation about martial magic, and sat in near-silence. The atmosphere was awkward, but Gaspi and Emea bravely soldiered on, trying to fill in the uncomfortable gaps left by the other two.

"Well, how do we know when it was last taught?" Gaspi asked. "None of the class has been here for longer than a few months."

"It's the older students who've been saying that," Emea answered. The older students shared private residences in the campus, studying specialised topics under their mentors, and generally didn't have much to do with the first years. Classroom teaching stopped after the first year, and the older students were more like journeyman magicians than pupils. "Do you think it could have something to do with what happened to us on the road?"

"I reckon," Gaspi said.

Taurnil grunted, staring out of the window.

"What's the matter, Taurn?" Emea asked. "You don't seem yourself."

Taurnil was quiet for a moment. "I've got the tournament coming up in a few days. It's all I can think about. Sorry if I'm a bit...weird."

"I thought you were looking forward to it," Gaspi responded.

"I was - I mean, I am. But Kristos beat me again today, and I want to win. I just can't seem to get the better of him."

Lydia let out a rich laugh. "You've only been a guard for a couple of months, and you want to win?"

"You wouldn't understand," Taurnil answered gruffly.

Lydia's mouth hung open for a second, before she closed it deliberately and turned to Emea. "Emea, I think I will go back to the dorm. Are you coming?" She was already gathering her things before Emea could reply. Lydia left in a bustle, her normal unruffled calm conspicuously absent. Emea trailed behind, throwing an exasperated look at Taurnil as she went.

"Are you an idiot?" Gaspi said, fixing Taurnil with a perplexed stare. "What's got into you?"

Taurnil flushed bright red. "Well, she...she was..." he blustered aimlessly.

"She wasn't doing anything," Gaspi said.

Taurnil folded his arms angrily, trying to think of a retort. "Damnit!" he said after a few moments, unfolding his arms "I AM an idiot!"

Gaspi couldn't help laughing. "We all are sometimes, mate, though it's normally me and not you. What's got you so riled? Surely not just the competition?"

Taurnil let out a long breath. "Well, it's partly the competition. I don't know why, but I just feel like I have to get good really fast."

"Why?" Gaspi asked.

"It's just a feeling I've got. And, I dunno...I've never really been the best at anything, and that's always been fine, but I just need to be the best at this. I know it doesn't make sense, but that's how I feel."

Gaspi put a hand on his friend's arm. "Fair enough, Taurn. I've never seen you like this, but if it means that much to you that's good enough for me."

Taurnil nodded gratefully, and still looked distracted. He opened his

159

mouth to speak again, but nothing came out. Gaspi waited.

"And…" Taurnil began, searching for words that didn't seem to want to come out of his mouth, "it's not just that." His eyes were fixed on the floor.

After a prolonged silence, Gaspi felt forced to prompt his friend. "What else is it?" he asked, as patiently as possible.

"It's Lydia," Taurnil said, braving an embarrassed glance at his friend.

"What about Lydia?" Gaspi asked, though he was pretty sure he knew the answer.

"Well…I like her," Taurnil said despondently, as if that explained everything. The two boys had never talked about this kind of thing, but Gaspi didn't think now was the time to get uncomfortable.

"So? Why's that such a bad thing?" Gaspi asked, trying to sound like this was a normal conversation.

"I just can't seem to help it," Taurnil responded. "Every time I'm around her my stomach ties in knots, and I don't know what to say. Do you know what I mean?"

Gaspi laughed and grimaced in that order. "Of course I know," he said. "I still feel like that with Emmy half the time. I'm waiting for it to settle down! But Taurn, I don't get what the problem is. So you like her. That's a good thing…right?"

Taurnil's face fell even further. "How can it be a good thing? She'll never be interested in me, and I'll never be able to relax around her. It'll just go on and on."

"Why wouldn't she be interested in you?" Gaspi asked, nonplussed.

"Because I'm not…you know…magical, like you all are."

"Are you being serious?" Gaspi asked. "Taurn, I don't think she thinks that way. Has she said anything like that to you?"

"Said anything?" Taurnil looked surprised. "Well, of course not. We've not really spoken at all. I've avoided her like the plague for the last few weeks. I don't really know her at all."

"Well, okay, that's true about the last few weeks," Gaspi said, "but didn't you get time on the road to get to know her a bit?"

"I suppose," Taurnil said. "It did seem easier then, but now it's different. You're all off learning about magic, and I spend all day with the guards getting beaten up."

Gaspi laughed. "Yeah you'd better start winning soon or you'll be one big bruise." Taurnil smiled despite himself. "But seriously, Taurn, maybe that's exactly what you need – to spend a bit of time together; get used to each other."

Taurnil looked like he was considering the thought. "Yeah, maybe," he said, with a slight smile. "That might work. So you seriously don't think she cares that I'm not magical?"

Gaspi looked at his friend's simple, honest face, shaped right now in such an expression of earnest hopefulness that it pulled on every one of his heartstrings. "I don't know, Taurn," he answered. "I don't think she's like that - but you should ask her, not me."

Taurnil grunted in what might have been agreement, and looked away. "And I can't dance, either," the large boy muttered.

"What?" Gaspi asked.

"Never mind," Taurnil said, staring thoughtfully out of the window for a minute. He turned to his friend. "Thanks, Gasp," he said, suddenly serious and without self-consciousness. "You've helped me out."

"Anytime, mate," Gaspi responded. "There's just one thing you're going to have to do, though."

"What's that?" Taurnil asked.

"Say sorry to Lydia."

The next few days passed in a blur. Taurnil was kept busy preparing for the tournament, which meant that he didn't get a chance to talk to Lydia. The young magicians were also practicing hard: the Test they had learned about on their first day at college was scheduled for only a couple of days after Taurnil's tournament. Gaspi and Lydia enthusiastically poured their energy into practicing every last bit of magic they knew how to perform. Both of them had a reasonable grasp of the lessons they'd been studying, and with Gaspi's block in place they were of about equal strength, so they tested each other rigorously whenever they got a chance.

It was not the same for Emea. Her friends were running headlong towards the day she dreaded. They went about their days with a kind of feverish excitement, never stopping to think that they might fail. But for Emea the days dragged by interminably, the passing of minutes and hours weighed down by the certainty that this would be the end of the road for her. Despite her initial success in probing injuries, she had been unable to heal more than the most minor of cuts and scrapes. She could just about summon a force strike and fling it at a shield, but by the time it reached the target it was so pathetic it barely evoked a change of colour; to her great embarrassment the darkest colour she had got out of the shield was a light straw-yellow! She was better at neuromancy, tuning in to another being's thoughts, and even influencing those thoughts a bit, but would that be part of the Test? It certainly didn't seem easy to measure. However she looked at it, she just couldn't see herself passing the Test. Then she'd have to leave the college, and Gaspi and Lydia would go on to great things without her.

Emea didn't want to puncture Gaspi and Lydia's happiness, so she put on the necessary smiles when they were expected, but in her heart she just felt sad and lonely. Not wanting to bring Gaspi down, she hadn't talked to him about it, and when he asked how she felt she lied through her teeth, swearing everything was fine. On the afternoon before Taurnil's tournament Gaspi was playing football, and Lydia was nowhere to be seen, so Emmy took the chance to visit Jonn, who was not on duty until the evening. She felt a little shy about dropping in on Jonn on her own, but Jonn was like a father to all of them in some ways. She felt safe with him, and she desperately needed to talk to someone.

She found him in the barracks, polishing his armour. His face brightened as he caught sight of her. "Emmy!" he said warmly. "What brings you down here to see me?"

"Oh, nothing much," she said, not willing to spill her guts just yet. "I just thought I'd visit. Am I in the way?"

"Of course not!" he said, with a warm smile. "And you're always welcome to visit me." He glanced up at the ceiling. "Do you want to take a walk on the wall?"

"That sounds nice," Emea answered, and, taking his offered arm, she walked with him out of the barracks. They went up the steps past the guards on duty at the gatehouse, and soon were strolling slowly along the broad path built into the top of the city wall. You could see for miles from the wall; a breathtaking view of distant, rocky mountains rising sharply from the plain. Jonn led her to a spot where you could sit on one of the raised benches of stone set into the top of the wall. He waited for her to sit, then took his place next to her. Placing his hands on his knees, elbows facing outwards, he drew in and released a deep breath as he took in the scenery. It was a contented sound. Emea struggled to relax, but the snarl of emotions inside her refused to be unwound.

Suddenly self-conscious, she tried to make conversation. "So, are you enjoying being a guard?" She wanted to kick herself for such a stupid question.

Jonn didn't seem to think it was a stupid question. "Enjoying? Well, yes; I suppose I'd have to say I am. I feel like I belong, I've got something to keep me occupied, and I've lost most of my fat belly, which is saying something!" he said playfully. "So yes, I'm enjoying it," he concluded, then looked at her shrewdly. "Are you enjoying being a magician?"

Emea let out a bitter laugh. "I'd have to be one to enjoy it," she said, and burst into tears.

Jonn put his arm around her. "Come on Emmy," he said, patting her awkwardly. "What's the matter?"

Emea gulped a few times, trying to get control of her runaway tears. She wiped her face on her sleeve. "I'm terrible at magic, Jonn," she said, fighting to stop her chin from wobbling. "Gaspi and Lydia can do everything, and Gaspi is still partially blocked! But everything I do is a weak, useless version of what they can do."

"Everything?" Jonn asked.

"Well, almost everything. Miss Emelda says I am good at using magic as a probe to explore wounds, and I'm okay at neuromancy. But you should see my force strike! It wouldn't hurt an ant!"

"Well, it sounds like Miss Emelda sees something in you," Jonn said comfortingly, "and the other stuff will come with time, won't it?"

"But I don't have time," Emea said, panic entering her voice. "The Test is coming up, and if I don't pass it I'll have to leave!"

"Ah, yes," Jonn said. "The Test. Has anyone told you what's in it, yet?"

Emea's forehead wrinkled. "No...but it's bound to include a test of strength, don't you think?"

"Maybe. Have you spoken to Gaspi about this? Maybe he could help you," Jonn suggested.

"I don't want to bother him with it," Emea insisted. "Besides, if I have to leave the college, then he'll be too busy with his studies to spend much time with me. I may as well get used to it."

Jonn looked genuinely surprised. "Emmy, I can't believe you'd think that. Do you think Gaspi would love you less if you weren't a magician? Do you love Taurnil less because he's not magical?"

"No, of course not," she said, going red in the face.

"Then maybe you should trust Gaspi a bit more, eh?" Jonn said.

Emea sniffed and nodded, wiping her face with her sleeve again. "You're right. I should probably talk to him."

"Good girl!" Jonn said. "And as for the Test, you'll just have to do your best, and let the teachers see your strengths." Emea nodded again, burying her head a little further into Jonn's chest. She didn't feel any more confident about the Test but her fear of being rejected by Gaspi had lifted, taking some of the burden away. She would talk to him that night. After a while she leaned away from Jonn, and they went back to the barracks.

"Thanks, Jonn," she said, grateful for the safety he provided for her.

"Any time, Emmy," Jonn said. "And try not to worry about the Test. Whatever happens, things will work out. You'll see." Emea even managed a genuine smile as she left him, making her way back up to the college.

After dinner she asked Gaspi to take a walk with her, and began to share her feelings with him. Gaspi stared at her in amazement when she explained her fear of losing him if she had to leave the college. With blazing eyes, he took her by the shoulders and held her gaze. "Emmy - I'd never abandon you like that! What does it matter if you're not living here with me in the college? And besides," he added with a shake of his head, "you're not going to fail the Test."

Emea kissed him warmly. "Thank you, Gaspi," she said, smiling sweetly. "I should have known it wouldn't make a difference to you, and I'm glad we've talked...but for what it's worth, I really think I might fail this Test."

"But why?" Gaspi asked, puzzled by her insistence.

"I'm just not very strong," she answered. "And that makes me nervous, and when I'm nervous it's even worse. This is so cruel, Gaspi. All I want is to be a Healer, and now I've had a taste of it I can't imagine living without it."

"Well...why don't you practice a bit more with me and Lydia over the new couple of days, and see if you can get a bit of confidence up?"

"Okay, Gasp," she said, not sounding much more hopeful. "I'll give it a go."

Chapter 20

On the day of the tournament the sky was overcast; sodden grey clouds loomed overhead, heavy with the threat of rain. But nothing could dampen the excitement of the students, who had been given the afternoon off so they could go and watch the fighting. Gaspi knew Taurnil hadn't apologised to Lydia yet and was worried she might not come along, but his fears were proved unfounded when she turned up with Emmy at midday, and the three friends made their way down through the city to the barracks.

As they neared the barracks, they found themselves surrounded by crowds of city folk also heading to the tournament. Apparently, it was quite popular! There were numerous magicians there too, some in colourful robes, but many more in brown. Gaspi recognised some of them from the refectory, where older students could eat if they chose to, though many didn't. The more garishly dressed magicians stood out amongst the more modestly dressed citizenry of Helioport, but the city dwellers were so used to magic-users that they jostled and pushed against them, as they did anyone else, in the rush for a good seat. The tournament itself was being held in a large open practice area surrounded by many dozens of benches already half-filled with spectators. They squeezed their way through to the front and found a bench they could all fit on. Lydia slid in first, followed by Emea, and Gaspi sat on the end. Gaspi glanced up at the lowering sky, wondering if they'd cancel the tournament if it rained.

The combatants themselves were sitting separately near another entrance to the large practice area, where they could enter and leave the arena without having to press through the crowd. There were about fifty guards sitting there at that moment, but Gaspi assumed others would come and go as the afternoon went on and different events were staged. They all looked alike, dressed in light mail over tan leather leggings and padded undershirts, and Gaspi struggled to identify Taurnil among them. It was Emmy who spotted him, her hand shooting out, pointing at the group.

"There he is!" she said excitedly.

"Where?" Lydia asked.

"Two rows from the back, sitting next to that massive guy with the red hair," Emea answered. Lydia raised a hand to shield her eyes and Gaspi squinted. It was Taurnil all right, though he looked very different in chain mail. To Gaspi's eyes he looked larger and older. The mail hung well off his strong shoulders and broad chest, making him look very…guard-like.

"Doesn't he look handsome?" Emea said, talking to Lydia.

Lydia looked like she was trying to smile and frown at the same time. "I'm sure he does," she answered rather haughtily, a fine red stain flushing her cheeks.

"Oh, come on, Lydia," Emea said impatiently. "I know he'll say sorry to you when he gets a chance."

Lydia flushed even more, elbowing Emea and indicating Gaspi with a flick of her head. "Not now!" she hissed. Emea sighed and leaned back against the bench. Gaspi thought it was simpler to pretend he hadn't seen or heard any of it. He thought he saw Taurnil looking over at them, and raised a hand in greeting. Taurnil nodded in response, and Gaspi could see even from a distance that he looked a little green around the gills. In fact, if he wasn't mistaken, his friend looked like he was about to lose the contents of his stomach.

The makeshift arena slowly filled up until all the benches were taken, and folk were standing against the walls. The hubbub and excitement built upon itself, until the whole arena thrummed with the murmur of anticipation. Finally, a stocky man in chain mail walked out into the middle of the open space and stood still, waiting for the crowd to quieten down. It took a minute or so for the loud buzz of conversation to drop off; slowly at first, and then descending rapidly into breathless silence as people looked around, aware of the sudden hush.

"Citizens of Helioport," the stocky man began, his strong voice carrying to the back of the arena, "I am Tobias Trask, Sergeant-at-Arms and Helioport's Drillmaster; and today I have the honour of presenting to you our annual tournament."

The crowd broke into loud cheering. Trask held up his hands until the noise subsided. "The bouts will be split into individual weapon skills: one-handed swords, two-handed swords, staff, and mace. At the end of the afternoon, the best two from each event will compete in a general melee, where one fighter will emerge as this year's champion." The crowd broke into an even loader cheer, which Trask let go on for longer this time.

"For the safety of the fighters," Trask continued, "the blades have been blunted, and cannot pierce the armour each man is wearing. So do not fear for your favourites. They will not be harmed." Again, the crowd cheered. Trask extended one hand towards the seated combatants, and one towards the dirt floor in front of him.

"Swords!" he shouted. "Brill, Sabu!"

Two men arose from the benches; a thickset ginger-haired man with a trimmed beard, and a tall, dark-skinned man with short-cropped, wiry

166

hair. They walked to the weapons rack, took out two short swords each and walked to the centre of the arena. An expectant hush filled the room, deepening as they squared off. Trask stood between the two men, arms stretched out towards the fighters. "On my command, you will fight until a winner is declared." He looked steadily at each man, then stepped back and dropped his arms. "Begin!" he barked.

Brill shifted into a fighting stance; one leg out in front of the other, bending at both knees, and holding his swords out in front of him. He looked like a coiled spring, ready to pounce. Sabu looked more relaxed as he began a graceful pacing, circling his opponent steadily, one foot sliding behind and past the other as he moved with an unbroken rhythm. His blades wove sinuously in front of him as he circled, every movement of his long, dark frame fluid and graceful. Brill was forced to circle too, or let his opponent get behind him, and although he moved with a certain grace too, it was a grace filled with tightly wound energy - each foot landing firmly on the ground, his arms and shoulders tense and ready to strike.

It was Brill who struck first, feinting with his left hand and, when Sabu moved to block, striking swiftly with the right. Faster than a snake, Sabu's other sword caught the second strike and turned the blade away with a ringing clang. Brill came in again swiftly, throwing a series of blows at Sabu's head and chest, which the slender fighter caught on his blades, deflecting all attacks with an economy of movement. The fight carried on in this vein for some minutes, Brill lancing out again and again with heavy strikes and Sabu turning each away without breaking stride. Some of Brill's attacks seemed to come very close to hitting his opponent, but somehow Gaspi knew it wasn't going to happen. Both looked like very good swordsmen, but there was something about Sabu that impressed him more. His fighting style was almost like a dance, and whereas Brill was starting to slow down, his breath coming fast and deep, Sabu looked like he was just warming up.

Gaspi sensed a sudden shift in the fight when one of Brill's strikes left him over-extended, and Sabu responded with a stinging riposte. Brill defended against the stroke, but had to leap backwards to avoid leaving himself open. Sabu didn't give him the chance to recover, but followed the stroke with another, and then another, forcing Brill to move backwards step by step, never regaining his balance. Brill retreated halfway across the arena, furiously defending against the whirlwind of Sabu's attacks, until the tall, dark fighter leapt forward, attacking with both blades at once. Both Brill's arms came up to fend off the double attack. Sabu's blades swept viciously across Brills, ripping the right hand one out of his hand and sending it spinning through the air to land point down in the dirt. The other blade was pushed up and away from the body, leaving Brill completely open. Sabu brought in his right hand sword, and poked Brill hard in the chest. Brill grunted and fell down to the floor, flopping heavily to his backside as a gong sounded and Drillmaster Trask's loud voice bellowed "Winner: Sabu!"

Gaspi roared and sprang to his feet, cheering wildly along with the rest of the crowd. He'd been so caught up in the fight he wondered if he'd even breathed for the last few minutes. He grinned wildly at Emea and Lydia, both of who seemed as impressed as he was. Lydia's eyes were wide with amazement, and Emmy held a hand over her open mouth.

The next fight wasn't nearly as impressive. The huge fighter sitting next to Taurnil took on a wiry, middle-aged guard, who couldn't compete with the strength of the larger man's strokes, and was beaten in under a minute when a heavy attack disarmed him. Five more pairs of swordsmen squared off and fought, bringing the total up to seven winners. Trask sent each of the winners to a separate bench, before calling out the next fight. Once the seventh winner was seated, he turned back to the face the crowd.

"And our last bout for this round of the swords: Erik and Jonn." Gaspi looked up in surprise as the two fighters stepped out from the other guards. In all the excitement of Taurnil's first tournament, it had never occurred to him that Jonn might fight too. He exchanged a look with Emmy, who was clearly as surprised as he was. But there Jonn was, weighing up two blades from the weapons rack along with his opponent. Gaspi had met Erik a couple of times while visiting Jonn. Gaspi liked Erik, and doubly so considering that without Erik's help he may never have reached Helioport alive after the attack at the gypsy camp. Not that it made any difference right now, of course. If Erik was fighting Jonn, then all that would have to be put aside until the fighting was over.

"Did you know he was fighting?" Gaspi asked Emea.

Emea shook her head. "I spoke to him yesterday, and he didn't say a word."

Jonn and Erik had reached Drillmaster Trask now, who stood between them with his hands raised. "Begin!" he shouted.

Gaspi was pleased to see Jonn immediately drop back into a comfortable fighting stance. He didn't think of Jonn as a fighter, but then he remembered the way he'd dealt with the thieves they'd met on the road. And Jonn had once told him that he'd spent a few years as a guard in another city, whose name Gaspi couldn't remember.

Jonn looked at ease with swords in his hands, circling Erik on the balls of his feet. He feinted in, probing Erik's guard before stepping back, letting Erik bring the next attack. The two swordsmen had a similar style, and seemed evenly matched. They circled each other carefully, stepping in for a ringing exchange of blows, before parting again. The pace of their circling gradually increased, as did the length of the exchanges, until they were standing blade to blade, circling and striking in a mesmerising display. The fight was going on longer than any of the other bouts, and Gaspi thought both men's arms must be ablaze with agony as they struck and defended, blocked and parried without a break. Gaspi grabbed Emea's hand as they watched, gripping her tightly as he willed Jonn on to win. It was hard to see exactly what happened, but in the middle of a particularly vicious exchange of blows Erik stumbled backwards as if struck, a sword clattering to the floor as he collapsed, and Trask was shouting "Winner: Jonn!"

Gaspi and Emmy surged to their feet again, along with the roaring crowd. He grabbed Emmy, giving her a massive hug as they cheered at the top of their lungs. Jonn helped Erik to his feet, before making his way to the winners' benches.

"That was amazing," Emea said breathily. "I had no idea he was so good." Gaspi just nodded, rendered speechless by the display of skill.

When the cheering had died down, the winning eight fighters were called forward two by two for a second round. Jonn knocked out a stocky young fighter from Helioport, to the dismay of the partisan crowd, who groaned noisily when their local favourite was dispatched. Sabu make light work of his opponent, and the other two winners were twin brothers Zlekic and Zaric. The twins' fighting styles were so similar it was easy to think you were watching the same man in both fights, until you looked at the winners' bench and saw the fighter's mirror image looking on. Both men were tall, broad and athletic with thick, straight blond hair so light it was almost white. They were handsome men in a hard kind of way, with light blue eyes and strong, straight noses.

The third round paired Jonn with Zlekic, and Sabu with Zaric. Sabu and Zaric were to fight first. The earlier bouts made Gaspi favour Sabu, who moved with such natural grace it looked like his blades were part of his body. His movements were so swift it made his opponents look clumsy and slow. His fight against Zaric lasted longer than his previous two fights. The blond swordsman was fast and very strong, and when Sabu deflected his strikes the clang of metal on metal rang loud and harsh. Sabu adjusted to the strength of Zaric's strikes by increasing the distance between them and pushing each of Zaric's attacks far from his body, slowing the tempo and making the blonde swordsman work hard to keep up the pace he had set. He tried to get his opponent to over-reach, but Zaric was disciplined and cautious. Neither did he appear to tire quickly, so Sabu couldn't outwait him either. Sabu remained on the defensive while testing Zaric's defences and stamina, but only a minute into the fight must have made up his mind about his opponent, and launched an all-out attack.

It was amazing to watch. The dark skinned swordsman's blades whirred through the air, spinning and slicing ferociously and with blistering speed. Zaric's defence was like his attack; disciplined and controlled. He blocked and parried, trying to lock up the blades so he could draw Sabu in close, but after each block Sabu would slide around him, attacking from another, unprotected angle. He never let Zaric rest, forcing him to constantly turn and shift his stance as he attacked. Confused by Sabu's constant movement, Zaric's defence began to lose timing. All it took was one clumsy overextension and the flat of Sabu's blade crunched down on Zaric's wrist, causing him to drop a sword. Zaric stumbled backwards, holding his remaining blade out in front of him in a desperate attempt to defend himself, but he stumbled over the fallen sword, falling onto his behind. One sweeping blow ripped the blade from Zaric's hand, and before he could react, the point of Sabu's other sword was at his throat.

"Winner: Sabu!" shouted Trask as the crowd cheered, calling out the dark warrior's name. Sabu stepped back and flashed a wide smile, white teeth glinting brightly in contrast to his dusky skin. He lifted a hand in acknowledgement, before returning to the winner's bench.

"Zlekic, Jonn!" shouted Trask. Gaspi's heart was thumping in his throat. If Zlekic was as good as his brother, it would be a hard fight. The two fighters squared off.

"Begin!" roared Trask.

They began to circle, slowly and carefully, neither of them keen to rush in without testing the other first. Jonn was the first to attack, his blows precise and fast, but Zlekic deflected them easily enough and swung a heavy riposte. Jonn leapt back, and they started to circle again. Zlekic attacked next with a series of hard, heavy blows, and Gaspi could see Jonn almost staggering under the weight of the strikes as he caught them on his blades. After a particularly brutal exchange, Jonn pushed Zlekic away from him, and Gaspi thought he could detect Jonn subtly changing his stance. He seemed to be gripping his swords more lightly and stepping on the balls of his feet. Zlekic attacked again, his strikes as hard and strong as his brother's had been against Sabu, but somehow Jonn's altered stance enabled him to deflect the blows without soaking up the majority of the force. Jonn was moving lightly and with speed now, making the heavy attacks of his opponent seem clumsy by comparison.

Zlekic started to come in heavier to try and wear down his fleet opponent, but Jonn just seemed to get faster and more light-footed. Jonn deflected a forceful overhand blow with the lightest of flicks, the momentum of the strike carrying Zlekic's blade down into the ground, where it struck hard. Zlekic's wrist must have been stunned by the impact, as he struggled to lift his blade up. Before he could recover, Jonn's foot lashed out against Zlekic's wrist, connecting with a sickening crunch. Zlekic yelped, involuntarily clutching his wrist against his body, giving Jonn time to prepare a thrust to the belly. Zlekic didn't wait for the blow to land, but stepped back, dropping his other sword to the ground and spreading his arms out in surrender.

"Winner: Jonn!" shouted Trask. Gaspi's voice was growing hoarse from all the cheering, but he gave it his best shot and was rewarded by a big kiss on the check from Emea. He couldn't believe that the quiet, private man he'd grown up with in Aemon's Reach was the same man as this elite, impressive fighter. It made him fiercely proud of his guardian. He had to blink rapidly to dry up the tears welling in his eyes.

Trask addressed the crowd: "The winners of the one-handed swords are Sabu and Jonn!" The crowd cheered once more, and the two fighters grinned at each other, remaining where they were on the winners' bench. Gaspi was disappointed that Jonn wouldn't be fighting Sabu, but at least he'd face him in the final melee.

The two-handed sword competition had fewer entrants than the one-handed competition, and was won by a huge, red-bearded guard called Baard. Gaspi couldn't help laughing while watching him fight. His massive strength and enormous arms made it impossible for anyone to contain him, and he barrelled over several smaller men, whose skill was probably greater, without much effort. The other winner was Zlekic, who was allowed to compete in more than one discipline as he'd not won the first.

Then came the staff. If Gaspi had been nervous watching Jonn compete, he was practically twitching waiting for Taurnil to fight. Emea looked sick, and Lydia had been stripped of her earlier coolness, concern and hope etched into every muscle of her face.

Emea grasped her hand. "I hope he does well," she said. "This really means a lot to him."

"Me too," Lydia responded breathily.

"I know he can do it," Gaspi said to both girls. He'd never seen his friend so determined about anything, and couldn't help feeling he'd be up to the challenge. The bruises Taurnil had been carrying these last few weeks told the story of relentless practice, which had to count for *something*, after all.

The first bout was between two evenly matched fighters; one lean and dark, and the other thick-set and blonde. The skills used for staff fighting were very different from those used for blades. The combatants pivoted and thrust, trapped and swung from a greater distance, leaping over their staffs and swapping positions every few seconds. It seemed as much a test of agility as anything else, and when the tall, dark fighter won out, Gaspi swallowed his concern at the obvious skill of the fighters, and waited excitedly for his friend to be called.

Taurnil sat on the bench, his heart beating so hard he thought people would be able to hear it. His palms were sweaty and he swallowed over and over, trying to moisten his bone-dry mouth. He'd been looking forward to this for weeks, practicing hour upon hour to get ready for the tournament, but now that it was here he wasn't even sure if his shaking hands could hold a staff, let alone fight with one. Suddenly, there was no more time left to think about it, as Trask's voice boomed out "Taurnil, Kristos," and he was walking to the weapons' rack. He collected a staff, and walked slowly out across the arena on legs that didn't even feel like they were his. Blood pounding in his ears, he forced himself to keep going, each step emphasised by the loud crunch of sandy, gritty floor beneath his feet. He reached the centre of the arena and faced off against his opponent, forcing himself to meet the calm gaze of the rangy fighter. He'd never beaten Kristos in a fight before, and he tried to force his nerves apart, daring himself to believe it was possible this time.

"Begin!" Kristos leaped in straight away, attacking Taurnil with an aggressive thrust. Taurnil blocked the thrust instinctively, and as wood clacked on wood and the reverberations shocked his arms, it was as if he suddenly woke up. He was fighting in the tournament, he'd been looking forward to it for weeks, and that moment was now. Nervousness fled him as his focus narrowed on the moment and on his opponent. He turned his block into a thrust, pushing Kristos' staff out to the right. Kristos allowed the momentum to carry his staff around, and he brought it swinging forcefully in towards Taurnil's exposed ribs. Taurnil snapped his staff up at the last minute, catching Kristos' strike and forcing his staff upwards. With incredible speed, Taurnil stepped in, reversing his staff and thrusting the butt of it into Kristos' chin. The tall fighter's head snapped up, his body frozen in mid motion. He seemed to float backwards, arms extended and legs hanging limply, before landing with a muffled thud on the arena floor.

The crowd was silent for a second, before erupting in riotous cheering. Taurnil looked to where his friends were sitting, filling with pride when he saw all three of them on their feet, cheering wildly and thrusting their hands in the air. His eyes rested on Lydia for a second, and his stomach lurched before he tore his gaze away. Now wasn't the time to be thinking about that.

"Winner; Taurnil," Trask announced, and Taurnil took his place on the winners' bench while the rest of the first round bouts were underway.

His next opponent was a dangerous little fighter called Ruberto. He was short and wiry, with a hooked nose and sun-burnt, olive skin. Taurnil squared off against his opponent. His heart was beating fast as Trask commanded them to begin.

"Begin!" Trask commanded, and Taurnil began to circle warily, his nerves on edge, ready for any sudden move. Ruberto attacked first with a sharp jab to the face, which Taurnil easily deflected. Memories of practice bouts told him that Ruberto was much better at defending than attacking, and decided to outwait him, forcing him into an aggressive position. Sure enough, Ruberto began to strike more often, and though the attacks were hard and fast, Taurnil kept up a strong defence. Taurnil could sense a woodenness in his opponent's attacks. They were strong and quick and could hurt if they connected, but he didn't have the kind of fluidity he'd learned to identify in the better fighters.

A couple of minutes into the fight, Ruberto leapt in with a strong thrust to the body, forcing Taurnil into a block; but as the staffs connected, Ruberto pivoted to the left, bringing the other end of the staff around towards Taurnil's exposed side. Taurnil tried desperately to bring his own staff round to block it ,but was too late, and Ruberto's staff crunched into his chain mail just below his armpit. Taurnil grunted as pain exploded in his side and chain links went spinning out across the floor as his vest ripped open. He staggered backwards away from the blow, putting distance between himself and Ruberto. Ruberto grinned predatorily and came in again on the attack, striking confidently now with a series of thrusts and sweeps. Every blow Taurnil caught on his staff sent a white hot stab of pain through his injured side, but he fought on with gritted teeth. If he could just get one good move in he could even the fight up, or even swing it in his favour.

He got his chance less than a minute later, when he caught his opponent in an overextended sweep, trapping one end of Ruberto's staff against the floor. He brought a foot down hard on the length of wood, snapping it noisily in two. He didn't pause but leapt in with a hard blow to the body, trying to finish the fight there and then. Ruberto dropped under the swing, landing on his back and thrusting out his feet, sweeping Taurnil's legs out from under him. Taurnil fell like a dead weight, throwing out his arms to catch himself. His eyes widened as he saw the jagged end of Ruberto's broken staff sticking up beneath him. He tried to twist out of the way as he fell, but the last thing he felt before blackness enveloped him was a brutal impact in his exposed side, as the splintered wood thrust deep into his flesh.

Chapter 21

Gaspi, Emea and Lydia all stood up, as the whole crowd gasped. Lydia shouted his name in the sudden, deathly hush, a bleak and desperate cry, and the three friends burst into a sprint across the arena. They arrived just as Trask pushed Taurnil onto his back, exposing the ragged wound under his armpit, where the broken staff had thrust deep into Taurnil's body.

"Oh God," Trask said fervently. Lydia flopped onto the ground like a rag doll, landing on her backside, legs folded around her in an unruly arrangement, staring without comprehension at the prostrate Taurnil. Jonn had run up from the winners' bench and stood behind Gaspi and Emea with a trembling hand on each of their shoulders, his breathing ragged. Gaspi stared in horror at his friend, at a wound that surely must be mortal. And then Emea stepped forward. Gaspi almost stopped her but then he saw something that held him back. Her face radiated a mixture of white hot anger and pure determination. She somehow didn't seem like the Emmy he knew. There was something else there too, something pure and frightening. Stepping up to Trask she laid a hand on his arm.

"Pull it out," she said, with a quiet certainty.

Trask stared at her uncertainly. "If I pull it out, he will bleed to death," he said.

"Will he live if you leave it in?" Emea asked.

"Probably not," Trask said.

"I want you to trust me," Emea said, holding Trask's gaze evenly for several seconds. Seeing something there that convinced him, he nodded.

"Now, pull it out!" she said. Trask turned to his task, bending down over the unconscious Taurnil, placing one hand on his flesh around the wound and curling the other around the staff.

"Now?" he asked.

"Now."

He leaned back, easing the length of wood out of the deep wound in Taurnil's body. It came out with a sucking noise, covered in blood. As soon as it was clear, Emea stepped in, kneeling beside her friend and placing her hands over the wound. Blood flowed through her fingers as she closed her eyes. Jonn's fingers were clenched tightly around Gaspi's shoulder. Lydia stared on with anguish, tears covering her cheeks and mouth.

Gaspi looked with desperate hope at Emea's cupped hands, willing her to connect to her magic. And, suddenly; there it was. Light burst into being under her palms, beaming through the gaps in her fingers. It blossomed in a moment, then grew until Gaspi could barely look at it. Instead he looked at Emea's face, a beatific mask of certainty and peace. The tingling sensation he felt when magic was being performed was so intense it resonated vibrantly out from his gut and through his whole body. Gaspi tried to look once more at the wound beneath Emea's hands, but the blazing light obscured all details, until after a few more seconds it began to dim. It waned to a glimmer, then flickered out of existence. Emea stared at her hands for a few seconds before slowly lifting them from Taurnil's body to reveal pink, unmarked flesh. Lydia sobbed loudly, collapsing completely in utter relief. Amazed by what he had seen, Gaspi reached out to Emea, who still knelt on the floor by Taurnil, a look of quiet surprise replacing the intensity of the previous few moments. She took his hand and let him lift her to her feet, allowing him to pull her into him and to hold her protectively.

Taurnil groaned and twitched, opening his eyes and blinking uncertainly. Trask and Jonn helped him to his feet. "What happened?" he asked, prodding himself under the arm where his wound had been.

"That's what happened," Trask said, pointing at the ground behind him.

Taurnil looked in surprise at the blood-soaked patch of floor. "Is that mine?" he asked, worried and confused.

"You were wounded badly, Taurnil," Trask answered. "And if this young lady hadn't intervened, you may be dead," he said, indicating Emea with his hand. Emea smiled shyly, her eyes filling with tears of relief now that the moment was over.

Trask was bowled aside by a flapping bundle of silk as Lydia pushed past the others and threw herself at Taurnil with a loud sob, flinging her arms around him and burying her head in his chest. Taurnil let out a grunt as the air was expelled from his lungs, his face a picture of bewilderment.

"Er...thanks Lydia," was all he could think to say, giving Gaspi an astonished look over the top of her head.

"You stupid, stupid boy," she said between sobs.

"There, there," Taurnil said awkwardly, patting her on the back.

"Sorry to interrupt," Trask said, "but I think it's time Taurnil goes to the hospital."

"But I feel fine," Taurnil said as Lydia reluctantly disconnected from him. "Well...a bit weak, maybe," he added, patting himself under the arm where the staff had speared him, "but there's no pain."

Trask indicated the patch of reddened floor behind him. "You've lost a lot of blood, unless this young lady replaced that while she healed you." Emmy shook her head. "And I can't have one of my guards get impaled and not be checked out by a physician. Off you go now. Jonn - will you take him?"

"Of course," Jonn said. "Come on, Taurnil."

"Just remember to come back for the melee," Trask added.

"I'll be back in time," Jonn answered.

Lydia placed a hand on Taurnil's arm. "I'll come and see you later, okay?"

"Okay...see you later," Taurnil responded, still looking bemused, and left with Jonn.

The city hospital was connected to the barracks, so Jonn didn't have to take Taurnil very far. The medics were quite accustomed to working in a city where Healer magicians lived and practiced their art, and so were initially not surprised to hear that Taurnil had been both wounded and restored to health that same day. However, when Jonn explained the extent of Taurnil's injury they became much more serious. They made him lie down while they prodded and probed and asked him lots of questions, muttering things like "quite astonishing" and "remarkable" as they worked.

While the medics fussed around him, Taurnil had some time to think. He kept remembering how fiercely Lydia had hugged him, and how she'd cried when he'd been healed. But what did that mean? He thought back over the last few weeks; the jealousy he'd felt at the circle, how they'd kept falling out after that, how inadequate he must seem around all those magicians. Nothing had really changed, and he didn't feel like making a fool out of himself again and making her uncomfortable all at the same time. She's probably just a caring person, he decided, and would have cried the same way if it was Gaspi or Emea who'd been hurt. He thought about asking Jonn what he thought, but what was the point? Injury or no injury, he still wasn't good enough for Lydia...so why drag it out?

An hour or so later Lydia walked into the room, her usual calm demeanour restored. Jonn stood up as she arrived, offering her the chair he'd been sitting on by Taurnil's bedside. "I'll head back now. Lydia, I leave Taurnil in your capable hands," he said, with a knowing smile.

Lydia took his seat as he left, arranging her skirts around her for what seemed an unnecessarily long time. Finally, she looked up. "So, how are you feeling?" she asked.

"Good," Taurnil answered, tongue-tied as always in her presence. "At least, I think so," he added lamely, trying to think of clever things to say. "So...how are you?" It was trivial and he knew it, but what was he meant to say?

Lydia seemed to warm to the question: "I'm much better thanks. I wasn't for a while back there. But now I know you're ok…"

It seemed to Taurnil she wanted him to say something. Should he ask her why she was upset? That seemed a bit too close to uncomfortable subjects. "I'm glad you're feeling better," he said at last. He must seem like a total idiot.

Lydia reddened, her eyes dropping to the floor as she began to shift uncomfortably in the chair. The seconds extended painfully, and Taurnil began to wish the ground would open up and swallow him. Without looking at him, Lydia stood up to leave, pulling her silks around her with plucking fingers. "Well, if you're okay then I should get going," she said, and turned to leave.

Suddenly, her head flicked back round, her beautiful green eyes brimming with tears, looking right into Taurnil's own. "Don't you like me at all?" she asked, somewhere between pleading and angry.

Taurnil was startled. "*Like* you?"

"You know, how a man likes a woman?" she said, definitely angry now, and looking like she was about to flee the room.

"Like you?" Taurnil said again incredulously, softness entering his voice. "I more than like you. You're the most beautiful girl I've ever met."

Lydia stood still as a statue. "The most beautiful…" she started to say. A slow smile started at the corners of her mouth, and spread across her whole face. "Well - why haven't you said so, you big idiot?" she said, planting her fists on her hips.

Taurnil stared up at her, utterly astounded. Was it really true? Could she feel the same for him? "I've felt this way from the first day I met you," he said, "but I never thought you'd feel the same about me."

"Why on earth not?" Lydia asked, still sounding angry.

"Because I'm not magical. And you're so amazing. I'm not good enough…" Taurnil trailed off.

Lydia placed a hand on his arm, leaned forward and kissed him fully on the lips. Taurnil's uncertainty diminished as the kiss lingered.

"Not good enough…" she said softly as she pulled away, sitting back down again in the chair. "Taurnil, that is for me to decide, and I say you're *more* than good enough. Besides - I'm a gypsy. We don't think that way. My mother has the Gift, but my father doesn't have a magical bone in his body. If you like someone, you like someone." She spoke with a kind of fiery certainty that Taurnil found easy to believe in. "And Taurnil, I like you. That has to be good enough."

"Oh believe me, it is," Taurnil answered, his tongue loosened by her words. "This is amazing," he said, sounding stupid in his own ears.

"Yes, I believe it is," Lydia said with a satisfied smile. "But don't keep me wondering like that again, okay?" she said, some of that fierceness returning to her voice. "If you've got something to say, just say it."

"I will," Taurnil said, nodding vigorously to convince her.

Just then, a nurse bustled into the room. "Well, young man you've had a lucky escape today. If it wasn't for that Healer, you might not be here at all."

"I know," Taurnil said, grateful all over again that Emmy had been there.

"But we can't find anything wrong with you apart from a bit of blood loss, and your body will sort that out on its own if you rest for a couple of days. So if you promise to avoid any physical activity for a few days, you are free to go."

"Thanks," Taurnil said, levering himself up out of bed. "Let's go back to watch Jonn," he said to Lydia, who smiled and took his hand.

"I'll send a note to Drillmaster Trask to keep you out of training while you recover," the nurse said.

"Yep, that's great. Thanks again," he said, and he and Lydia left the hospital and headed back to the arena.

Chapter 22

Gaspi and Emmy sat on the benches in the arena, completely ignoring the two guardsmen battling it out with maces in front of them.

"That was amazing, Emmy," Gaspi said, not for the first time since she had healed Taurnil.

"I'm more amazed than anyone else," Emmy said. "It was like it all just suddenly made sense. Taurnil was injured, and I just knew I could do it."

Gaspi remembered the blazing power and certainty that had shone in Emea's face as she'd performed the healing. It was unlike her in every way, and remembering the moment sent a shiver down his spine. It was as if an outside force had entered her in that moment, something bigger than him, than her, than all of them; something that made him feel very, very small. He was about to talk ask Emmy about it, but then thought better of it. He didn't want to say anything that might take away the confidence boost she might get out of what had just happened. There would be plenty of time later to resolve mysteries.

"Well, you picked a good time to find some confidence," he said. "I think Taurnil would have been a goner without you there."

Emea frowned, staring out at the red patch still staining the ground where Taurnil had fallen. "I can't even think about that," she said.

"No, me neither," Gaspi said, with a shudder. "So do you feel more confident about the Test now?" he asked, changing the subject.

Emea laughed. "I hadn't even thought about that, but yes. I mean, I still don't know about casting a strike...but somehow I think it will all be fine."

Gaspi leant over and kissed her, breaking into an expansive grin. "Nice one, Emmy," he said, slipping his arm around her and leaning back against the bench to watch the fighting. The two winners of the mace had been decided, and it was time for the general melee between the finalists. Gaspi noticed Jonn had made it back to the arena, sitting with Sabu on the winners' bench along with the other six combatants. Both the twins had made it through; one with the two-handed swords, and one with the mace. Ruberto had won the staff along with a tall gypsy fighter called Simeon, and the remaining two fighters were Baard, who had also won the two-handed swords, and a stocky fighter called Brant, who had won the mace along with Zaric.

Gaspi was looking at the impressive group of fighters, when the gateway to the barracks opened, and out walked Taurnil and Lydia. Gaspi did a double take when he saw they were holding hands, hardly able to believe what he was seeing. His giant lummox of a friend must have finally drummed up the courage to talk to Lydia about his feelings. Emea let out a squeal of joy when she saw them. She was practically bouncing up and down on the bench with excitement as they drew near, until she couldn't restrain herself any longer. She popped off her seat and ran over to Lydia, wrapping her in an explosive hug which Lydia returned with interest. Gaspi thought he should save Taurnil from standing there like a fool, and waved his friend over.

"So you finally managed it, then," Gaspi said mischievously, when Taurnil had sat down next to him.

"Er...yeah, I did," Taurnil said, looking at Gaspi sheepishly.

Gaspi laughed, and clapped his friend on the back. "Well done, mate!" he said. "I thought she liked you all along."

Taurnil's sheepish smile turned into a grin. "I didn't...but what do I know?"

Gaspi laughed again. "Well, it only took a near death experience to get you two together," he said.

Taurnil smacked him on the shoulder, nearly knocking him off the bench. "Shut it!" he said, with mock sternness.

"That hurt!" Gaspi said, rubbing his shoulder.

"That's right," Taurnil said, with the smallest of smiles.

They were interrupted by Trask, who had stepped out to introduce the final melee. "Ladies and gentleman, it's been an eventful afternoon, but now we have our eight finalists ready to battle it out to the finish." He paused while the crowd cheered. "Wielding the one-handed swords we have Jonn and Sabu," he continued, announcing the first of the day's winners. "Wielding the two-handed swords are Baard and Zlekic. Wielding the staff are Ruberto and Simeon, and finally wielding the mace are Zaric and Brant. Fighters - to your positions!"

The combatants stood in a circle in the centre of the arena, facing outwards towards the crowd. Trask addressed them again. "You will pace on my count. On twenty, turn around and begin. I will declare each of you out when a killing blow is landed, until only one of you remains. That last man standing will be the winner. Ready?" All the fighters lifted their weapons in assent.

"Begin pacing. One...two..." Each of the fighters walked away from the circle with strong, steady steps, as Trask counted. Gaspi found the stalking warriors impressive. Each of them carried themselves and their weapons with a kind of easy deadliness, though none looked as deadly as Sabu. The graceful, dark-skinned swordsman moved like a panther, gliding over the ground with effortless balance.

Trask's countdown came to an end: "Eighteen...nineteen...twenty. Turn around! Begin!" Gaspi noticed that Sabu and Jonn were nearest to each other, which he hoped didn't mean Jonn would have to fight the other swordsman first. The dark skinned swordsman caught Jonn's eye, and the two exchanged a quick nod and stepped towards each other. Gaspi's heart was in his throat as they drew near each other, but the two men didn't square off. Instead they joined ranks and stepped in carefully together towards the centre of the arena, looking in all directions as they moved. It looked like they were going to work together, which made more sense when he looked at the other fighters: The twins had quickly found each other and were standing back to back, one with a mace and the other wielding a huge, two handed sword. Ruberto and Simeon had also paired up, standing about ten feet apart and spinning their staffs around their bodies.

Brant turned to Baard, the only other fighter not to have paired up, and raised his mace in salute. His expectant look turned to alarm as Baard locked eyes with him. The giant man roared, raising his enormous sword over his head, and rushed in, flaming red hair and beard trailing behind him as he ran. Brant raised his shield just in time but one massive swipe of Baard's sword ripped it off his arm. A second swipe snapped Brant's weapon in two, and sent the mace head bouncing across the ground. Brant stepped back, arms spread as Baard levelled his sword for a killing blow. Trask called him out, and, giving Baard a hard look, he stamped out of the arena in a fury.

Jonn watched Baard dispatch Brant with brutal efficiency. His decision to fight alone changed the shape of the battle, and he wasn't sure who would attack who next. The decision was made for him, however, when Baard swung around, fixing his gaze on Jonn and Sabu. He raised his sword with another wild roar, and raced towards them. Sabu and Jonn exchanged the quickest of glances and separated left and right, forcing the enormous swordsman to pick one of them and leave himself exposed to the other. Baard veered towards Sabu, who waited calmly in a fighting stance, blades held out before him and knees bent, balancing on the balls of his feet. The swordsman didn't even try to catch Baard's blade, but stepped under his wild swing, trying to snag his feet out from under him as the big man ran past. But Baard was no fool, jumping over the leg sweep with surprising grace.

He turned to face Sabu again, coming in more carefully this time, swinging his blade in low, even swipes as he came. Jonn tried to manoeuvre himself behind the large swordsman but Baard would not let him, keeping one eye on each of them and slowly retreating. Suddenly, he sprang towards Jonn, cutting a ferocious arc at chest level. Jonn had to leap backwards to avoid being hit, and as he landed his ankle twisted beneath him. Jonn let out a cry of pain as he fell over his ankle, landing hard on the ground. Rather than finish him off, Baard span to meet Sabu, who had stepped in with a blistering counter attack. Baard tried to use the extra range and weight of his sword to keep the duel-wielding swordsman at bay, but Sabu was already inside his range. Using his two hander like a cudgel he thrust the pommel at Sabu's face, but Sabu ducked under the blow and brought both swords up hard into Baard's ribs. Baard let out a wounded roar. Dropping his weapon to the floor, he fell backwards onto his rump, landing with an undignified thump. Clutching massive arms over his bruised ribs, he gave Sabu a grin, and let himself fall back onto the ground.

Sabu came over to Jonn, extending a hand and helping him to rise.

"Well done," Jonn said, limping alongside the dark fighter.

"He was faster than I thought," Sabu said. While they'd been fighting Baard, the twins had taken on Simeon and Ruberto. Jonn and Sabu finished Baard off in time to see Simeon leave the arena floor with a broken staff in his hands. Ruberto had already been beaten, leaving only the four fighters left.

Jonn wasn't sure if his ankle would hold up against the heavy swings of Zlekic's two hander, but thought he could handle a mace. "I'll take Zaric," he said.

"Okay," Sabu responded, as the two pairs of fighters approached each other. Sabu lifted a sword in salute to Zlekic, and attacked, not giving him a choice between himself and Jonn. Zaric swung a testing blow at Jonn's chest. Jonn found himself weaving around Zaric's blows, taking steps only when he had to, but the mace was a heavy weapon and Zaric's best attack was to throw in broad swinging strokes and keep Jonn on the defensive. Jonn knew from drill sessions that Zaric was more comfortable with a blade than with a blunt weapon, so when Zaric swung a little too wide he switched from evasion to attack, testing his opponent's defences with a flurry of well-placed blows.

Zaric defended well at first, catching Jonn's strikes with a combination of both his shield and mace, but Jonn could feel that he was a fraction of a second quicker than his now fully defensive opponent, and increased the intensity of his attack. Zaric began to be hard-pressed, catching Jonn's attacks at the last possible second - until finally one of them got through, Jonn's sword slicing down hard on his shield arm.

Zaric dropped the shield with a yelp, his arm hanging limply at his side. Zaric's only chance now was an all-out attack, and he launched himself at Jonn, swinging his mace wildly. Jonn anticipated the move, however, and stepped out of range of the heavy weapon. As soon as its head had passed him he stepped into Zaric's space, not giving him time to bring his weapon round again for a second swing. He jabbed a sword hard into Zaric's side, and stepped back. Zaric didn't need Trask to tell him he was beaten, and, stepping back from Jonn, nodded once before turning his back and walking off.

Jonn turned to find Sabu standing alone, Zlekic already defeated and departed. The dark skinned swordsman smiled a wide smile. "It's just you and me, my friend," he said. Jonn smiled in return and lifted his weapons, dropping into a fighting stance. Sabu didn't start circling as Jonn expected, but shuffled forward, dancing lightly on the balls of his feet. Jonn suspected Sabu was trying to give him an even chance by not forcing him to circle on his bad ankle. They engaged directly, swords glancing lightly off each other in a quick exchange of blows. The blades rang brightly in the (now breathless) silence of the arena.

Sabu led the pace of the fight, his rhythmic strikes teasing Jonn into a hypnotic interplay of thrust and parry. Jonn allowed himself to be led, enjoying the testing rhythm Sabu had set for him. He constantly made minor adjustments in grip and strength, matching his style to Sabu's. Without warning, Sabu shifted a gear, throwing a burst of harder, faster strikes. They were out of kilter with the rhythm he had established, and Jonn found himself constantly on the back foot, struggling to anticipate Sabu's attacks. He was only just blocking some of them, holding them on the last few inches of his swords, and then one got through, Sabu's sword running along the edge of his blade and deflecting down across the chain mail vest covering his side, sparks trailing in its wake.

Jonn knew it wasn't a killing blow, and didn't look up to check if Trask had called him out. Even with sharpened blades his mail would have held against a blade at that angle. The strike had broken Sabu's momentum, and Jonn used the moment to gather himself. It was blindingly obvious to him that he wouldn't hold for long against Sabu's bewildering attack, and the only option left to him was to take control of the fight. Without hesitating he launched his own attack, striking hard at Sabu, whose face tightened into a mask of concentration as he was forced to step back, fending off Jonn's aggressive thrusts.

The crowd gasped appreciatively as Jonn turned the tables on the dark-skinned fighter. Jonn knew he had to push Sabu hard to have any chance of winning, so he didn't hold back any strength or effort. He struck high and low, swinging in wide and then narrowing the angle, varying the rhythm of attack and using his full strength and speed to break through his opponent's defences. Sabu stepped back steadily, ducking and weaving, parrying and riposting. He tried to force Jonn's blades wide after each attack, but was unable to create an opening for a counterattack. As he forced Sabu backwards, Jonn thought he might be able to detect a wavering in Sabu's defence; and, digging deep, he summoned up an extra reserve of strength, putting everything he could into each blow.

Sabu stepped back and Jonn stepped forward once again, using both swords to deliver a double attack. Sabu caught the blades hilt–to-hilt on his own. Pushing out and to the right, he forced all four weapons out and round over their heads in a glittering arc of steel, stepping sideways as he did. Jonn was forced to pivot as his swords came down, to avoid leaving his side exposed to an attack. He span quickly, anxious to keep up the momentum of his attack, but as his right foot landed his ankle gave way beneath him. He fell to one knee with a gasp, and, as quick as thought Sabu's sword crunched into the exposed chain mail of his vest.

"Winner: Sabu!" Trask announced, followed by the explosive roar of the crowd. Sabu helped Jonn to his feet, a look of chagrin on his face.

"I'm sorry, Jonn," he said into his ear, only just audible over the wild celebration going on all around them. "I tried to hold the blow when I saw you'd fallen, but it was too late."

Jonn smiled at the dark-skinned swordsman. "You're a gentleman, Sabu, but in all honesty you deserved to win. It's my fault I twisted my ankle. A better fighter would have avoided it."

Sabu returned the smile and grasped him hand to wrist, a grip Jonn returned. "Well fought, brother," Sabu said.

"Well fought," Jonn replied, unexpectedly moved by Sabu's declaration of kinship. He shifted the grip he had on Sabu's hand and thrust it into the air, the cheering crowd bursting into another, even louder shout. The cheering continued as they raised their weapons in salute to the other fighters, who stood and saluted in return. Trask took out a plain metal box from his jerkin, opened it, and retrieved a set of simple steel wristguards. He asked Sabu to extend his arms, wrists turned upwards, and he clamped them on onto the winner's forearms. These plain ornaments were the only trophy the winner would receive, but they were a badge of honour among the guard, and the bearer would wear them proudly until someone took them off him the next year. Sabu held his arms aloft one more time, and then as the crowd cheered he, Jonn and Trask joined their fellow fighters, and left the arena.

The four friends met with Jonn in the barracks, hugging and congratulating him on coming second. Jonn was swamped by other guardsmen wanting to talk about the fight, and so he told them to meet him in the Traveller's Rest that night. Buzzing with excitement, they walked back up to the college, reliving every moment, and even Taurnil was babbling away as they looked back on each fight. Gaspi looked at his friend with a heart full of happiness. It wasn't often Taurnil got to be the hero of the moment, but right now he was being bombarded with questions from both girls, his face seemingly fixed in a massive grin.

They met with Jonn in The Rest that evening, as planned. He was waiting for them when they arrived, having secured a large table in the front room by the windows, and they were soon tucking into a beautiful roast beef dinner. It was pink and juicy, wonderfully flavoured with a peppery sauce, and they washed it down with ale.

When he'd finished eating, Jonn leaned back with a contented sigh, arms behind his head. "Good day!" he said, with satisfaction.

"I still can't believe how awesome it all was," Gaspi agreed. No-one seemed to have grown tired of the topic, even though the tournament was all they'd talked about through dinner. "Both of you were good. The way you took out that first guy, Taurn!"

"Yeah...and then I fell on a stick and nearly died," Taurnil said, and they all laughed.

The big difference in that evening's gathering was the change in Taurnil and Lydia. They had barely been able to be in the same room for weeks, and now they sat comfortably next to each other. They weren't holding hands anymore, but Gaspi couldn't help noticing the looks they kept flicking at each other when they thought no-one was looking. Lydia had regained something of her usual dignified calm, but Gaspi could detect a faint flush in her cheeks that gave away the lie.

"I didn't know you were such a good fighter, Jonn," Emea said.

Jonn shrugged, still smiling. "I used to think I was good," he said, "but then you meet people like Sabu."

Taurnil focussed on the conversation for the first time in half an hour. "But you'd hurt your ankle," he said. "If you'd not fallen like that, maybe it'd be different."

"No, Taurn," Jonn said with certainty. "Sabu is a master. I've only fought someone as good as he is once before, back in the old days when I was a guard with Gaspi's Da." Jonn's eyes had a faraway look for a few moments as he drifted into memory, and then sharpened again as he turned his gaze to Taurnil. "No matter how hard, I try I'll never beat Sabu unless I get very lucky."

After a moment's silence Jonn clapped his hands together, looking round at all four of them with a smile. "Well, Taurnil and I have had our moment of glory. Now it's your turn," he said, looking at the three trainee magicians. They returned his look quizzically. "The Test!" he said.

"Oh yeah, right!" Gaspi said, a fluttering awakening in his stomach. He glanced at Emea, who straightened her skirt nervously. "How are you feeling about it, Emmy?"

She was quiet for a moment. "You know, I feel much better after what happened today. I still haven't got a clue how I'll do in anything except healing, and I have a feeling I wouldn't be able to repeat what I did today anyway, but I guess we'll just have to wait and see. At least I know I can do magic when it really matters." Gaspi smiled, relieved that Emmy had taken a confidence boost. It was no surprise she was feeling better really - healing Taurnil like that was pretty special.

"How about you, Lydia?" Taurnil asked.

"I feel good about it," she said. "I mean, we came here to learn magic and if I can't pass the test I shouldn't be doing it." Sometimes Lydia's poise mystified Gaspi, whose stomach was still performing little jumps. How could she not feel nervous, even if she was confident? "How about you, Gaspi?" she asked him in turn.

Gaspi thought about it for a minute. He'd noticed in the last week or so that his block must be eroding fairly quickly, as his spells had suddenly increased in potency. Out of all the class, he'd got the deepest colour out of a force shield in martial magic. If he was completely honest, he was just nervous because it was a test, but didn't actually feel afraid that he'd fail it.

"Pretty good, I guess," he admitted. "I'll be nervous on the day, of course, but I'm not worried about failing. I mean, we know all three of us can perform magic, right? And that's what the Test is for."

They talked on for a bit longer before the magicians left Taurnil and Jonn, and headed back to the college. Emea and Lydia were both worn out from what had been a massive day for both of them, so they didn't linger outside the dorms, but said a quick goodnight and went in for a well-earned night's sleep. Gaspi's head was full of thoughts as he drifted off to sleep that night. It had been an extraordinary day after all, one whose effects would probably be felt for a long time afterwards. The image of Taurnil bleeding on the arena floor was replaced by one of blinding, healing light blazing from Emmy's hands. Then Jonn was fighting again, and Lydia and Taurnil were holding hands, and everything seemed well with the world. Images and feelings melded into one as sleep drew Gaspi down into the void, and his thoughts became rambling and scattered as he let them go one by one, falling at last into peaceful oblivion.

Chapter 23

The day of the Test was one of those rainless, blustery days, where grey clouds scudded overhead, driven by restless winds, but never shed their load. Those same winds were also fickle, whipping leaves and debris into the air, throwing them this way and that, only to discard them in corners like unwanted toys. Gaspi emerged from the dorm that morning and squinted defensively to keep the airborne dust out of his eyes. The wind had a chill to it, so, wrapping his coat tightly about him, he ducked his head and pushed across the quad towards the refectory. He pulled the heavy wooden door open, resisted by a particularly violent gust of wind, and slipped through. Everyone looked up as the door banged shut forcefully behind him, and sifting through the wide eyed faces he quickly found the two he was looking for.

He filled a plate with fried egg and sausages and sat down with Emmy and Lydia. "Lovely day!" he said sarcastically, tucking into a particularly juicy looking sausage.

Emmy made a face. "Why can't it be summer all year?" she complained half-heartedly. Gaspi had been watching the leaves in what he thought of as his meditation garden slowly change colour for weeks now as summer inevitably faded into autumn, even though the weather had remained mostly mild and sunny. Emmy obviously didn't mind autumn, until it started to get cold and nasty.

"I like it," Lydia said. "It's dramatic."

Emmy stuck out her tongue. "Well, I had enough of cold in Aemon's Reach!" she said with a pout. "I like it warm."

Gaspi laughed. He couldn't help thinking this was all a diversion from what they were all really thinking about. He knew they couldn't avoid the topic forever, and decided to broach it now and get it over with. "So...how're you both feeling about...you know...the Test?"

"Oh, don't," Emmy said, putting her cutlery down on the table and pushing her food away. Lydia looked at her friend sympathetically.

"But we talked about this the other night," Gaspi said, a bit surprised by Emea's jumpiness.

."I feel okay about the things we talked about, Gasp," Emmy explained. "But the Test still makes me nervous. I can't help it. I feel like I swallowed an eel, and it won't stay still."

Gaspi kissed Emmy on the cheek, and went back to his food. There wasn't much point in saying anything, really. Emmy just got nervous about things like this, but she'd be fine. Seeing Emmy made him realise that he didn't feel all that nervous. There was some anticipation, but nothing like what Emmy was obviously feeling. If he was honest, he felt pretty confident. Most of his spells worked pretty well now, and he didn't think it was likely he'd fail the Test. He just hoped it would go better for Emmy than she feared.

They didn't have to wait long, as the bell for class rang shortly, and they headed out to the quad. They stepped out of the door into a ring of Everand's friends. Everand himself stood at their centre, a sneer twisting his otherwise handsome face into a picture of nastiness. "Going to go fail the Test, hedge wizard?" he jeered. Ferast had started that particular piece of name calling. A hedge wizard was a dabbler in magic, going from town to town offering dubious remedies and a few small spells for pennies or a meal. Ferast obviously thought he was being clever, demoting Gaspi from Nature Mage to hedge wizard. Emea pulled at Gaspi's arm, trying to tug him away from trouble, but Gaspi wasn't having any of it. He pulled free of her grip and took two long steps towards his tormentor.

Pushing his face right up to Everand's he spoke quietly and fiercely into the larger boy's shocked face. "Take this as a warning Everand," he hissed. "If you don't back off I'm going to make you regret ever starting this." Gaspi rode his boiling anger, finding deep satisfaction when Everand blanched. Gaspi forcefully held eye contact for a few seconds, then turned on his heel and stalked away, Lydia and Emea hurrying to catch up behind him.

"Why did you have to do that?" Emea said angrily as they walked. "You'll just make him worse."

"Don't start, Emmy," Gaspi said furiously. He didn't want to hear one of her lectures about being nice to that idiot.

"I think it was good," Lydia said. Both Gaspi and Emea looked at her in surprise.

"What?" Emea said, obviously taken aback.

"You have to stand up to bullies, sometimes," she said firmly. "If a gypsy acted like he did, someone would knock him out soon enough. It doesn't do any good to let a bully go on like that."

Emea looked like she'd been bitten by her favourite dog. "But...but..." she spluttered, then turned on Gaspi. "Whatever Lydia says, I don't want you to hit him –okay, Gaspi?"

"Fine," an exasperated Gaspi said. "I won't hit him, okay!"

Emea looked between him and Lydia, clearly not satisfied.

"Not unless he hits me first," Gaspi mumbled rebelliously.

"Gaspi!" Emea said angrily.

"Leave it out, you two," Lydia said firmly but calmly, gaining another double set of incredulous looks. "He probably did it to wind you up before the Test to make it harder to pass. I think we should just focus on what we've got to do."

Gaspi felt some of the tension flow from him. Lydia was right, and he could see from Emea's body language that she knew it too. "You're right," he said. "Thanks Lydia, and sorry Emmy. I don't want to argue with you."

"Me neither," Emmy said sheepishly. "It's just that I feel strongly about...well, you know."

"I know," Gaspi said, putting an arm around her. "Let's try and stay relaxed before the Test."

Emelda had given them clear instructions the previous day. Head for the tower instead of the classroom when the bell rings. Don't bring any books, or a stylus, or ink. She'd even said they needn't meditate that morning - the Test would take care of everything, including their preparation. So the three friends walked the rest of the way to the tower in silence, putting the morning's unpleasantness behind them. They were grateful for the thick, ankle-length coats they wore over their robes, as the fretful wind buffeted them mercilessly with every step.

They stepped into the tower's large atrium, thankful to be out of the wind. Gaspi took one look at the two girls, and burst out laughing. Their hair was sticking out all over the place, blown into bizarre tangles by the errant wind. Lydia gave him a withering look that told him she thought he was being childish, but when Emmy broke into a fit of giggles too the gypsy girl couldn't help but smile, as she tried and utterly failed to pat her hair back into place. The girls helped each other out while they lined up at the reception desk. The atrium wasn't too busy, however, and there was only one student in front of them - a large boy a couple of years older than them but who still wore the brown robes of a student. He was only handing in some forms, and when he walked away from the receptionist she turned her attention to them, squinting at them through bottle-thick, round-rimmed glasses.

"Can I help you?" she asked, in a reedy voice.

"We're here for the Test," Gaspi said.

"The Test, eh?" she said, peering more intently into each of their faces. "Eighth plinth; password is *testing suite*," she said briskly, jabbing her quill in the direction of the plinth with a bend of the wrist. "You can all get on at once," she finished, her attention already on something else, eyes glued to a piece of paper on her desk.

Gaspi shrugged, and led the way to the plinth. After counting to make sure he'd got the right one, they stepped on and linked arms. "Shall I say it?" Gaspi asked. Emmy looked pale as a ghost, her nerves obviously threatening to get the better of her, and she just swallowed and nodded.

"Go ahead," Lydia said calmly.

"Testing suite," Gaspi said, and they were swept up by the uncomfortable sensations of transportation. When it was over, they found themselves in the corner of a large room that was furnished entirely in deep red fabrics. Velvet drapes hung from the walls and thick carpets covered the floor. In the centre of the room there were three deep burgundy armchairs, separated from each other by a space of several feet.

"Shall we?" he asked the girls, indicating the chairs.

"I think we're meant to," Emmy said quietly, and they each took a seat.

Gentle harmonics sounded in the air, harmonics that seemed to draw him into a meditative state. The sound was underpinned by deep bass sonorities that insistently drew him inwards, more powerfully and quickly even than the musical enchantment of Emelda's classroom. It seemed clear to Gaspi that the preparation room was designed to help them enter an optimum state before facing the Test. Glancing at Emmy and Lydia, he saw that they had reached the same conclusion; they were both sitting there with their eyes closed, chests rising and falling with each deep, rhythmic breath.

Even if they weren't using the time well, he didn't think he could say anything to them anyway. Something about the enchantment of the room made him feel strangely detached from the two girls. He felt that same something pulling at him, calling him inwards. Heeding that call, he closed his eyes and let out a deep breath. Far more quickly than ever before he found himself in an altered state, the tips of his fingers and toes tingling as refreshment rushed through him in an irresistible wave.

With each breath his experience deepened, his imagination flooding with the sounds and colours of his secret place. The lake and secluded valley formed around him, cool water lapping over his bare feet, as he breathed deeply in contentment. He wanted to linger, to lie back on the shore and watch the clouds drift across the pale blue sky, but the inward call continued to tug at him irresistibly, and he released his hold even further. The imagery dissolved around him and he quickly approached and was immersed in the depths of his own spirit, a rich green swirling of colour and life, magic and sprit intermingling inseparably. Power played around his fingers, waiting to be called upon, eager to be released but no longer out of control. The partial block enabled him to contain the strength within him, taming his once-rampant magic, though if he peered intensely enough he could see depths of colour and radiance beyond his grasp – the magical potential that his eroding block still held at bay.

A noise in the room brought him briefly back to consciousness. Opening his eyes a crack, he saw the double doors had swung open, but he distinctly felt he was not to rise from the chair. To his right, Lydia stood to her feet and walked through the doors, which swung soundlessly shut behind her. Gaspi re-entered his trance, content to do nothing but bask in the presence of his power, and it didn't seem like long before the door opened again. Once again he felt to stay where he was, and Emea stood up and walked through the door. It could have been five or thirty minutes later when the door opened a third time; this time he felt the deep trance state lift a little, and he knew it was time.

Standing up, he gathered his thoughts and walked through the door into the next chamber, a small room whose walls glowed the same deep burgundy as the chair he had just been sitting in. The doors shut behind him, and he stood facing another door on the opposite side of the room. Between him and the door was an opalescent barrier, swirling gently with pale light. Instinctively, he knew what this was; it was a form of force shield, and he was required to send his power into it. He could only assume that if he did well enough the barrier would disappear, letting him move on. He briefly wondered how Emmy had coped with this, given her struggles with this type of magic; but, realising there was nothing he could do to help her now, he pushed his concern aside.

He held out his hand and let power flow into it, forming a pearly ball of force that span in his palm. He sent all the power he could into it, knowing his block would keep him safe from losing control, and it swelled responsively in his hand until it was over half the size of the leather ball the boys kicked around the courtyard at break-time. He lifted his hand, aware that the block must have eroded a little further once again, as the ball of power resting against his palm was larger and more potent than any he had conjured before. When he was sure it would get no bigger, he flicked his wrist purposefully, sending it hurtling towards the barrier. When the force strike hit the barrier it resonated sonorously, like a gong being hit with a padded hammer. Deep red light lanced out from the point of impact, spreading all the way to the walls of the room, and the barrier dissolved into nothingness in an instant. Smiling, Gaspi walked forward to the single door at the other end of the room - which swung open silently, as he expected it to do - and stepped through.

Gaspi didn't have time to register the details of the next room, as it was not lit in any way, and the dim red glow flowing from the previous room was cut off the moment he crossed the threshold. He was plunged into blackness. It wasn't the kind of dark you experience at night, where the light from the moon and stars give everything a silvery sheen, but it was the absolute absence of light. Gaspi felt a surge of panic nipping at the edges of the calm state he'd been in up to that moment. Holding his hand up in front of his face, he opened his eyes as wide as possible, but it was no good. He couldn't even see the outline of his hand.

Forcing himself to breathe deeply, he thought about his options, quickly settling on the simplest solution. Just as Emelda had showed them in their first lesson, he conjured a light. It wasn't like the force strike, surging with power and intention, but was a benign glowing sphere that took very little power. The globe formed quickly, a pale green sphere that pulsated gently, revealing a single narrow pathway snaking through a long wide room. The path twisted and turned unpredictably, winding its way across the room to the other side, and on either side of it there was a drop. Gaspi peered down into the drop, trying to see how deep it was, but it was impenetrably black, just as the whole room had been before he had summoned the globe light. Instinctively, he knew that non-magical lanterns would not work in this place, and that without the light of his globe he wouldn't be able to navigate the narrow and tricky path across the room. He also thought that it would be a bad idea to fall into the inky black drop.

Holding his hand before him, he took a small step onto the path. The surface of the path glimmered faintly in the light of his globe, tiny sparkling facets of light glinting from deep within it. It looked slick and polished, and curved away into nothingness on either side, so that it appeared to have no clear edge. Sticking to the very centre of the path, which was never more than two feet wide and sometimes as narrow as one, he edged his way carefully round the room, following the sinuous curves of the pathway. Halfway round the room he began to grow confident, stepping a little faster than he had previously, when suddenly his foot slipped. Letting out a panicked yelp, he let his concentration falter and the globe light blinked out, plunging Gaspi into blackness.

Wobbling from the slip, Gaspi's arms pin-wheeled desperately in an attempt to regain balance - but in the blackness he was unable to keep his centre of gravity, and he fell backwards. He threw his arms out desperately to try and land flat on the path, and grunted in relief when he slammed into the floor without slipping off into the blackness. Breathing heavily, he let his head fall against the ground. How could he have been such an idiot?

After a moment he gathered himself and held out his hand, channelling magic into it again to form another light. For a moment it wouldn't work, and he felt the sharp edge of panic. Pushing the panic aside, he deliberately steadied his breathing, allowing his focus to reform, and the light popped into existence; flickering at first, and then growing stronger, its light revealing his position in the centre of the snaking path. Pushing himself to his knees, and then to his feet, he made sure he kept his concentration on the light. Slowly and steadily he took small, certain steps around the remaining curve of the path. It was with some relief that he finally stepped off onto the platform at the other end of the room, and the next door swung open before him. When he stepped through the door, it was with less of the confidence he'd felt earlier.

The next room was a glimmering white, and it took Gaspi's eyes a few moments to adjust. It was perfectly circular with three small, square tables standing at waist height at equidistant points along the wall. There were two things about the room that Gaspi found surprising. One was that directly in front of him against the wall was a transporter plinth, and the other was that he was not alone. Sitting in an upright white armchair was Hephistole, smiling benignly as Gaspi gave an involuntary start of surprise.

"You weren't expecting to see me, then?" Hephistole said, stating the obvious.

"Er...no," Gaspi said, feeling thrown off his stride by the Chancellor's presence, but deciding to take advantage of his being there. "Hephistole, I fell in the last room and my light went out. Does that mean I've failed?" he blurted anxiously.

"Now stay calm, young Mage," the Chancellor said calmly, but without giving any obvious reassurance. "We will talk about your performance after the Test is complete." Gaspi opened his mouth to ask a question.

"Now, Gaspi, you need to keep your focus; so take a breath and relax, and I'll tell you what is expected of you in this third and final part of the Test." Gaspi wilfully took a deep breath, and tried to let go of his worry about what had passed. It wouldn't do him much good to get so wound up about the second Test that he failed the third.

"Much better," Hephistole said. "Now you've already been through the Test of Power and the Test of Control and this," he said, gesturing expansively around the room, "is the Test of Precision. Are you paying attention?" Gaspi said he was.

"Well, it's simple enough," Hephistole continued. "On the first table is a magical tool - a device used to draw and collect energy from deep in the ground. The tool is broken, and has been separated into three parts. Only one of those three parts is non-functional, and it is your first task to identify which piece that is. You are not to touch it, and have to use your magical senses alone. When you think you know which part is broken, just say your answer out loud, and move on to the second table. Is that clear?" Gaspi indicated that it was.

"The second table is perforated with hundreds of holes, each of which emits a tiny flame," the Chancellor continued. Pausing for a moment, he gesticulated towards the second table and neat rows of miniscule flames rippled into being, standing to attention like tiny soldiers. "Of all the hundreds of flames, a single one will not be orange, but will in fact burn green," Hephistole said, carrying on with his explanation. "Your task is to use your power to snuff out that single flame without extinguishing any of the others. You can keep trying this until you feel you've done as well as you can, and then simply say out loud that you wish to move on to the third. Do you understand?"

"I think so," Gaspi answered, "but how do I use my magic to put out the flame?"

"I'm sure you'll think of something," Hephistole said, expressionlessly. He obviously wasn't going to give anything away. He closed his hand with a flourish, and the flames went out.

"Now, on to the third table," he continued prescriptively. "You'll find an injured bird lying on its surface, currently held in magical sleep. Your task is similar to that of the first table. Simply use your power to identify the injury, announce it out loud; and when you are done, step on the transporter, and you will be automatically taken away. Is everything clear?"

Gaspi looked back at the transporter. "Yes, but where does it..." Gaspi trailed off. The Chancellor and his armchair had disappeared in the few heartbeats it had taken to look at the plinth.

"Blooming heck," Gaspi muttered under his breath. All the mystique was just making him more nervous. He took a deep breath and tried to push all thought from his mind. The first and the second parts of the Test were gone now, beyond his reach. He knew what he had to do, and all that mattered was what was happening right now, here in this room.

Managing to re-establish a semblance of genuine calm, Gaspi moved to the first table. He didn't recognise the device lying on it. It was inelegant and clunky, made of some kind of dark metal, and - as Hephistole had said - it was currently split into three pieces, though Gaspi could see how the pieces all fitted into each other. Gaspi didn't delay, but summoned his power, delicately forming it into a kind of probe, running it through and over each part of the broken device. After the first pass, Gaspi was already sure he had the answer. Both the first and second parts of the tool gave off what he could only think of as a magical hum. There was something alive about them, but the third piece didn't have that kind of feeling at all. It just felt…dead. He checked a couple more times in case he was making a stupid error, but quickly confirmed that he'd been right the first time.

"The third part of the tool is broken," Gaspi announced clearly. When he received no response, he figured he'd done what Hephistole had asked, and moved on. Gaspi stood looking down at the second table, eyeing the hundreds of evenly spaced holes spread across its smooth surface. Gaspi was unsure if he needed to do something to activate the device, and nearly jumped in the air when hundreds of flames all burst into being under his nose. So much for staying calm! The rows of flame burned uniformly orange, but then with a strange sputtering noise one tiny flame towards the back of the board flickered and turned a wicked green colour. Gaspi wondered how he was going to snuff it out. If it was a normal flame he'd pinch it between his thumb and forefinger. Unable to think of anything more precise, Gaspi summoned a small amount of power, forcing it into a shape like a miniature thumb and finger. It hovered invisibly in front of him, more a focussing of power than an actual device.

Feeling nervous, Gaspi moved it carefully out over the board until it hovered over the single green flame. He lowered it over the flame and tried to quench it, but at the last minute he snatched at the flame, his carefully shaped magical pincher turning into more of a grasping fist. The flame went out, but so did about twenty of its orange neighbours. Wincing, Gaspi guessed this had not been a successful attempt. Kicking himself, he reformed his delicate magical tool, and waited for the flames to reset themselves.

Seconds later, the tiny flames had all re-emerged from their holes, and this time the green one appeared at the front of the board to his right. Taking a deliberate breath, he moved his pincher slowly over the flame and began to lower it. When his magical pincher was level with the board, he squeezed. The green flame went out again, and this time only took seven others with it.

"Better," Gaspi murmured to himself, but he still felt that more precision would be needed to pass the test. He focussed on his tool, making it tinier, flaring the ends to make them just the right shape to cut off the flame at the base. The next green flame appeared right in front of him, and without pausing he guided his tool to the spot. Making it as small as he possibly could, he lowered it over the flame and carefully closed the magical finger and thumb over it. The flame went out, and to Gaspi's pleasure only two other flames around it went out too. He tried it five more times, but he couldn't improve on his third attempt. He wasn't quite sure if it was enough, but it didn't look like it was going to get any better. He decided enough was enough, and announced he was moving onto the third table.

As Hephistole had said, a small bird lay on the table. It lay unmoving, held in a magical sleep, and Gaspi couldn't see any obvious clues about the kind of injury it had. Compared to most of the students, and especially Emea, Gaspi was practically inept at healing. He wasn't even very good at probing wounds with his power, and so didn't feel particularly confident when confronted with the injured bird. Nevertheless, he had to have a go.

He formed and sent out a probe, trying to treat the bird like the magical tool on the first table, looking for something that stood out. Gaspi searched through the bird's small body, trying to sense any breaks in the bone structure. This proved difficult as he didn't really know what it should look like, so he ended up just looking for something broken. He couldn't see wounds from the inside like Emea did, so if it was an internal flesh wound he had no chance, and he just had to hope it was a broken bone. He was just starting to get desperate when he felt something half way along the right wing where the wing had a joint. He compared it against the other wing and could swear that the right wing joint was bigger than the left. It seemed like it was swollen, and given the length of time he'd already spent on this part of the task, Gaspi was pretty sure he wasn't going to find anything else.

Hoping that he'd somehow managed to luck out and get the third table right, he announced his findings more confidently than he actually felt. "It's the right wing, around the joint."

When silence greeted his announcement, Gaspi walked over to the transporter. Before he stepped on, he ran his mind back through the Test. The Test of Power had been fine, but he'd fallen in the second test and had to re-summon his globe. In the third he hadn't managed to single out the green flame, and who knows whether he'd got the injury right. He realised in that moment that he'd always had a kind of confidence - or maybe even arrogance - about the Test. He was a Nature Mage after all, and secretly he'd assumed he'd blast through it, but now he wasn't sure he'd even passed two out of the three parts of it. He'd always thought it would be Emmy that would struggle. She might have a bit of trouble with the Test of Power, but there's no reason she'd struggle with the Test of Control, and she'd probably be amazing at the Test of Precision. Maybe she would pass and he would fail! Well, there was no point putting it off any longer, Gaspi mused to himself. Stomach clenched with anxiety, he stepped forward onto the plinth.

Chapter 24

When Gaspi's senses returned to him, he found himself standing in Hephistole's office. The Chancellor was already seated in one of two comfortable chairs, pouring out two cups of steaming tea. Seeing Gaspi, he placed the teapot down on a small, delicately carved side table.

"Gaspi, come on over," he said in a neutral tone, beckoning the young Mage towards the other chair. Gaspi walked over obediently and took a seat, his heart thumping in his throat. He tried to read Hephistole's expression, but the Chancellor was giving nothing away.

Hephistole pushed a cup and saucer across the table. "Have some tea," he said, holding Gaspi's gaze thoughtfully for a few seconds. Gaspi picked the cup up, but didn't take a sip. "So...how do you think you did?" Hephistole asked seriously, peering at Gaspi intently as he waited for an answer.

"I'm not sure," Gaspi answered honestly. "I think I did the Test of Power okay, but, like I said before, I fell down in the Test of Control and let my globe go out." He looked at Hephistole for reassurance, but his expression was unreadable. "And then in the Test of Precision, I don't have a clue how well I did."

"Mmm," Hephistole said, leaning back in his chair and stroking his chin. "Yes, the Test of Precision is hard to master," he said, leaving another pause.

Gaspi was trying to be patient, but his need to know got the better of him. "Hephistole, please just tell me. Did I pass?" he blurted, flushing bright red in the face.

Hephistole leaned forward slightly, peering over his steepled hands. "Did you pass? Let me see..." His serious expression was suddenly transformed as a twinkle fired in his penetrating eyes. The corners of his mouth were pulled upwards in a broad grin. "Of course you passed!" he said, throwing his head back with a hearty laugh.

Gaspi sat back with a massive sigh of relief, all of the tension flooding from his body at once. "Why not just say?" he asked weakly, passing a hand over his forehead.

"Ah well, we mustn't make things too easy for you, eh? And this way you'll appreciate passing all the more, having spent several minutes fearing you wouldn't!" Hephistole answered, still grinning almost maniacally. Gaspi wasn't sure he agreed with the Chancellor, but decided it was best to hold his peace. Hephistole thrust out a long-fingered hand, and shook Gaspi's hand vigorously. "Well done, young Mage! Well done!"

"Thanks," Gaspi said, a smile creeping over his face as relief gave way to joy. "How did the others do?" he asked, his thoughts turning immediately to Emmy.

"They have also passed," Hephistole said, still smiling. Gaspi experienced another surge of relief on hearing that Emmy was through as well. "But let's talk about how you did," Hephistole continued. "What do you think you did well?"

Gaspi thought for a second. "I think I did well at the Test of Power," he said, remembering how the force shield had dissolved so easily.

"Yes, you did," Hephistole agreed. "I'd say you blasted through it, wouldn't you? Your block must be eroding nicely, or you couldn't have summoned nearly so much power." Gaspi was a little embarrassed by the praise but couldn't help feeling elated at the effectiveness of his force strike. "I might have to go and check it's still working properly!" Hephistole said conspiratorially to a grinning Gaspi. "So, how about the Test of Control?"

"It started well," Gaspi answered. "I kept calm when it went dark, and thought of globe light pretty quickly, but I think I was a bit cocky after the force shield and tried to go too fast. And that's when I lost control and fell down."

"Yes, you did," Hephistole said, the corners of his lips twitching before he brought them back under control. "And do you think that means you failed that part of the Test?"

"I really don't know," Gaspi answered. "I mean, I didn't fall off the path did I? And I managed to summon another light and keep going. Actually, what would have happened if I'd fallen off the path?" he asked.

"Well asked," Hephistole said enthusiastically. "Curiosity is always a good thing. If you'd fallen off the path you would simply have reappeared at the beginning of it. You don't think we'd actually allow you to be in any danger during the Test, do you?"

Gaspi laughed out loud. "No, I suppose you wouldn't," he said. "I really should have figured that out, but for some reason I was desperate not to fall off."

"Yes...we may have lent some apprehension about the depths surrounding the path to the fabric of the room," Hephistole explained, "and the power of suggestion would make you want to stay on the path anyway - so you were only reacting naturally. As for passing that part of the Test, all you have to do is make it to the end, even if you fell in and had to start from the beginning. So yes, you passed that part too. And finally...the Test of Precision," Hephistole said. "How do you rate your performance there?"

Gaspi sat quietly for a moment. "Not so good," he answered. Hephistole waited for him to continue. "The first table was probably ok," he said. "Did I get the right part of the tool?"

"Yes, you did," Hephistole answered. "How did you work it out?"

"Well, I could feel a kind of energy flowing through the other parts, but the last bit felt kind of dead," Gaspi answered.

"That's a good way of putting it," Hephistole said thoughtfully. "It shows you are sensitive to magical energy, which can only be a good thing. What about the fire table?"

"I'm not so sure about that," Gaspi answered. "I tried to shape my magic into a form where I could squeeze the green flame out, like it was my thumb and finger, but I never managed to put it out without hitting some others. I think the best I did was to get the green one and two more along with it."

Hephistole rubbed his chin with his hand. "There are lots of ways to put out the flame, but your solution is not inelegant," he said. He paused for a moment before continuing. "You are right that you could have done better. Emea, for instance, singled the green flame out on the first try - but you were far from terrible." Gaspi looked a bit crestfallen. "Now, come on Gaspi!" Hephistole said cheerfully. "You can't be good at everything, and precision can be improved over time."

Gaspi smiled wryly at his own pride. "Fair enough," he said. He didn't wait for Hephistole to ask him about the third table. "I don't have a clue how I did with the bird. Did I get it right?"

Hephistole grinned at him. "Not even close!" he said emphatically, letting out that single bark of a laugh that always made Gaspi jump.

"Oh!" Gaspi said, a bit discouraged.

"No, no, we'll have none of that!" Hephistole said brightly, his good cheer seemingly unquenchable. "The bird had a broken ribcage. But you did well enough on the first two tables to just about pass the Test of Precision. And even if you'd failed it, we'd consider how well you did on the other tests and how much potential you have before making any decisions. The Test is designed not only to query your basic magical ability but to reveal strengths and weaknesses. And yours are obvious. You have a lot of power, which is only going to get stronger as your block erodes. Your concentration is decent but could be strengthened, and in terms of precision you are fine with magical energy, but not so sensitive to living matter. You could also learn a bit more finesse; but all of that will come with time."

Gaspi still wasn't sure whether to feel encouraged or discouraged, and Hephistole must have read it in his expression. He leaned in closer, his animated, enigmatic face grabbing every last bit of Gaspi's attention. "Gaspi, my boy," he said in an engaging whisper, "you are going to be a great magician. You have tremendous ability and determination, and you have good friends to learn with, whose strengths and weaknesses differ from your own, so you will be good for each other. You've done very well today, Gaspi. Take it from an old hand like me. When you hit that force shield, I'm sure my hair stood on end!" Hephistole held Gaspi's gaze with a beady eye for a few seconds, and sat back in his chair with a satisfied sigh. "Well done, young Mage! Now - go and celebrate with your friends!"

Gaspi felt much better, gratified by Hephistole's sincerity. "Thanks, Heppy," he said, feeling pleased with himself on the whole. He couldn't wait to see Emmy, and almost bounced out of the chair. "This way?" he asked, indicating the plinth.

"That'll be fine. Cheerio then," Hephistole answered, pouring himself another cup of tea as Gaspi stepped onto the transporter and disappeared.

Gaspi found Emmy and Lydia in the refectory, talking animatedly over a cup of hot cocoa. When she saw Gaspi, Emea sprang up from the bench and hurried over to him. She gripped his arm insistently. "Did you pass?" she asked.

Instinctively, Gaspi decided to play a little of the game Hephistole had played with him. "The thing is, Emmy," he said after a few seconds of dramatic pause. He rubbed the back of his head with his hand, staring down at the floor. "The thing is…" he started again, still staring at the floor. He glanced up and saw Emmy's face cloud with worry, and couldn't keep the game up any longer. "The thing is that I passed!" he said, a broad grin splitting his face from ear to ear.

"Gaspi!" Emea said indignantly. "That's not nice!" Then she was hugging him tightly. "That means all three of us are through!" she said happily, pulling back to kiss him on the cheek.

He grinned back at her. "Yes it does! Come on, let's join Lydia," he said. The three friends sat at the table, exchanging stories for the better part of the next two hours.

Lydia had performed solidly in all three tests, but Emea's experience had even more ups and downs than Gaspi's. She had to try three times to summon a strong enough force strike to break through the shield. In the Test of Control she'd lost her concentration just as Gaspi had, but in the darkness had actually fallen off the path, only to find herself back at the start. At that point she'd really thought she'd failed, but she'd summoned another globe and got through to the final room. Hephistole had told her that in the Test of Precision she'd excelled way beyond the ordinary. She'd identified the broken part of the tool in seconds, put out every green flame on the fire table without extinguishing any others, and identified and healed the injury at the same time at table three. They'd had to replace Emea's newly healthy cat with the bird before Gaspi reached the third room.

Gaspi laughed out loud at that part. "Heppy said we had different strengths and would be good for each other. Sounds about right to me. I was pretty hopeless in the Test of Precision," he said wryly, pulling a face.

"I'm not sure how I fit into that," Lydia said quietly. They both looked at her in surprise. "My strengths are only strengths one of you already has," she continued. If Gaspi didn't know better, he would have sworn Lydia was being a little insecure. Was that a flush he could detect in her cheeks?

"That's not true," Emea answered quickly. "I bet your light didn't waver for a second in the Test of Control."

"Well...no, it didn't," Lydia answered honestly. "It was obvious, really. I mean, that falling off the path wouldn't harm you. I just walked slowly, and made it round."

Emea laughed. "Exactly! You're good at pretty much everything, but your real strength is the way you see things. You're so level-headed and...what's that term...self-possessed. You know who you are and what you're doing. Gaspi and I can both be a bit...unreliable."

Lydia looked at them both for a moment before answering. "Yeah, I suppose you're right. A couple of flakes like you need someone reliable like me around to keep you grounded," she said, smiling wickedly.

Emea reached over and tugged on a lock of Lydia's hair. "Flake!" she said, with false indignation. "That's a fine thing to call your friends." Lydia's smile broadened.

"So, let me see if I got this right," Gaspi said. "Emea's inconsistent, I'm clumsy, and you're boringly good at everything. Glad we got that sorted out." All three of them laughed.

They shared their good news with Taurnil and Jonn that evening over an ale in the Rest. Sitting there, looking around at his companions, Gaspi couldn't help feeling a warmth that had nothing to do with the beer suffusing him; spreading out in radiating waves from his belly right out to the tips of his fingers and toes and the crown of his head. Taurnil was fast becoming a great fighter, and had found something special with Lydia. Emea and he were sharing an amazing journey into magic, and she had a gift so incredible it amazed him. Jonn was clearly happy as a guard, and had done well in the tournament. It was as if destiny had picked them up by the scruff of the neck and dumped them down somewhere far better than they could ever have hoped. There had been times on the journey with robbers and magical attacks, or even more recent times like when Taurnil was mortally injured, when it looked like things had gone horribly wrong; but right there, right at that point, it looked like everything was going to work out all right.

Chapter 25

After the Test, time seemed to speed up for the three trainee magicians. The weeks and even months fled by as they explored their expanding skills, and discovered whole realms of new knowledge. Emea had taken a liking to enchanting, and seemed to be trying to put a little bit of magic into every ordinary thing she got her hands on. Gaspi was woken up one morning by a gently fluttering butterfly made entirely of paper resting on his nose. It lifted off as he awoke, hovered over him for a second and then fell apart as the enchantment lifted, leaving three pieces of paper on his chest that said separately *I, Love,* and *You.*

Lydia was thoroughly enjoying her tutorials with Professor Worrick. Prophecy wasn't something you could make happen just because you happened to be studying it, so they filled most of their time exploring the broad array of magical disciplines the professor knew about and was willing to teach. Lydia had embraced the idea that she was "good at pretty much everything," and was keen to learn everything she could. Her passion for magical learning rivalled Taurnil's for martial skill and, aided by Professor Worrick's own scholarly curiosity, she was fast becoming the most knowledgeable student in their class.

Gaspi was encouraged by every little increment in power as his block continued to erode. His spells were becoming increasingly effective, and in class he was beginning to outshine even the more powerful students, at least when it came to sheer strength. Like Emea he'd taken to enchanting, but he was more interested in creating useful objects than paper butterflies. In the last week he'd made a pair of glasses that let him see in the dark, and a compass that pointed to wherever Emmy was instead of north.

He'd also discovered a love of all things botanical. Hephistole had told him that the plants from his meditation garden had been transported from Boranavia, a far flung land, part of a distant continent that was the homeland of one of the many long-term residents of the sprawling campus. The Mage in question, an expert in neuromancy, loved the foliage of his homeland so much he'd had some examples shipped here, and used his magic to sustain and nurture the garden he'd planted. Gaspi discovered in the course of his studies that many plants had natural properties that were useful for magical purposes, and that some plants, if magically enhanced, could become something very special indeed.

It was his love of meditation that drew him to botany. Hephistole's teas were grown and harvested in a large greenhouse in the campus, and having visited there several times, and seeing the steamy rows of foreign plants growing under the expansive glass roof, Gaspi was fast becoming fascinated by both the possibilities and the process of magical botany.

Conversely, his mentoring sessions with Voltan had not turned out to be as exciting as he hoped. Voltan was a warrior at heart, and although this branch of magic interested Gaspi, he found himself more passionate about enchanting and with growing things than with all things martial. Their mentoring sessions often entailed lengthy examinations of tactics from great magical battles of the past, and Gaspi struggled to find this very interesting. He just wanted to do things with his magic, not theorise endlessly. Voltan wouldn't teach him any martial skills out of fairness to the other students, as he said it was going to come up in class, and so his sessions with the naturally serious Voltan had not turned out to be his favourite part of the week.

Autumn inevitably turned into winter, but not as the Aemon's Reachers knew it. There were no heavy snows and no icy ponds. An occasional dusting of light snow feathered the ground in the morning - but it was always gone by midday - and on the days when the sun shone uninhibited in the watery blue skies, the shafts of winter sunlight were still strong enough to beam through the tall classroom windows, warming the necks of drowsy students, and sending them to sleep. The rare glimpses of snow made Gaspi miss the mountains. He longed for a good game of Koshta. There were a few ponds in the campus that were big enough to hold a match on, but midwinter came and went and the water still hadn't frozen over. Disappointed, Gaspi had to make do with football, which was never interrupted by something as inconsequential as weather.

"Gaspi!" Owein yelled as he sent the football soaring over the head of an opposing player, right down into Gaspi's path as he sprinted towards goal. Gaspi could see the leather ball turning in its flight, spinning over and over as he leapt up and forwards, trying to smack it hard with his forehead. He'd learned from previous attempts that you had to get it just right or it really hurt, so he put his full effort into it, stretching out as far as he could to make a good contact. As the ball neared his face he drew his head back and thrust it forwards. The ball made contact with a loud slap, but even though he hit it pretty squarely Gaspi could feel it sliding off the centre of his forehead, angling off to the right. It bounced once, heading to the right hand side of the makeshift goal. The goalkeeper leapt towards the ball, stretching his whole body out in a desperate attempt to reach it, but he landed short with a thump, sending clouds of dust flying into the air around him.

Gaspi landed from his leap, hungrily eyeing the ball as it rolled forwards; but to his disappointment it was just a little too far to the right, and bounced over the pile of coats marking the edge of the goal. The cheers of his team mates fell into a collective groan as they saw the ball miss.

Gaspi jogged back to the centre of the courtyard, past a smug Everand who called after him "Better luck next time, hedge wizard." Gaspi bridled at the insult, reminded once more that it was the weasely Ferast who'd invented that particular piece of nastiness. He tried to push his annoyance aside, and was determined not to let it show. There would be a time and a place to show Ferast up for what he was.

The hardest thing about it was that Emmy shared private classes with him and Emelda, as they both had a primary healing gift, and Emmy insisted on seeing the best in him. Normally that was one of the things Gaspi liked best about Emmy, but in this case it was driving him mad. He increasingly suspected that Ferast was the driving force behind Everand's bullying behaviour. He was always whispering in his ear and throwing little manipulative suggestions into every conversation. He was a snake in the grass, but every time he mentioned it to Emmy she got annoyed and said he was just misunderstood, and was hiding behind a more popular boy. As far as Gaspi was concerned, Ferast had pulled the wool right over her eyes; but trying to remove it only made Gaspi look bad.

That didn't mean he had any more liking for Everand, who continued to taunt him at every opportunity, though after Gaspi had threatened him on the day of the Test he always made sure he had plenty of friends with him when baiting him. Gaspi was struggling to contain his anger at Everand. He wasn't by nature a violent person, but years of bullying had worn away any tolerance he may once have had for such things, and his emotions rose right to the surface every time he was mistreated. He had grown physically over the last half year, and with his magic to back him up he didn't feel like running away anymore like he used to do with Jakko. It had been over three months since the Test and Gaspi's block had thinned to the point where he wasn't sure how much more there was to go before he was able to use his full power. Right now, he was itching for a confrontation.

Gaspi stopped and walked up to Everand, holding his gaze without flinching. "Want to try saying that without your friends around Everand?" Gaspi asked quietly, so only the large boy could hear. That said, he held the bully's gaze for a few more seconds, then turned away and carried on jogging back towards the middle of the pitch.

"Yeah...keep running!" Everand said bravely. Gaspi considered making something of it there and then, but saw Emea and Lydia watching from the sidelines, and swallowed his pride. Everand would have to wait, but not for long.

Emea opened her eyes and took her hands off the now-sleeping deer's side, a beatific smile lighting her pretty face.

"Very good, Emea," Emelda said quietly, almost reverently. In the months she'd spent learning from Emelda, Emea had come to understand just how much her mentor loved healing. It was some sort of spiritual experience for her, and every time they saved a life she was transfigured for a short while, filled with a quiet joy. At those times Emea could see the beautiful woman she must once have been, before ill-health and weight masked her femininity. It was an irony that someone so generous and gifted in healing found it impossible to receive the same for herself. She had hinted at this difficulty once or twice, but Emmy didn't feel comfortable enough to ask her about it directly, in case she was being invasive.

Emelda's eyes flicked to her other pupil. "Were you watching that, Ferast?" she asked. Ferast's gaze had been glued to Emea's face, but at Emelda's question he quickly looked back to the animal in front of them, a slight flush of embarrassment - or anger - colouring his pale visage.

None of that showed in his voice, however, which was controlled and unctuous. "Yes, of course. That was impressive to watch, Emea." Emea smiled warmly at him. Ferast was a more than capable Healer and was particularly precise with his magical interventions, though he lacked some of Emea's instinctive talent for the discipline.

"Yes, it *was* impressive," Emelda said thoughtfully, "though for me the word *wonderful* feels more appropriate." She looked at both her pupils. "It will be your turn in a moment, Ferast. But first, let me ask; how did you find that, Emea?"

Emea's brow furrowed as she thought. "It was easy enough," she said, "but I still have to think really hard and control the flow of magic carefully. Whatever I do, it's never like it was in the arena when Taurnil was hurt. That was just...effortless."

"Well, Emmy, I've said it before, but I'll say it again," Emelda said. "That was verging on a miracle, and you'd be best to lower your expectations for now. You'd barely had any training, and most Healers would never be able to attempt such a grievous wound even after years of practice. But you have a profound gift, and you feel deeply, and somehow your care for your friend enabled you to tap into that gift more deeply than you should have been able to. It was simply amazing,

207

Emea." Emea let her memory drift back to that event, amazed once again by the way she had been caught up in the moment. It was as if some agency had taken charge and used her gift for her.

"But you can't rely on that," Emelda continued. "What if you have to heal someone you don't love as much, or if it simply doesn't all fall into place next time? No - you need to practice, like everybody else."

Emea nodded. "I know what you mean. I'm not sure I'll ever understand what happened that day, but I'm glad it did."

Emelda smiled. "Okay, Ferast," she said. "I'm going to go see what other creatures we have in need of your help. I'll be back shortly. Can you two entertain yourselves?" They both nodded, and Emelda left the room.

Ferast scraped his chair round so he was facing Emea. "That was beautiful to watch," he said, leaning forward intently as he sought her attention.

"Oh, thank you," Emea said, with a slight flush of embarrassment.

"You have a special touch," Ferast continued, seemingly unaware of the discomfort he was causing her. "The way you wove the flesh back together..." he said, sliding his fingers between each other in demonstration, his eyes never leaving Emea's face.

"Oh, it's nothing," Emea said, her flush deepening. "I've seen you do the same thing many times. You're a very good Healer, Ferast," she insisted, caught between discomfort and the desire to affirm this strange and lonely boy.

Ferast sat up a little straighter, flicking the greasy flop of hair from his eyes with a toss of his head. "I know I am," he said. "But you're the only one who can understand."

"Because I'm a Healer?" Emea asked uncertainly, not feeling entirely comfortable, but not entirely sure why.

"Yes, that's it," Ferast said after a pause, his attention back on Emea after his brief moment of preening. "You know, I've often thought we should spend more time together," he continued. "So we can practice, I mean," he added smoothly.

"Erm...yes, maybe," she answered noncommittally, not wanting to either offend Ferast or commit to anything. "I get quite busy though," she added, knowing instinctively she shouldn't just leave it hanging. "I have my other studies – and, of course, there's Lydia and Gaspi." Ferast made a barely audible sound of displeasure. "What is it, Ferast?" Emea asked. "Do you have a problem with Gaspi?"

Ferast turned his head away slightly, his eyes narrowing as he looked out through the window. He continued to look away while speaking: "I don't want to speak out of turn, but Gaspi is always looking at me as though he hates me," he said, swinging back round to face Emea. "As if he'd like to hurt me."

"Gaspi doesn't hate you!" Emea insisted, but without absolute conviction, as she knew that at the very least Gaspi really did dislike Ferast. "I certainly don't think he wants to hurt you," she continued, much more sure of herself this time. Gaspi felt strongly about things, but he wasn't violent. "I know he and Everand sometimes clash, but they are both physical boys and they get competitive," she said, trying to justify the one aspect of Gaspi's behaviour she didn't like.

"Rand feels the same way as I do about Gaspi," Ferast said.

"That's not really fair," Emea said in Gaspi's defence. "Everand usually starts it, and tries to wind Gaspi up. I can't say I like it though," she said, more quietly. "Why do boys have to fight?" she asked with a sigh. She returned her attention to Ferast. "But there's nothing to worry about, Ferast. You don't treat Gaspi like Everand does, and I'm sure he'd never do anything to you."

Before Ferast had a chance to respond they were interrupted by the door swinging open and Emelda returning, preceded by a levitated fox, dried blood matting its rich red fur.

"Okay Ferast," she said briskly. "Your turn."

Hephistole lay in his four-poster bed, enveloped in a maroon velvet dressing gown and propped up by many pillows. He was reading late into the night, as was his custom, when a familiar chime sounded in the room, shimmering in the air around him. Hephistole spoke out loud, projecting his response magically as well as verbally.

"Come on up, Voltan," he said, putting his book to one side. He was busy rearranging the golden tassels of his robe when the hawk-featured Mage entered the bedchamber.

"I'm sorry to disturb you so late, Chancellor," Voltan said.

"Not at all! Not at all!" Hephistole said. "This book has lost its sense of narrative anyway. A little distraction will do me some good. What brings you to my chamber at this time?" he asked, indicating a chair at his bedside with a wave of his hand.

Voltan sat down. "You asked me to report any kind of unusual arcane activity in the surrounding villages," he said. Hephistole nodded. "Well - there is a lot of it - and dotted all around to the north."

"What kind of activity?" Hephistole asked, suddenly focussed.

Voltan frowned. "It sounds like the kind of thing we're looking for. Local Healers and weather-watchers dying in the night, every last one of them looking like they had been terrified at the moment of death."

Hephistole swung his legs out of bed, and began to pace slowly. "Do they seem to be increasing?" he asked.

"Yes, exponentially," Voltan said. "Each night there are more attacks, and the people are starting to be afraid. The attacks are spread out in the outlying villages so news doesn't travel too fast, but even so, people are starting to perceive a pattern."

"Have there been any in the city?" Hephistole asked.

"Not a single one," Voltan answered. Both men were quiet for a while.

Hephistole stopped pacing. "Double the guard at night, but do it quietly. We don't want people to notice. And let's step up the combat training. Also, speak to Trask and find out which of his fighters we should trust the enchanted weapons to. I don't like this, Voltan."

"Neither do I," Voltan said. "But all we can do is be ready for whatever may come."

Chapter 26

Gaspi, Emea and Lydia lined up with the rest of their classmates in the courtyard. Voltan had been drilling them on martial magic, teaching them about a wide array of magical attacks and defences.

"In short," the dark haired teacher said, "the variety of attacks you can use is limited only by the imagination and skill of the caster. I could, for instance, use the air around me as a weapon or a shield. Matthias, come here!" he said, beckoning the student out into the middle of the courtyard. The short, curly haired boy did as he was told, facing Voltan with a look of anxious determination. "See what you can do to defend yourself," Voltan said, then swept both arms forward. The dust on the courtyard floor swirled upwards in great spirals, as Voltan's magic sent a gust of wind surging across the distance between teacher and pupil. The strike ripped into an unprepared Matthius, sending him staggering backwards. After the gust passed he steadied himself, looking embarrassed that he didn't defend himself in time.

"Let's try again," Voltan said, "but this time, defend yourself." Matthias looked confused. "I'll give you a clue," Voltan said. "I'm attacking you with air, so why not defend with air?" A look of understanding dawned on Matthias' face, and when Voltan sent a gust of air surging at him again, he thrust both palms outwards towards his attacker. It was hard to see exactly what happened, but when Voltan's strike reached Matthias he staggered backwards once again.

"Better," Voltan said. "But why didn't it work?" he asked, looking round at the class. Lydia put her hand in the air. "Yes, Lydia?"

"Because he tried to create a shield out of air, but that just acted as a normal shield would; it caught the wind and was blown backwards by it, like the sail of a ship."

"Very good," Voltan said. "Using magic won't help unless you also apply it intelligently. Okay, Lydia - you come and replace Matthias, and see if you can think of a way to use air to defend yourself." Lydia swapped with Matthias, who returned, red-faced, to his classmates.

"Are you ready?" Voltan asked. Lydia nodded, holding herself with a total absence of self-consciousness. Voltan swept his arms forward once again, and a third gust of wind swept across the courtyard. At the last second, Lydia simply held one hand up, little finger pointing towards Voltan and thumb towards herself. When the gust reached her the dust on either side of Lydia flew up from the ground, but the spot she stood in stayed calm, and even her hair didn't flutter.

"Excellent," Voltan said, a rare look of genuine pleasure on his hawk-like face. "Tell us what you did," he said.

"I formed the air into a kind of pointed shield to divide the strike, like a snow plough."

"Well, class," Voltan said. "that's not only clever, but efficient too. Your device didn't try and counter my strike, which would take as much energy as making one in the first place, but it diverted it, which takes much less force. Well done, Lydia."

Voltan was not often generous with praise, and where Gaspi knew he would be unable to hide his pleasure, Lydia simply took it in her stride and re-joined the class.

"Okay - form up in twos, and practice both striking and defending with air," Voltan said. Gaspi looked around to find everyone already pairing up, and no-one left for him to partner with. Emmy had already paired with Lydia, and when she saw him standing there on his own she gave him an apologetic look. Gaspi thought he could sense a bit of pity in that look too, and tried to look nonchalant, hiding any hint of vulnerability.

"Sir," said a familiar, oily voice from behind Gaspi. "I don't feel so well. Do you mind if I sit this one out?"

"No, that's fine, Ferast," Voltan said, "Gaspi can take your place with Everand."

Ferast gave Gaspi a smug smile as he passed him on the way to the benches that surrounded the courtyard. Gaspi realised Ferast was play-acting and felt a surge of anger, but he was also confused. What was Ferast up to? Gaspi had been avoiding conflict with Everand as much as possible, but why would Ferast want to throw them together like this?

Gaspi was faced with a grinning Everand, and didn't have time to think about it further. The only comfort he could take from the situation was that Everand's grin looked a little forced. Gaspi knew he'd shaken the bully when he'd stood up to him on the day of the Test, and for all his bluster Everand must have noticed Gaspi's power increasing almost every day in class as his block eroded. Part of Gaspi was glad of the chance to face him, but Emmy was so touchy about fighting that he felt hamstrung. Pleasing Emmy mattered more to him than showing this idiot up; but there was no way he was going to let Everand humiliate him either.

"Stand about ten paces from each other," Voltan said, as the pairs of students spread out across the open area. "Now, face each other." Each pair faced off in readiness for combat. "Decide between yourselves who is going first, and you can begin."

"Do you want to..." Gaspi started to say, when Everand thrust his arms out and sent a burst of wind flying at Gaspi. Gaspi didn't have time to defend himself, and staggered backwards as it hit him. As he staggered he caught one foot on the other, and went flopping onto his backside in the dirt. Most of the class burst out laughing, and Gaspi angrily pushed himself to his feet, glaring at a grinning Everand.

"Idiot!" Gaspi hissed to himself. Why had he acted the gentleman? He should have known Everand would play dirty. He dusted himself off, and stepped back to his place.

"Okay... it's my turn", he said flatly. Everand didn't look exactly nervous, but Gaspi could tell he was concentrating with every ounce of his strength. Gaspi swung his arms around in a circle, bringing them back round until his hands were almost touching. He thrust them forwards, using his magic to compress and push the air at his opponent. He put all his will into it, shoving it out with as much force as he could muster. The strike flew away from him, ripping up the dust from the ground in an impressive trail. Gaspi had deliberately contained the edges of the strike to make a harder, narrower stream. Everand tried to replicate what Lydia had done and part it around him, but Gaspi's strike burst right through whatever Everand had tried to construct, hitting him like a punch in the stomach. The taller boy grunted loudly, span around backwards, and fell face-first to the ground.

"Everybody stop!" Voltan shouted. The students started gathering around Gaspi and Everand, as Voltan helped the prostrate boy to his feet. Everand's face was covered in dust, and he looked furious.

"He cheated," the tall boy said, spitting out a mouthful of dust as he pointed at Gaspi, hate flashing in his eyes.

"No...he didn't cheat," Voltan said. "He just sent a very hard strike." Gaspi couldn't tell if Voltan was angry, or pleased. "How did you do it, Gaspi?" he asked. "Everand's shield would have been pretty strong."

"I forced the air into a narrower strike, so it would hit harder," Gaspi answered without embellishment, not taking his eyes off Everand, who looked ready to jump on him.

"That was good thinking," Voltan said, gaining a look of stupefied surprise from Everand. "A narrower stream means more force, like when you pinch a water pipe," the teacher added.

"But sir!" Everand said, spluttering incoherently.

"But nothing, Everand!" Voltan said firmly. "This is the kind of thinking we want from you all. Make your attacks harder to defend against. Be creative," he said. "Okay - back to your places. Everand take a break, and I'll partner Gaspi," he said.

Once the other students had walked away, Voltan leaned in to Gaspi. "And Gaspi," he added, "be careful how much power you use. We don't want anyone injured now, do we?" he asked, holding Gaspi's gaze long enough for the young magician to understand that his feelings towards Everand had not gone unnoticed.

"No sir," he answered, trying not to show the lingering pleasure he felt at the memory of Everand dropping like a sack of potatoes. For the rest of the lesson Voltan put Gaspi through his paces, trying different strengths and shapes of air strike. He got Gaspi several times by slipping around or under his shields, and Gaspi, forced to concentrate hard on the exercise, began to enjoy himself, any residual anger at Everand slipping away in the wake of genuine satisfaction. After another hour, Voltan dismissed them, and the students started to disperse. Gaspi joined Emmy and was walking away with her, when a blast of air caught him from behind and sent him sprawling onto his face. He sprang to his feet to find Emmy had also been hit and was sitting in the dust with a look of surprise on her face, blood trickling from one of her nostrils. Gaspi span around to find Everand standing nearby, the obvious culprit of the attack.

"Emea, I'm sorry," he said sincerely. "I didn't mean to hit you." Gaspi paid no attention, his long-stored anger at the bully bubbling over into a white hot rage. He thrust a finger at the sky, and beckoned towards the clouds scudding overhead. If Everand wanted to play with breezes, he would show him how it was done. Everand looked perplexed, glancing upwards in confusion. Gaspi reached out instinctively with his senses, feeling for the powerful flow of the winds blowing far above him. It was easy to do, the thick flows of air so much stronger higher up than they were nearer the ground. Entranced by the sheer amount of energy he found, he called it to his service. He drew some of it down, gathering in enough to form a violent gale. The wind responded to the call of a Nature Mage, moving under the direction of its natural master.

Gaspi brought the gale swirling down above him, until it beat furiously in a wide circuit of the courtyard, chasing its own tail as it circled him. Sensing the turbulence, Everand looked up - firstly in confusion, and then in fearful comprehension, as the head of the gale swooped over him with an ear-popping rush. Gaspi brought the gale round behind him once more, controlling it with wide motions of his arms, before leaping forward and thrusting both hands out at Everand. Everand held up a hand in futile denial, eyes wide with fear as the windstorm come boiling down over Gaspi's head and along the ground towards him. It ripped up the dust in massive, roiling clouds, racing towards the helpless magician. Just before it reached him, Gaspi heard a faint cry of "No!"

Everand was picked up and sent tumbling backwards across the yard, falling head over heels several times before Gaspi closed his hand, and Everand rolled to a stop. Everand got to his hands and knees and looked up in Gaspi's direction, his face white with shock. Gaspi gave a flick of his hand, and one last slap of wind sent him flying onto his back once more. Releasing his held breath, Gaspi turned both hands palms upwards and the remaining trapped forces were released, dissipating into the air. Dust settled slowly back to the ground like mist, mirroring the calm that was returning to Gaspi's thoughts.

There was total silence in the courtyard. Everand still lay on his back, and the other students stood frozen, staring in shock at Gaspi. Gaspi slowly turned around, looking at each face until he found Emea's. Gaspi smiled at her tentatively, hoping to get a response, but she had a look of such seriousness that his smile faltered and died. Without saying a word, Emea turned her back and walked away from the courtyard. The sound of the girl's dormitory door closing had the effect of waking everyone from their shocked state. Gaspi heard it like a portent of doom, and the other students sprang into motion. Several of the girls hurried past Gaspi to the prostrate Everand, one of them shooting him a look of disgust as she passed. The others fearfully avoided looking him in the eyes.

Gaspi was still looking for a friendly face when a harsh voice sent a cold shiver down his spine. "Gaspi, stay right there!" Voltan said.

Gaspi turned around to find his intimidating mentor standing with folded arms at the edge of the courtyard. Gaspi had totally forgotten about Voltan, and with a nod and a gulp stood stock still, while the hawk-faced teacher walked over to Everand. He helped Everand to his feet, asking him a question Gaspi couldn't quite hear, then with a sharp nod stalked back over to Gaspi. "Follow me," he said in hard, flat tones. Gaspi picked up his things, and followed him away from the courtyard.

Voltan led Gaspi through the campus without saying a word, rudely ignoring the magicians they passed who called out a greeting. As Gaspi followed, a sense of dread grew within him. What had he done? Would he be punished? Expelled? That last thought turned his blood cold. Several minutes later, Voltan led an almost-frantic Gaspi into the tower. When Gaspi realised which plinth Voltan was leading him to, his worry ratcheted up another notch.

"Step on," Voltan said brusquely. Gaspi had no choice but to obey, and almost as soon as his feet had landed Voltan spoke a command, and he was caught up in the vibrations of transportation. Gaspi was so worried that he barely paused to take notice of the uncomfortable experience, and a moment later he was standing in Hephistole's study.

The Chancellor stood waiting for them, and although he wasn't showing the same kind of sternness as Voltan, Gaspi couldn't see any of his usual sparkle. He indicated Gaspi should take a seat, and though he also took a chair, Voltan remained standing.

"What's this all about, Voltan?" Hephistole asked, obviously not yet fully familiar with the situation.

Voltan told of Gaspi's confrontation with Everand without embellishment, then turned to Gaspi. "There's just no excuse for that kind of attack on a classmate," Voltan said, anger still flashing in his dark eyes. "I can't allow this to go unpunished."

Gaspi's nervousness diminished slightly in the wake of a resurgence of his own anger. "It's not fair!" he said. "Everand's been having a go at me for months."

"Watch your tone, Gaspi," Voltan said, and Gaspi bit back a retort that he knew would land him in even deeper trouble.

"Now, hold on a minute, Voltan," Hephistole said reasonably. "I agree that Gaspi has gone overboard, but let's hear him out." He turned to Gaspi, the hint of a kindly smile on his well-lined face. "What's behind all this?" he asked. "This is your chance to tell us your side of the story."

Gaspi let it all out in a flurry of angry words. "He's picked on me from day one. He excludes me, he encourages the other students to make fun of me. He calls me names. He says I am not a Nature Mage, and calls me hedge wizard instead." As Gaspi talked his words began to sound increasingly pathetic in his own ears. "He attacked me today, not the other way round. He threw a strike at me when the class was over and I was walking away. I just didn't feel like putting up with it anymore." Gaspi felt a bit better about that last reason.

Hephistole looked at Voltan. "Have you observed any of this, Voltan?" he asked.

"In part, yes. I have noticed some friction and, yes, Everand is often rude to Gaspi in class. It's also true that Everand was the first to attack today. But that's still no excuse," he said, turning back to Gaspi. "You are by far the more powerful Mage, and you are responsible for using that power carefully." The warrior Mage still looked angry, but the hard line of his jaw had relaxed a little.

"You are right in saying that it is not an excuse Voltan, but it *is* a reason," Hephistole said calmly. "Gaspi," he said, addressing the young Mage again. "I remember from hearing your story the first time that your magic first erupted when defending your guardian against someone in your village. Is that right?"

"Yes sir," Gaspi said. "It was the Brock and Jakko; the blacksmith and his son."

"And would you say that they were picking on you?"

Gaspi paused for a long moment before answering. "Yes. Brock was picking on Jonn, and Jakko was always bullying me."

"I see," Hephistole said. "It seems you have a history of being mistreated, and it's not a surprise that you are sensitive about it. It also seems that our Everand has been carrying on that grand tradition." Gaspi, feeling embarrassed by the feebleness of his excuses, merely shrugged. "Well, Gaspi," Hephistole continued, "I want you to know I can imagine something of how this might make you feel. We are vulnerable in some ways, and there are those who would exploit our weak spots. But Voltan is right. The past haunts all of us, but you must put it aside. You have inherited a mighty gift, and it cannot be used without maturity. The other students just don't have the same kind of firepower...something Everand learned the hard way today." Hephistole leaned forward, holding Gaspi's attention with his piercing green eyes. "Gaspi," he said gravely, "like it or not, with power comes responsibility. Do you understand?" He held Gaspi's gaze, giving his words time to sink in.

Gaspi was unable to avoid the truth of his words. "Yes sir," he said, after a pause. Somehow the usual informality seemed inappropriate, and he gave the Chancellor his proper honorific title.

"Good," Hephistole said, leaning back in his chair. "Then try and understand this, also. There may come a day when you have to fight side by side with Everand, or with any of the other students. Not everyone can be friends, but I'm asking you to be the peacemaker here. Will you do what you can to put this animosity aside?"

Gaspi felt that Hephistole was trying to communicate something to him, but wasn't sure exactly what it was. He was so captured by the older man's sincerity that he found it much easier to agree than he would have believed possible half an hour previously.

"I'll try," he said, and found that he meant it. His own power had shocked him today, and however much he wanted everyone to see Everand for the idiot he was, he didn't actually want to hurt him. He even started to feel a little ashamed.

"Good man," Hephistole said, radiating approval. "Voltan I agree that Gaspi must be punished for this, but let's not make it too arduous. Repairing the containment cages?"

"That sounds fair," Voltan responded. He looked at Gaspi again, and Gaspi was relieved to see his mentor's face showing only its usual sternness. "Cancel whatever you had planned this afternoon. I'll meet you in the main classroom in an hour. Now, go and have your lunch."

Chapter 27

Gaspi left the room in thoughtful silence. Walking back to the refectory, he ran the events of the morning through his head. The most important thing was making things right with Emea. He knew she was upset with him, but not knowing exactly how upset gave him an uncomfortable, squirming sensation in his stomach. That feeling injected a sense of urgency into his thoughts, and he broke into a jog. She would probably be in the refectory with Lydia, maybe nearing the end of their lunch, and if he rushed he just might catch her.

When Gaspi reached the refectory he wrenched open the doors, looking round for Emea. He heard her tinkling laugh and, turning to see where she was, found her sitting with Everand and his usual crowd of followers. Gaspi's insides turned to ice, all of his good intentions to make peace with Everand blown out of his mind by an unstoppable surge of jealousy. Lydia spotted him, and nudged Emea. When she saw him Emea flushed, looking sheepish for a moment, but then some kind of resolve seemed to kick in and she tilted her chin up in defiance, a flush still showing on her pale cheeks. Gaspi couldn't think of anything except getting away from the scene in front of him, and without saying a word he turned and fled the room. The last thing he heard as the doors shut behind him was another wave of laughter erupting from Everand's table. Gaspi felt tears start in his eyes. Not wanting anyone to see him, Gaspi broke into a run, angrily wiping away the tears that wouldn't stop pouring down his face. He didn't know where he was going until he found himself in his meditation garden. Relieved to find it empty, Gaspi walked numbly to the spot he always meditated in, and sank to the ground. He stared into space for a long moment, haunted by the image of Emea sitting with Everand, laughing at his jokes; and before he knew what was happening, he broke into uncontrollable sobbing.

Gaspi didn't know exactly how long he stayed there, but with a flicker of panic he realised it had to be way past the time he was meant to meet Voltan for his punishment. The momentary panic was submerged by a much more powerful wave of self-pity. What did it matter what Voltan thought? He'd probably just lost the girl he loved. Thinking of Emmy brought more tears to his eyes, and he fiercely brushed them away. He couldn't just sit there and cry, but what should he do? Then, suddenly, he knew. He'd go and speak to Jonn. He'd know what to do, and down in the barracks he'd not bump into Everand or Voltan, or anyone else he didn't want to see.

Gaspi managed to avoid being seen as he left the college, but when he arrived at the barracks Jonn wasn't there. He looked around for

Taurnil instead, and after asking a guard where he might be, found him sharpening swords in the armoury.

Taurnil looked up as Gaspi entered. "What's the matter, Gasp?" he asked, sensing his friend's distress straightaway.

Gaspi told him all the details, somehow managing to hold back his tears until he'd finished. "I think I've lost her, Taurn," he said in utter despair. Suddenly he couldn't fight it anymore, and broke down into wracking sobs. Taurnil patted him awkwardly on the back, clearly not knowing what to do in this situation. It took a couple of moments for Gaspi to get a hold of himself, but he eventually managed, and looked at Taurnil plaintively.

"What do I do, Taurn?" he asked.

Taurnil looked thoughtful. "Well, Gasp," he said. "I don't think you've lost her, but you probably have some making up to do." He paused for thought. "You know what Emmy is like. Remember the time she found that lame duck back home, and nursed it all spring?"

Gaspi couldn't help smiling. "Yeah. It was obviously a goner but she wouldn't let Jonn put it down. And when it died we had to have that ceremony."

Taurnil laughed. "She's a soft person, Gaspi. She just can't cope with any kind of violence."

"Well, she managed okay at the tournament," Gaspi said, with a touch of indignation.

"But that was an organised event. No-one was out to get anyone else for the sake of it. She doesn't like the fact that you deliberately used your powers to harm someone, just because you felt like it."

Gaspi was quiet for a moment. "I get that, but she should know I don't like being bullied. If I lose my temper because some toe-rag won't leave me alone, why can't she understand that?"

"I dunno, mate. You're gonna to have to talk to Emmy about it. But for what it's worth, I really don't think you've lost her."

"You think?" Gaspi asked hopefully.

"Yeah. But it's probably best not to leave it. It'll only get harder if you do."

Gaspi peered at his friend as if seeing him for the first time. "When did you get so wise?"

Taurnil pulled a wry face. "I'm not wise. Remember the fool I made of myself at the gypsy dance? It's just easier to see when it's not you."

Gaspi felt sure that Taurnil had the right of it, and decided not to wait for Jonn. He went back up to the college, anxious to find Emmy. When he reached the campus he headed for the girls' dorm, but as he crossed the courtyard he saw the silhouette of Voltan standing in the doorway of a classroom. He didn't even try to pretend he hadn't seen him, and, changing his course, walked with his head hung down towards his mentor.

Without saying a word, Voltan stood aside to let Gaspi through the door. Closing it behind them, Voltan took a seat, indicating with a gesture that Gaspi should do likewise.

"Where were you this afternoon?" Voltan asked without preamble.

"I'm sorry sir," Gaspi said, anxious to get it all out in the open. "I had a bit of a problem." Gaspi told Voltan what had happened, just about managing not to get upset again. Gaspi knew Voltan was strict, but hoped he would be able to appeal to a well-hidden, softer, side of the warrior Mage. "It wasn't deliberate, I promise," Gaspi finished. "I just lost it."

"Okay, Gaspi," Voltan said in an even tone. "I'm not going to add anything to your punishment for not turning up today. I understand that matters of the heart are...difficult, and you seem to be having a hard time at the moment. But don't let it happen again." That last statement sounded very much like a command, and Gaspi knew that a line had been drawn that he would be unwise to cross.

"Thank you sir. I won't, I promise," he said, with sincerity.

"Get going, then," Voltan said, gesturing towards the door. "You can do your detention tomorrow."

Not needing to be told twice, Gaspi picked up his things, and headed out of the door.

He knocked on the door of the girls' dormitory, but the girl who answered told him frostily that Emea wasn't there. Gaspi took off round the campus, desperately hoping to bump into her, but he couldn't find her anywhere. Several times he caught sight of someone whose profile was similar, or who wore her hair the same way as Emmy, and his heart would start to thump, before he realised it wasn't her. Suddenly, he remembered the compass he'd enchanted to point in her direction. Cursing himself for being an idiot, he set off at a jog back through the campus.

The light was failing by the time he reached the courtyard, dusk quickly passing into night. He was about to head into the dorm to get his compass when he saw her. He'd know that silhouette anywhere. She stood in the doorway of the girl's dormitory, looking out into the night, framed in warm light spilling out through the door, her head turning slowly from side to side.

"Emmy!" he called out plaintively from the other side of the courtyard. She looked directly at him for a second, then turned around and headed back into the dorm. Gaspi's heart sank in despair. He started to walk with heavy feet towards the door, trying not to give in to the gut-wrenching sadness that pulled at him. He'd just have to knock and call her name until she'd speak to him, even if it took all night. But as he neared the door she came out again, wearing a thick coat. The sharp edge of Gaspi's pain diminished slightly. Maybe she would hear him out.

"Emmy, please listen to me. I need to talk to you," he said, sounding desperate in his own ears.

Emmy placed a hand on his outstretched arm. "Don't worry, Gaspi," she said, her tone comforting, but more distant than he was used to. "We're going to talk, but not here. Let's go to the garden."

Gaspi found some of the tightness in his chest easing. "Okay, the garden," he said. Normally they would hold hands or link arms, but this time they walked apart and in silence. Gaspi was bursting to blurt out all his thoughts, but managed to wait while they walked.

The entrance to the garden was narrow, and as they passed through Emmy put her hand on his arm to steady herself. Gaspi realised in some distant part of his mind that he'd never been with anyone else in the garden before, but in the face of his demanding emotions, the thought didn't hold his attention. Emea led him to the nearest bench, and they sat down two feet apart.

They both started talking at once, and then stopped awkwardly. "You go first, Gaspi," Emea said after a moment, her manner quiet and reserved.

It was like taking the cork out of a bottle. "Emmy...I'm so sorry!" Gaspi began. "Sorry for upsetting you, sorry for storming out of the refectory, sorry for staying away all day...I'm even sorry for attacking Everand! All this – the fighting with Everand, my pride, jealousy, everything. It all means nothing. The only thing that matters to me is us. The only thing that matters to me is you." His words spilled out in a rush. "I've acted like an idiot today because I'm terrified of losing you. Just thinking about it makes me go nuts! I can take anything you have to say as long as you don't tell me it's over."

Gaspi was staring intently at Emea's face as he spoke, anxiously searching for some clue about how she was feeling. Running out of steam, he sat dead still, waiting for words that might break his heart.

Emea let out a long sigh and her shoulders slumped, her posture losing the reserved rigidity she had maintained until that moment. "Gaspi, there's no need to be so sorry," she said, looking chagrined. "Or at least, I need to say sorry too."

"Really?" Gaspi asked incredulously. "But..."

"Please, just let me talk for a few minutes," Emea interrupted. "It'd be easier that way." Gaspi nodded, and sat in silence.

"I should trust you more," Emmy said. "I hate violence and what you did today really upset me, but I need to trust that even if you do things I don't like, you are still the same big-hearted person I've always known." Gaspi resisted the urge to respond, his heart inflating with hope as Emmy spoke.

"I know Everand winds you up, but I want you to understand how much it would mean to me, and how much I'd respect you, if you don't fight back. But even if you do, I'm not going to dump you because I don't like it. I might get angry with you, but there's no need to get in such a panic. After all we've been through, how could you think that? I love you, Gaspi."

Gaspi's self-control fled him completely in that moment. "I love you too, Emmy," he said, choking on tears he couldn't restrain. She reached out and cupped his face with her hand, drawing it smoothly along his jaw. With tears brimming in his eyes, he drew Emea into an embrace. They cried uncontrollably, hugging each other tightly for what felt like hours. When they separated, Emea's hand remained in Gaspi's.

"I came looking for you after you left the refectory," Emmy said, "but you weren't anywhere. I've been waiting for you all day."

"I was with Taurn," Gaspi said. "I reacted so badly to seeing you with Everand in the refectory. I was convinced I'd lost you, and needed to get away. Poor Taurn," he said with a wry smile. "I cried like a baby, and he didn't know what to do."

Emea laughed. "What did Taurn say?" she asked.

"He told me I probably hadn't lost you, but that I needed to find you as soon as possible, to sort things out," Gaspi said.

"Sensible boy, that Taurnil," Emea said. "Look, Gaspi, the thing that upsets me most about today is how you panicked. I hate the thought of you feeling so desperate and alone all day. Why did you react like that?"

Gaspi was quiet for a moment. "I really don't know. It wasn't deliberate. It just sort of...happened. It's not something I can control," he added. "I've never felt like I did today, and I never want to again."

"Well - promise me that you will trust me not to dump you, even if we fall out, and I'm sure we can work through everything, Gasp. Okay?" Emea smiled as she spoke.

"Okay...I promise," Gaspi responded, breaking into a warm smile that spread from ear to ear.

"Now...what are we going to do about you and Everand?" Emea asked, playfully, but with a hint of seriousness. Gaspi told her about his conversation with Hephistole and Voltan.

"I can't mess around with this kind of power!" he said seriously. "Today showed me that pretty clearly. I even frightened myself!" he said. "I think Hephistole was trying to tell me something, you know. All that stuff about having to fight alongside my classmates. Something's brewing. I know it!"

"What do you think it might be?" Emea asked, sounding a little nervous. Gaspi was surprised at how vulnerable she suddenly seemed. For someone who had showed much more strength and common sense than he had today, she certainly still made him feel protective. He put his arm around her.

"I don't know, Emmy; maybe something to do with the thing that attacked us on the road. But even if it was, and one of those things was right here, right now, it'd better think twice before attacking this time."

Reassured by his confidence, Emmy wriggled in under his arm and rested her head on his shoulder. "Ah Gaspi," she said softly. "How can I be scared, with you to look after me?"

Gaspi kissed the top of her head. "We'll look after each other, Emmy," he said, and there they stayed, sat together in the night, comfortable once more in the silence.

Everyone was surprised when Gaspi and Emea sat together at breakfast the next day. Everand looked annoyed, though he was trying to hide it; but not nearly as much as Ferast, whose eyes glinted with bitter fury whenever he looked their way. Gaspi had mentioned Ferast's involvement in setting up the conflict with Everand in class the previous day, but Emea still wouldn't hear anything of it. Not wishing to rock their newly stabilised boat, Gaspi wisely chose to leave it alone.

But every time Ferast glanced at them, he could feel his hateful scrutiny; a form of attention both boiling hot and icy cold at the same time. It made Gaspi shudder just thinking about it. More than ever, he couldn't escape the conclusion that there was something very wrong with his mysterious classmate. He was worried about the time Emmy spent with him in their healing class, but he had no choice but to trust that Emelda would protect her if Ferast decided it was time to show his true colours.

That afternoon in his mentoring session, Voltan talked at great length about the use of air strikes in battles of the past. Gaspi found it much more interesting than usual, however, having seen first-hand how effective his own powerful strike had been the previous day. He could well imagine how useful it could be in the heat of battle, and as a Nature Mage he could tap into the strong currents moving in the skies above, harnessing them as no-one else could. The natural forces available to someone with his talent were phenomenally powerful, and the limits to their use were only defined by his own ability. Gaspi got so into his lesson that he completely forgot about detention. As he opened the door to leave his mentor's study, hoping a game of football would even now be underway, an amused Voltan called him back and told him what the rest of his afternoon would involve.

He was going to be cleaning the containment cages. Voltan wouldn't tell him yet what they had once contained, but only that they needed a proper scouring. He wasn't even going to be allowed to use magic, as the cages apparently held an enchantment that might be disturbed by other forms of magic. Gaspi looked round Voltan's small office for anything that looked like a cage, but nothing stood out as an obvious candidate. Voltan's office was small and scrupulously neat. The walls were panelled with some kind of dark wood, and hung with well-placed banners and a few small tapestries.

There was nothing that resembled the ornate, comfortable furnishings of Hephistole's study. The seat Gaspi sat on for his mentoring sessions had the thinnest of cushions, and always left his buttocks numb. He would have complained if Voltan had anything more luxurious for himself, but his mentor's chair looked even less comfortable. Gaspi supposed the room suited its occupant, and certainly it was the study of a warrior Mage. The tapestries were all of battle scenes, the carefully selected books stacked neatly on heavy-looking shelves were all related in some way to martial magic, and there were even a couple of ancient weapons suspended from the wall behind Voltan's squat, square desk.

"Where are the cages, sir?" Gaspi asked.

"Not here," Voltan answered, before standing up and walking to the door. "They're up in Hephistole's study. I'll take you to them," he said, swinging the door open.

Gaspi swiftly gathered his things, and followed his mentor. Voltan's office was on the third floor of the large tower in the centre of the campus. To get to Hephistole's study they could use the transporter on their floor, which was only paces from the door to Voltan's study. They transported up to the observatory, as Hephistole named his own study, and Voltan began to lead Gaspi round the long curve of the tower's bulbous top floor. Gaspi had been to the Chancellor's study several times now, but he'd never gone further than the part immediately by the transporter, where Hephistole had his long, bean-shaped desk, and several comfortable chairs for visitors.

Jonn had once described the rest of the office to him, with its sinuous walls falling back into seven deep recesses filled with all kinds of interesting sounding things. Jonn had also spoken of the hole at the other end of the office that he'd "flown" down from with Hephistole after his first and only visit to the Chancellor's office. Gaspi was hoping Voltan would let him go out that way instead of using the transporter. He was craning his neck, trying to catch a glimpse of what lay around the broad curve of the office - but, disappointingly, Voltan stopped him at only the second recess.

The wall swept back into a wide recess lined from floor to ceiling with shelves, each housing several cages. The cages were all of a similar size, large enough to contain a small dog perhaps, and most of them were covered in a red velvet cloth. The few that weren't were stacked on the left side of the recess, and they were charred and sullied enough that they looked as if there'd been a small bonfire held in each of them.

"What's in the other cages, sir?" Gaspi asked.

"Take a look," Voltan answered. Gaspi had expected Voltan to refuse to tell him, and he looked back at his mentor a couple of times before going to the nearest covered cage. Suddenly nervous, he slowly lifted the edge of the red cloth, peering under his hand as he did so. He could see what looked like a knobbly little knee poking out towards him. Curiosity got the better of him, and he pulled the cloth off in one quick motion, revealing an ugly little creature, its distended pigeon chest rising and falling with each ragged breath.

"Is it a dJin?" Gaspi asked, taking an involuntary step back from the cage. He couldn't see much of its face; but the heavy claws on the end of its hands and feet and the grey skin, pulled so tight it looked like it was about to burst, were exactly as he remembered from Professor Worrick's first lesson.

"Yes, Gaspi, it is," Voltan said. "You don't need to worry, though. The cages are enchanted to keep them asleep, which gives us a chance to study them."

Gaspi took a step nearer the dJin again, peering closely at the vicious little demon. He remembered the sheer hatred and violence that the first dJin he'd seen had displayed, and shuddered. Why would anyone want to keep one of these, even to study them? And then he remembered what Professor Worrick had said; it was illegal to summon a demon. "How did they get here, sir?" Gaspi asked, not confident Voltan would tell him the answer.

Voltan paused, his mouth twisted, as if reluctant to speak. "Hephistole seems to want you to know things that other students do not, so I will answer you question - but only if you promise to keep this to yourself."

"I promise," Gaspi said, without hesitation.

"That means Emea, too," Voltan said firmly.

"Okay," Gaspi said, eager for the answer.

Voltan still didn't look particularly keen to speak, but he started nonetheless.

"There used to be a teacher here at the college who became secretly obsessed with things that are best left alone; one of which was Demonology." Voltan's serious tones brought the dark subject matter of the story to life, capturing Gaspi's imagination completely. "Unbeknown to the other teachers, this magician explored deeply into mysteries that are better left unearthed, seeking ways to control other beings. Learning how to summon and control demons was an inevitability for someone of his proclivities." Gaspi didn't know what proclivities were, but they didn't sound like good things.

"He was caught eventually, and fled the college and the country," Voltan continued. "We found these demons in his basement, kept in these enchanted cages, along with a lot of other strange and dark things."

"What things?" Gaspi asked.

"Things you don't need to know about," Voltan said sternly. "Hephistole asked me to tell you about the demons, but beyond that I draw the line."

Gaspi wasn't put off by Voltan's answer. He could still ask about the demons. "So, why keep them?" he asked.

"A question many have asked," Voltan answered thoughtfully. "Some people think we should destroy them all, but Hephistole wants us to learn as much as we can from them before that happens."

"But isn't that…cruel?" Gaspi asked.

"That's certainly a good question to ask," Voltan said approvingly. "Hephistole would happily talk with you all night about that, but I'm not really a philosopher and I can only give you my view. They are pure evil. There is nothing redeemable about them. They cannot be rehabilitated or feel sorry for their actions. They are quite simply the enemy, and if studying them - even causing them pain - gives us an advantage in the long run, then we must do it."

Gaspi didn't know how to feel about that. Certainly Emmy wouldn't like it. She would probably see a dJin as a naughty dog or something.

"You're probably wondering what happened to the dJin kept in these few cages," Voltan said, interrupting his thoughts and indicating the charred cages Gaspi had seen on first entering the recess. Voltan didn't wait for a response from Gaspi before continuing. "Hephistole has recently wanted us to study more of how to fight and defeat these creatures, and so we have woken a few of them up, and eventually killed them."

Gaspi looked at the filthy, burned cages in distaste. "Aren't the cages broken now?" he asked. "They look pretty beaten."

Voltan let out a single bark of a laugh. "Nice try, Gaspi. These cages hold a powerful enchantment, and are too precious to throw away. We could mimic the enchantment and make new ones, of course, but it would take much more time and effort than we wish to expend. I think you'll find they'll clean up just fine," Voltan finished, indicating a bucket of steaming water and several scourers with a sweep of his arm. "Now, I must attend to other duties and will leave you to yours. I'll come and get you when it's time to finish."

Voltan swept out of the room, leaving a disgruntled Gaspi in his wake. Gaspi took off his robe and pushed up his sleeves with a grimace, ready for what was going to be hours of unpleasant, dirty work.

Chapter 28

In the wake of Gaspi's confrontation with Everand, the weeks rolled by in relative peace, a steady regime of ever-more-challenging classes keeping Gaspi's head full of new learning. His spells became increasingly impressive as the block on his power continued to erode. He'd done as Hephistole had asked and been very controlled in martial magic; but in other classes, where no-one was on the receiving end of his spells, Gaspi hadn't felt any need to hold back. In terms of pure power, he had started leaving the class behind in almost every lesson. Even if his skills were not very refined in some of them, the potency he brought to the table made his spells brutally effective most of the time. Gaspi remembered what he'd promised Hephistole, and didn't stir things up with Everand, but he'd have been lying if he claimed he didn't feel smugly satisfied when his spells outshone Everand's and the large boy tried to hide his impotent frustration. Gaspi thought that by not bragging about it he was in a way making it even harder for Everand to keep his cool, but at the same time it pleased Emea, so he won on both fronts. He didn't want to start another fight with Everand, but he certainly didn't mind seeing the overblown idiot eat some humble pie.

One morning, the class met in the courtyard for martial magic, and Voltan surprised them all by leading them into the classroom. Martial magic had been in the courtyard since the very first lessons, when they'd moved on from the force shield and started learning more sophisticated kinds of new forms of attack. They filed into the classroom and took their seats, wondering what the warrior Mage had in store for them today.

Voltan faced the class. "You've all done a fair job of learning new strikes, so I decided it's time to see how you've improved against the force shield."

Several students groaned, but quickly shut up under Voltan's flat stare. "Why the groans?" he asked, surprising Gaspi by indulging the class instead of just telling them what to do.

Temalia's hand went up. "Yes, Temalia?" Voltan said.

"It's just that we started with this, and it's much easier than all the other strikes we've been learning," the willowy girl said.

"Yes...it is easier," Voltan answered. "And no doubt while you've been learning air strikes and earth shocks your strength and skill will have increased. With the exception of Gaspi, who can actually use the wind, you have to use force to summon and shape your air strike, or to send a shock into the ground. Force is just a summoning of magical power, untamed, untailored; and you will all do measurably better against the shield after all this practice. Matthius, we'll start with you," Voltan said, while lifting the ornate force shield out from behind his desk, and placing it on a table at the front of the room.

The small, curly-haired boy shrugged and walked to the back, turning to face the shield while summoning magical force into his palm. His strike swirled in his palm, an opaque ball of power ready to be cast at an enemy...or in this case, a practice shield. It certainly seemed to Gaspi that Matthius' strike was a fair bit bigger than when he'd last seen him summon one. Matthius seemed to think so too, as he was staring at his strike with wide eyes, clearly pleased by what he was seeing.

"Cast it, don't play with it," Voltan said, and Matthius flushed, the strike almost flickering out as he lost concentration. He managed to hold onto his strike, and lifted his eyes to the shield. With a look of particular focus, he threw his hand out at the target, sending his ball of power spinning rapidly through the air. It hit the shield with a deep, dull detonation, and the shield coloured a deep orange as it absorbed the force.

"What colour did the shield turn last time you did this?" Voltan asked.

"It was a much lighter orange than that," Matthius said, with a shy smile.

"Good work," Voltan said. "I expect you will all see a similar improvement. Emea - you're next."

Gaspi suspected that Voltan knew how much Emmy would be dreading her turn if left to wait for long, and was grateful for his consideration. His mentor was certainly stern, and you didn't want to cross him, but he showed moments of sensitivity that made Gaspi remember that there was more to Voltan than just being a teacher or a warrior Mage.

Emea took her place at the back of the room, and closed her eyes. Despite all the progress she'd made, Emea's weak spot was combative magic. She was so good at enchantment, and at healing of course, but anything that was just a raw show of strength still threw her off. To her credit though, she didn't look half as nervous as Gaspi thought she would, and if anything she was just being really deliberate and trying to concentrate. When she opened her palm a ball of force began to grow there. It swelled to the size of an apple and kept going, slowing down and eventually stopping at about twice that size. Emea opened her eyes and looked down at her force strike, eyes narrowed in concentration. She lifted her eyes to look at the shield, extended her palm slowly until it was lined up with the target, and then flicked her wrist. It was an elegant, sudden movement that sent the strike spinning off her finger and flying at the target. At the moment of impact a detonation sounded that was every bit as deep as the one the shield had made for Matthius' strike, and it turned an almost identical shade of orange.

Emea spun around to look at Gaspi in delight. Gaspi grinned and gave her a wink. The whole class knew how hard this was for her, and several of the girls broke into applause. Gaspi looked around in surprise. He knew that some of the girls were really nice and would probably have liked to be friends with Emmy and Lydia, but Everand had always kept them from crossing that unspoken divide; or, at least, in class. Emea and Lydia were Gaspi's friends, and Gaspi was the enemy. Emmy had told him before that the girls were much nicer towards her in their dorm, but they'd never shown such public support before. For a moment, he thought that could mean there really was a thaw coming on, but one look at Everand's stormy expression showed him otherwise. The only other thing it could mean was that Everand was losing his control over the class. Gaspi supposed it was inevitable after he'd been so humiliated by Gaspi in martial magic. He was no longer the most powerful magician in the class, and every lesson that passed was making that clearer, as Gaspi continually outperformed him.

The rest of the students were called up for their turns one by one, getting a better result out of the force shield than they had previously. Gaspi wondered if Voltan was saving up his turn for the end of the class, giving him a chance for a bit of dramatic victory. He glanced at Voltan, who briefly made eye contact with him, and Gaspi could have sworn he saw the ghost of a knowing smile. Another tick in the box for his mentor. And then, it was Everand's turn.

The large boy stalked out to the back of the room with exaggerated confidence. He immediately summoned a large strike, waiting only long enough to make sure he couldn't make it any larger, and then thrust it dramatically across the room. Gaspi watched the powerful strike surge across the room, wondering in that infinitesimal moment why Everand had to be so pompous about everything he did. It landed with by far the deepest detonation so far, and the force shield glowed a deep red colour that lasted for several seconds, as the force was slowly absorbed and safely dissipated.

"Very strong, Everand," Voltan said matter-of-factly. "Ferast!" he called immediately, not giving the large boy a chance to posture. Ferast slid into position, pushing his greasy hair back out of his eyes and hooking it behind his ears. He squinted at the shield and then flipped his hand over, so that his palm was facing upwards. Gaspi was accustomed to the tingling sensation he felt deep in his belly when someone was performing magic nearby, but he couldn't help noticing that the sensation was the most pronounced when Ferast was summoning his strike, even more so than when Everand had taken his turn. The ball forming in Ferast's palm grew until it was as large as the one Everand had summoned, and then carried on a little further, stopping at an impressive size. Ferast bent his elbow, brought his hand up behind his head, and flicked out his arm with whip-like speed, releasing the strike at the last possible moment. It flew across the room much more rapidly than Everand's had, and when it hit the shield there was no doubt in Gaspi's mind that the detonation was the loudest and the colour the deepest of the whole class. There was an extended moment of silence after the shield had returned to its normal, colourless, state. Ferast was not universally popular and only kept his position by being Everand's sidekick. Beating the boy whose coattails he clung to didn't seem the smartest idea in the world to Gaspi, and the silence in the room as Ferast slunk back to his seat seemed to bear that out.

"Gaspi, your turn," Voltan said, distracting Gaspi from his thoughts. Gaspi pushed himself out of his chair, and went to the back of the room. He'd never actually cast a force strike at one of these miniature shields before. The only time he'd attempted it was just after his block had been taken off, and he'd had to spell-sing his block back in place when the spell-casting had got out of control. He'd cast one against the large shield in the Test of Precision, of course, and he didn't feel the slightest bit nervous, but he just didn't know how the shield was going to respond to his strike.

Gaspi started to summon his power, gently calling it to form in his hand. It coalesced into a swirling ball of force about the size of his palm, mesmerising to look at as it turned and span, driven by its own shifting energy. He fed it slowly, watching it shift and grow in his hand. Soon it swelled to twice the size of his palm, and then larger. He could feel the reservoirs of strength within him, far too much for this simple bit of conjuring, and marvelled at the total control he now felt over his power. It was only eight or nine months ago that summoning a force strike had been a nearly catastrophic undertaking for him, but now it was as easy as breathing. He fed more power into the strike, enlarging it until it was clearly bigger than those summoned by Everand and Ferast. He glanced at Voltan, who gave him a nod, and stopped feeding the strike. He lifted his palm, took careful aim, and, imitating Emmy, sent it flying across the room with a simple flick of his wrist. The strike span away from him, bearing swiftly down on the force shield. Gaspi

231

was waiting for a loud detonation, but in the moment of impact a deep crack sounded, making everyone in the room jump. The force shield had split right down the middle, and black smoke curled out of the jagged edge of the split metal.

"Sorry, Gaspi," Voltan said. "I thought the shield could take it. That's my fault."

Gaspi felt slightly disturbed by the cracking sound, which, like the detonating sound, seemed to resonate from inside him as much as from outside. He felt a bit shaken, and as he took his seat he could tell the rest of his classmates felt the same. On the other hand, he'd broken a force shield with what was only a small portion of his power, and the whole class had seen it. Voltan ended the lesson after that, and as the pupils filed out Gaspi could hear the muted buzzing of excited conversation that would inevitably be about what he'd just done. Following them out with Emmy and Lydia, he couldn't help thinking that, in the long run, it wasn't a bad thing.

Gaspi's impressive display against the force shield was the final nail in the coffin of the class's taunting that Gaspi was just a hedge wizard. That had died down after he'd called down the windstorm on Everand in martial magic, and tailed off even more now that Gaspi was performing strongly in almost every class. The result of breaking the force shield was the class's final acceptance that Gaspi was what he claimed to be - a Nature Mage. Even Everand seemed to have backed down. He was grudging about it, and maintained a rude attitude towards Gaspi, but he no longer taunted him publicly.

The change in attitude towards him made Gaspi's life a bit easier, and he found himself increasingly excited by the exploration of magic. An idea he'd had after Taurnil fought in the tournament motivated him to work particularly hard at enchantment. He'd read about magical weapons in one of the historical texts set by Voltan, and hadn't been able to shake the idea since. If he could enchant a stone or a piece of chalk, why not a weapon? He stayed behind to speak to Professor Worrick about it one day after class.

"Yes, Gaspi, how can I help you?" the professor asked. Professor Worrick had been impressed by Gaspi's increasing skill as an enchanter, and had been particularly pleased the previous week when Gaspi had enchanted his robes to be impervious to getting wet, and somehow managed to add an enchantment that made them warmer or cooler to the wearer, depending on the temperature of the room. He hadn't yet worked out how Gaspi had done it, as the clothes didn't change thickness or weave, but somehow warmed or cooled the wearer without changing state. Gaspi didn't really know how he'd done it either, and couldn't seem to repeat the trick once he knew how difficult it was. This didn't frustrate Professor Worrick, who loved a good conundrum, and whose passion for magic was as much academic as practical.

"What magical marvel have you unearthed today, young Mage?" he asked amiably. Gaspi liked Professor Worrick. He was straightforward and honest, and always enthusiastic about his pupils' achievements, even down to the most mundane of spells. Gaspi also liked his curious mind, which reminded him very much of Hephistole; although where the Chancellor had a kind of fierce, burning energy, Professor Worrick's curiosity expressed itself as a constant sense of quiet delight and surprise.

Gaspi went straight to the point. "I was hoping, sir, that you could teach me to enchant weapons."

"Weapons, eh?" Professor Worrick reflected. "There's no reason why not, Gaspi, but can I ask why?" The professor sounded curious, rather than concerned.

"It's for my friend, Taurnil," Gaspi answered. "He's a city guard, and I thought it would make a great gift for his Nameday."

"No doubt it would," Professor Worrick answered thoughtfully. "Did you know that Hephistole has some magically enhanced weapons in his study? They're artefacts from another age, powerfully made."

"No, I didn't," Gaspi answered, excited now. "Well - I want to make another one."

"I admire your determination, Gaspi," Professor Worrick said. "It's not an easy thing to do, however. The reason we only have a few is because of the difficulty involved in the enchantment. There are no rules stopping you doing it, but just remember that the kind of enchantments you're likely to put on them would be exhausting. A normal magician would be unable to do much spell work for several days afterwards, and there's no guarantee the weapons would pick up anything of power." He peered at Gaspi with a sparkle of interest. "But you're hardly a normal magician, now, are you Gaspi?"

"I guess not, sir," Gaspi answered, pleased by the recognition. "Even if it was exhausting I'd like to give it a try - maybe at the end of the week, when there are no classes for a couple of days."

"Good idea," Professor Worrick answered. "So - what do you know of enchantment that will help you turn a normal weapon into a magical one?"

Gaspi thought for a second. "Well, you always say that different materials take different types of enchantments, and that some materials are better than others full stop - like the stone used to make the wall."

"Yes, so that means you'll have to choose your materials well," Professor Worrick responded. "The problem you have is that if you want a truly powerful weapon you'll first of all have to have it made of the right materials, which means you'll have to pay for both the materials and for a weaponsmith's services. I don't know how your resources are, Gaspi, but I'd guess that they won't stretch that far."

"No, they won't," Gaspi answered, furrowing his brow in thought. "What if I just enchanted a normal weapon?" Gaspi asked. "How powerful might it be?"

"Well, almost anything will take a degree of enchantment," Professor Worrick answered. "The general rule is that the purer the substance, the stronger the enchantment, but this doesn't always hold true. Also, metals tend to hold an enchantment better than wood."

"Taurnil fights with a staff!" Gaspi said, frustrated..

"Well, you can only try your best, Gaspi, and see what happens," Professor Worrick said. "For now, that may be all you can do. What enchantment do you think will effectively enchant a staff?"

"Staffs break a lot, so maybe I should make it stronger, less breakable, or make it hit harder?" Gaspi said.

"Interesting," Professor Worrick said. "Remember that energy cannot be created. It all comes from somewhere,, and goes somewhere. I know Voltan has been teaching you how to use an air strike. When you summon an air strike, you still have to use raw magical force to trap the air into a narrow space and then to push that out, but you use a lot less raw energy than when performing a spell that is entirely crafted by magic such as a force strike. The air strike uses the energy captured in the air to create the substance of the attack. The magical element is just in the shaping and moving of that energy - energy you did not have to create. Do you understand?"

"Yes," Gaspi said. "Is that why Emmy always feels more tired using a force strike than almost anything else?"

Professor Worrick started to speak, and then stopped himself. He looked at Gaspi intently for a minute, and then seemed to make a decision.

"I'm going to tell you something that you are not to share with your fellow students, except when you are in great need, Gaspi. That's my condition for answering your question." He peered at Gaspi, waiting for an answer.

"Okay, sir," Gaspi answered, unhappy with being asked to keep anything from Emmy; but he supposed that if something happened where she really needed to know, then he could tell her.

"We don't tell this to students in their first year, Gaspi, in case the knowledge is abused. But seeing as you are particularly gifted, you may actually need to know this before we'd normally expect." Professor Worrick paused for a moment to collect his thoughts. "You're right that the reason a force strike tires you is because you are drawing your energy from yourself. This can be very dangerous, and if the magician draws too much they can either burn themselves out for good, and never be able to use magic again, or they could even die, which might be better!" Gaspi swallowed anxiously, remembering how close he had come to this on two separate occasions.

"There are some spells where the energy is drawn from the environment, but others - like most blocks, or other types of strikes - draw energy from the caster. What you are not aware of yet is that you can chose to draw energy from any other source. For instance, you could focus your spell to take the energy for your strike from the person you are attacking." Professor Worrick paused, letting Gaspi absorb this. "Can you see why this is so open to abuse?"

"Yes, sir," Gaspi said. It wasn't hard to imagine what someone like Ferast might do with this knowledge.

"It's not easy, but once you get the hang of it you can direct a spell, or even an enchantment, to draw from any source of power. So let's say you wanted your friend's staff to hit with a force that doubles the force of the actual swing of the weapon. If you simply enchant the staff to do this, the enchantment will draw the energy from the obvious source - the fighter. Your enchantment would drain your friend with every swing, which would defeat the purpose of the enchantment, and maybe place your friend in danger. See?"

Gaspi nodded impatiently. Sometimes he wished teachers would just tell him the answers without all the rambling. "So, where can the energy come from?"

"Well, that's the question, isn't it?" Professor Worrick said, scratching his head. "The good thing about enchantments is that they can be as sophisticated as you like, as long as you have the deftness of touch required for the spell. You could enchant the staff to draw energy from everything except the bearer, but that would indiscriminately take energy from friend and foe. That wouldn't be a good thing if your friend was fighting alongside others on the same side." Gaspi nodded, waiting for information he could use.

"I think the best place to draw the energy from is the ground," the professor continued. "It means that if your friend is fighting on soil, he will be taking energy that is normally used by plants and growing things, or if he was fighting on rock, he'd be weakening the structural integrity of the rock. But there's so much energy stored in the ground that, if the draw was spread nice and wide, he shouldn't do any real damage; unless he was fighting on one spot for a long time. I think that's probably the best solution, don't you?"

Gaspi didn't like the idea of draining the ground of life, but if Professor Worrick said it wouldn't have any real effect, then that would have to be good enough for him. "That works for me, sir," Gaspi responded. "But how do I make sure the enchantment draws from the ground? Is there some kind of special spell?" he asked.

"No - it doesn't work like that," the professor answered. "Just make sure that when you're casting your enchantment that you are imagining the draw, and the enchantment will follow your leading."

Professor Worrick must have spotted Gaspi's uncertainty. "You'll be fine, Gaspi," he said with confidence. "Some of your recent spell work has been as sophisticated as it is powerful, and adding a draw is well within your abilities."

"Thanks sir!" Gaspi said, sure now that he knew what he needed to do a good job of it.

"You're welcome," the professor answered. "Just promise me you'll show me the staff once you're done."

"I promise," Gaspi said cheerfully, and with that he took his leave.

Gaspi met with Jonn that night at the barracks to tell him about his plan for Taurnil's Nameday. Jonn wasn't on duty, so they went to a café near the city gate, and sat in the warm spring sunshine. Winter had been well and truly pushed out the back door now, and they were able to sit outside on the street and watch the passers by. Over a cup of bitter coffee, Gaspi explained what he had in mind for Taurnil's present.

"That's a great idea Gasp," Jonn said, clearly approving. "I've never seen anyone work so hard in training, and Taurn still prefers the staff over other weapons." Jonn scratched his chin. "In fact, that helps me with my own present."

"Really?" Gaspi asked.

"Well, you won't be able to use his weapons as they are city property, and you definitely can't afford a new one. If I buy him a decent staff from a weaponsmith you can do…whatever you do to it, and we'll give it to him together. What do you think?"

Gaspi grinned. "Sounds good," he said.

"So, if you magic up this staff," Jonn asked, "will it really hit more forcefully than a normal weapon?" Jonn seemed intrigued by the possibility.

"It's called 'enchanting'. And yeah, that's the idea," Gaspi said. "I don't know how well it will work out, though. It could go horribly wrong, and Professor Worrick says I will be exhausted for days afterwards."

"Is that dangerous?" Jonn asked quickly.

Gaspi knew what he was thinking. It wasn't that long ago when casting a spell had drained Gaspi so badly he'd nearly died in Jonn's arms. "Professor Worrick would have said if there was any danger. But I'll check, if you like?"

"Please do, Gaspi," Jonn said, then sat back again, allowing himself to relax. He took a deep breath, and let it out in a contented sigh.

"You seem happy, Jonn," Gaspi said. In all the time he'd known Jonn, his guardian had been a bit of a loner. Oh he cared about Gaspi, for sure, but Jonn kept a lot of private pain to himself, and preferred to be alone most of the time. Gaspi knew it was to do with the loss of his wife and Gaspi's parents, both killed in the same tragic attack by thieves in the forest, and had often thought that maybe Jonn blamed himself for not being able to protect them. But since coming to Helioport, Jonn seemed like a different man.

Gaspi saw him a couple of times a week, usually with Emmy and their friends, but occasionally they caught up like this – just the two of them – and Gaspi loved those times especially.

"Happy?" Jonn mused. "Yes, I suppose you can say that I am." Gaspi sat attentively, hoping Jonn might say more.

"I've been thinking," Jonn continued after a minute's pause, "that living in the village wasn't doing me any good. Too many memories," he said quietly, falling back into his old brooding manner. He caught himself and snapped his attention back to Gaspi. "I'll never forget your Da, nor your Ma. And most of all I'll never forget Rhetta," he added emphatically. "But being here has shown me that I still have a life to live. Being a guard is a good thing for me, Gasp. I'm part of something, doing something really useful. And besides, I need to be here for you lot."

It was unlike Jonn to reveal so much of himself, and Gaspi could tell the revelation was at an end. Jonn took a sip of his drink, and resettled himself in his seat. "Now about that staff…"

Chapter 29

Gaspi opened his eyes, focussed and restful after a particularly deep meditation. He sat alone in Voltan's office, which his mentor had loaned to him for the afternoon, and the object of his attention lay on the desk before him. It was a sturdy length of polished ash wood, its naturally light shade deepened by layer upon layer of resin, rubbed into the wood to treat it and make it both stronger and more flexible. Its golden colour was made even more attractive by the appealing grain of the wood; sinuous lines of deeper colouration snaking along the length of the staff. It was thick enough to be sturdy and slender enough to be light, and each end was capped by finely wrought metal fastenings. Jonn had explained that ash was a hardwood, providing natural force, but was more supple than oak, and would not break easily. Gaspi thought it was perfect.

Before attempting the enchantment, Gaspi spent a few minutes in a restful state, and, coming out of his meditation, he felt ready to give it a try. Magic was gently flowing through his body, tingling at the fingertips he reached out to take hold of the staff. He placed it on his lap, curling his hands round the smooth wood, and let himself imagine. He imagined it striking an enemy, drawing power from the very earth beneath the wielder, from soil and stone, enhancing its force and impact and making it hard to break. He released magic into both his fantasy and into the staff, tying the two together and forging the ordinary wood into something else altogether, infusing it with the mandate of his vision. Gaspi spoke to the staff to trigger the release of magic – "Be strong!"

Gaspi knew he was in some way successful as he felt power pour from him into the staff, leaving him weakened, but nowhere near incapacitated. Gaspi thrilled in the moment, letting the magic continue to fill him as he imagined Taurnil using the now enchanted staff against an enemy. Without consciously doing so he called to mind the demon that had attacked him on the journey to Helioport, his imagination placing Taurnil in combat with such a creature, defeating it with raw power.

Suddenly, Gaspi was channelling a riotous flood of energy, coursing violently through his fingers into the wood. The staff flared with a bright, almost blinding, blue light, as Gaspi felt his strength drain to dangerously low levels. He tried to let go but the spell had him in its grasp, taking his energy with it. Just as spots began to dance in front of his eyes, the light emanating from the staff flared even more brightly for a final moment, then winked out as if it had never been, leaving Gaspi holding an ordinary-looking piece of wood. His breathing was ragged, his heart labouring in his chest for a moment, before stuttering and resuming a normal rhythm.

The door burst open, and Voltan ran into the room. He looked round hurriedly and, seeing Gaspi, strode over to him and picked up the staff. "What on earth did you do?" he asked. Gaspi shrugged weakly. Voltan looked at him anxiously. "Are you okay?" he asked. "I felt a deep surge of power."

Gaspi croaked as he tried to speak, forced himself into a more upright position, and tried again. "Something unexpected happened," he said. "I was enchanting it to hit harder, and then I imagined Taurnil fighting with it, and something else happened."

"Something else?" Voltan asked, the sharpness of worry replaced by a kind of intense focus, a professional interest.

"The staff glowed brightly. Really brightly. I could barely look at it."

"Mmm," Voltan murmured to himself, lifting the staff up to his eyes and turning it around, looking at it from every angle. "Well, whatever you did, this staff is now holding some kind of powerful enchantment." He handed it back to Gaspi. "Your friend is lucky indeed to have a Nature Mage for a friend." Sensing dismissal, Gaspi tried to push himself out of the chair, but fell back on the first attempt. "You really put everything into it, didn't you?" Voltan asked rhetorically, as he helped Gaspi out of the chair.

"It looks that way," Gaspi said wearily. Voltan insisted on taking him to the infirmary just to have the Healers check him over, leaving Gaspi there to rest up. Despite his exhaustion, Gaspi couldn't help feeling pleased with himself. He was surprised he felt so drained, but also very pleased he'd done what he set out to do. The staff was almost certainly going to hit hard, but then there was the second part of the enchantment too. It would hopefully be something even better than adding force to the strike. One thing was for certain: Taurnil was going to love it!

It turned out that Gaspi had weakened himself much more than he'd expected. Five days later he was still weak as a kitten, and had to spend most of the day lying down. Since the day Voltan had moved him to the infirmary, Gaspi had only been out for meals and classes. In class, Gaspi felt like a prize idiot. Emelda had found a special chair for him that was somewhere between an armchair and a bed, and although anything was better than staring at the ceiling in the infirmary, the sniggers of the other students, and especially Ferast and Everand, occasionally provoked him to anger. Every time they started he thought about the staff he'd enchanted and how much Taurnil would love it, and sometimes that helped calm him down. When that didn't work he thought about what Hephistole had said about being a peacemaker, and when that didn't work he just lay there, quietly seething. After class and in the evening he'd take a brief walk to the refectory where he sat upright just long enough to get some food down, before his friends helped him back to his bed.

It could have been worse, he supposed, as he lay once more in his infirmary bed. Emmy and Lydia had practically moved into the infirmary, and Taurnil came when he could - this night was no exception. Taurnil had brought some painted squares of card from the barracks, and was teaching them a game the soldiers played when they were off duty. The aim of the game was to swap the cards dealt to you with others from the deck to make combinations of colours and shapes that were worth different numbers of points. It was a game of luck but the rules made it fairly complicated, and Gaspi found he really enjoyed it. Of course he'd much rather be kicking a football, or whacking a Koshta seed. Koshta! Gaspi hadn't thought of it in some time, and found himself longing wistfully for a set of skates and an icy pond, and for legs that would hold him upright for more than a few minutes as well!

Taurnil interrupted his musings. "So, for the last time, Gasp, are you going to tell me how you got like this?"

"Nope," Gaspi said with a grin. It was something Taurnil had asked him every day since the enchantment, and winding his friend up was one of the few compensations for being so incapacitated. "If you just wait till Feast-Day, it'll all be made clear."

Taurnil screwed his face up in thought. Gaspi didn't think that Taurn would assume it had anything to do with his Nameday, even though it fell on this coming Feast-Day. "Why Feast-Day?" Taurnil asked. "Bah!" he said in disgust when he got no answer. "You're not going to tell me, so why bother? I give up!"

Lydia let out a rich laugh, and smoothed the hair back from Taurnil's forehead. "Now, now, Taurnil dearest," she said teasingly. "Don't be so demanding."

Taurnil immediately lost his frustrated expression, driven to a kind of slavish distraction by Lydia's touch. Gaspi wanted to laugh at the asinine look on his friend's face, but he held back. He and Emea had been together longer than Taurnil and Lydia, but he still managed to look pretty stupid often enough. Emea, on the other hand, was less restrained and laughed her tinkling laugh, a sound that Gaspi adored.

He caught himself staring at her and, realising he must look something like Taurnil had a moment ago, let out a barking a laugh of his own.

"What's funny, Gasp?" Taurnil asked, his guileless face framed by freshly tousled hair.

"Dunno mate," Gaspi answered, breaking into an extended fit of giggles. Emea started giggling too when Gaspi kept chortling to himself, and even Lydia seemed to catch the bug. It wasn't long before they were falling about laughing for no apparent reason, until tears were streaming down Gaspi's face. It took a while to stop, but eventually they'd calmed down to the point where a snigger would get them all going again.

Taurnil wiped the tears away from his face with the back of his hand. "Dunno what that was all about," he said.

"Me neither," Gaspi said, "but we should do it more often."

Feast-Day came around, and although Gaspi was feeling a bit stronger, he wasn't well enough to walk through the city to the barracks. They'd planned to meet Taurnil and Jonn there and spring Taurnil's Nameday surprise on him, and knowing Gaspi couldn't make it down in his condition, Jonn had organised for a land-dhow to come and pick them up. A land-dhow was basically a colourful wooden box on three wheels pulled by donkeys. Helioport sat in the middle of the broad flood plain of the river Helia, which meandered in huge lazy swoops across the wide-open stretch of fields that supplied the city's many inhabitants. In history class they had learned that in ancient times Helioport used to sit right on the ocean, giving it the suffix "port," but some catastrophic event way in the unrecorded past had caused the sea to retreat and the great city to be landlocked. The river, red with the rich clay of the plain, snaked around the outer curve of the west side of the city, and was its last remaining link to the sea that once surrounded it. Historically there would have been lots of the small sea craft known as dhows plying their trade in Helioport's waters, but now traffic along the river was vastly reduced, and there were many more land-dhows than their seagoing cousins.

The dhow drew up outside the infirmary, its arrival announced by the loud braying of the donkey pulling it. Gaspi refused to lean on Emea, and walked himself out to the dhow unsupported, lowering himself into its waiting seat with his dignity intact. The young boy who led the donkey flashed a gap-toothed grin at Gaspi, a shining contrast to his well-tanned skin and dark curly hair.

"Huy!" he cried loudly, rapping the donkey smartly on the rear. It brayed and started forward, dragging the dhow into motion with a lurch. Lydia and Emea kept pace with it, chattering excitedly as they walked.

They passed out of the gates of the college and wound down the broad road that led them through the town to the barracks. In Aemon's Reach no-one worked on Feast-Day or Rest-Day, but here in the city most of the shops remained open for trade, so the streets were teeming with people. Many folk stopped to stare at the unusual sight of a young man dressed in magician's robes being drawn in a land-dhow, and Gaspi started to feel like a bit of a spectacle. Trying to ignore the scrutiny of the crowd, he peered around at the shops, until his eyes fell on a most unwelcome sight. Ferast was emerging from an apothecary, his skinny arms bundled with brown paper bags. He blinked in the bright sunlight for a moment, and then his eyes fixed on Gaspi. His mouth began to curl up in its customary sneer, but before that unpleasant expression could fully spread across his sallow face, he caught sight of Emea, and quickly brought his features under control.

Ferast shuffled over to them, careful not to drop or spill his acquisitions. His dark eyes were for Emea alone. "Hello, Emea," he said. "What are you doing?" he asked, without looking at either of the other two.

"Hi Ferast!" Emea said brightly. "We're going to the barracks to visit Taurnil for his Nameday."

"Taurnil?" Ferast responded in a puzzled voice. "Oh yes, the guard," he added, in a tone that revealed - at least to Gaspi - that he considered such company beneath him.

"Yes, the guard!" Lydia interjected dismissively. "Now, if you'll excuse us, we need to be getting on."

Lydia grabbed Emea by the arm and was already moving away, the dhow-driver taking his cue from her and smacking the donkey on the rump. Looking back over her shoulder, Emea called back to Ferast "See you later," leaving the gangly boy standing bemused in the middle of the street. Gaspi watched Ferast through a gap in the boards of the dhow as they pulled away, and he saw what Emea didn't. He saw the way Ferast's hard black eyes narrowed hatefully on Lydia's back; he saw him angrily flicking his lank, dark hair out of his eyes, spinning on his heel and stalking furiously up the road.

"Lydia!" Emea exclaimed in surprise. "What's gotten into you?"

"The guard!" Lydia spat in disgust. "I'm sorry Emea but that boy is a nasty piece of work. Did you not hear how he spoke about Taurnil, as if he was nothing?" Gaspi said nothing, highly pleased that someone apart from him could see Ferast for what he was, and hoping that Emmy would listen to her friend, even if she wouldn't listen to him.

Emea's face was a mask of confusion. "But all he said was that Taurnil is a guard, which is true."

"Emea...you are blind about this boy," Lydia responded firmly. "How long has he been sharing private classes with you, or finding ways to talk to you? He didn't even remember who Taurnil was for a moment there, as if he doesn't matter at all. You have mentioned Taurnil, haven't you?"

"Of course I have," Emea answered defensively. Her frown deepened for a moment as she stared into space, and when she next spoke it was more softly: "You might be right, but I just don't want to give up on him unless I know for certain he's as nasty as everyone seems to think he is. I just know there's a good person in there somewhere."

Lydia and Gaspi shared a telling glance over Emea's head. "Never mind," Lydia said. "Let's drop it. We don't want anything to spoil Taurnil's Nameday, do we?"

Emea smiled, the little wrinkle in the centre of her forehead disappearing. "Okay...let's forget it," she said. Gaspi didn't think Emea would see Ferast for what he was unless he did something truly terrible, something he considered the strange boy entirely capable of if he thought he could get away with it. He just hoped that if that happened, it wouldn't be something that would hurt Emmy.

Chapter 30

Jonn met them when they reached the barracks. He paid the dhow driver, and helped Gaspi out of the seat. Leaning on his guardian, they walked to the arena where Taurnil was practicing. Taurnil was going through a series of exercises on his own, warming up for practice; but seeing his friends enter, he stopped in surprise.

Lydia and Emea ran onto the arena floor, and engulfed him in two massive hugs.

"Happy Nameday!" they cried exuberantly. An embarrassed but pleased Taurnil let them hug him for a moment, before gently shrugging them off. Gaspi was struck by how big Taurnil was. Months of weapons practice had cut his once sturdy frame into a much more defined shape. His shoulders were enormous, and his arms thicker than Jonn's by some way. He had continued to shoot up in size too, and was a couple of inches over six foot. He still had the benign, bumbling quality Gaspi loved about him; a sort of childlike simplicity that had nothing to do with a lack of intelligence, but reflected a man who preferred to keep everything in its rightful place. That innocence was now coupled with a kind of manly strength that made it seem robust and well-balanced. He was in every way the opposite of scheming, self-important Ferast.

Jonn helped Gaspi over to Taurnil, where he clapped his friend on the back and wished him a happy Nameday.

"Well, this is a surprise!" Taurnil said with evident pleasure.

"Trask has agreed to give you the day off," Jonn said, "but I thought perhaps we could start the day with a demonstration of your skills with the staff," he finished, with a small smile.

"Really?" Taurnil said, looking at his friends confusedly. "You want to watch me and Jonn spar?"

"Yes, they do," Jonn said as his friends all responded enthusiastically. "Now, why don't you go over to the rack, and see if you can find a decent weapon?"

Taurnil still looked a little confused, but went over to the rack, where he stopped in his tracks. Among the regular weapons was looked like a staff wrapped in brown paper, with his name written at the top. Picking it up, he turned back to his friends. "But this wasn't here when I started," he said.

"Someone must have snuck it in there while you were warming up, eh?" Jonn said by way of explanation. "You'd best open it...don't you think?"

Taking the gift in both hands, Taurnil peeled off the brown paper at one end, exposing the warm golden glow of the wood and one of the metal caps. Exclaiming breathily, he ripped off the rest of the paper, until he gripped the exposed staff with eager fingers. He looked up at Jonn in disbelief. "It's beautiful!" he said quietly. He turned it in his hands, running his fingers over the polished surface of the intricately patterned grain. "Beautiful," he said again. Standing back from the group he span it round his body in the comfortable practice manoeuvre of a skilled fighter. "Perfectly weighted," he murmured.

"We'll give it a try in a minute, Taurn," Jonn said, interrupting the young guard's reverie, "but you need to know that this staff is not just from me. It's from Gaspi as well."

"Really?" Taurnil asked, looking at Gaspi questioningly.

"I, er, altered it a bit," Gaspi said with a grin. "You know, made it more powerful."

"You can do that?" Taurnil asked excitedly. "But what does it do?"

"Well, it'll hit much harder than it should," Gaspi answered. "But also something else happened that I don't understand. It might have some hidden powers."

Understanding dawned in Taurnil's eyes. "Is this how you got like this?" he asked, indicating Gaspi's weakened body with a wave of his hand.

"'Fraid so," Gaspi answered sheepishly.

"Mate...this is an amazing present," Taurnil said, his eyes shining with excitement and gratitude.

"Come on, then," Jonn said. "Let's give it a try." And with that, he sprang from his seat, and took a staff from the weapons rack. "Just take it easy, okay? We don't know how effective Gaspi's spell is yet, and I don't feel like being brained."

Taurnil grinned. "Okay, Jonn - I'll keep it light."

The two men squared off. The first exchange of blows had Jonn grunting and staggering backwards. He let down his guard, and they stopped fighting. "Can you feel anything different when you hit with it, Taurn?" Jonn asked. "It's like fighting against an ogre at this end."

"No, it just feels like normal," Taurnil said. "I can tell the difference in your reaction, but other than that there's nothing different."

"Amazing!" Jonn said. "Let's try again." This time he leapt in and attacked Taurnil properly, forcing the young fighter into a defensive stance. "It's less obvious this way," Jonn said, talking as he attacked. "It feels like I'm hitting a tree trunk, but there's nothing coming back at me."

Jonn span into an aggressive attack, striking hard at Taurnil's midriff. Flicking the end of Jonn's staff upwards in a clever defensive move, Taurnil swung back hard in return. Jonn raised his staff to defend against the blow, but as it landed his staff exploded into splinters in his hands. Taurnil only just managed to hold the strike before his staff slammed into Jonn's chest. Jonn held the broken ends of his staff in astonishment.

"Wow!" Taurnil said, eyeing his golden staff meaningfully.

"I think your enchantment worked, Gaspi," Jonn said dryly.

Gaspi laughed. "You're telling me!" he said.

"Let me have a go, Taurn," Jonn said, holding out his hands.

"Sure," Taurnil said, handing Jonn the staff, before retrieving another from the rack. The two men squared off once again, circling slowly, until Jonn stepped in with an attack. After several exchanges of blows, Jonn called a stop to it.

"How does it feel, Taurn?" he asked. "You don't seem to be struggling."

"Just like normal," Taurnil answered, looking confused.

Jonn turned to Gaspi. "Is it possible you enchanted it so it only works for Taurnil?" he asked.

"I really don't know," Gaspi answered. "Professor Worrick says enchantment is unpredictable, so I guess it's possible. I was imagining Taurn using it when I cast the enchantment."

"That's even better!" Taurnil said, brimming with the kind of focussed excitement he only ever showed about martial matters. "Now it can't even be used against me if I dropped it."

Gaspi always got the feeling that when Taurnil talked about fighting he was imagining a battle where he was defending Gaspi and Emea, a battle he truly believed would come to pass. The vision Martha had shared with them before leaving Aemon's Reach seemed to be much more real for Taurnil than it was for Gaspi, motivating him to work extra hard at his weapons skills in preparation for the day Taurnil was so sure would come. It was a little unnerving at times, but Gaspi supposed it had to be a good thing really. If that day ever came, they'd be well protected by Taurnil, especially now he had a magical weapon.

That wasn't the only surprise Taurnil had that day. They had lunch at the Rest, during which a boy ran in and whispered in Jonn's ear, before running off again.

"What's that all about?" Gaspi asked.

"Never you mind," Jonn said mysteriously. "But when you're all finished, let's head down to the gate." Emea exchanged a quizzical look with Lydia. Gaspi finished his food impatiently, keen to see what Jonn had in store. The only one not in a rush was Taurnil, who loved his food, and wouldn't rush it if the building was falling down around him.

By the time he was ready Gaspi was tapping his foot impatiently, and even Lydia was fidgeting in her seat.

"At last!" Gaspi said explosively as Taurnil mopped up the last of the juice on his plate with a hunk of bread, and popped it in his mouth.

He looked at Gaspi indignantly. "What?" he said with a mouthful of food. "It's my Nameday, and you expect me to rush my food?"

"Come on, you big ox," Lydia said in amusement, standing up and tugging on one of Taurnil's ham-like hands until he lumbered to his feet, tripping over the table as he followed her out of the room. Gaspi and Emmy exchanged a glance, and burst out laughing as they followed their friends out of the inn.

Jonn wouldn't give anything away, despite each of them pestering him constantly all the way to the gate. "Wait here, you lot," he said. "I'll be right back." And with that he walked into the gatehouse, leaving them more perplexed than ever. It was only when he emerged with three people in tow - one man and two women - that the realisation hit.

"Ma!" Emea screamed, flinging herself past Gaspi, and running into the arms of her mother.

Taurnil's mother jogged to her son, pulling her astounded progeny into a warm embrace. Gaspi looked away when he saw a hint of moisture in his friend's eyes, as he wrapped his big arms round his mother. He was happy for his friend, but didn't want to intrude in what was a very private moment.

Taurnil's Da walked over to his wife and son, joining in the embrace briefly, before drawing back. "Let me look at you, son," Seth said. Taurnil stood away from his mother, both proud and self-conscious as his parents looked him up and down.

"You're enormous!" his Ma said, and they all laughed.

"Jonn tells us you're a city guard," Seth said, with more than a hint of pride.

Taurnil drew himself up straight. "Yep, that's right," he said, looking his Da proudly in the eye.

Seth clapped him on the shoulder. "Let's go somewhere and talk about it," he said. They had to separate Emmy and her Ma, who were still hugging each other, tears streaming down their faces.

"Come on, ladies," Jonn said jokingly. "Let's go and get you a room and then you can go right back to it, okay?"

Emea's Ma stepped back from her daughter, and glowered at Jonn playfully. "Lead on, sir," she said, wiping the tears from her face.

Jonn led them straight to the Traveller's Rest. Emea became all emotional again when the three visitors booked long-term rooms, announcing that they were planning to stay for a month or two. Emmy's Ma explained that her Da had to stay at home to look after Maria, who was too young to travel, but she and Taurnil's folks were here for a nice long visit. The innkeeper led them upstairs, and half an hour later the villagers were settled in their new abode.

Seth had travelled a bit in his time and was happy to settle into a snug with Jonn and chew the fat, but the two women had spent their entire lives in the mountains, and wanted to see the city. As Seth wanted to catch up with Jonn, Gaspi found himself, along with Emmy, in the role of tour guide, showing the ladies the sights of Helioport. They walked along behind him, arm in arm, in open-mouthed amazement, pointing and exclaiming at every last thing. From the clay smoking pots and their snaking pipes to the rounded terracotta dwellings of the outer city, and from the glowing wall encircling the college campus to the enormous tower in its centre, everything was worthy of an "Ooh" or an "Aah!"

Gaspi didn't mind showing them around, but in all honesty he felt a bit excluded from the emotional reunion, and was glad when the light faded and he could leave them all at the Rest. Emea was normally sensitive to his feelings, but she was so caught up in the excitement of seeing her Ma that she seemed oblivious to what was going on with him. This suited Gaspi, who didn't want to cast a shadow on her joyful experience. When Emmy's Ma dragged her up to her bedroom, he was quick to say goodnight, and headed up to the campus and to his dormitory.

Gaspi lay in bed that night, wishing he could control his emotions better. Why couldn't he just turn off that feeling of vulnerability? He knew in his head that he had Jonn, and Emmy and Taurn, but something about families always made him feel lost and alone. Perhaps everyone felt this way sometimes? Gaspi sighed deeply. He'd just have to hope he felt better in the morning, so he could enjoy the long visit from the villagers along with everyone else.

Chapter 31

The next few weeks turned out to be much more enjoyable for Gaspi than he'd thought they would. After that first night he didn't feel so vulnerable again, and enjoyed hanging out with Jonn and Seth, who seemed to have taken up permanent residence at roadside cafés near the barracks where they chewed the fat and smoked tabac whenever Jonn was off duty. They welcomed Gaspi whenever he wanted to join them, and around his classes and studies he found his life wasn't that much changed; he just had a few more people to hang out with. Seth had a kind of dry humour that made him laugh, and he treated Gaspi like an adult; something Gaspi pretended not to notice, when in fact it made him swell with pride and contentment every time it happened.

He saw Emmy a bit less than before, as she was often with her Ma, but they still had plenty of time together. Taurnil's Ma had taken to stealing Lydia whenever she could, and disappearing off into the city. Taurnil complained to Gaspi that they were probably hatching plans about the rest of his life, but Gaspi had no sympathy, and teased his friend endlessly until the day Taurnil quite seriously threatened to hit him, which put an end to that little bit of fun. All in all, it was a good time. Despite his initial feelings, Gaspi felt included and part of it all, and was happy when the visitors decided to extend their stay from one month to two.

Several weeks into the visit from the folk from Aemon's Reach, Gaspi was lying in bed, unable to sleep. Without really knowing why, he took his Koshta seed out from his bedside table, and examined it in the faint light filtering through the large dormitory windows. He turned it over in his hands, observing with pleasure how the smooth, dark wood caught and reflected the silvery glow of moonlight. He missed playing Koshta. Football was fun, but he missed the feel of a good whacker in his hand, and the skittering of the seed across the ice as it slid into goal.

Ice! That was the key. If he could get ice to form across the courtyard, he could set up a game. Suddenly excited, he started thinking of the possibilities. He was a Nature Mage, after all. All he'd have to do is place and hold a layer of water on the ground and freeze it. He'd have to tap into an energy source to tie it off and make the spell self-sustaining, but there would be plenty of those available deep in the ground.

Mid-thought, an uncomfortable prickling sensation made him suddenly aware that someone was watching him. Keeping his movements slow and subtle, he turned his head just enough to scan the room; and, as he expected, there was a brief glitter of unblinking eyes from Ferast's bed, before the skinny boy realised he was being observed in turn. Feigning sleep, Ferast groaned quietly, and turned his back to Gaspi. Uncomfortable that Ferast had caught him in such a private moment, Gaspi put his seed away and tried to sleep; but unbidden thoughts of playing Koshta again skittered through his mind like a seed whacked back and forth across a frozen pond, keeping him up well into the small hours of the night.

Emea sat between Gaspi and Lydia in class, listening carefully to Professor Worrick's lesson on spirits. It was no surprise to her to hear of demons, after their experiences on the road and after seeing the dJin, but she was surprised by the existence of other types of spirits. Apparently there were spirits of water, wind, earth and fire called elementals. They held different shapes depending on their exact nature, but they all fell broadly into one of these categories.

Emea glanced at Gaspi, who listened with his usual intelligent curiosity. Emea loved the way he saw into the heart of things, and asked all the right questions. His hand was up right now.

"Yes, Gaspi?" Professor Worrick asked.

"Why do we never see these spirits?" he asked.

"That's a good question," Professor Worrick answered. "Spirits are by nature shy and avoid human contact. There are a few people – we call them druids – who spend their lives working alongside these spirits, to preserve and nurture the land. Their branch of magic is often underrated by the practitioners of traditional Mage craft, but that's just an old prejudice. They are powerful in their own way, and they tend to be as reclusive as the spirits they commune with. Gaspi, you are in a unique position among us with your particular calling. It may be that in the future you will have more interaction with elemental spirits than any of the rest of us."

Gaspi nodded thoughtfully, as Emea put her hand in the air.

"Yes, Emea?" Professor Worrick said.

"How are these spirits different from demons? I mean, are demons a bad version of the same thing?"

"Ah, well, that's the crux of the matter right there," the professor said. "That may well be the case, but little is truly understood about the origin of any kind of spirit. There are theories, of course, but all we know for certain is that they are different from us. They don't eat or drink and aren't corporeal in the same sense. They don't procreate, and they don't need to relieve themselves."

A couple of the girls broke into titters at this. The professor looked

250

up, bemused, and carried on.

"One difference between demons and these other spirits is that demons must be summoned and are not comfortable in our realm for any extended period of time. They inhabit this plane for brief periods, and then return to wherever they come from. Elementals, however are fundamentally comfortable with this physical realm - they are an integral part of it, in fact – and do not seem to come and go as demons do. But that is all I can say with any clarity, without departing into conjecture. Perhaps you can take this up with Hephistole, Emea," Professor Worrick said, with a smile. "He is the most able philosopher among us."

At the end of the lesson Emea waited for Gaspi, who was asking Professor Worrick a question, when she caught an odd movement out of the corner of her eye. When Everand's back was turned, Ferast quickly slipped something into his friend's satchel. She couldn't make out what it was, but it was dark and no bigger than his hand, and it certainly seemed odd behaviour between friends. Ferast left the room with Everand and his gaggle of girlfriends while she was still waiting. In all honesty, Emea wasn't all that curious about what Ferast or Everand got up to, and quickly put it out of her mind.

After lunch, Emea found herself in a tutorial with Ferast again. However much she felt sorry for him, something about the scrawny boy was making her increasingly uncomfortable. He stared at her too much, and spoke in a kind of secretive half-whisper that made her have to lean in to hear properly, and she didn't like being too close to him. Miss Emelda was talking them through the basics of bone reconstruction – a very tiring process – when Ferast interrupted her.

"Miss Emelda, what can you tell me about using healing power as a weapon?" he asked in his quiet, intense voice. He hadn't quite spoken over her, but she had clearly only been pausing for breath in the middle of explaining something, and both Emelda and Emea looked at him in surprise.

"Where did you hear that, Ferast?" Emelda asked quietly. Her expression was deadpan, but Emmy couldn't help sensing that her normally jolly teacher was not happy with this line of questioning.

"I read about it in a book about the Ancient Arcane Wars," Ferast answered, his gaze losing none of its intensity.

"Yes, I suppose you could have come across it there," Emelda said hesitantly. "I will answer your question," she said, making up her mind. "But just so you can fully appreciate the importance of using your power for the right purposes. Is that clear?"

251

"Of course Miss," Ferast responded, the very picture of respect.

Emelda was quiet for a long moment, before beginning. "There was a time, long ago, when some magicians treated with dark powers, engaging in unwholesome rituals until they became something other than human. More than human, or perhaps less. The powers they treated with were demonic, and the terrible rites human magicians willingly underwent lent them extraordinary powers. But they also corrupted their souls, rendering them a twisted form of creature; neither fully human nor fully demonic. Their powers were such that ordinary magicians couldn't stand against them, and in those desperate times it was discovered that the magic we use to heal could damage these perverted creatures."

Emelda paused for a moment, clearly troubled by what she was saying. "It was a horrible choice to make. The soul of the Healer is not designed to destroy, but when our very existence was at stake, we struck back, putting our Healers in the front line like holy knights, throwing bolts of pure healing energy at the demonised Mages, causing them great pain and even destroying them. It was a close-run thing, but eventually we prevailed."

Emelda took a deep breath. "It is my sincere hope that we never have to use healing energy in that way again. The calling of the Healer is to mend what is broken, not to tear down and destroy. Can you understand this?" Her gaze flickered between both of her pupils. Emea found it easy to agree. There was not one single part of her that wanted to kill. Ferast smoothly responded that he also understood, but even in Emmy's trusting heart she found a degree of doubt. The strange boy she shared these classes with seemed filled with a kind of restrained, glittering energy, reflected in the over-bright gleam of his eyes - eyes that could only be called hungry. Emelda looked troubled as she continued her lesson.

After the lesson, Emea stepped out of the classroom to find the boys in her class milling around, ready to play football. Gaspi spotted her and waved as he jogged onto the makeshift pitch, waiting impatiently to start the game. As usual he was on the opposite side to Everand, the large athletic boy stretching his long legs before play began.

"We need bags for the goal," someone shouted from Everand's end of the pitch. She watched Gaspi's nemesis jog lightly to the sideline and pick up his bag, carrying it back with him onto the pitch. Emea noticed a furtive movement nearby, and glanced over to see Ferast flicking his fingers and muttering under his breath. The movement was well disguised, but it was clear to Emea that he was performing some kind of magic. A snort of disgust brought her attention back to the pitch, where the contents of Everand's bag has spilled out onto the floor. He held up his bag in annoyance, exposing a large rip along the bottom. Emea watched him grab as many of his books and belongings as possible and start to carry them to the side of the pitch, when all of a sudden Gaspi came boiling in from his side of the courtyard.

"What are you doing with that?" Gaspi asked, furiously snatching up a dark, hand-sized object that was still lying on the ground.

"With what?" Everand asked.

Gaspi thrust out his hand at Everand. "My Koshta seed!" he said indignantly, his voice loud and angry.

"I never saw that before," Everand said, defensively.

"Yeah right," Gaspi said, taking a step towards the larger boy.

Emea glanced once more at Ferast, who was watching the argument unfold with avid attention, and all of the pieces suddenly fell together in her mind, filling her with a cold anger.

"Stop!" she shouted, stepping onto the pitch towards Gaspi and Everand. The two boys looked at her in surprise.

"Emmy," Gaspi began, but didn't get any further.

"Everand didn't take your seed," Emea said.

"What?" Gaspi said in surprise. "But he's got it right there!"

"Someone else put it there," Emea said with certainty. "To start a fight between you two."

"Eh?" Everand said, as confused as Gaspi. "Who would do that?"

Emea turned to face Ferast. "I saw you put something in Everand's bag at the end of class," she said. "I wasn't sure what it was, but it was the same colour and shape as Gaspi's seed."

"Rast?" Everand asked, his face a picture of confusion as he struggled to believe what he was being told.

"Of course I didn't," the skinny boy said. He turned to Emea. "Why would I do that, Emea?" he wheedled, and Emea shuddered at his unctuous, oily tone.

"Because you want me for yourself," she said quietly. Ferast froze. "You've been jealous of Gaspi since the moment you found out we were together. You know I hate fighting, and you're always talking him down behind his back, trying to get me to think badly of him. You saw how upset I was when he and Everand fought in Voltan's class, and you've been planning a way to get them to fight again so that I'd leave him."

"Emmy...no! It's not true," Ferast said, unconvincingly.

"Don't call me Emmy!" Emea said icily. "Only my friends call me that. And I can't be friends with a boy who wants to hurt the person I love most in all the world."

253

She turned to Everand. "I saw him cast a spell just as your bag ripped open. Your friend has been trying to set you up."

Everand strode angrily across the courtyard. "Ferast, tell me it's not true!" he said, his eyes fiery with anger.

Ferast glanced at him as if he barely heard him, all of his attention reserved for Emea.

"Emea, please. I'm only trying to help you. He doesn't deserve you," he said, with contempt. Emea was in no doubt who Ferast was referring to. "You should be with someone who understands you," the greasy-haired boy said, with frightening intensity.

Gaspi strode across the pitch to stand beside Everand, who looked an inch away from pouncing on his former ally. Emea held out her arm, stopping both boys in their tracks.

"Ferast," she said in clear tones. "Even were I not with Gaspi, I would never want to be with you. You are nasty and self-obsessed and arrogant, and I don't want to be friends with you ever again."

Ferast visibly blanched, his already pale face whitening to a ghostlike pallor. Pain wrote expressively across his face for a moment; pain and disbelief. Dragging his eyes away from Emea, he looked towards Everand. "Rand?" he said, plaintively.

"I'm done with you Ferast," Everand said coldly. "I'd take you apart, but you're not worth it."

Ferast looked as if he would fold in on himself and implode. With one last, agonised look at Emea, he turned and fled the courtyard, disappearing into a gap between buildings with a ragged cry.

A shocked silence reigned in the courtyard, rendering everyone motionless. Gaspi could have sworn nobody was even breathing. It was Everand who broke the silence.

"Sheesh!" The large boy let out an explosion of breath. He and Gaspi eyed each other with a remnant of the combative, suspicious air they had allowed to develop between them. And then, surprisingly, Everand let his shoulders drop, all the stiffness draining from his face.

"Gaspi, this isn't easy for me, but I need to apologise to you," he said. Gaspi was so taken aback, all he could do was goggle at Everand. The handsome boy pushed on. "I know I've been an ass to you, and I can't blame all of that on Ferast, but he hasn't helped things, and he was always stirring me up against you. I can see that now."

Gaspi still hadn't recovered from the surprise of hearing those words from Everand's mouth, and just nodded stupidly.

"I'm not expecting us to be friends or anything," Everand said, looking uncomfortable, but determined to finish. "But I think it's time to call a truce. Stop all this fighting. What do you think?"

Everand extended a hand, holding Gaspi's gaze as well as he could. For a second Gaspi didn't respond, totally unprepared for this sudden turnaround. Realising he was leaving Everand hanging, he pushed past his surprise, and seized the moment. If Everand was man enough to apologise, he was not going to let the moment pass. Gaspi grabbed Everand's hand, pumping it enthusiastically. A grin split Gaspi's face from ear to ear. Their classmates behind them broke into a loud cheer, which made Everand look a bit sheepish, and Gaspi burst out laughing.

"Thanks, Everand," he said, when the cheering stopped. "A truce it is! And I'm sorry for my part in keeping this going as long as it has."

Now it was Everand's turn to look surprised. "You really don't need to apologise!" he objected. "I called you a hedge wizard and made fun of you from the day you arrived. I only shut up because you beat me so badly in martial magic!"

"That's true; but every time you had a go at me, I responded," Gaspi said. "I've got a short fuse, and Emmy's always telling me I need to control it better."

"Ha!" Everand laughed loudly, and then his expression clouded over. "I'd never have thought it of Ferast, though. What a..."

"Toe-rag?" Gaspi supplied helpfully.

"Yep, that just about sums it up," Everand said, shrugging off his momentary introspection. He glanced over his shoulder. "So, fancy a game of football?"

"You know it," Gaspi said. "Just hold on one second." He stepped over to Emea, whose eyes were red and who was trying hard to subdue a sniffle. "Are you okay, Emmy?" he asked.

"Yes," she said in a wavering voice. "I'm just so happy you two have made up," she said, then burst into tears.

Gaspi laughed, and gave her a big hug. "Go on then, go play," she said, more in an effort to escape everyone's scrutiny than anything else.

Gaspi kissed her on the top of the head, and walked onto the pitch with Everand. "She gets emotional," he said, with a conspiratorial smirk.

"So I see," Everand responded, in a matter-of-fact manner. The two boys split off to opposite sides of the pitch, both burning to win the game. Friendship was one thing, but football was something else altogether.

Chapter 32

Voltan surveyed the scene before him with deep concern. Yet another demonic attack had been reported, but this one by villagers from a settlement only three miles from the walls of Helioport. He'd set out early that morning to investigate, and had taken the unusual step of bringing Emea, Lydia and Gaspi with him. Gaspi had suggested they bring Taurnil along with his magical staff, in case any of the creatures attacked again, and Voltan had called in a favour with Drillmaster Trask and had Taurnil released from duty.

The villagers were clearly terrified, speaking over each other as they tried to tell the magicians what had happened. Voltan had quickly brought order to the chaos, and had them speak one at a time until he had captured all the details. The victim had been the village Healer, and the sheet thrown over the body couldn't erase the memory of a terror-blasted face, frozen in death to gruesomely capture the moment her mind was broken beyond repair. Neither could it hide the twisted limbs petrified in a final agony so violent it left limbs and torso in a shape no living person could emulate.

The various garbled reports of the villagers agreed on a few things about the creature that killed their Healer: it was blacker than sin, colder than ice, and scared them all half to death.

"So, what do you think?" Voltan asked Gaspi and his friends. "Does this sound like the creature that attacked you?"

"Pretty much," Gaspi answered. "Big and cold and nasty."

"But what about the monkey?" Emea asked.

"The monkey?" Voltan asked, but didn't wait for an answer. "Oh yes; I remember now. The monkey acted as some kind of sentinel."

"The demon wouldn't need a sentinel in this case," Lydia said bleakly. "The monkey had seen me doing a reading, or it wouldn't have known I had magical ability, but there's no secret that this poor woman was a Healer. It's on a sign outside her house!" she finished, pointing at the etching of two cupped hands carved on a plaque that swung gently above the Healer's front door.

"Yes, that might explain it," Voltan said, deep in thought. "Well...it seems that evil has finally come knocking on our own door," he said, decisively. "The time for speculation has passed. It is time to act."

"Act in what way?" Taurnil asked.

"We need to open our gates to all comers, and prepare to fight. This incursion has been moving in our direction for months now, and we would be foolish to wait any longer to prepare for it." Taurnil's hands curled tightly around his staff, his face settling into hard, determined lines.

"But my Ma is still in Helioport! Emea said worriedly. "And Taurnil's folks too." The visitors from Aemon's Reach had been in Helioport for six weeks now, and had been planning to stay for another two or three before starting the long journey back home.

"She won't be forced to stay, Emea," Voltan said. "But it may be advisable," he added. Emea didn't look comforted.

"Time to go!" Voltan said, and led the young magicians and their protector back to the city.

Voltan and Gaspi sat in Hephistole's study, sipping on cups of what the Chancellor called his 'thinking tea.' Within hours of Voltan's return from the trip to the village, Hephistole had sent out the guards with official requests for all villagers within twenty miles to move into the city. Some had resisted, but Hephistole was not leaving anything to chance, and had ordered the guards to do everything they could to persuade them, short of using force. Within a day the wagons had started rolling in, and the lower city had become a kind of shanty town of tents and wagons. Some of the immigrants were complaining about the situation, but no-one could remember Hephistole ever issuing such an invitation before, and most were sensible enough to keep an open mind. Not a few were treating it as an adventure, getting drunk in the taverns each night and having parties around the tents long into the night.

"I think we need to control the drunkenness," Voltan was saying. "We don't want a city full of hungover peasants when it comes to a fight."

"I can ask the innkeepers to keep a close eye on people drinking too much, and the guards to be extra vigilant, but I don't want to start locking people up for having fun," Hephistole said. "It's a fractious enough situation already, without starting a riot of our own."

Voltan harrumphed in annoyance. The Chancellor turned his piercing eyes on Gaspi. "The reason I've invited you here today, Gaspi, is to pick your brains."

"My brains?" Gaspi asked, not sure he had anything to offer these two clever, experienced Mages.

"You and Voltan here are the only ones who have faced one of these creatures. So, I wanted to gather your thoughts about the best ways to combat them."

"You fought them, sir?" Gaspi asked Voltan.

"Yes I did, and only just lived to tell the tale. My companion did not," Voltan responded.

"How did you beat it?" Gaspi asked.

The heavy crags in Voltan's serious face seemed to deepen into even sharper relief as he furrowed his brow. "I tried all kind of strikes and defences, but at best it just held the creature at bay. It nearly took me then, and in the end I had to use the power of a very precious artefact I carry to destroy it." He reached a long-fingered hand into his breast pocket, and pulled out a small oval of silver metal. It had previously acted as a surround for a picture or symbol, but whatever had been contained within its frame was twisted and blackened beyond recognition. He caught and held Gaspi's gaze meaningfully. "I don't have another one," he said.

"Can't we just get more of those?" Gaspi asked, and Voltan let out a bitter laugh.

"More of those?" he asked. "This is a very rare object, picked up on my travels in the most dangerous of circumstances. No...we can't get more of those," he said.

Gaspi felt he was on precarious ground, but carried on nonetheless. "But what about the source of that power? If none of your defences really worked but the power of the artefact worked, why can't we...tap in to that source? What kind of magic is it?"

Voltan was about to respond, when Hephistole held up his hand. "That is good thinking, Gaspi, and perhaps in the future we can look into that, but suffice it to say that this particular source of power is not available to us right here, right now. We will have to make do with what we have." Hephistole waited for that to sink in. "In that light, what effective weapons do you think we could use against the creatures that threaten us?" Hephistole asked, his probing, sea-green gaze lingering on Gaspi as he waited for an answer.

"Well, I used fire, but that is the something I can do because I'm a Nature Mage," Gaspi said. "I'm not sure what use that will be to anyone else."

"We've been thinking about that," Hephistole said. "The other students, and even the teachers, won't be able to manipulate fire as you do, but if we set barrels of tar around the city, and light them in the event of an attack, any magician should be able to manipulate the tar and use it in whatever way they see fit."

"Oh yeah," Gaspi said. "That should work."

"And if we're unfortunate enough to be under attack, perhaps you could take it on yourself to reignite the barrels if they are put out by magical means?" Hephistole said.

"Sure thing," Gaspi said. "But are you letting the students fight?"

"The older students will all be fighting. Most of the first years won't, as you won't be strong enough to make a difference, but several of you will be given the choice. That is, if you want to, Gaspi," Hephistole said carefully.

"Of course I want to fight!" Gaspi said fiercely.

"We thought so," Hephistole responded, "but it's never good to assume. So - what else do you think might work against them, Gaspi?" Hephistole asked. "I know you only fought one of them, but did you perhaps get an instinct for what kind of creature it was - what its strengths and weaknesses were?"

Gaspi thought back to the battle he'd won against the demon at the gypsy camp. On the one hand it seemed an age ago that he had faced the monster; but on the other, it felt like it was just yesterday. He remembered the hungry, draining creature and its mind-splitting howl. He remembered how it froze everything around it, sucking out life and warmth from every source. Most of all, he remembered the numbing fear that drove him into the hidden recesses of his own soul. But nothing about the memory gave him much of a clue about how to beat these creatures.

"Sorry, I just can't think of anything," Gaspi answered. "I suppose when it attacked me before, I chose the right way to fight it. I think that's as far as my instinct goes. I don't think a force strike would do much against it."

"No, a force strike doesn't do much at all," Voltan said grimly. "Force, earth, and air strikes are for creatures with physical bodies. These demons have some kind of form, but it is made more of energy than matter. The small part of them that is physical responds to regular strikes, but all you can really do is slow them down that way. Physically attacking them won't do much more, and would probably be a very bad idea."

Gaspi had a flash of insight. "What about the wall?" he asked, remembering the way the dJin had burned itself to death trying to pass it.

"Yes; there's always the wall," Voltan said. "We are going to try and bring as many of the city folk as possible behind it in the next two days. If it came to it, and the lower city was lost, the demons will have to try and pass it, and some will die in the attempt."

"Some? Why not all?" Gaspi asked. The effects of the wall on demonic creatures seemed pretty clear.

"The wall was enchanted a long time ago," Hephistole said. "The secret of that particular enchantment has been lost, but what does seem to be true is that it doesn't draw its power from an outside force. Whatever enchantment was laid on it was done by some very powerful

Mages, and they gave of their own power to do so. Do you understand what this means?" Hephistole asked, his piercing eyes looking steadily into Gaspi's own. Gaspi was reminded of a bird of prey, and at the same time was made aware of the fierce intelligence behind those eyes.

"That once the power has been used up, it will be gone?" Gaspi answered.

"Exactly," Hephistole said with a small smile. "The power held in the wall was undoubtedly great, but we don't know how much of it has been used over the years, and it would be foolish to rely on it."

Gaspi suddenly remembered something Professor Worrick had said. "What about enchanted weapons?" he asked. "Professor Worrick said you had a few."

"Another good thought," Hephistole said. "We've had a look at the few we have, and the enchantments have faded on all but two of them. There are a pair of scimitars enchanted to be so sharp they can cut through anything, and a two-handed axe that has a similar enchantment to the first one you placed on Taurnil's staff - it hits very hard. We don't know the origin of the swords, but the axe is centuries old. It used to be handed down from War Leader to War Leader of the Uurgal empire. In our language it is called Bonebreaker. We've loaned the swords to the winner of this year's tournament, a blade master called Sabu. Bonebreaker is in the hands of a giant called Baard."

"I remember both of them," Gaspi said excitedly. "They were amazing."

Voltan leant forward. "They are good fighters, and weapons will be a help, but they're only two people. We're looking for more of a strategic advantage."

Gaspi furrowed his brow, wracking his brains for anything else that might be useful against the demons, but absolutely nothing came to mind. "So, basically, we're going to light a bunch of fires and turn force strikes into fire strikes by using magic to manipulate burning tar, and then run behind the wall and hope it kills some of them. Then we start fighting again, inside the college?" Gaspi summed up.

"Unless we can think of anything else, that is exactly what we're going to do," Hephistole said. "I have to admit that it would be nice to have another weapon in our arsenal. But if this is all we've got, then we'll have to make do. Thank you, Gaspi, for your time," Hephistole said. "Please be careful not to alarm your classmates; but be ready, young Mage. If the alarm sounds, leave everything you're doing, and prepare to fight. The most important thing is that you keep those fires burning."

"Got it!" Gaspi said, with more confidence than he felt. He tried to swallow, but his throat was dry.

As he was about to step on the transporter Hephistole called out behind him. "Oh, and Gaspi...I hear you made peace with Everand."

"It was more him than me," Gaspi said, "but yeah - we made peace."

"Thank you, Gaspi," Hephistole said with a warm smile. Gaspi nodded, unsure why such a small detail mattered at a time like this.

"No problem," he said, and stepped onto the transporter.

Chapter 33

Gaspi and Taurnil were sitting on the city wall, overlooking the crowd of people gathered outside its gates, trying to get in before the lowering sun finally set and the gates were closed. Footsore villagers led wagons full of personal belongings and provisions, and after up to two days travelling, they were not feeling very patient. Raised voices, bleating goats, and braying donkeys made quite a cacophony, punctuated by the barked commands of city guards trying to bring some order to the scene.

"Glad I'm not on duty today," Taurnil said, his legs dangling over the edge of the wall as he overlooked the milling crowd.

"Totally," Gaspi responded. "Wonder how many more we can take in?" The last week had seen the city filling up with more tents and wagons than Gaspi had imagined could fit into the overcrowded city. He couldn't see Hephistole turning anyone away, but the city just wasn't big enough for any more people.

Jonn had persuaded Taurnil's parents and Emea's Ma to stay in the city rather than risk the journey home. If there were demons out there in the countryside, then trying to leave right now would be madness, especially when the people who could protect them would all be locked up here in the city. Hephistole had found them an empty residence within the college grounds, and both Taurnil and Emea had been particularly happy that they would be safely behind the added protection of the wall.

A lot of the residents wanted to stay in their homes, so the villagers were the ones who had been steadily moved into the college, which was now brim-full of strangers. Gaspi thought the city residents would have been happy to leave their homes to these visitors and move up into the college themselves if they understood what might be coming, or just how important the wall might end up being in any defence. The irony of it all was that there might not be an attack at all.

Taurnil ran his hands along the length of his staff. "Do you always have to carry that with you?" Gaspi asked, thinking once more that his friend was being a bit overzealous.

"Do you always carry your magic with you?" Taurnil asked.

"Never mind," Gaspi said, sensing the inevitability of a losing battle. "Sorry Taurn...I don't mean to be tetchy. All this is just making me nervous, and you being battle-ready all the time doesn't help."

"Better to be battle ready without a battle, than not ready when the battle comes," Taurnil said.

Gaspi couldn't really argue with that. "Fair enough," he said.

They sat on the wall after the sun set, and into the first hour of darkness. Several groups of villagers were still lining up to enter the city, but after they were through the heavy gates would swing shut for the night, regardless of who came knocking. A long howl sounded faintly in the night. Gaspi sat up straight, his eyes scanning the darkness outside of the city walls. It was probably just a plains wolf, but something about the sound had sent a shiver down his spine. He could tell from Taurnil's posture that he was alert, too.

"Did you hear that?" Gaspi asked.

"Yup," Taurnil said, staring out into the night. They waited like that for a few long minutes, but nothing else happened.

"Probably just a wolf," Taurnil said gruffly, but just then it sounded again, and this time it was much nearer. Every hair on Gaspi's body stood up at the sound. It was like the howl of a dog or wolf, but deeper and harsher; a ripping, painful sound that made him think of broken glass and ragged flesh.

"Who goes there?" shouted a magician stationed along with the guards on the gate. Gaspi and Taurnil were on their feet in a moment, staring out at the dark, waiting for it to resolve into some kind of recognisable shape.

"Taurnil...your staff!" Gaspi exclaimed. Taurnil's staff was glowing a faint blue - the same colour it had flared when Gaspi had enchanted it. "That can't be good," Gaspi said, scanning the darkness even more keenly now, his stomach writhing in nervous anticipation of what he was sure was coming for them. A bright globe of light flew from the hand of the magician below them, illuminating the ground for hundreds of meters around the gate. What it revealed was a scene from a nightmare, causing every muscle in Gaspi's stomach to clench.

Staggered along the length of the wall was a ragged line of creatures Gaspi recognised all too well. The man-shaped bulk of heavy-shouldered figures were revealed only by their refusal to reflect the light. Each of them was revealed as a swirling abyss of impenetrable darkness, its bulky shape tapering away to nothing below the waist, gliding leadenly over the ground, heavy as a mountain. Gaspi looked right and left, seeing as many as ten demons spread out along the wall, inexorably approaching the city. Between them were hundreds of fearsome dogs; dogs at least half again the size of the biggest hounds Gaspi had ever seen. They seemed to be covered in a kind of fibrous armour, and were unnaturally heavy at the shoulders. As light flared around them, they broke into a vicious snarling that ripped hoarsely out of ruined throats, and spoke to Gaspi of a rapacious hunger to tear flesh and crush bones beyond repair.

The demons lifted their black, featureless heads, and howled. No memory of the attack at the gypsy camp could prepare Gaspi for the impact of that sound. It ripped at his sanity like a freezing wind, tearing the loose edges of his self loose and spinning them off into darkness. Next to him, Taurnil's staff flared bright blue and his friend held it up in front of them, shielding them with light. Protected by the magic of Taurnil's staff, Gaspi felt the impact of the sound decrease noticeably, and his senses returned.

"Taurnil, get down there. I have to go and make sure the fires are lit," Gaspi said, aware in that moment that he may never see his friend again. Their eyes met in understanding.

"Stay safe, my friend," Taurnil said. With that, he vaulted over a low wall and sprinted down the stairs, his glowing staff leaving an imprint on Gaspi's vision even after he'd disappeared from view.

Gaspi jumped as a loud warbling sound started abruptly, vibrating through the air, as if it came from all sides. The magician on the gate must have triggered the alarm. Everything in Gaspi wanted to run out after Taurnil, but he knew what his duty was. He ran down the steps and away from the gate, heading to the nearest barrel of tar. He found it quickly and set it alight with a flick of his wrist as he ran past. Residents were stumbling out from their houses, looking around in sleep-dazed confusion.

"Get inside, and stay there!" Gaspi shouted, and seeing his magician's robe, they obeyed without question. Gaspi ran from barrel to barrel, calling flame to them with the lightest touch of his power. The streets were filled with tents and wagons, and Gaspi was forced to shout at people until he was hoarse, telling them to abandon their belongings and get into a house. Most people did what he said, but there were plenty who seemed to think they knew best, or who weren't willing to leave their wagons. Gaspi didn't have time to persuade them, and ran on.

He ran upwards into the city, lighting barrels. He came across one that was already crowned with flickering flame. Voltan had drilled all the college's magicians apart from the Healers in the defence plan, and seeing they had reached their stations, Gaspi had to make a choice; run around and make sure the fires didn't get put out, or go and fight where he was most needed. There wasn't really a choice to make; turning on his heel, he sprinted back towards the gate.

Emea was with Lydia in the dormitory when the alarm sounded. "It's started," she said, as both girls leapt to their feet. Both girls had been asked if they wanted to take part in the fighting, and they'd said yes. Emmy had been asked because of her exceptional healing powers and Lydia because she was strong at most spell work and mature enough to handle herself under pressure. Of all the students only they, Gaspi, Everand and Ferast had been given the chance to help out, and Ferast had refused. "Gaspi's down at the gate with Taurnil," she said frantically, her heart knotting with fear. "We've got to get to them," she urged.

Lydia placed a restraining hand on her arm. "They both know what they're doing, Emmy," she said firmly, "and we need to be here." All those who were going to be involved in the defence had been prepared for the eventuality of battle, and whereas Gaspi's role was to keep fires burning and to directly combat any demonic forces head on, and Taurnil's was to fight with the guards, Emea was assigned to the infirmary to heal the injured, and Lydia was to defend the college at the gate should the incursion get that far.

Emea tugged at her arm, trying to pull away, but Lydia strengthened her grip. "Emmy!" she said, firmly.

Emea stopped struggling, her shoulders dropping in defeat. "Okay...you're right," she said. "But I'm at least coming with you to the wall, until people start getting wounded."

"Alright - let's go," Lydia said, and the two of them marched through the campus to the college gate. Other magicians assigned to the gate were already milling around when they arrived, including Everand, who gave them a determined smile. Emea was relieved to see Voltan there, his face intense and furious as a thundercloud. His warlike countenance was very reassuring in this situation. She recognised a couple of the older students she'd seen around the campus, as well as a few teachers. Lydia stood at her side, a determined look on her face, and Emea wondered how her friend managed to keep calm.

Voltan had taken a flaming brand from a sconce in the gatehouse, and lit two large barrels of tar. "Listen up!" he said commandingly, and everyone fell silent, giving him their full attention. "Try not to use the tar up too fast. Shape a sphere like this," he said, gesturing with a hand to bring a globe of tar up about three times the size of his fist. Flames flickered from it, causing the air around it to shimmer in the heat. "We don't know exactly how effective this will be until we try it, but it should hurt them. If they break through the wall and we run out of tar, move back to the next set of barrels. Everyone clear?" he asked, looking round the group, as everyone gave their assent.

Seeing Emea, he made a beeline for her. "Shouldn't you be at the infirmary?" he asked.

"No-one is injured yet," Emea answered as firmly as she could in the face of his fierce gaze. "And what if someone gets injured here and needs me right away?"

He looked at her steadily for a long moment. "So be it!" he said, and moved on to speak to another magician.

Emmy smiled weakly at Lydia, who gave her a quick hug. "Looks like we'll fight them off together, then," Lydia said bravely.

The sounds of battle could be heard from the lower city. There was a dreadful baying that sounded like a pack of demented dogs, the screams and shouts of men fighting for their lives; but worst of all were the unearthly howls that made her shudder right down to her toes. As those particular howls drew nearer, so did the screams. These weren't the battle screams of fighting and wounded men, but something more primal; the kind of sound she imagined a person could only make if they were being broken by unbearable terror. She and Lydia shared a glance as an especially long scream pierced the night. They both knew what kind of creature could cause a person to make that sound, and it wouldn't be long before they'd be facing it once again.

All the magicians at the gate were silent now, scanning the darkness between buildings for the first sign of their enemy. It seemed to Emea that they'd been standing like that forever, every nerve afire with adrenaline; and then it was upon them, and the waiting was over far too soon. The darkness in front of the gate seemed to move, a greater darkness gliding out of the general murk, taller than the tallest of the Mages by at least another head, boiling and swirling with a power that spoke of the theft of light and life. Emea broke into a sweat as the first wave of fear passed over her, an icy chill stabbing right into her belly. The creature emerged fully into the lamplight, its dark head swivelling to take in the crowd of magicians standing in its path. The ground at Emea's feet crackled as an icy coating spread its fingers over everything, and her breath misted in the moonlight. It seemed to swell even larger for a moment, before the heavy head dipped and thrust forward from the weighty bulk of what might be shoulders as it let out a heart-stopping howl. Emea would have fallen over if it wasn't for Lydia, who had grabbed her arm – whether to help Emea or to steady herself, she didn't know.

All thoughts of fighting fled from her mind, as she simply fought to hold onto sanity. Her soul shrank to a faint glimmer as fear forced her back into the deepest recesses of her mind, her body unresponsive to the urge to run for her life. As if from down a great distance she heard a human shout, and dimly recognised Voltan in the sound. A great ball of fire, much larger than the one Voltan had summoned minutes earlier, swept past her towards the dark creature, and in its wake she felt her terror diminish. The creature's fearsome howl changed to a cry of pain as the flaming tar-ball struck it in the chest, where flames now crackled in a wide circle. Its head snapped up, glaring at Voltan, its bottomless eyes black vortices of hatred that seemed to pulse with dark power. Charging at its antagonists, the demon roared in agonised fury, anger and pain driving it to put an end to those that opposed it; but it was halted in its path by several fireballs flung by other magicians, freed from the grip of horror by Voltan's bravery. Red hot flame flared all over its body in a conflagration, as the balls of burning tar hit it. Its howl of pain escalated into a jagged, wheezing roar that was no less horrible for its brokenness. It writhed in agony for unendurable seconds, turning this way and that in an effort to escape the pain it hadn't known it could feel, but in the end the demon collapsed in on itself. Its death howl ended in sudden silence, and all that was left were a few remnants of burning tar flickering fitfully on the ground.

Emea patted herself, as if to make sure she was still all there, and turned to look at Lydia, whose face was unnaturally pale beneath her dark, gypsy complexion. Before either of them had a chance to say anything, Voltan hissed in warning and she turned to see a sight that froze the blood in her veins.

Three more demonic creatures were emerging out of the blackness between buildings, converging on the gate from different directions. For a brief second before the madness began, Emea wondered how many more of them there were. Then fireballs were flying through the gate as the magicians shouted in defiance, borrowing courage from their victory over the first of the demons. Lydia lifted a hand purposefully, her fingers splayed widely as she summoned a burning ball of tar from one of the barrels. Her friend looked to be filled with a cold fury as she gestured with her upraised hand and flung the ball of burning pitch right at the head of one of the creatures. Emea glanced across at Everand. He was pale-faced and clearly terrified, but with gritted teeth he was throwing fireball after fireball at the demons.

Realising she was doing nothing to help, Emea reached out with her power as well, containing as much burning tar within a strike as she could manage. It wasn't quite as big as the sphere Voltan had used to demonstrate with, but it would have to do. Flicking her wrist, she threw it out at the same creature Lydia had attacked. Although it moved slowly, her strike hit the demon below the waist, leaving a second patch of flame on its dark bulk as it rushed forward. For a moment it looked like the magicians had the upper hand in the fight, as fireballs landed on all three of the demons, but then two more slid heavily out of the darkness, moving quickly towards the gate.

The combined fear effect of five of the creatures was unbearable. Emea felt frozen on the inside as well as the outside, except for her labouring heart, which was trying to beat itself right out of her chest. It seemed as if the other magicians were similarly affected, as the flow of fireballs had all but dried up. Only Voltan continued to fight, throwing fireball after fireball with his teeth gritted, every tendon standing out in sharp relief on his neck as sweat poured down his face. But it wasn't enough. One of the five demons was out of action, covered in a rippling wreath of flame that looked likely to kill it as it howled and writhed in pain and anger. The remaining four converged on the gateway at the same time, and then were suddenly caught in mid-motion. Dark heads swivelled this way and that, accompanied by harsh roars of anger as the magic of the wall was activated. The wall itself, and the slender span of enchanted stone spanning over the head of the four creatures, flared with a searing radiance - a kind of fierce golden glow. Roars of rage swiftly turned to howls of pain as the ancient enchantment fought them, searing them as they tried to push through into the college.
    The fifth demon had perished outside the gate now, and with the four creatures battling to break the enchantment of the wall, Emea felt the dread that had immobilised her loosen its grip. She watched with a horrified fascination as the creatures started to steam and smoke, as the dJin had done all those months ago. Even Voltan had stopped attacking and was grimly watching the magic of the wall do its work. The demons were boiling with a fathomless hatred that was in itself terrifying to behold. How could any creature be filled with such black violence, and not be destroyed from the inside?
    Steam was pouring off the demons in clouds now, as they continued to be resisted by the magic of the wall. Emea couldn't see how they could last much longer. The one on the right suddenly burst into flames and was consumed, and Emea felt a momentary surge of hope. But wait; had the glow of the wall flickered? Emea stared at the glowing stone, hoping beyond hope that she'd imagined it, but no...there it was again. The bright radiance of the wall was no longer constant. It kept dimming and then blazing back into light again, and each time the light returned it was a little less bright than it had been previously. As if sensing victory, the three creatures howled in concert, their combined sound causing Emea's heart to lurch into her throat in an uncontrollable spasm of fear.
    Suddenly Voltan was shouting orders. "THERE IS ALMOST NO

268

TAR LEFT. IF THEY BREAK THROUGH THE GATE SPLIT UP AND FALL BACK TO THE NEXT BARRELS. WE HAVE TO SPLIT THEM UP. THEY ARE TOO POWERFUL TOGETHER. WHEN I SAY RUN, RUN!" And with that he summoned up the remaining tar into a large flaming strike, holding it ready to throw if the magic of the wall failed.

A sharp crack sounded through the night, and Emea looked up in horror to see a jagged break in the stone arch splinter right through the upper part of the gateway's span. The golden light shone defiantly for one last second before flickering out completely, and broken rock tumbled down on the demon's heads.

"RUN!" Voltan yelled, as he sent the last fireball surging into the demon that looked most weakened by the battle with the enchantment of the wall. Emea watched in stupefied fascination as it was engulfed in flame. Lydia was tugging at her arm and shouting something in her ear. She found the strength in her legs, turned, and ran for her life.

When Gaspi arrived back at the gates, the fighting had already moved inside the city wall. The Mage stationed with the guards was nowhere to be seen, and all but one of the demons had already moved on into the city. The one that remained was surrounded by dozens of the dog-like creatures, boiling over each other in a killing frenzy. The guards had been joined by reinforcements from the barracks, and were holding their own. It was easy to see Taurnil, whose blazing blue staff swept through the night in a broad arc. In the light of the staff Gaspi could see Jonn fighting alongside his best friend, and he was pretty sure that was Erik right next to them.

Everything in him wanted to join them, but he was stopped in his tracks by a sudden jolt of realisation. The demons were sent to target magic users. Perhaps they could harm normal people and perhaps not; but the creature in front of him was not attacking any of the guards, but seemed to be making straight for Taurnil, whose staff advertised him as some kind of magical adversary. Gaspi desperately wanted to help Taurnil, but there were nine more of those creatures, all of whom looked like they would bypass the defences of the lower city and head straight for the college...for Emmy! He knew he should get up there and help defend the college, but he was still torn. How could he leave his best friend to fight this thing alone?

A wild flash of blue caught his attention, as Taurnil's staff connected with one of the dogs. Its ribs snapped loudly as they broke, its snarls turned into strangely pitiful yelps as the creature fell writhing to the floor. Taurnil leapt over the fallen dog, pausing only to crush its skull with the metal end of his staff. He let out a coarse yell, sprinting straight at the demon at the centre of the melee. It howled in response, and Taurnil's staff flared with an even greater brightness. Although Gaspi couldn't make out any expression in the featureless black vortex of the demon's face, there was something in its response that looked like hesitancy. Taurnil sprang forward with a shout, and his staff burst into bright blue flame. Convinced now that his enchantment had given Taurnil the power to face this foe, Gaspi made the difficult choice, and turned away from the fight. He ran towards the college with every last bit of speed he could muster. He'd always been fast, but no village competition had ever spurred him on to such a pace. The demons were heading straight for the college, and Emmy was there. Nothing else mattered to him now.

He sprinted past burning tents and wagons, past groups of people running terrified through the streets, or sensibly hiding in buildings, peering fearfully out of darkened windows. There were bodies everywhere; guardsmen ripped and mauled lay dead across the ground. The wounded cried out in agony, reaching out to Gaspi for help as he vaulted over their sprawled limbs and carried on towards his goal. He rounded the final corner of the road leading up to the college to find that the enchanted archway that used to span so elegantly over the gateway a broken, useless piece of rock. The once glowing stone was piled at the foot of the gateway, lifeless now, drained of all enchantment. With a cry of despair, Gaspi jumped over the failed barrier, and stepped into carnage...

Chapter 34

Hephistole stayed in his tower when the fighting began. Some instinct he daren't ignore compelled him to stay and watch the battle as it unfolded, waiting for something that would tell him what to do. He couldn't put his finger on it, but something didn't feel right. Using a scrying device, he watched with tears flowing freely down his face as the guards bravely gave their lives to defend the city against what he recognised as Wargs; a perversion of nature bred from wolves, and altered by dark enchantments. He watched with pride as Voltan organised a brave defence at the wall, and with grim satisfaction as Taurnil wielded his magical staff with deadly efficiency, destroying one of the demons in a fierce duel. After dispatching the demon the young fighter left the fighting at the gate, which was now under control, and sprinted up towards the college.

He sent out his senses throughout the college, marking out where their enemies were gathered. The Wargs had been held at the city gates, three demons had been destroyed at the wall, and Taurnil had killed another. Two had penetrated the wall and were being fought by magicians stationed in the college, so that left four unaccounted for. He searched for them carefully, letting his consciousness roam through the campus, alert for any demonic presence, and then he found them. They must have missed the gate when moving up through the city towards the college, and were circling the once-enchanted wall. It didn't appear that their corporeal embodiment enabled them to climb, as they were even now circling the wall, looking for an entrance. Hephistole could see that they would soon stumble across the broken gate, and there would be six demons loose within college grounds. It looked like it was time for him to join the fight.

He sent his perception out for one last sweep of the city and college grounds, and sensed two things that caused his breath to hitch in his throat. One was Gaspi sprinting up towards the gate, on a collision course with the four demons still coming round the curve of the wall, and the second was a sudden surge of powerful magic emitting from the abandoned pyramid - Shirukai Sestin's pyramid. He froze, unable to look away from either sight. The sense of wrongness his instinct had alerted him to earlier now swelled and surged into full bloom as dark power flooded from the long-abandoned structure. Panels that had sealed themselves shut decades earlier slid open without a sound on each side of the pyramid, and a tide of Wargs poured from the openings. They followed one much larger Warg built on the same twisted canine model, but bulking twice the size of the others, its armour-like hide tinged a blood-red colour.

Hephistole didn't feel he had a choice. Gaspi was going to have to use the powers that had been bestowed on him; a Nature Mage was never defenceless. They had been tricked, and only he knew they were being attacked from within. With a sick feeling that he might regret his decision, Hephistole stepped onto the transporter, and was magicked to the atrium. The large entrance to the tower was deserted – all the magicians would be spread throughout the city and the campus, stationed by the barrels of tar.

Hephistole sent out a mind probe to Voltan. "We're attacked from within. They're coming through the pyramid. Rearrange the defence."

Voltan's response arrived in his own head like a thought he didn't think. "We're all split up. I'll be there; will bring others."

Hephistole was a powerful Mage, much more so even than Voltan, but even he knew he couldn't take on what looked like forty or fifty Wargs on his own. He moved quickly back towards the wall, gathering magicians as he went. Some of the guards had been stationed in the campus in case of attack, and they joined him too. Halfway to the wall he met Voltan, who had brought five magicians and about twenty guards. Hephistole was relieved to see that Taurnil was among them.

"Taurnil, go back to the college gate and help Gaspi. He will be fighting there," he said. Taurnil turned on his heels and sprinted off. The Chancellor looked round at the rest of them. The complement of guards was bolstered by the presence of Sabu and Baard, fighters who, along with Taurnil, carried magically enhanced weapons. Sabu's curved scimitars were unsheathed, emitting a faint white glow that announced the presence of magic. The massive two-handed axe Baard carried had a kind of dark, heavy aura that made it hard to look at directly for more than a few seconds. Hephistole knew Bonebreaker's history, and seeing it glowing darkly in Baard's hands, he felt uncertain about using it in their defence. A moment later he dismissed the thought; desperate times make for desperate measures. He looked around at the gathering of fighters and magicians. "This will have to do," he said.

He spoke quickly to Voltan, who addressed the group of guards and magicians.

"There's been an incursion of about fifty Wargs - the dogs - inside the campus. They came through the pyramid." Several of the older magicians drew a collective intake of breath through clenched teeth.

"There don't seem to be any more of the demons, but there are still six of those around here somewhere. So be on your guard, and check behind you as you go. Follow!" he ordered. Hephistole fell in next to him, and the group followed behind, as Voltan paced rapidly towards the pyramid.

Within minutes, a group of seven Wargs came streaming around a corner, baying and growling at the sight of flesh and blood. The one in front sprang into motion, flowing over the ground towards them with unnatural speed. Voltan threw a heavy force strike at it, powerful enough to blast a man off his feet; but the Warg was only slowed briefly, pushing through the strike with a kind of grunt.

"They're resistant to magic!" Voltan cried. "Guards forward!" he ordered.

Led by Sabu and Baard, the guards jumped out past the magicians without hesitation and ran at the Wargs with a loud shout, swords brandished before them. Bonebreaker was a flowing streak of night that cut one of the Wargs in half with a single stroke, and Sabu's glowing white scimitars whirled in the blade master's dance of death, slicing another one up in seconds.But between the two fighters the other guards were being slaughtered; ripped to pieces by the vicious rending teeth and claws of creatures designed for only one thing. The magicians did what they could, trying different strikes and spells to slow the Wargs' advance until Sabu and Baard could deal with them. However, their spells had little effect, and Voltan quickly stopped them, urging them to save their spell power until it was really needed. This fight was up to the guards. Baard and Sabu dispatched a second pair of Wargs, and the other guards had killed two in the course of the fight, leaving only one Warg to kill. Seeing it was alone, the last Warg broke and ran, and Baard started to chase after it.

"Hold!" Voltan commanded, and the huge fighter reluctantly stopped. "Keep order. There are many more of them, and we don't want to run into another pack unprepared."

Chastened, Baard re-joined the group, and Voltan led them forward once again. They'd won that battle, but as they passed the corpses of the six Wargs they'd killed, Hephistole looked at the four dead guards who lay among them, and wondered how many more would die before they could win this fight. *If* they could win it.

Gaspi stepped through the broken gate, his heart full of anxiety for Emea. The area around the gate told the story of a hard-fought battle. Broken stone lay shattered all around, and patches of the ground were scorched, remnants of burning tar still flickering around the edges. He couldn't see any bodies, so the fight must have moved further back into the campus. He was bending down to examine one of the scorched areas of ground when the hairs on the back of his neck stood on end, and a frigid chill puckered his skin. Whirling around, he was faced with a terrifying sight. Four of the demons were passing through the gate behind them, their dark bulk drawing all warmth and light into a ravenous vacuum. As one the creatures saw him, and, lifting their heavy heads, let out a chorus of grating howls that threatened to curl a fist around Gaspi's soul and rip it right out of his body.

Fear battered Gaspi like a hurricane, but he had been expecting it, and kept a tight grip on himself. Reaching out with his magic, he summoned the flickering remnants of flame from the ground, forging them into a single hovering ball of fire. He flattened it, shaping it into a wide shield between himself and the demons, who stopped their advance, uncertainty making them hesitate. Gaspi didn't show any such hesitation, but reached out with his magic to an old tree planted near the gateway. With a thought he shattered the heavy trunk into jagged shards of wood, summoning them to his side. He siphoned flame away from his shield, lighting them with magically enhanced flame. He whispered to the burning shards of wood, urging the fire to burn hotter, and in moments they were transformed into blazing spears, sizzling with super-heated sap. With an angry motion he let his shield drop away, and flung his burning arsenal at the four creatures.

They didn't have a chance to flee, rearing up in surprise as they were peppered with the burning shards. A two–foot-long shaft of flaming wood flew straight into the face of the nearest demon, piercing so deeply it thrust out the back of its head. The creature didn't even have time to react, collapsing in on itself so rapidly Gaspi almost lost his concentration. One second it was there; the next it was not. The other three creatures were not so easily banished. Hurt, but by no means vanquished, they rushed at Gaspi, howling fiercely as they came. They made a frightening spectacle, looming figures of darkness punctured by burning spears of wood, filling his vision as they slid heavily towards him.

For a moment Gaspi was immobilised, horror stealing his strength of purpose, and then they were on him. Gaspi shuddered as they reached out for him, his back arching in agony as the touch of dark hands froze him inside and out. Incapable of movement or action, Gaspi's mouth opened in a silent scream as he felt his power, his precious magic, being siphoned out from the very core of his being. Anger pierced his incapacitating fear, and with a roar of defiance Gaspi found his strength. He reached out and grabbed a large shard of burning wood, pulling it from a demon's body. Uncaring of the searing pain in his hand, he thrust it with a yell into the face of the demon right in front

274

of him. He pulled his hand back, willing the flaming spear to blaze, and as it flared white hot , the creature stumbled back from him, clawing ineffectually at its face until it too collapsed to the ground and dissolved into nothing.

The pain in Gaspi's hand was suddenly unbearable. He knew he should be attacking the remaining two demons but it was all he could do to keep from sobbing, clutching his ruined hand to his chest. Sensing victory, the demons let out a twisted howl of rage mixed with a rapacious hunger for Gaspi's power, and fell on him again. When the cold grip of fear paralysed Gaspi again, he couldn't find the strength to resist. He felt his power being drawn out of him once more, dragged up from his most private of inner places. A spark of anger rose in him again, but it was not enough. Abused in every part of his being, Gaspi was immobilised in horrified stasis, willing that the darkness take him, willing that it be over.

And then it was. A bright flare of vivid blue light swept across his vision, and the freezing cold receded. Gaspi was so far gone he almost didn't care, his eyes closing in brokenness and exhaustion, but someone was yelling, shouting his name. Why were they making all that noise? When the yelling didn't stop, Gaspi forced himself to focus, opening his eyes a crack to once again see the vivid flare of blue cutting bright swathes through the night. He forced his eyes open further. The blue fire was blazing from a weapon; a staff. Taurnil! Summoned back suddenly to full consciousness, Gaspi took in the scene before him.

"Taurnil," Gaspi said weakly, watching helplessly as Taurnil battled the two remaining demons. His initial attack had surprised them, the bright blue fire of his staff inflicting unexpected pain. They approached him warily from both sides, looming menacingly over Taurnil, their arms outstretched hungrily towards their prey. Taurnil stepped back carefully, trying to draw them nearer to each other. Blue flame rippled over his staff, apparently not burning his hands at all. Taurnil continued to step backwards slowly and methodically, manoeuvring the demons into a better position. Gaspi could see the concentration on his friend's face, the tightly clenched muscles of his jaw bunching with tension. Suddenly, Taurnil sprang to the right, putting one of the creatures between himself and the other one. Even through the haze of his unbearable pain, Gaspi's heart lurched in fear for his friend. Taurnil brought his staff up, blazing with searing blue fire, and slammed it down across the head of the nearest demon. The blue flame burned even more fiercely as the blow landed, hungry to destroy its enemy. The demon let out a fearsome howl of pain - a sound so broken and grating it hurt Gaspi's bones just to hear it.

Taurnil didn't relent, pressing his staff down hard against the demon's face as it twisted and shrieked, blue flame spreading out from the staff across its head. The other demon didn't attack, frozen in a kind of dumb uncertainty. The first demon was now fully ablaze, shrieking in agony as it burned. Taurnil held the staff in place, his face a mask of fierce anger as the creature finally collapsed in on itself, burned out of existence by the bright blue fire. Taurnil lifted his head slowly, his angry gaze stopping on the last demon, which was already backing away from him. Turning, it started to flee, gliding over the ground as fast as it could, heading into the depths of the campus. Taurnil flipped his staff up into the air, catching it over his head. Hefting it like a spear, he bounced it against his hand a couple of times, getting the measure of its weight, and then with one swift motion he flung it at the fleeing demon. The flame made a roaring sound as the staff flew through the air, a sound that should have alerted the demon to its impending doom. The staff flew straight and true and caught the demon between the shoulders, piercing right through its dark torso, and protruding from its chest. The creature couldn't even make a sound. It spun slowly in one heavy circle, blue fire sheeting up its torso, and consuming its heavy head. Within moments it simply disappeared and Taurnil's staff fell with a clatter to the cobblestones; its magical fire dying out, leaving them in darkness.

Gaspi gasped as pain throbbed agonisingly through his hand with every heartbeat. Taurnil was quickly by his side.

"Are you okay, Gasp?" he asked, with obvious concern.

"No," was all Gaspi could say, his breath hissing through clenched teeth.

"We've got to get you to the infirmary," Taurnil said, picking up his friend as easily as if he were a child. Gaspi moaned and held his hand to his chest. Taurnil started to walk briskly towards the infirmary.

"The staff," Gaspi hissed. "Get the staff."

Taurnil turned, and carried Gaspi over to where the staff lay on the floor. "Hold on mate," he said. Gaspi put his good arm round Taurnil's neck as he bent down to retrieve the staff. Taurnil had to carry it in awkwardly, pressed up against Gaspi's side, bruising him with every step, but that was better than leaving it behind. If more of the demons came, they'd be in trouble without it. Gaspi really didn't think he'd be able to draw on his magic through the pain he was feeling. He passed in and out of consciousness as Taurnil carried him, the pain in his hand pushed back by moments of dark oblivion, and then the darkness took him completely.

Gaspi came round, lying on a bed in the infirmary. The first thing he noticed was the diminishing pain in his hand. Looking down he saw Emea kneeling by his side, determination on her face as she cupped her hands over his burnt hand and forearm. White light shone brightly from between her fingers, and with every second the pain receded further and further, until it disappeared altogether. Emea gave a start as Gaspi sat up. "Oh, you're conscious!" she said, with relief.

Gaspi kissed her warmly. "Thanks, Emmy," he said. Emea flashed him a grim, but triumphant, smile.

A loud cry of pain from across the room grabbed his attention. Looking around, he realised that every bed was occupied with wounded guards, all sporting gruesome injuries. The cry of pain came from a man in the far corner, whose face was furrowed with deep gouges from chin to forehead. There was only a ragged, wet hole where his left eye had been. Gaspi gagged and looked away, shocked by the gory sight. Healers in white robes bustled from bed to bed, tending to the wounded as quickly as they could.

Gaspi pushed himself off the bed, wanting to get out of there as quickly as possible. He signalled to Taurnil. "Let's go mate. This time we stick together." Taurnil nodded, and picked up his staff.

"I'm needed here," Emea said. Her eyes landed briefly on each of them with a curious intensity, as if burning their faces into her memory. "Look after each other," she said, and then she was at the bedside of the guard with only one eye.

Gaspi and Taurnil headed out into the night. There was no obvious direction to go in. "Where should we go?" Taurnil asked, looking up and down the path.

"The tower," Gaspi said on instinct. "Any kind of fighting will probably end up there."

They set off at a steady trot, looking left and right as they ran, but they didn't come across any demons or Wargs. Minutes later they arrived at the tower, and still found themselves alone. A sudden motion to the right caused them to jump. Taurnil's staff was already in his hands, ready for battle, as Gaspi drew deeply on the magic within him, summoning power to his fingertips as they whirled to face their attackers. But instead of a pack or Wargs or the dark bulk of a demon, they were faced with the backs of several guardsmen and Voltan, carefully retreating towards the tower, stepping backwards as if expecting attack from the front at any moment. As if sensing someone behind him, Voltan looked over his shoulder, and saw them.

Taurnil lowered his staff. "Stay ready!" Voltan ordered. "They've split up and could come from anywhere." Taurnil lifted his staff once more. Gaspi kept his power tingling at his fingertips. A second commotion had them whirling in another direction, but this time it was Hephistole and another handful of guardsmen. Hephistole's hair hung wildly round his face, his eyes blazing with a fierce light Gaspi had never seen before in the normally genial Chancellor. Gaspi was taken aback by the aura of sheer power emanating from Hephistole's crimson-robed frame. He was almost crackling with magical energy, lively as storm-tossed air before a lightning strike.

Seeing Gaspi, Taurnil and Voltan, he strode over towards them, leaving the guards behind him to cover their retreat. "Gaspi, Taurnil. Good," he said as if ticking off items on an inventory. "Voltan, how did you fare?"

"We killed twelve but lost ten guards," he said, business-like but grave.

Hephistole looked around at the remaining guards. "So we have thirteen men, three magicians, Sabu, Baard, and Taurnil," he said as if measuring them against an unknown standard. "The other magicians?" he asked.

"Robyn and Thieron saw one of the demons and went to battle it. Beth was taken down by the Wargs," Voltan reported, pain showing through his brusqueness.

Hephistole said nothing for a moment, absorbing the news, and for a moment Gaspi could see deep sadness flowering behind his eyes. The Chancellor gathered himself, shelving his emotions.

"Voltan, stand guard at the foot of the tower. I'm going to use the scryer to see where the fighting is. Gaspi, come with me," Hephistole commanded, and strode into the tower. Gaspi hurried to keep up as the tall Chancellor strode purposefully towards the transporter. Speaking the word of command, Hephistole initiated the device, and they were quickly at the top of the tower. He led Gaspi around the broad curve of the office, until they reached what Gaspi assumed was the scrying device - a large white sphere resting on a bronze, three-legged stand. It was filled with a misty white substance, like smoke captured in glass, glowing gently as it swirled.

"This will show us how things stand," Hephistole said. He placed the tips of his fingers against the device, and closed his eyes. Gaspi watched intently as the glowing mist span more rapidly, responding to Hephistole's magic as he began to search with his inner sight...

Taurnil stood guard at the entrance to the tower, surrounded by the surviving guardsmen. He was in good company: Sabu stood to his right, and Baard to his left. The blademaster looked relaxed, but Taurnil knew this was an illusion, and that Sabu kept his energy contained like a coiled spring, waiting to be unleashed when it was needed. Baard was formidable enough on his own - an enormous, red-bearded, fighting man with incredible strength and a reputation for unpredictability - but, carrying that glowing black axe, he looked like a god of war. Voltan stayed with them, watching the possible routes the Wargs could take to reach the tower in a state of transparent readiness. Taurnil looked at the heavy lines etched into Voltan's serious face; lines currently hardened in determination and anger. Taurnil was glad they were on the same side. Voltan would make a formidable enemy. A loud growl brought him back to attention. A chorus of snarls and yelps sounded from one of the nearby passageways. A louder, deeper growl ripped through the others, quieting them in an instant.

Voltan hesitated for a moment, then signalled to eight of the guardsmen, including Baard. "Come with me," he said. "The rest of you stay with Taurnil. Taurnil; you're in charge."

Taurnil was momentarily taken aback by the decision, but he was also well-drilled in responding to the voice of command. "Yes, sir," he said.

As Voltan led his group of guards in the direction the sounds had come from, Taurnil glanced covertly at the remaining guards. Every one of them was older than him, some more than twice his age, but not one of them showed any discomfort at being placed under his command. Perhaps it was because of his staff, but Sabu had the swords, so that didn't completely make sense. He caught Sabu's eye, concerned that the blademaster might be unhappy with the arrangement, but Sabu just gave him a small smile and a nod, letting Taurnil know he was fine with it.

There was no need to say anything. They were already standing in a defensive formation, and Taurnil wasn't about to start shouting orders for no good reason. Instead, he scanned the various entranceways to the open area in front of the tower, alert and ready for action. The Wargs could come out of any entrances, at any moment.

The sounds of fighting erupted from somewhere in the maze of streets in front of them. Some of the guards started forward instinctively, anxious to support their comrades. Taurnil held them back with a simple hand gesture. "We can't leave the tower defenceless," he said. "Voltan told us to hold." Everyone settled back into position.

The minutes ticked by with unbearable slowness. Loud cries and the occasional boom of a magical concussion punctuated the waiting, setting Taurnil's teeth on edge. If only something would just happen!

And then it did. Twelve Wargs came boiling out of a passageway, silent as the grave, and heading straight for the tower. "Guards, ready!" Taurnil cried, each of his group of fighters bravely readying themselves in the face of overbearing odds.

Taurnil had a few surreal seconds to watch the Wargs silently eating up the ground between them, before the first deafening collision of battle pushed all thought from his mind. His staff connected with the first Warg, its magically enhanced strength smashing right through its ribs, and killing it on the spot. With the exception of Sabu, his guards didn't share the advantage of magical weapons, however, and were immediately battling for their lives with creatures stronger and faster than they were; armed with vicious teeth and cruel claws, and powered by iron-hard muscles built for destruction. Taurnil leapt to help one guard, just as he saw the brutal teeth of a Warg clamp onto the throat of another. The Warg shook the guard like a cloth doll, ripping his throat right out with one powerful wrench of its jaws.

Taurnil span back to help the struggling guard, gagging as he fought. He broke one Warg's spine with a single heavy blow of his staff, so that it could only drag itself along the ground using only its front legs, its limp torso and hind legs a dead weight behind it. Filled with horrifying malice, it snarled and snapped at the ankles of any guard who got too near, desperate to cause pain and injury to the hated humans. To his right Sabu span and swirled, magical blades aflame with white light as they cut effortlessly through hard muscle and sinew and even bone. Two Wargs already lay dead by his hand, one of them beheaded by a single swipe of those formidable blades.

Taurnil assessed the situation in a glance. The odds were still against them. There were eight Wargs left, but two guards were down, and others were hard pressed, bleeding from numerous injuries. Another Warg suddenly sprang out of the dark. It was twice as big as any of the others - more like a small horse than a dog - and something about it filled him with loathing and dread at the same time. Taurnil stepped back and raised his staff, bracing himself for a brutal impact, but it sprang right past him, rushing into the interior of the tower. Taurnil knew in that moment that, above everything else, he had to stop this Warg.

He left the other guards to battle the remaining Wargs, and raced after the big one. It was heading straight for the last of the twelve glowing plinths set into the floor round the periphery of the room. Taurnil took long leaping strides towards the monstrous Warg, lifting his staff above his head like a spear, ready to throw it as soon as he was in range.

The Warg reached the plinth and spun around, its baleful eyes filled not only with the same driving hatred as the other Wargs, but with an undeniable intelligence. Taurnil took one more pace and threw his staff, sending it slicing through the air towards his adversary. The Warg glared at Taurnil with a kind of wilful mockery, before growling a word Taurnil couldn't make out, and disappearing. Taurnil's staff sizzled through the air where the Warg had been just a second before, and clattered against the wall, dropping to the floor. Taurnil raced to pick it up, and jumped onto the plinth. What was the damn word?

"Follow!" he said. Nothing happened. Roaring in fury, knowing he'd failed in his most important duty, he raced back towards the other soldiers. At least he could make sure none of the other Wargs survived.

Chapter 35

Gaspi stood by Hephistole, watching intently as the Chancellor's enigmatic face was drawn in fierce concentration. His eyes moved back and forth beneath closed eyelids, hands splayed widely over the scrying sphere. Suddenly, his eyes sprang open.

"The demons have been banished, but the Wargs are attacking the tower. We have to get down there," he said, and then froze in mid-motion. "The transporter!" he said, his voice edged with sudden fear. Gaspi never thought he'd hear that tone of voice from Hephistole, and his guts clenched anxiously in response. Summoning his power to his fingertips, he turned to face the direction of the transporter.

The scryer was right around on the far side of the office from the transporter, but in a matter of seconds they could hear the sound of something heavy ripping up the polished wood of Hephistole's exquisite floor, an unknown something that was getting rapidly closer. Hephistole also summoned his power, a nimbus of gently glowing light surrounding him as he drank deeply of the magic within. A huge creature sprang from round the curve of the office. In a surreal moment that seemed to last forever, Gaspi noticed every detail of the massive Warg; the sheer size of the thing, the bunching of muscles thicker than his torso, the thick, hooked claws and brutal teeth, the slaver dripping from its snarling mouth, the reddened, intelligent eyes. Everything about it shouted of killing. A large medallion hung from its neck, bouncing against its chest as it rushed towards them.

The moment passed in a heartbeat, and Gaspi started to forge his power into the biggest force strike he could muster. Hephistole, similarly, was summoning some form of attack, when the Warg skidded to a stop. With a dip of its head it ripped the medallion from around its leather thong, and flipped it across the floor towards them. Gaspi watched in dull apprehension as the device skidded and span across the polished wood, stopping at their feet.

Hephistole's strike flew from his fingers; a golden, misty substance that Gaspi had never seen the like of before. It formed into a serpentine shape and whipped across the room, wrapping itself around the giant Warg's neck. Gaspi released his force strike, a massive ball of energy that hit the Warg square in the head.

A loud buzzing drew Gaspi's attention, and after a moment he realised it came from the device near his feet. Too late, Hephistole reached out to grab it, but red light burst out from its core, surrounding them in a crimson radiance. Gaspi tried to summon another strike, but his magic was untouchable, blocked away beyond his reach. He tried again.

"It's no good," Hephistole said quietly. "It's the device. It blocks magic."

Gaspi didn't hesitate and kicked at it, trying to send it spinning away from them. As his foot connected, Hephistole looked at him with a mixture of chagrin and acceptance. The device skidded away as intended, but when the periphery of the light reached the two magicians it was as if a wall slammed into them, dragging them along with the edge of the sphere of radiance. The pain Gaspi felt wasn't just physical; it was as if his thoughts and feelings were scraped along the floor with him. When they stopped moving, Gaspi looked at Hephistole apologetically. The Chancellor just smiled grimly, and turned his attention to the Warg.

The massive creature was growling in annoyance, snapping at the constricting golden mist around its neck. Gaspi's force strike had done almost nothing, but somehow Hephistole's summoning still existed beyond the circle of red light, strangling the Warg in its intangible grip. The Warg growled deeply, a sound as visceral as Gaspi could imagine, and then with a final shake of its heavy head, the spell dispersed.

"Resistant to magic," Hephistole murmured quietly to himself.

Gaspi almost jumped when the thing spoke. "I wish I could rip you apart," the Warg snarled, a hoarse and broken sound emitting from a throat that was never designed for speech, "but my master has other plans."

"Your master?" Hephistole asked, almost conversationally.

"You'll find out soon enough," growled the Warg, advancing towards them. Gaspi's stomach clenched in fear. There was no way they could fight this monster if they couldn't use magic. Even with it, they could only slow it down. Gaspi glanced around hurriedly, looking frantically for a solution.

And then he saw it. They were not far from the other way out of Hephistole's office – the hole you could drop through and float down to the atrium. Jonn had told him about it after his first and only visit to the Chancellor's office. The red light emitted by the magic-subduing device had an edge. It beamed unwholesomely for several metres, and then stopped at a clearly defined point. They were encased in a dome of light, and he'd already found out that it could be moved. One good kick in the direction of the hole could move the dome so that it extended over it, and perhaps he could drop through. The dome may negate the magic of the hole, but he remembered what Jonn had told him all those months ago; the plinth at the bottom should stop anyone falling before they hit the floor. It was a massive gamble, but much better than letting this Warg get them.

The Warg was stepping through the curtain of red light now, a hungry expression on its vicious face. Gaspi gave Hephistole a meaningful look and glanced first at the hole, then at the medallion, and then at his foot, which he swung slightly. Understanding dawned on Hephistole's face, and he gave the tiniest nod of assent. Gaspi didn't hesitate, but stepped over to the buzzing device. He took aim, and lifted his foot.

"You don't want to do that," growled the Warg, not understanding Gaspi's intent. Gaspi judged the distance, and deftly swung his foot.

"Run!" he shouted at Hephistole, who needed no urging to keep pace with the skittering object. Gaspi's kick looked like it might not have been hard enough, the skidding device slowing down earlier than he'd expected, but it slid just far enough that the edge of the dome of light extended out over the hole, leaving just enough room for someone to drop through. Seeing the danger, the Warg growled and leaped at Gaspi, just as Gaspi threw himself into a slide along the floor, the Warg's jaws snapping loudly in the empty air where Gaspi had just been standing. He spun onto his front as he slid, looking backwards at the monstrous creature as it bounded towards him, its savage jaws opening wide as it reached for him. Gaspi braced himself for the inevitable bite, but then he felt his feet slide out over nothing. He slipped out of the hole like a trout from a fisherman's hands, and just had enough time to flash the briefest of smiles at the dread creature's furious face.

Falling through the air, his stomach flying right up into his throat, Gaspi had an infinitesimal moment to acknowledge that the device had indeed negated the magic of the hole, before the panic of a person falling to his death overtook him. He tumbled head over heels, rooms and ceilings flashing past in bewildering succession, the floor of the atrium rushing up beneath him. Gaspi screamed, too panicked to be able to draw on his magic. The impact was only a microsecond away, his heart thumping madly in his chest; and then suddenly the air thickened around him, slowing him so abruptly that his flesh felt like it was pressing into his bones. And then he stopped completely, hovering for a brief second about a foot above the ground. He let out an enormous breath before the magic let go of him altogether, and he landed face first on the hard plinth.

Bouncing to his feet, he ran to the entranceway, where Taurnil and the guards were still battling the last two Wargs. Taurnil was just finishing one of them off with a blow to the neck, when Gaspi ran out of the tower. Voltan arrived at the same time, stalking out one of the passageways with three guards on his tail, including the enormous Baard, whose wild red beard was matted with blood that ran from a cut on his head.

"Taurnil, Voltan, we've got to get up to Hephistole's office. He's trapped up there!" Gaspi said urgently. Taurnil immediately broke away from the fight with the last Warg, which was surrounded by too many guardsmen, snarling its anger and hatred even in the face of inevitable death. Gaspi led Voltan and Taurnil to the transporter.

"What are we facing up there?" Voltan asked brusquely.

"Hephistole's caught by a massive Warg. There's some kind of device that stops him using magic," he said. "The Warg's really resistant to magic - so Taurnil, you'll have the best chance at fighting it."

"Okay...let's go," the fierce magician said, urging them to get onto the plinth. He spoke the word of command, and the three of them appeared a moment later in Hephistole's office.

"It's round the other side," Gaspi said, leading them quickly round the interior of the Chancellor's long office. He could hear the sounds of struggle from up ahead, and was fearful of what that might mean. "It's just a bit further," he whispered. "By the hole."

Urgency sped their steps as they neared the spot, both Gaspi and Voltan summoning power to the tips of their fingers, and Taurnil bringing up his staff in readiness. They stepped round the last part of the curving wall, and found Hephistole flat on his back, using his long legs to scurry backwards away from the enormous Warg. Somehow he had escaped from the magical field and was now fighting for his life, throwing spells into the snarling creature's face that would have floored anything else, but which only slowed the magic-resistant Warg down. It snapped and snarled its way through each spell, bearing inexorably down on the chancellor.

Gaspi's hair stood on end as Voltan released a spear of blazing white light. He shouted in defiance as he released it, catching the Warg full in the face as it turned to face him. The Warg dipped its head, seemingly in pain, giving Hephistole the time he needed to scramble to his feet and back away.

"Go for its eyes!" Voltan shouted. All three Magicians cast their spells at once, and the Warg was struck in the face by a three-pronged attack. Voltan had thrown another blinding white spear, Hephistole a stinging globe of sparkling red particles, and Gaspi had seized an ornate letter opener with his power, and sent it flying right into one of the creature's eyes. The Warg reared up in pain, the letter opener quivering in its right eye, fluid running down its face from the terrible wound.

With a loud shout, Taurnil leapt forward, his glowing staff held high above his head. The Warg turned to face him, an avalanche-like growl rumbling in its throat as it launched itself towards this new attacker. Taurnil stopped short, judged the momentum of the Warg, and brought his staff down in a crushing blow, aiming for its neck. The Warg shifted to the side at the last second, and Taurnil's staff slammed heavily into its ribs. The Warg let out a doglike whimper, as a loud snapping noise punctuated the sounds of battle. Limping backwards in obvious pain and surprise, it turned its baleful eye to its tormentor, glaring at him as if searing him into its memory.

"This is not the end," it growled in its broken voice; and, spinning around, it leaped into the dome of light. Taurnil hefted his staff above his head once again. All three magicians summoned power to their fingertips, but the Warg ran quickly to the device, pressing on its centre with a heavy paw. With an intense buzzing vibration it disappeared, the red light winking out of existence.

Taurnil lowered his staff, as the three magicians stood for a long moment of frozen shock. "That was a transporter," Hephistole said hoarsely, breaking the silence. "It was meant to take me with it."

"Take you where?" Gaspi asked.

"There'll be time for all that later," Voltan said firmly, ushering the shaken Chancellor to a seat. "You two get to the infirmary," he said.

"But sir..." Gaspi said. Voltan raised a hand to quiet him.

"I promise you, you will find out everything later - but for now, please go to the infirmary," he said. "I will check on you later."

"Okay," Gaspi said grudgingly, eyeing the fragile-looking Chancellor, who looked shaken for the first time since Gaspi had known him. He turned and started walking away with Taurnil, heading for the transporter.

"Gaspi," Hephistole called gently after him. Gaspi turned around. "Thank you," he said.

Gaspi nodded, smiling wearily. "You're welcome, Heppy," he said, and walked away.

Emea waited anxiously in the infirmary. It seemed like forever since Gaspi and Taurnil had walked out of the door, and as the stream of new casualties slowed and then dwindled to almost nothing, she had far too much time on her hands and nothing to do except worry. She wouldn't allow herself to finish any thought that started with *what if*, but despite her resolve she couldn't stop tension building up, until she was blinking back tears that seemed determined to form in her eyes every few minutes. Jonn came in at one point to check on her and let her know he was okay. Grateful for his visit, it wasn't long after he left to look for Gaspi and Taurnil that worry consumed her again. When the door swung open and her two battle-stained friends walked through it she abandoned restraint altogether and flew into their arms, kissing them both over and over amidst a constant flow of unchecked tears.

It was Taurnil who broke away first, looking around anxiously. "Where's Lydia?" he asked.

"Have you seen Jonn?" Gaspi added.

"Jonn's fine," Emea said, placing a reassuring hand on Gaspi's arm. "Taurn," she continued gently. "There's nothing to worry about...but Lydia was brought in not long ago."

"What happened?" he asked, stricken with worry despite Emea's assurances."

"She was fighting one of those demons," Emea said with a shudder. "It got the better of her and started draining her power, but two magicians came along just in time and killed it. She'll be okay, Taurn," Emea said gently, placing a hand on his tense forearm. "The other magicians got there in time, and she just needs to rest."

"Are you telling me I can't see her?" Taurnil said, tension straining his normally gentle manner.

"Good grief, no!" Emea said. "She won't stop asking about you. Come and see her right now, so she can sleep."

Emea led Taurnil and Gaspi to an annex of the infirmary, where Lydia lay abed, staring out of the large window into the campus grounds. Taurnil took four enormous strides across the room, falling to his knees by her bedside, and engulfed her in an enormous hug before she could even fully register what was happening. As she realised whose arms it was that held her, she slowly lifted her own, and slid them around his back.

"Thank heavens you're alive, you big bear," Lydia said softly, kissing him gently on the cheek.

"Are you okay?" Taurnil asked solicitously.

"I was stupid," she said. "I took on one of those demons by myself, and it cornered me. It was awful," she said, her eyes growing troubled as she thought back on the experience. "But some magicians saved me," she said, "and as far as I understand, I'll be fine with a bit of rest."

"Which is exactly what you're going to get," Emea said, with mock sternness, from the doorway. "Come on, Taurnil," she said. "Lydia needs to sleep, and not even you are allowed to get in the way of that."

Taurnil looked back at Lydia, his eyes locked onto hers as she smiled gently. "You'd better go, or we'll both get into trouble," she said. "I'll be fine now, knowing that you're okay." Taurnil looked like he wouldn't leave her for all the world.

"Go on, Taurn," Lydia said. "We'll have plenty of time later."

Taurnil stood slowly, bending to give Lydia a soft kiss before walking out with Emea and Gaspi. Taurnil cleared his throat. "Sorry I was rude before, Emmy," he said. "It's just…"

"Don't be sorry, Taurn," Emea said, slipping her small hand into the crook of his arm. "You never have to apologise for loving my friend."

Taurnil smiled, saying nothing more, as the three friends headed back out into the entranceway. Emea sent Gaspi and Taurnil off to get some rest, but she would check to see if anyone else needed her before she left. She wasn't going to leave the infirmary until the last patient had been healed.

Chapter 36

The next couple of weeks passed slowly for Gaspi and his friends. The city was reeling in shock after the attack, and despite the tireless work of the Healers, many guardsmen had been killed by the Wargs. Two magicians had also been killed, drained of all life by the demons, and signs of destruction were evident throughout the city and the campus. People spoke in quiet voices, relieved to be alive, but not wanting to disturb the mourning of those who had lost loved ones. Even as the remaining guards and civilian volunteers brought order back to the damaged parts of the city and campus, and things began to appear as they had done before the battle, the smashed gateway into the college still spoke eloquently of the events that had brought the great city to a standstill. Its tumbled stones no longer glowed gently with protective magic, but lay strewn across the ground, and no slender arch of rock gracefully spanned the entrance to the College of Collective Magicks.

All classes had been stopped, and Gaspi and his friends spent time talking in the Traveller's Rest or hanging out in the barracks, reliving the dreadful night they'd somehow made it through alive, feeling increasingly grateful that none of them had been killed. A quiet Feast-Day afternoon found the four friends talking quietly in the Rest, when a messenger arrived from Hephistole, summoning Gaspi to his office.

"Just me?" Gaspi asked.

"That's all he said," the white-robed messenger said, with a shrug.

Gaspi hadn't been back to the office since the battle, and found himself unaccountably nervous. "Tell Jonn where I am when he gets here?" he said to Taurnil.

"Sure, Gasp," Taurnil said. "See you later."

Gaspi kissed Emea, and left his friends in the tavern. On arriving at the tower, the receptionist was expecting him, and waved him straight over to the transporter. When the vibration of the transporter wore off, Gaspi found himself facing Hephistole and Voltan. The Chancellor seemed to be recovered fully from his encounter with the Warg. He lounged in one of the deep chairs near his desk, resplendent in a maroon brocaded gown. Voltan was dressed all in black and sat opposite Hephistole, sipping a cup of fragrant tea.

"Ah, Gaspi," Hephistole said with a warm smile, not rising from his chair. "So good of you to join us."

He indicated that Gaspi should take the third of a trio of chairs ranged around a low circular table, and poured a stream of steaming tea into a fine porcelain cup as Gaspi sat down. Gaspi lifted the cup to his mouth. The steam smelled of autumn leaves and woodsmoke, filling

Gaspi with a deep sense of comfort and peace as he breathed it in.

"A good tea for flagging spirits," Hephistole said, with a wink. Gaspi smiled, and took a sip of the golden brew, letting its fragrant warmth slide over his tongue and down his throat. A restful type of tingling sensation flowed out languidly through his body, spreading down his limbs and to the very tips of his fingers and toes. Gaspi let out a deep sigh of satisfaction. He loved coming to Hephistole's office.

"So...how are you feeling?" the Chancellor asked.

"All right thanks, Hephistole," Gaspi answered. "How about you?"

"I'm pleased to say I'm very much recovered," Hephistole answered. "And no small thanks goes to you, my young friend."

Gaspi flushed with pleasure at being called Hephistole's friend. "It was nothing," he said, somewhat abashed.

"Nothing? I hardly think so," Hephistole countered. "That was quick thinking, moving the field of negation over the exit, and very brave letting yourself fall like that, and equally resourceful bringing the best possible aid. If it wasn't for you, and the help of Voltan and your impressive warrior friend Taurnil, I dare say I would not be here right now."

Gaspi knew Hephistole was referring to the transporter the Warg had used to escape from Hephistole's office, a transporter built into the same device used to block their magic. "Where do you think it would have taken you?" Gaspi asked, uncertain as to how much information he was going to be given.

"Where I would have gone is less important than who was trying to take me there, Gaspi," Hephistole said, suddenly grave. "I've asked you here today, as I've chosen to place my trust in you." He held Gaspi's eye. "Voltan here thinks I should do otherwise; not because you are untrustworthy, but because you are still in training. I have decided on this occasion to ignore his counsel. But before I carry on, I need to ask you if you are willing to hear what I have to say."

Eager for information, Gaspi opened his mouth to respond. "Don't answer too quickly, Gaspi!" Hephistole admonished. "This is the most serious of business, and even hearing what I have to say will place an enormous burden on your shoulders. I think that the moment of this revelation is inevitable, but the timing is not. The choice is yours."

Gaspi sat silently, looking from the Chancellor's earnest face to Voltan's stern one. He forced himself to think seriously about what Hephistole had said. Would he want to hear something that would make everything more intense, that would put pressure on him and maybe on his friends, maybe even place them in more danger? Maybe he could just enjoy the summer away from college before classes started again, hang out with Emea and Taurnil and Lydia, go hunting with Jonn, have some romantic time with Emmy. The thought was enticing, but on the other hand here was a chance to really find out what was going on, and to be involved in the heart of things. It wasn't just his curiosity that drove him, but also an instinctive feeling that his being a Nature Mage was something of consequence, and that things would work out better if he was involved.

Gaspi made his decision. "I want to know," he said, firmly.

"I'm glad that's your decision," Hephistole said, "and in turn I will do you the service of telling you everything." He must have seen a flicker of cynicism in Gaspi's face. "Yes, everything!" he said, with a wry smile.

Gaspi didn't say anything, not wanting to give Hephistole a chance to change his mind. When the Chancellor was sure Gaspi wasn't going to say anything else, he began to speak again.

"Shirukai Sestin was my mentor," he began. "He was a strange and reclusive man, and a very powerful Mage. He specialised in combining healing with neuromancy, and his experiments took him down a dark road. He was obsessed with exploring the effects of pain on another being, while subduing their ability to respond."

Hephistole's gaze took on a faraway look. "I was dreadfully impressed by him and not a little scared of him too, and even when I saw a glimpse of who he really was I held my peace, to my great shame." He fell silent for several moments, brooding over some unspoken detail, but then he pushed himself up straight, shook his head like a dog getting out of a river, and carried on.

"It happened in my third year as a Mage, when I was on the cusp of becoming a fully fledged magician in my own right. A young guard had been missing for several days, and would probably never have been found if he hadn't married a wife with latent magical talents. She was distraught when she came to us, saying that she could sense that her beloved husband was in unendurable agony and was reaching out to her. His pain must have awoken an empathic ability in her, and she could sense which direction he was in and how far away he was. She insisted that he was somewhere within the college campus.

Several of us went with her as she followed her instinct, searching through the campus for her lost husband. The search led us ultimately to the door of Shirukai's pyramid, a place that few magicians were ever allowed to enter. We forced our way past the door, and found him performing unspeakable magical experiments on the guard.

We tried to capture him, but Shirukai was more than a match for even several magicians together, and fought his way past us, killing one of his fellow teachers in the process. He escaped, and as there was no alert for him in the campus, he was able to leave without being stopped. He fled the city and the country, and as far as we know was never seen again.

The guard was so far gone he wasn't aware of who or where he was, chained to the wall like an animal." Hephistole paused, his face fractured by lines of sorrow. "We never found a way to heal him," Hephistole said. "Sestin had experimented on him, pushing the limits of human pain and then healing him over and over, controlling his mind all the while so he couldn't take back any kind of control. We looked after him in the infirmary for a several years, but something in him was broken beyond recovery, and he eventually just stopped living."

"That's terrible," Gaspi said, deeply shocked by what he'd heard.

"That guard's fate is a source of great shame for me, Gaspi," Hephistole said heavily, his long face suddenly childlike and filled with sadness.

"But why?" Gaspi asked gently. Someone else Gaspi's age might have felt uncomfortable with an adult showing such vulnerability, but growing up with Jonn as his guardian had taught him early on that some adults were burdened by terrible regrets.

"Ah, Gaspi," Hephistole said with a brief smile, "your compassion becomes you. I am old enough to know that I cannot take full responsibility for what happened, but when Sestin was my mentor he involved me in an experiment that caused me great personal distress. It was probably the beginnings of his exploration into torture. I wasn't quite sure what I'd seen, but it was enough to stop me going to him for mentoring, and it troubled me for months. If I had said something, then perhaps he could have been stopped before he did any real harm.

But there's no real value in self-questioning at this point," Hephistole said more briskly, rousing himself from his uncomfortable reverie. "We closed up his pyramid after Shirukai fled. He was a powerful Mage, and we couldn't undo or even understand all of the enchantments he'd placed on it, so it was never taken down. We removed many artefacts, some of which had very dark purposes, and sealed it up for good - or so we believed. No-one has ever liked working near it ever since, as there is some fell enchantment about the place, so that part of the campus has remained largely unoccupied even to this day."

"I know what you mean," Gaspi said. "We explored around there one time soon after we got here, and there was no-one to be seen. Lydia leaned on the wall around the pyramid, and got ill."

"That's very interesting," Hephistole said. "Voltan, perhaps you can have a talk with young Lydia, and see if we can learn something. She may have some kind of empathic ability." Voltan nodded in agreement.

"As you know," the Chancellor continued, "that seal was broken during the attack last week, and a secondary force of Wargs was transported directly into it from somewhere else. I have no idea how Sestin has managed to preserve his life, or how he managed to transport the Wargs over any kind of distance, but we can only assume that he is still very much alive, and even more powerful than he was before. We also have to accept that, for some reason, he has decided to make war against us."

Gaspi tried to weigh up this news, as Hephistole lapsed into silence. Hephistole was right; telling him this placed a shadow over everything.

"How can we stop him doing it again?" he asked. "Couldn't he just transport some more Wargs into the pyramid? Or demons?" The thought was very disturbing.

"Good question," Hephistole said, but with none of his usual enthusiasm for such a thing. "First of all, I don't believe the demons can be transported, as they are not material in any true sense. None came through with the Wargs, and we were aware of their growing activity for the last year, as they found and destroyed people with magical talent. At this point Voltan believes, and I agree with him, that the demons needed to drain those poor weather workers and Healers in order to gain strength for the attack. It appears that this is how they feed, and gain power. If this is so, you can probably see why a city of magicians would be a powerful lure.

Secondly, we had been complacent about Shirukai's pyramid, as no-one believed him to still be alive. We have already found and destroyed the device he used to transport the Wargs. It was built into the floor of his study, something we failed to identify all those years ago after he fled. I am fairly certain that he cannot use the pyramid again."

Gaspi breathed out a sigh of relief. "What do you think he wants? And I don't mean to sound rude, but what do you think I can do to help?" Gaspi asked.

Hephistole ran a long-fingered hand down his face. "I wish we knew, Gaspi, I wish we knew. But we have to be on the alert now. We will be enchanting weapons throughout the summer, recruiting and training new guards, and preparing all our Mages for combat. I will be doing what I can to discover more, but for now we have to do everything we can to be ready. As for what you can do...we've decided to disband your class. You're all at about the level we'd do that anyway, and I think the student's parents will want to spend some time with their children. We're sending all the first years home for a couple of months, so you can go home and rest for a while with your friends, and come back ready to study again next year as a journeyman Mage. I'm including you in this because it seems that destiny has brought you to us at a time when we need you most, and I'm not foolish enough to ignore that. Something tells me you will have a very important part to play in all this before long."

"But don't you need me here, enchanting weapons?" Gaspi asked. He didn't want to stay when his friends would be going back to Aemon's Reach, but if it was necessary then he'd do what he could to help.

"No, Gaspi," Hephistole said, with a warm smile. "You've done more than enough, and we have plenty of magicians who can enchant."

"About me having an important role in all this...I'm not really sure that can be right," Gaspi said, pulling a wry face.

"What makes you say that?" Hephistole asked, looking genuinely surprised.

"Well, I nearly died, didn't I?" Gaspi said, expressing something that had been quietly bothering him since the attack. "There were four of them, and I only killed two of them before the other two got me. If Taurnil hadn't come along when he did, I'd have been a goner!"

Voltan barked out a laugh, and leaned forward in his chair. "Gaspi - it took several Mages to take down a single one of those demons. The fact that you managed to deal with two of them is amazing. And the weapon you produced is so powerful that Taurnil managed to defeat the other two. The two of you together are a force to be reckoned with!" Voltan leaned back in his chair. Gaspi felt a little encouraged; praise from Voltan was rare.

"Gaspi, I think you greatly underestimate your part in last week's events," Hephistole said. "If you hadn't been so resourceful, I'd probably be suffering Shirukai Sestin's cruel ministrations as we speak." Hephistole didn't quite shudder at the thought, but he looked like he wanted to. "In short, Gaspi, Shirukai's mission failed because of you, and I owe you my life."

"But I owe Taurnil my life," Gaspi said, "and we probably all saved each other at some point during the fight. I really didn't do anything more special than anyone else."

Hephistole smiled from ear to ear. "I should have known you'd see it that way," he said. "If I thought it was false modesty I'd have to chastise you, but I think you mean exactly what you say. I happen to think you did something pretty remarkable, and so does Voltan, but we won't force our opinions on you any longer. Modesty is a strong quality."

Gaspi flushed, but didn't bother with any further denials. "So, I can go back home for the summer?" he asked.

"Yes, Gaspi, you can go back home," Hephistole said. "Whatever Sestin's reasons are for trying to capture me, I think it's fair to say he's had a major setback. He has lost the advantage of surprise, and knows that we are now aware of both his existence and some of his plans, and he can no longer use the pyramid. On top of that, we've destroyed the force he sent to us. The demons, at least, will have cost him a lot of energy to control, and he'll no doubt be licking his wounds for a while. So yes; go home, and enjoy the summer with your friends!" Hephistole beamed a beneficent smile at him, and Gaspi was surprised to see something more reserved, but similar, on Voltan's face.

"Well done, Gaspi," Voltan said, his tight smile warming up his normally stern face. "I'm proud of what you've done this year."

Gaspi was taken aback by this open praise from his normally reticent mentor.

"Thanks," he said with a smile of his own. "I'll get going, then."

He walked over to the transporter and stepped onto it, turning back to face the two magicians, his stern mentor and the enigmatic Hephistole. "See you, then - Voltan, Heppy," he said with a grin, which was answered by an even broader grin than his own from Hephistole. Speaking the word of command, he was transported out of the office.

Chapter 37

It was quite a large group that set out from Helioport. Jonn had been given leave for the summer months to accompany Gaspi, Taurnil and Emea on their trip home. Roland and his large family of gypsies were not due to visit until the next year of college began, and Lydia had decided months previously that she would go back with Taurnil to Aemon's Reach when class was eventually disbanded. Taurnil's folks and Emea's Ma were travelling back with them too, and so all in all there were eight of them setting off on the long journey back to the mountains.

As they stepped out onto the road Gaspi couldn't help looking around at them all, and wondered at how much they'd changed in the last year. Taurnil had lost most of the doughy look he'd always had back in the village, and looked more like a fighter. He looked somewhere in-between the boy Gaspi had known and the fighting man he was becoming. He carried himself with a kind of quiet confidence that was reassuring, and since he and Lydia had been together that assured quality had deepened even further. Gaspi thought he looked like a man who knew his place in the world.

Jonn seemed to have banished his old ghosts. He smiled more freely than he'd ever done and Gaspi couldn't imagine him ever getting lost in drink again. He was truly happy for his guardian, who'd given everything to look after Gaspi for as long as he could remember. The changes in Emea were subtler, but no less profound. She'd never be the type of person to be brashly confident, but there was a kind of underlying calm that grounded her sometimes nervous nature in something more peaceful and stable. It was as if there was a kind of glow around her. Gaspi knew she'd found a kind of contentment in healing that went beyond an enjoyment of magic. It was almost...spiritual. Emea must have sensed his scrutiny and caught his gaze with a puzzled look, the familiar frown line appearing down the middle of her forehead, and Gaspi found himself welling up with emotion for her. He was very lucky not to have lost her this year, and swore inwardly to do his best never to put her through that kind of upset again.

Lydia was perhaps the least changed of all of them, but that was because she'd been way ahead of them when they'd met. She'd always shown a self-knowledge that was a bit frightening, and had a kind of strength that rarely faltered. Once or twice he'd seen her crack around the time she and Taurnil were working things out, but Emmy had said that even in the heat of battle she had been calm.

Gaspi couldn't help comparing himself to his amazing friends. Had he changed as much as they had? He'd certainly become a capable magician, but the most important changes were more personal than that. He'd learned how to meditate, and found he had inner resources he'd never known about. He'd also learned that he could be insecure and jealous, and short-tempered too, and that he needed to be aware of those things in future if he wanted to avoid getting all bent out of shape again.

It's no surprise they had grown so much, considering everything that had happened, and it looked like the coming year was going to be even more challenging. Gaspi didn't know quite what to make of Hephistole's talk of destiny. Instinct told him the Chancellor was right, and that some unknowable force had chosen him and given him his natural talents for such a time as this, but sometimes it was hard to believe. Whether any of that was true or not, Gaspi was determined to do everything he could to help Hephistole and Voltan in the war they said was coming.

Shrugging his shoulders, Gaspi pushed away thoughts of darkness and danger. Now was the time to relax and enjoy the summer with his friends. Depending on what next year brought, they may not get another chance for a while.

Gaspi enjoyed every part of the journey home. He'd not seen much of the scenery along the Great South Road on the way to Helioport as he'd been unconscious, rushed towards the city by a desperate Jonn. The red soil of Helioport's flood plain soon gave way to loamy ground and pale green scrub, which grew over the low rolling hills that stretched away for miles on either side of the road. The hills grew steadily taller as they travelled, a prelude to the majestic mountains that awaited them further north.

Each night Jonn made a campfire, and Lydia insisted on cooking for them. At the outset of the journey she'd made her intentions clear, and when Emea's Ma couldn't talk her out of it, no-one else had tried. Thankfully, she was pretty good at it. She'd bought some spices from a travelling merchant before setting off, and Jonn had brought along plenty of supplies, and so Gaspi had the unexpected treat of richly flavoured and beautifully cooked food at the end of each day's journeying. One evening, after wolfing down a particularly juicy stew, he looked over at Taurnil, who was reclining against his backpack, licking his fingers in obvious contentment and appraising Lydia with a proprietorial eye.

"You're a lucky man, Taurn," Gaspi said carelessly, earning him a raised eyebrow from Emea. Ignoring the warning sign, he turned his attention to Emea. "Can you make stuff like this?" he asked.

Emea's raised eyebrow was joined by the other one. "Why do you ask?" she said. Jonn secretly caught Gaspi's attention from behind Emea, grimacing and drawing a finger across his throat. Gaspi cottoned on at last, realising he'd inadvertently stepped onto thin ice and needed to backtrack before it cracked beneath him entirely. "No reason," he said quickly. "No reason at all. I was just curious."

Emea's Ma chuckled warmly. "Smart boy," she said, and Taurnil's parents joined in the laughter. Seth leaned forward and cuffed him across the back of the head. Emea flushed bright pink, but couldn't contain a little smile, which pulled the corners of her lips upwards against her will.

Gaspi caught her eye, and seeing that the danger had passed, laughed nervously at his own helplessness. Later that night, Gaspi fell asleep wondering if he'd ever feel on stable ground again.

It took them four days of leisurely travel to reach the point where they were to diverge from the Great South Road. They paused to find the gypsy encampment where Gaspi had fought off the first demon they'd encountered, and Jonn told the tale of that dark and fateful night. After a bit of searching, they came across the spot. Emea's Ma stared in horrified fascination at the wide patch of scorched earth where the grass still refused to grow back. It was surrounded by a thick fringe of lush green growth and stood out in stark contrast, a magically inflicted scar on the virgin soil. After Jonn told the story, Lydia left Taurnil's side to give Gaspi a kiss on the cheek.

"You saved me that day," she said, her voice rich with sentiment. "Thank you, Gaspi."

Gaspi put his arm round her and gave her a squeeze. He didn't really understand Lydia a lot of the time, but she was very important to Taurnil, and she was Emea's best friend. He supposed that you don't have to understand someone to grow to love them; and standing there, remembering that dark night of over a year ago, he recognised that she had made an inroad deep into his affections.

"You've had quite a year," was all that Seth had to say.

They turned off the road after that, trekking through thickening forest for two days and nights, before emerging onto the broad plains that skirted the great mountain range that cradled Aemon's Reach. They camped at the base of the mountains, not wanting to start the most arduous section of their journey until they were fully rested. Emea sidled up to Gaspi round the campfire that evening, and snuggled up under his arm.

"Can you believe it?" she asked excitedly. "Tomorrow we're going to be back in Aemon's Reach? I can't wait to see my Da and Maria. She'll be so much bigger by now!"

"Jonn says it'll take two days to reach the village," Gaspi said, "but yeah... it's gonna be strange." He was quiet for a long moment. "Do you think people will really believe we're magicians?" he asked, voicing a concern that had been niggling at him.

"What?" Emea asked incredulously. "Why wouldn't they?"

"I'm pretty sure some people won't," Gaspi said. "Or will pretend they don't – Jakko, for one."

Emea pushed herself off his chest, and looked seriously into his eyes. "Now, Gaspi - you're not going to stir up all that nonsense again, are you?" she admonished.

Gaspi thought about it for a minute. "Nah...I guess not," he said with a grin. "Heppy said I had to grow out of that, and so did you in your own way! I'm just winding you up."

"Mmm," Emea murmured disbelievingly, resting her head back on his chest. "As long as you are," she said, sleepily.

Gaspi mulled it over before he slept that night. He *had* been winding Emea up, but there was always that little voice in him that wanted things to be seen for what they are, that wanted fair treatment. He couldn't afford to listen to it anymore, and he'd never use his magic to pick a fight with someone again, especially if that person wasn't a magician themselves. But he hoped that one day that voice would go away altogether, and he wouldn't be bothered about what people thought anymore.

They set off up the mountain the next morning, and it quickly became clear that it wasn't going to be easy. Taurnil's training meant he was much fitter than the other three and he wasn't too troubled by the climb, but Gaspi and the two girls were soon pulling in massive lungfuls of air as they struggled up the slope. Seth and Jonn were doing fine, but the two ladies were struggling even more than the magicians, so they had to keep the going really slow and take a lot of breaks.

Despite the exertion, Gaspi found himself enjoying it after a while. There was something invigorating about the feeling of blood pumping through his veins, and the views just kept getting better. He struggled to keep his eyes on the trail, wanting to look around at every moment, but after tripping twice and almost falling down the side of the slope, he forced himself to wait for the breaks to drink in the view. In those breaks he would sit facing back the way they'd come, the heaving of his lungs slowing down gradually as he looked out over the scene. The tops of tall trees stood way below him, and even the birds were circling beneath their vantage point. At the base of the mountain the plains stretched away endlessly until they met the pale blue dome of the sky. The best time was at sunset, after they'd made camp, when they all sat in contented silence, bewitched by shimmering reds and oranges smeared across the underside of mountainous, billowing clouds. The colours deepened to purple and then to black as night fully eclipsed the day, leaving them bathed only in the warm light of the fire, and later the silver glow of the stars.

The next morning, Gaspi awoke with a kind of nervous tingling in his belly. He shouldn't be nervous really, but the idea of seeing his home again set a thousand anxious butterflies free in his stomach. Emea was excited and Taurnil was obviously looking forward to showing Lydia his home. Only Jonn seemed to share his mixed feelings. Gaspi caught his eye a few times as the day wore on, and they drew nearer to the village. Jonn smiled at him on each occasion, but his smile seemed a little tight, and Gaspi couldn't help feeling that for Jonn this was less fun than it was for anyone else. He'd just have to make sure he looked after his guardian while they were there.

They climbed for most of the day, stopping often to rest. Gaspi was surprised at just how much cooler it was up in the mountains. It was still fairly balmy, but it was the middle of summer, and at that moment in Helioport people would be sitting under shady awnings to escape the heat.

As the afternoon was drawing to a close, the party of travellers rounded the last switchback in the trail, and pressed on into the forested inner valleys of the mountain range, within which lay the small network of villages that had marked the boundaries of Gaspi's world for most of his life. It wasn't long before every knoll, ditch, and clump of trees was familiar; the landscape of his boyhood wanderings announced itself with every step. Mixed feelings aside, Gaspi couldn't help feeling sentimental. He walked closely with Taurnil and Emea, pointing out hollows they'd hid in and trees they'd climbed. It was only when Gaspi caught a glimpse of Jonn's strained face that he remembered that these trees hid other, less palatable memories, too.

The first they saw of Aemon's Reach was smoke rising through the trees ahead, smoke that they knew was rising from numerous chimneys as families settled down to share an evening meal. Emea tugged on his arm in excitement, almost wriggling with pleasure. She stood on tiptoes to kiss him on the cheek, then grabbed his hand and dragged him into a run. They ran through the last few hundred yards of forest, emerging into the village green. Gaspi turned full circle to take it all in. The cottages seemed smaller than he remembered, but otherwise all was as it should be. There was Emea's home next to Hahldorn's, and there was the Moot Hall, standing tall in the shadows of an even taller Koshta tree. And there was the pond, the sight of all those winter Koshta battles. They stood hand in hand, drinking in the familiar sights of home, while they waited for the others to catch up.

Dusk was well underway by the time they all stood on the green. Emea and her Ma went straight to their house to find her Da and Maria. No-one was about, so the rest of the travellers knocked on the door to Hahldorn's house, where they were greeted with a loud exclamation of pleasure, and quickly ushered in.

"There's someone to see us, dear," he called out, winking conspiratorially at Gaspi. Martha came bustling out of the kitchen, drying her hands on a large apron that covered her from neck to ankles. Seeing who it was, she rushed forward and embraced each of them in her ample bosom. She hugged Gaspi first, and then Taurnil, placing a hand on the outside of each of his arms.

"And here's my bear," she said appraisingly, eyeing him up and down. "It looks like you're up to the job."

Taurnil flushed and mumbled something incoherent, before shoving Lydia in Martha's direction. "Lydia's my girlfriend," he said, his face still bright red. Lydia held out her hand, but Martha swept her up in an engulfing embrace. Lydia stood stiffly for a second and then relaxed, giving in to the warmth of Martha's hospitality. Just then Emea and her family bustled in through the front door, completing the party.

Once Martha had made a proper fuss over Emea, she left her guests in Hahldorn's hands, and disappeared to the kitchen to cook up a feast for them all. As the evening went on, she managed to pick up all the important parts of their story. She sat next to Emea as they ate, patting her hand often, glowing with happiness at the fulfilment of her vision all those months ago. She only let them go at the end of the night when Emea had promised to spend the next day with her and Hahldorn and tell them about her healing gift.

They slept in their own houses that night, Gaspi and Jonn lighting lanterns in their kitchen and bedroom; but it seemed clear to Gaspi that neither of them felt particularly attached to the old place. Both he and Jonn had found more of a home in Helioport than they'd had in Aemon's Reach, and though it remained unspoken, Gaspi was sure that Jonn was thinking the same thing. They didn't linger that night, and went to bed fairly early.

The next morning they gathered in Martha's house for breakfast, and after wolfing down bacon and eggs, Taurnil was keen to go out exploring. Lydia said she wanted to stay with Emmy and Martha, so Gaspi and Taurnil would have the day to themselves.

"What are we going to do, then, Taurn?" Gaspi asked.

Taurnil scratched his head. "Go hunting, maybe?" he said. "I wish it was winter."

"How come?" Gaspi asked.

"So we could play Koshta," Taurnil answered, as if it was obvious. "The pond's not frozen."

Gaspi rapped Taurnil round the side of the head. "There's something I can do about that!" he said sarcastically. Taurnil looked at him blankly. "I'm a Nature Mage, you idiot!" he said.

Taurnil's face lit up, as realisation dawned. "Let's go," he said, and they sprang up out of their chairs, rushing out of the door without a backwards glance.

Emmy shared an exasperated glance with Lydia. "Boys!"

Lightning Source UK Ltd.
Milton Keynes UK
UKOW051946040812

197085UK00001B/26/P